For Vivian

...and in recognition of many years spent in the remote hamlet of Paglesham on the Essex coast, a place I wish I had never left.

FREDDIE'S END OF THE PIER SHOW

A novel by Keith Warren
https://www.amazon.com/author/keithwarren

Originally published as "Whispering of Fields Unsown" by Arima Publishing (U.K.) 2011. This edition is a revised work.

This is a work of fiction, although some of the characters of Paglesham in Essex are based on real people, all of them now deceased. Historical events and locations, whilst bearing some resemblance to reality, have often been altered to suit the narrative.
Otherwise, any resemblance to persons living or dead is entirely coincidental.

Published by Keith Warren, Guimaras, Philippines.

ISBN–13: 978-1517616687
ISBN–10: 1517616689

Cover image from an old postcard posted on Facebook. With thanks to Ros Harman and Jo Milton.

Acknowledgements

"Pieces of Paglesham" by Anne Boulter and "Under the Flight Path" by Mark and Rosemary Roberts (Roberts, 1995) have both provided historical material in addition to that gleaned from my own experience of the village of Paglesham where we had a family home for more than forty years.
"The 50's" by Peter Lewis (Heinemann 1978) has been a useful reminder of things I had forgotten or never knew when I was growing up in Westcliff-on-Sea.
I am indebted to my good friend Paul Toplis for his enthusiastic support and his tireless help with proof-reading.

KW
Guimaras
Philippines

Caution

This novel contains some robust language, some politically incorrect narrative and a modicum of naughty stuff, much in the mould of 1950's saucy postcards and music hall.

Crowds of trippers thronging the pier head, circa 1960.
With thanks to Natalie Evans at Facebook's *The Shrubbery* page.

Introduction by Dr.G.I.Soper

What follows is the story of the early years of my parents' lives. Most is directly transcribed from my father's journals.

Those journals are almost entirely written in pencil in cheap, school notebooks, each one covering one calendar year. Some were evidently written hurriedly and carelessly; the circumstances surrounding their creation may explain that. Certainly he did not look after them very well. I recall them from my youth but assumed, as one does, that they had been lost or thrown out. I had no idea that they still existed until they came into my possession, about three years ago.

Many are damaged. Sometimes pages are missing; in some cases they appear to have been savagely ripped out. Whether this was because they contained something my father changed his mind about or whether the damage was simply because he was in urgent need of a scrap of paper, I cannot say. Some were water-stained to the point where it was almost impossible to decipher his script.

Sometimes whole years were not referred to at all. Whether this is because individual notebooks have been lost or because he chose to jump ahead in his story, again, regrettably, I have no way of telling.

Thus, in order to provide some continuity and depth, I have taken it upon myself, for the purposes of this narrative, to fill in the gaps. That is, I have created events and conversations in order to flesh out my father's autobiographical accounts and to make the whole more like a work of fiction than simply a diary. But what is contained in "my" chapters is not just simple invention, although that does play a part. I have gathered material for them from my own, probably patchy, memories of what my parents told me of their early lives. It is a truism, I'm sure, that in adulthood we wish we had listened more closely to what our parents or grandparents told us when we were children.

My father Frederick Tanner was an intelligent and well-read man who was particularly fond of poetry. Tucked into his journals I found many poems he had copied and annotated in his spidery hand. It seems he saw them as relevant to his own life and where appropriate, they are included here, in the manner in which he used to employ them.

Perhaps the most important of my father's favourite poems is Matthew Arnold's *Dover Beach*. There is little doubt in my mind what the most significant line within that poem would have been for him, but I hope that the force of my parents' story will enable readers to work that out for themselves.

Dr. Grace Isobel Soper
Westcliff-on-Sea
2000

PART ONE

THE CLIFFS
OF ENGLAND

1936 - 1943

FROM UNDER THE SLAB
July 1936

I'd gone with Benny and Kathy down to the cemetery, to throw stones at the rats as they scampered over the gravestones. We'd do that sometimes after school, if we didn't feel like going home. After all, there wasn't much to go home for: whatever dreams we had, they'd not be found in our grubby, terraced streets. But I wish I hadn't gone ratting that day because by the time I did go back home, it was too late to be sure what had really happened.

It's funny how the events that spin your life on a dizzying pivot always occur on ordinary days; or at least, they start as ordinary days. Burnt toast for breakfast; no clean shirt; in a hurry to get out of the house; can't find your school books...all the usual stuff and then this thing jumps up from nowhere and bites you right on your rear end.

Truth to tell, it wasn't really the rats or the other macabre attractions of the cemetery that stopped me going back to Bamford Road that afternoon. It was Kathy. Benny had to look after his twin sister because his Dad had to go up West for some reason. Benny wanted to go and mess about in the cemetery and I liked to be where Kathy was. Simple as that, really. Simple as Kathleen, some of them used to say.

When we darted into the cemetery we made for our favourite spot in the overgrown, far corner under the staggering yew trees where the cemetery officials would be less likely to see us. We were out of sight, so that was good, but the yew trees, with their feet worming inexorably into the hollow, broken-toothed mouths of the dead around them, always gave us the creeps. I suppose that was part of the attraction of the place because kids like to be frightened sometimes. Another attraction was that most of the grown-ups lying there, having "gone to another room", wouldn't complain, nag, strap us or call us inside.

It seems odd now, many years later, to realise that we found comfort, or the space to exercise our fantasies or hopes, such as they were, in a cemetery. As Benny would have put it, a cemetery is a "place for dumping stiffs". Let's be honest, a graveyard is often a reason for sadness, pointing up, one might think, the temporary nature of Man's Life and the ultimate futility of his hopes and dreams. But that's an adult's view and as kids we saw it differently: it was a mysterious, spooky, quiet, untended place where we could live a little inside our heads. A place where the slapping hands of teachers and parents could not reach us.

Benny and I sat in the shade, leaning up against one of the trees, discussing the day's events at school. There'd been a vicious fist-fight in the playground, one boy calling another a "bloody fascist". We'd been hearing the word a great deal. After a while, we started skirmishing between the graves, our arms outstretched like a plane's wings, stuttering fascist bullets at one another when we had a clear line of sight. Kathy, being a girl and therefore a more advanced life form than we were, wasn't really interested in our silly boys' games. She was wandering aimlessly amongst the graves, picking dandelions and daisies for a posy. After a while, she came trotting over to where we had collapsed after our dog-fight, sprawling once more in the long grass.

"I just saw a man," she said, rather inconclusively.

"So what?" replied Benny, spitting chewed fragments of grass against a tree. "Wiv a uniform, you mean?

"No. He had his thingy out; his...you know!" She giggled and put her hand up to her mouth.

"Ey? 'E was...'aving' a wee?" queried Benny.

"In a graveyard!" I offered. "No respect, some people."

"No," she murmured, her attention already distracted by some butterflies dancing in the breeze. "He looked at me and wiggled it."

"What?" shouted Benny, jumping to his feet and scanning the surrounding area. There was nobody to be seen. "I can't ignore you for a bloomin' second, can I, without dirty old men jumpin' up at yer! Did he touch you or anyfing like that, Kathleen? Did he...?"

Benny ran aground on the quick sands of his sister's probable incomprehension. He was already many months, if not years, ahead of his peers in understanding and physical maturity, but his sister was well behind – mentally, anyway.

"No."

Kathy had already lost interest in the man. For her the butterflies were much more engrossing than someone exposing himself.

The way Benny told it, as he'd been told it himself, was that Kathy was the second to be born, some considerable time after he had been delivered. The midwife, who was looking in vain for an after-birth, realised that Mrs Soper had not finished her labour and that there was another life there somewhere, clawing in the restricted throat of the womb, struggling to get out into the light and air. Some months previously, a small part of her had propelled its way in without any difficulty, but now she couldn't locate the exit.

It seems extraordinary that nobody knew she was there. Back then, in the crowded streets around Bow, most women would know they were expecting a baby but if in truth they were carrying two, they might not know it. So, the second one would emerge, dripping blood and slime, as an Unforeseen Event.

It wasn't just the difficult birth that affected Kathy. Somehow the fact that she wasn't supposed to be there at all shaped her temperament. As a child, she could sometimes be quite steely and stubborn but more often she was apologetic, diffident and withdrawn. I think Mr. Soper resented her in a way, given what her birth caused, although he probably didn't acknowledge it until Kathy was well into her teenage years. So she must have sensed at a very early age that her arrival was not an occasion for unbridled family joy.

People called their Mum "Mrs Soper" but I don't think that she and Benny's Dad were ever married. That's what people said, anyway. She was from Bow but he wasn't; I think he came from quite a privileged background in rural Essex or Suffolk or somewhere like that. Certainly he was different and spoke differently from the other men I knew at that time. He'd had an education and he was a thinker, a man who reasoned out a problem rather than just using his fists like Pa. His preference for calm reasoning was something I would be very grateful for eventually.

I've often wondered – even as a child, once I understood these things – whether he'd got their mother in the family way and was cut off by his relations because of her poor, working class background. They say that class doesn't matter any more but it's still there under the surface or called by another name. In those days, before the social levelling that was supposed to have come out of the war, your social class was everything. Archie was Upper Middle and Grace was Working. That was that. In showing interest in her, let alone impregnating her, he was betraying his background and descending to the gutter. It would have been a shameful scandal and pretty well unforgivable.

But my reckoning now is that Archie Soper was a man of some principle for whom personal ties and commitment were more important than the travesties of class. So, unwilling to abandon the beautiful creature who was carrying his child, he found himself renting a scruffy little terraced house in the East End and getting a job with Inland Revenue Collection to support his new family. And then the girl for whom he'd sacrificed a comfortable life died when he needed her most.

They said that Grace Soper was very young, very pretty and very small. "Petite" is the word the fashion houses use these days, on the basis that's it's not fashionable unless it's foreign and therefore slightly mysterious. Anyway, something went terribly wrong for Kathy. It took ages to haul her out; her mother was past pushing and Kathy herself was feeble. The midwife panicked and Benny said there was something nasty involving forceps but he didn't really understand what.

So, she suffered some sort of minor brain damage. Lack of oxygen at the crucial moment, Benny said, or maybe it was the forceps. Or both; anyway Grace Soper died three days later. Archie, despite his consuming grief, managed to arrange some help with the twin babies. And then, as the years went by, it was inevitable that Benny would find himself looking after his sister. After all, their father was out all day working in an office or chasing people who hadn't paid their tax. He was always busy — a job for life, Pa reckoned, like being an undertaker. They lived only four doors down the street from us and we all went to the same school, so I probably spent almost as much time with Kathy as Benny.

Like her mother, she was slender of frame and very beautiful. Everybody said so and I certainly didn't need convincing. There was a quiet and calm physical perfection about her that made her seem almost unworldly, as if she had been designed and constructed by some alien influence and then placed upon Earth to silence us with admiration. Of course, as the years went by and she grew from a little girl to a young woman, almost every man who passed her in the street would look in her direction. But Kathy herself remained blissfully unaware of the effect she was having. Her simplicity and innocence generally shielded her from the lascivious inclinations of the men around her. She had a constantly bemused expression, as if she had never seen our grimy streets before or as if she was wondering how she came to be born at all.

I don't mean to suggest that she was crazy or mentally dislocated or anything like that; not at all. She was just a bit slow on the up-take, and as a kid, she was always way behind at school. It took her a long time to grasp what the teachers were telling her. So, she was simple and sweet, not simple and dribbling. In nubibus.

"Like she just got on the wrong blinkin' bus and dunno what ter do about it," Benny would say, laughing and putting his arm affectionately around her.

It didn't matter to me. Kathy and I had a bond going back for as long as we could remember.

Benny was as unlike his sister as a donkey is unlike a swan. He was big-boned and cumbersome with skin like sandpaper. His feet kicked out in all directions as if they had motors of their own. His hair was wiry and bristly, standing up from his head in all directions like Dennis the Menace. His nose was flat and bulbous and was permanently glistening with mucus, which offending slime he would wipe on his sleeve, thereby giving the impression that he lived in the garden with snails. As I say, he was ahead of his years and his ability to do things with his body that the rest of us boys would have to wait a year or two to emulate gave him a decided kudos in the playground and the bike sheds where most of his demonstrations took place. One might have thought that such a physically unattractive, precocious and gangling boy would find that girls ran away from him and yet, curiously, as he arrived at full manhood, some girls found him quite irresistible. I suppose it takes all sorts.

Kathy started peering into a round hole under the stone edge of a grave. There were bits of dried grass and leaves straggling from its opening, so you could tell it was used by rats building a nest underground. She poked a stick into it very slowly and gingerly. "Why do the rats want to go in the graves, Benny?" She looked at him, her bright blue eyes wide open in expectation.

"Gawd, Kathleen, 'swhere they live, innit?" Benny picked up a large stone and looked about him for a suitable target.

"Why?"

He gave an exasperated little sigh. "They gotta live somewhere, ain't they? They like 'oles. You wanna watch out they don't spot yours, squatting there like that!"

Kathy looked puzzled and didn't respond. She almost certainly hadn't understood Benny's vulgarity; she rarely did.

"Well," I said cautiously, "maybe they can find things to eat. Like worms and stuff."

Benny snorted contemptuously. He lumbered towards a headstone and began tracing the weathered lettering with his finger. Slowly, he read the inscription.

"Here lies Josiah Maltby, Schoolmaster of this Parish. Depart...er...departed this life 10th January, 1845. Loved and re...respected by all. Blimey! Bleedin' rats won't find much meat on 'im! 1845! An' I bet 'e wasn't loved by all the kids wot he strapped."

I laughed my agreement.

"I mean, why do people say that when it ain't true? He was probably a 'orrible bloke and then on 'is grave they say 'e was loved by all! Makes you wanna puke, don't it? Then it says...er...At rest until the day break and the shadows...flee away. Wossat all about, then? Flee?"

"You just read it! Flee; fly!" I said, probably rather patronisingly.

"Yeah, well, I know each word, don't I, but not when they're all together. S'alright fer you, clever dick. All the same now, though, innit?" Benny observed after mouthing the words to himself again. "I mean ter say, whatever 'e did or tried ter do and whatever 'e worried about for 'is whole life, it don't matter no bleedin' more, do it? It's all gone, into this 'ole in the ground." He kicked the bottom of the headstone and spat into the long grass again. Benny could surprise you sometimes with his profound little remarks. And then he'd go back to teasing his sister or being sarcastic and profane.

"Well," I said, affecting a degree of boredom, "people often use words that twist the truth. Sometimes you have to look behind their masks."

"You don't say?" grunted Benny.

"And I suppose that about daybreak and so on means that he has left behind the darkness of this life but dawn will soon break in Heaven. Or something like that, anyway."

"Oh, yeah, right. All that stuff. I fink it's all rubbish, that. When yer dead, yer dead an' thassit. So while yer 'ere, you might as well enjoy yersilf."

When I think of that remark now, I am reminded of something that Grandpa once said to Vinny around about the same time. We'd gone to visit and I was supposed to be in bed but I'd crept halfway down the stairs to listen to them talking.

" 'Ow old are you now, son?"

"Fourteen, Grandpa."

"Humph!" Grandpa made a snorting noise. "So, well, you know a fing or two about 'ow yer body works, then, eh?"

Vinny gave an embarrassed laugh.

"Whadja mean, Grandpa?" he said archly.

"You know wot I'm on about, son. Well, it don't last like that is all I'm sayin'. Do what you've got to do, right and take note of yer responsibilities, like yer should, see? But don't go bustin' yer guts with it. When the girls and the ladies comes callin' – an' they will – don't pass 'em by. Don't bovver yerself too much with all the rights an' wrongs of it, is what I'm sayin'. Have yer fun, see? When yer young you got plenty of energy and plenty of spunk and when yer old like me, you ain't got nuffin 'cept regrets about lost opportunities. An' then yer bleedin' dead an' it's too late."

"Yes, Grandpa."

"I mean it, son. Most of us can see that we're gonna die, but we think it'll 'appen to the other bloke, right? Not us. We don't imagine that some day some geezer will say, "Oh, yeah, Harry Tanner? Poor old sod; I remember 'im. Cor! He must've been dead...what? Forty years?" But they will; for all of us; you, me, everyone. We can't begin ter unnerstand it, see? So when them girlies are givin' you the eye – chase 'em, 'cos one day you – and them too – will have been dead for bloody ever. An' when yer dead, yer don't get yer end away, see? An' thassall that matters; that an' beer."

Vinny gave another embarrassed giggle but it seemed he knew what Grandpa was talking about. No wonder Pa behaved like he did if he'd had the same advice when he was a lad!

Benny was still kicking at the headstones. He grinned slyly to himself.

"Oi, Freddie? What about this one, look? It says, "Here lies Hannah Anne Bartholomew, 1823 – 1875. Born a virgin, died a virgin; returned unopened." Must've died of boredom, I s'pose."

I laughed, but Kathy was looking puzzled. "Very funny, Benny," I chuckled. "Anything to do with virgins and you're there, aren't you?"

Kathy wasn't really listening. She put her hand out to catch hold of my arm.

"Freddie? Do the rats eat the dead people? Do they really? Really, really?"

" 'Course they blinkin' do!" yelled Benny. "Like all them soldiers in the war, you know, like in the trenches at Wipers 'n that. Remember we done it at school, Kathleen? Go fer the eyes first, don't they and then the soft guts. Eat their way inside the corpse, right?"

"Don't, Benny! Don't talk about the dead soldiers!" squealed Kathy, putting her hands over her ears. When Miss Dawson had talked about it in school, even though she didn't give much detail at all – she certainly didn't describe a rat's etiquette at table – Kathy was sick. Irene Smedley had to take her to the toilets outside and sit with her. They were gone a long time and Irene said Kathy was sick twice more. It was February and they came back in with bits of frost in their hair.

So, at times like this, I always felt I had to protect her. Benny meant no harm, but he couldn't resist teasing her, often to the point where she'd become confused and hysterical.

"It's alright, Kathy," I murmured. "Benny's just pulling your leg."

I was the only one to call her Kathy. She wouldn't let anyone else do that, ever. It was a special thing between us.

"Yeah," said Benny, "and rats like girls' legs an' all. If you stand still too long, they'll be up your skirt!"

"Benny, stop it, you filthy toad! Freddie, make him stop, he's frightening me!"

"Come on, Benny, leave her alone."

"Alright, alright! Keep yer 'air on, four-eyes!"

I adjusted my glasses self-consciously while Benny went back to inspecting the graves. Kathy snuffled and wiped her nose on her sleeve.

"Benny, look, there's a big one!" I whispered.

Usually, if you made a noise, the rats all shot into their holes under the slabs. We'd been making a lot of noise but this fat grey one was sitting up, smoothing its whiskers and looking right at us.

"Just finished 'is dinner, look, Kathleen," whispered Benny. "Josiah Maltby with chips 'n vinegar!"

Kathy wailed again and clutched at her stomach.

The game we played was based on the idea that if the rats really had been feasting on the remains of the corpses below, then, in a manner of speaking, we were lobbing stones at our reconstituted, former neighbours. Each rat was given an identity; that was all part of the fun.

" 'Ere's one in the eye fer you, Mr. Liebstein, you fat old creep!" Benny suddenly shouted, bringing his right arm back in an impressive bowler's attack. The fat rat took a direct hit and flipped over onto its side, twitching.

Solly Liebstein had lived further down the street. He was the first man around our way to own a car and he was flashy and arrogant. He died of a heart attack, on the back seat of the car, on top of the blowsy young woman who ran the bakery in Pelmont Road. He'd managed to drive the car to a quiet spot, late one night, somewhere in Mile End Park. There was nobody around to hear the woman yelling for help. Solly was so big and heavy she couldn't shift him or get out from under him. When eventually she did manage to attract attention, it took three men to lug and manoeuvre Solly from the back seat and out through the driver's door. It was only a small, two door car. According to the story, Solly was still in a state of arousal, although, of course, the woman was not. She was unavoidably pinioned on the seat, an unusual, naked distraction for Solly's rescuers.

Our friend Morry Bloom was intrigued by this scurrilous story. He was wiser than us; wiser even than Benny. He had already had "The Talk" from his Dad, although, apparently, it consisted of precious little information. Morry had been cleaning his shoes before going to bed and his father had suddenly appeared, looking shifty and embarrassed.

"Time for the Facts of Life, son," he said. "When you want to make a baby you put what you've got into what she's got. That's about it, really. Goodnight, son." With that he left their little scullery, Morry staring at him open-mouthed, the shoe brush poised in mid-air.

For several weeks, Morry kept on about this event and especially the signs of Solly's physical excitement. We thought that perhaps he was focusing unduly on that piece of Solly's anatomy least likely to have been the problem; we thought his gargantuan bulk and elephantine backside were more likely to have hampered operations. But either way, the blonde from the bakery wasn't telling; overcome with shame at her literal and metaphorical exposure, she left the area soon after.

Benny went to inspect the rat and gave it a nudge with his toe.

"Still alive, then, Solly?" chuckled Benny. "You fat old f...fornicator." Benny's academic standard was low, but nevertheless, he knew all the necessary words for human intercourse.

He looked around him, finally picking up a large piece of broken-off headstone. I could see what he was intending to do and tried to wrap myself around Kathy so she wouldn't see, but ever curious and trusting, she pulled away from my grasp.

Benny lifted the stone high over his head and dashed it down on the rat. Bits of flesh and bloodied fur splattered over his shoes.

"Benny! Oh, I don't like that!" cried Kathleen, tears already brimming in her eyes.

"Just a stinkin' rat, innit?" said Benny, pushing the stone off the crushed creature.

"But it was still alive, Benny," she spluttered and then turned away to be sick behind one of the gravestones.

Benny sniffed impatiently, flicking the mess of flesh and fur into the grass with his shoe. Then, as was ever his wont, he broke wind theatrically. I suppose he thought that was a fitting requiem for a rat.

RICTUS

I remember very little now of the house where I was born, except that it was the place where, when I was chasing rats, Vinny found Ma dead at the bottom of the stairs, her neck snapped and her mouth contorted in a rictus of agony. Something had ripped a long strip out of the faded blue wallpaper in the stairwell, and under that, a deep slice in the fleshy pink plaster. He wondered whether she'd had a broom in her hand that had gouged the wall as she fell, but if so, there was no sign of it.

The last time I'd seen Ma was at breakfast time that morning – if a few scraps of burnt toast can be called breakfast. I wolfed it down, yelled a cursory goodbye and was gone. By the time I got home that evening, the undertakers were struggling to load her into their black wagon. They weren't disrespectful or anything like that, but you might have been forgiven for thinking that they were about to transport a particularly heavy and cumbersome sideboard. They were in a hurry because they were bothered about blocking the narrow road.

For my whole life, I've regretted that morning's dismissive haste; wished I'd known somehow what was going to happen so that I could have said goodbye to her properly, put my arms around her one last time to show how much I cared. I've been trying to say that goodbye ever since, but I haven't been able to find her anywhere.

Pa was still upstairs at breakfast time. He must have been on the late shift; if he was on earlies, he was out of the house by five. He was snoring like a hog and no doubt stinking of drink, filthy clothing and cigarettes. He took no care at all over his appearance or his personal hygiene. Invariably unshaven and unwashed, he would bathe reluctantly only once a week and even then his ablutions were minimal. He had suspicious, tell-tale marks all across the front of his trousers and sweat stains in the armpits of all his ragged shirts. What a pig! I could never understand why he had such a way with women. Animal magnetism, perhaps.

We'd heard him come in during the night; heard him shouting at our Ma; heard him slapping her about and then heard her pleading and whimpering as he took his pleasure. Of course, we didn't really know at the time how to interpret all the sounds coming through the flimsy wall. I don't mean we were innocent: like all kids, we'd picked up some facts and even more myths in the playground, but nevertheless, our understanding was limited. In those days you knew only what you were told, what you saw with your own eyes or what you read in books considered suitable for children. So you didn't know much. Not like kids today, flaunting themselves with their knowing looks, up and down the seafront. Then, you were still a kid at fourteen: treated like one and kept largely in the dark about the grim world of the grown-ups.

We knew Pa was hitting Ma because we'd seen it before and we recognised the noises: her shrieks; his fist making contact with her stomach, her face or her breasts and then the crashing sounds as she fell to the floor and things were sent flying. But the sounds that followed the short silence that ensued after he'd knocked her down, we were not so sure about, although we'd heard them before as well. I know now, in adulthood, that what we heard that night and many others, was our father raping our mother. Well, one day it'll be understood that rape can happen in a marriage bed. Then, it was just a man exercising his conjugal rights.

All this that I'm talking about was in East London, in the summer of 1936. Most of the people I knew as a kid are long dead now and many of the houses aren't there either. A lot were smashed and bull-dozed away just before the war and then Hitler knocked the crap out of the rest during the Blitz. A whole community ripped apart like a cadaver on a mortician's slab. "Slum clearance" was a phrase you heard in those days, but if those little places had been in Bombay or Manila, they'd have been best-quality housing.

Strange and sad to think that nothing now remains of the houses that were there: the bricks on the corner of the outhouse, scraped where the old man left his bike every day for forty years;

the cracked front path; the green wallpaper in the upstairs bedroom, peeling off at the side of the door. And nothing remains either of the lives that were conceived, lived out and ended there. There it is. How do we make sense of the critical importance of events in each life as it's lived and then, for most, the insignificance of it all when the sun goes down? I suppose that's why Man invented God – to try to give some meaning to the endless abyss.

Vinny reckoned our mother must have been dead some time. He tried to move her from the corner at the bottom of the stairs. When he touched her she felt quite cold. But she was too heavy for him and wedged too tight. Vinny just stood and stared, not quite sure what to do. She grinned back at him, her head all twisted round in a funny position, her eyes bulging from her skull and her pinafore hitched up right round her waist from where it got tangled when she'd fallen. Her arms were under her and much later I wondered about that, because if she'd fallen headlong, then surely she would have put her arms out to try to save herself?

Vinny yelled and screamed until one of the neighbours came to investigate. In a manner of speaking, he never stopped screaming after that: what he saw that evening affected him forever until he met his own violent end. But more of that later.

For days and weeks, endlessly, he went over and over everything he'd seen and plenty that he hadn't. He rambled; he repeated himself; he got confused and tearful but one thing he was clear about: he kept saying he could see blotches, bruises and blood on the inside of Ma's upper thighs.

"But howja get bruises there from fallin' down the stairs?" he said, that puzzled expression on his face where his eyebrows seemed to ride up a ridge above his nose. "I mean, yer arms or yer face or your back or somethin', but up there, right inside; don't make no sense, do it?"

It didn't make much sense then for two little boys huddled together in one filthy bed for warmth and comfort, but, as I've said, it made sense later. The only unanswered question was to what extent those bruises shed any light on Ma's fall to her death. I learned some years later that at the post-mortem Pa was asked about it. He brushed it off with comments about Ma's frequent refusals to allow him his conjugal rights: he was obliged to use "a little persuasion". This was East London in the thirties, don't forget.

There was talk, of course: speculation and gossip as well as official questions and investigations. Pa held to his story: he'd woken as Vinny and I slammed the back door. He'd got up and was out of the house by nine, leaving Ma doing the washing. And it's true that there was still laundry on the line in the back yard when I got home, something that I was surprised about at the time, because Ma usually had it in and aired well before five.

"She's always had giddy spells, 'specially after the youngest was born," he kept saying to officialdom and neighbours alike. "So I 'spect she came over faint, like she does...did...and toppled down the bleedin' stairs. An' once you've slipped on those beggers, you ain't got no chance! Poor woman," he added, shaking his head a touch too melodramatically.

And this was true too. Ma was given to what she called "the vapours", particularly in hot, airless weather. Well, it was hot that day and she'd been boiling water in the copper for the laundry. And the stairs, steep and turning, were lethal. They didn't even have a thread of carpet to soften your fall. We'd all tumbled down them or slipped a few treads. The neighbours, whose houses were built to the same design, could tell similar tales. Pa would say no more and so that was that. The coroner pronounced a verdict of accidental death and that's what's on the certificate.

In a tight community like that you couldn't hide much. Everyone knew that Pa would beat Ma until she was almost senseless: there were bruises, broken teeth and black eyes enough to give visible evidence without anyone having to look under her pinafore. Screaming and shouting at all hours. Pa was known to be a violent drunk and a womaniser. He was quite open about it, but in that and all his other failings, he was not unusual. That's how it was in those days; people saw it, knew of it and kept quiet. What happened in your neighbour's bedroom was his business alone and the marriage certificate sanctioned almost any behaviour on the man's part, once the door was closed.

And there, as they say, is the rub. Vinny and I wanted to believe our father's story but were more inclined to the view that he'd knocked Ma down the stairs in a fit of rage when, after we'd left, she'd refused to come back into his bed to satisfy his raging, early morning lust. Maybe she was already knocked senseless as she fell, which, we thought, would explain why her hands were not where we thought they ought to be. But what did we know? Anyway, there was no way of telling and Ma wasn't around to ask. Even if we had spoken out, who would have believed a couple of ragged kids?

If, in the days following her death and her funeral, Pa had behaved like a man distraught, we could have given his story more credence. But he didn't. Far from it.

About four days after she died and before she was even buried, I was awoken from a restless, tearful sleep by unfamiliar noises. We were accustomed to the sounds of violence but what I heard that night was entirely different: whispering and giggling. Pa's voice was urgent, cajoling. The other voice was coquettish, simpering, teasing.

"Oh, come on, Alice," cajoled Pa.

Vinny and I, our ears pressed against the wall, decided this was Alice Jordan, the daughter of Arthur Jordan who ran the shop on the corner of Arrow Road. We knew no other Alice. She was flame-haired, provocative and aged about eighteen. After a while, the whispering and giggling stopped. Vinny grabbed my arm to pull me towards the door, putting a forefinger to his mouth to indicate that I should keep quiet. Once on the little landing, Vinny let go of me and bent down to look through the keyhole. So tight was the space that he almost nudged me down the staircase.

He kept his eye to the keyhole for some time, his breathing getting faster. On the other side of the door I could hear soft squealing noises. Eventually Vinny stood up and, adjusting himself inside his pyjamas, he went back to our room, saying not a word. I supposed that this gave me the all-clear and so I bent to take his place.

A few years later, on the pier, I would laugh as I dropped a penny into "What the Butler Saw". I was older and wiser by then, of course, and I knew that the flickering, sepia image inside the machine would show very little and certainly not even a quarter of what Vinny and I saw through the keyhole that night in Bamford Road.

Pa had his back to the door and was kneeling on the floor between Alice's knees, his head and shoulders partially hidden under the hitched-up folds of her skirt.

"What's he doing?" I whispered urgently to Vinny as I wriggled back beside him a few minutes later.

He spat venomously. "And Ma's still cold over at Micklewhite's. I'll get him for this, one day, you bloody see if I don't. Stinking swine!"

The metal bed frame began to squeak furiously.

I managed eventually to fall back into a troubled sleep where images of my mother's bruised thighs intermingled with another of Alice Jordan leaning against her father's shop doorway, her head thrown back, her pinafore held aloft, partially revealing the dark, damp spaces between her shivering loins.

It was about this time that I began to be troubled by strange dreams and severe headaches.

INCISIONS
October 1936

When Mum died, I was ten years old, the same as Benny and Kathy. Vinny was almost fourteen. Perhaps it was to be expected that he would go a little wild following what he'd seen and with Ma's influence suddenly removed. Pa disciplined us from time to time but it wasn't a concerned and consistent fatherly hand that we felt; rather, he'd lash us with his belt when he was drunk or kick us with his boots when he discovered that there was no food in the house.

Vinny spent more and more time on the streets; sometimes we hardly saw him for days at a stretch. Pa didn't care one way or the other whether he was there or not. I trotted down the road to be with Kathy so as to be out of the way of Pa's unpredictable rages.

A better man, of course, would have sought to try to comfort us and in some way to compensate for the sudden and violent cessation of Ma's love. Or, if he couldn't do that, I think we might have understood and respected a withdrawal into grief and pained silence. That didn't happen either. In many ways, he just abandoned us to our own devices, although Mrs Johnson, who lived between us and the Sopers, kept "an eye" on us, as well as Benny and Kathy, and would occasionally pop round with a pot of stew, or she'd offer to do some laundry. But she had her own family to care for, including Mr. Johnson who was blind. She did what she could, but she couldn't do everything.

It was a bleak and miserable time. Whatever hopes Vinny and I may have harboured as kids, they died with Ma on that staircase. I don't imagine I'd be where I am now if she'd survived. That seems to be the gist of it.

Pa managed to keep his job although it's difficult to see how. I suppose not much is expected of a platform and toilet cleaner at a station, other than that he should turn up each day and push a mop or a broom about. I don't think for a moment that he hung onto the work because he realised he'd need money to feed himself and his sons or to pay the rent. More likely he wanted the money for drink and to oil the wheels of seduction. Those were the things he gave his attention to.

Alice Jordan was followed by a succession of other young women, some of them younger than they ought to have been. Hardly a night passed at Bamford Road in sleep and silence. Gruntings, groaning, squeals of surprise and pleasure were the lullabies coming to us from Pa's room right up until the early years of the war. His appetite appeared to be insatiable.

As he got older and more aware of the kind of husband that Pa had been, Vinny held him in almost absolute contempt and rarely spoke to him, except to berate him about his promiscuity and his failure as a father.

Unfortunately, as the years went by it was clear to everyone that Vinny was a chip off Pa's block. A few months after Ma's funeral, he fell in with a crowd of other feral kids whose primary interest was stealing from corner shops and markets. He kept moving, never hanging about in any one place too long. Anything that came his way that was dishonestly obtained he would eat or sell as quickly as he could. He never carried anything back home that he couldn't dispose of straight away; if he had to store it, then it went into an old space he'd found under some railway arches where someone once had fixed a kind of door.

The only exception to this would be bikes. He couldn't resist stealing them from outside shops or even when they were leaning against people's front walls. He was very good at it and never got caught; perhaps because the bikes he stole were from other places like Bethnal Green or Shoreditch. The bike would be his for a day or two, left in our back yard, and then he'd return it to more-or-less where he'd stolen it, dump it and filch another one. Pa never even noticed.

"It's like a game, see? Keeps me amused and me mind occupied. No time to think about stuff I don't wanna think about."

He was forever involved in gang fights and skirmishes, careering along the streets, alleys and canal paths, usually accompanied by a group of like-minded cut-throats, all yelling abuse and threats as they sought out the enemy. Rarely did he come home without another black eye, a newly-bloodied nose or lacerations and bruises. One night, after what must have been a particularly vicious encounter, he came staggering into our room, a blood-soaked rag wrapped around his left hand.

"Tom Cotton," he said venomously. "Reckons I stole his cousin's bike down Limehouse. Gets a meat cleaver out his old man's shop and tries to cut me 'and off!"

Tom was only partially successful, having merely severed the very ends of two of Vinny's fingers. Tom put it about that Vinny would now have trouble interfering with girls. Vinny wasn't left-handed and he didn't have a regular girlfriend, although he had spent a long August night under some bushes in Victoria Park with Tom's sister Eileen. He said it was his fourteenth birthday present to himself. It was probably that, rather than any theft of a Limehouse bike, that occasioned Tom's attack. Needless to say, it was never reported to the police.

Local violence was, of course, mirrored by what was happening nationally and in Germany at that time. At the beginning of October that year the British Unionist Party was making a lot of noise in the East End. Oswald Mosley's rallying call was heard on every street corner, in every pub and probably every playground too.

There's a good deal of crap talked about those days. In the elections in 1937, almost a quarter of the electorate in Bethnal Green supported Mosley. But the plaque that's in Cable Street now, the street where the "riots" were supposed to have taken place, gives the impression that the East End rose up as one man against the Blackshirts. I don't remember it that way. Most of the trouble that day was caused by Communist infiltrators, not local people, if you ask me.

Not that Vinny gave too much of a toss for the politics of it all. Nor did most other ordinary people, as is always the way with these things. All he knew was that the proposed Mosley rally gave him a good enough excuse and apparent legitimacy for acts of violence. No doubt he wasn't the only one to see it like that.

I don't know for sure what happened the afternoon that Vinny got injured because I wasn't with him. I was with Kathy, Benny and

Mr. Soper. He was a pacifist and could sense that there was going to be trouble. He took us down to Southend on the train from Bromley where we'd be out of harm's way and Kathy could stop shaking with fright. Like I say, he was alright, Archie Soper.

All I know is that Vinny got caught between two groups of mounted police somewhere near the Commercial Road. A lorry had been overturned, some wooden staves had been stolen from a builder's yard along with bricks which were being thrown at the horses. Vinny did not ever say whether he'd been hurling missiles, but it wouldn't have surprised me. Anyway, he was knocked to the ground by a policeman wielding a truncheon, he said, but again, Vinny's account may be questionable. What is certain is that his leg was badly fractured when a rearing police horse trod on him. Vinny said that all he could remember, before he lost consciousness with the pain and shock, was the underside of the horse. He said he wouldn't mind being equipped like that stallion. A typical Vinny remark. A typical Pa remark, actually. As I say, it was strange in a way that Vinny could be so like the man he said he despised.

The fractures took months to mend but even when they had, he was left with a very slight limp, much worse in damp weather.

I don't know to this day how he managed to get into the Navy in 1940. With a limp and the ends of two fingers missing, you might have thought he'd have been declared unfit. But, as he would have seen it, he got lucky and managed to disguise the injuries; he could always put on a convincing show.

He was never happier than when he was on the ships at sea. He liked the fact that his job involved killing people.

MOUTHS
July 1939

When we went to the cemetery, it wasn't always to chase rats.

One stiflingly hot afternoon, during the summer holiday in 1939, just before war was declared, Kathy and I wandered down there for want of something better to do or somewhere else to go. Force of habit, I suppose, although in fact, as time had gone by, we visited the place less often. That afternoon, because it was so clammy, I had a terrible headache. We thought we might find it cooler under the cemetery's spreading trees. It would have been cooler still under the bridges over the canal, but loads of the other kids would be there and we just wanted one another's company. Not that either of us said so; we just knew. Benny was playing cricket in Victoria Park and, of course, Mr. Soper was at work so we didn't need to engineer it. Unusually, it was just the two of us. I don't remember that it had happened that way before.

"I don't need looking after, Freddie," Kathy said suddenly and, for her, almost petulantly as we ambled through the dusty, oppressive heat of the Mile End Road. She pulled her hand away from mine. "I'm not a baby, you know."

"Alright, Kathy."

Perhaps my grip had been more like a parent's than a friend's. I let things be for a while and didn't respond further to her challenge. It was the best policy. A few minutes later, I crossed to her left side and held the other hand, but just by the finger tips because I knew she liked that. It usually made her giggle.

A couple of rather swarthy men were setting out mouldy, bruised fruit in rickety display trays at the front of their unkempt shop. One of them looked up as we passed and whistled through his teeth, licking his lips and passing a greasy hand across his stubbled, sweating face.

"She your girl, then, mate?"

"I'm just looking after her for a while," I said rather stupidly. Realising my error, I shot an apologetic glance at Kathy who flicked my hand away from hers in irritation.

"Oh, yeah? Is that what they call it now? Well, when you get fed up with it, son, pass 'er this way. I don't mind a spot of baby-sitting!" He guffawed and scratched his belly.

Kathy was thirteen and, I now fully understand, she looked older physically than she was.

"I'm sorry, Kathy," I said when we were out of the men's hearing. "I shouldn't have said that."

"It's alright."

We walked under a shop's striped awning to be out of the sun for a few seconds. I kicked at some paper bags that had fallen from a rusty nail on the shop-front. Dust blew at us from the oven-door of the sun.

"Why do men stare at me all the time, like that, Freddie?" she asked after a while, linking her arm in mine, which I took to mean that my tactless remark had been forgiven, or forgotten.

"You don't know why?"

"No. I don't know. I don't like it. It's very rude."

"Yes, it is. But in a funny way, it's a kind of compliment too, Kathy, you see," I muttered, uncertain about whether I truly felt that it was or whether in fact I was angry about it on her behalf. She gave me one of her puzzled looks and ran her hand around the crenulated top of a pillar box as we passed, but she didn't say any more.

A few minutes later, we were sitting in our favourite place under the yew trees in the dappled shade. Even though we were in the middle of the East End, close to the railway lines and Bow Road, it was strangely quiet, even for an afternoon so hot. You could have sliced the motionless air with bread knives.

"That gravestone there; Josiah Maltby. Remember?"

"Not really."

"I looked up that stuff about the day breaking and shadows that flee away. It's from the Song of Solomon. In the Bible."

"I don't really understand the Bible. It's got hard words. Why didn't they make it easier to understand if it's so important?"

"I don't know. Yes, some are very hard. Even grown-ups can't decide or agree. But it's easier than it used to be. Once it was all in Latin."

"What's that?'

"An old language. The Romans. So all the ordinary people in the church – the ones without a posh education – hadn't a clue what the service was all about. They didn't understand it."

"I don't believe you. That's too silly to be true," she said, pulling at the grass around her. "What's the point of going to church if it's all in a foreign language? Stupid, that is."

"Well, I'm not sure. I suppose they just had to work it out from the actions. You know, like watching a play but with no words. Mime. And like we do stuff at school but we don't really know what it's all about. I asked Mr. Browning but he didn't seem to know either. Or want to tell me much. I think he said it might be about the Church trying to control people."

"It all sounds silly. How can you know about something if you can't understand the words? It can't be, Freddie."

"Well, sometimes the words don't help much either, do they?"

Kathy looked at me with that expression she had which indicated that she didn't know what on earth I was talking about and that it might therefore be a good idea to change the subject.

"You remember that place we went to with your Dad, last summer? Out on the River Roach, wasn't it, the other side of Rochford where we got off the train?" I said after a while.

"Yes!" she replied, flicking her hair back in excited recollection and gratitude that we were talking about something she understood. "We had to get in that cart with the horse. It was beautiful, that place by the river. Boats...and I remember the swans, Freddie, the lovely white swans! And some other birds that made a noise like, like kittens mewing."

"That's right. Curlews, wasn't it? And it was so, so quiet. Country quiet. Just the river slapping that jetty. Different from here. I could live in a place like that. But this afternoon, it's very quiet like that here too, isn't it? Strange. Listen!"

Kathy sat up straight and turned her head dutifully from side to side. There was hardly a sound and no movement either; just a feeling of moist heat rising from the lush grass around us. The sun was beating down on the graves. In the shimmering haze, it appeared that some were stirring, as if they were being pushed up by trembling fingers from below. There was a click as the fierce sunlight popped a chip of stone from a headstone. My glasses kept sliding down my nose.

"Mr. Browning said at the end of term that this holiday might be the last quiet one for a while. The lull before the storm."

Kathy considered this for a while, twisting grass into tight bunches around her fingers.

"Is there going to be a war, Freddie?"

"Mr. Browning thinks so. I expect he's right. If he is, I don't know how long it'll be before those shadows flee away from us. But it does feel like...well, like it's getting dark, kind of," I sighed, not too sure quite what I was saying. Kathy looked at me, frowning in puzzlement.

"Oh. Sometimes you say funny things, Freddie. I don't know what you're talking about."

"Sorry, Kathy. Yes, I think there is going to be a war but...what do I know about it? We're just kids; I suppose the grown-ups will decide."

"What happens in the war? What's it for?"

I could tell from Kathy's tone and her expression that she'd gleaned enough from adult conversation in the last few weeks to deduce that people were more than anxious. But I didn't see any point in telling her about bombs blowing people and their houses to a bloody infinity. According to our teacher, she was going to find out soon enough anyway. As for its purpose, well, I trotted out what I'd heard, but as each day went by, I was beginning to form my own, different opinions.

"It's because of Germany, Kathy. We have to stop them invading other countries. They're bad people, it seems. Trying to persuade them to stop bullying isn't working."

Kathy looked sceptical. "Are they all bad, Freddie, even the children?"

"No, of course not. Well, I suppose not. But there's this thing called the Hitler Youth and they..."

"Will you have to go to the war?" Kathy's hands came up to her mouth so that she could bite her fingernails.

I laughed ruefully. "Well, I'm too young, aren't I? Depends how long it lasts, I suppose. Anyway, I'm as blind as a bat. Probably shoot myself instead of the enemy! But, you see, I don't agree with fighting. On principle."

"What do you mean?"

"Fighting is not the way to sort out arguments. It just causes more hurt because of revenge."

"Oh."

"Mr. Cooper says that history shows that clearly. He should know, because he's the head teacher."

"There you go again. I feel frightened, Freddie. Will it hurt me? Or hurt you? I don't want us to be hurt..."

I put my arm around her shoulders. "I'll make sure you're alright," I said. I meant it too; if it was humanly possible, I'd shield her from bombs with my own back. I thought to try to deflect the conversation a little.

"You've never been frightened here, in the cemetery, have you?" I asked after a few minutes of silence.

"Nothing to be frightened about in here," she murmured. "Dead people can't hurt me."

"Maybe not. What they did before they died might hurt you later on, though," I suggested, wondering whether she'd grasp this point. Actually, I wasn't too sure I knew what I meant myself. It happened like that sometimes: a thought would come to me and I'd spit it out and then be puzzled over exactly what my brain was trying to say.

"Sammy hurts me now because when he was alive he wagged his tail and it makes me sad. I loved him too much."

"Poor old Sammy," I said.

"Mmm." Kathleen brushed a tear from her cheek, stood up and took a few steps out into the cauldron of the afternoon. The sun shone through her curls, turning them gold and yellow. She bent down to scratch at her leg. Suddenly, I wanted to put my arms around her; not like a protective brother, but as a boy showing affection for a girl.

"Freddie? Why do men look at me? Do I look funny?"

"Of course not."

"They do it a lot. I don't like it."

"No, I suppose not."

"It's too hot out here." She turned round and came back to where I was sitting. She knelt on the grass facing me. She looked down at my scuffed knees and put out a finger to smooth an old graze, running it around the crusted wound very gently. Slowly she raised her head until her gaze met mine. I felt myself tingle.

"Why then?"

"Well, because you are very pretty, I suppose. Nice to look at." I felt that there was much more to it than that but it would be a few years before I had the full understanding or the words to articulate a man's baser desires.

"You think I'm pretty, Freddie?"

"Yes, Kathy, I do," I croaked.

"Are all girls pretty?" she said quietly. It was an entirely innocent question. She wasn't fishing for compliments or being flirtatious. My dry mouth wouldn't properly form the words that were in my head.

"Well...um...no, I suppose. Some are ugly! Like Audrey Fossett! I..." My voice trailed away, silenced by the spell of her proximity.

She thought about this for a while. "My Mum was pretty. I've got a photograph."

"Yes. You get your looks from her, your Dad always says. Thou hast doves' eyes within thy locks, Kathy. That's from the Bible as well; the Song of Solomon. I saw it when I looked up about Josiah Maltby's gravestone over there."

"Crikey! Doves' eyes? Have I?"

"Yes."

"Doves are just pigeons, though, aren't they? Dad says pigeons are the rats of the sky."

"Trust your Dad! Well, doves are associated with love and beauty, Kathy, that's why."

"Asso...see..? What's that?"

"Oh, more words. You say one thing and it's connected to another."

"Mmm. Sounds silly as well, but thank you, then. I think your Mum was pretty too," she replied. She didn't want me to feel left out in the cold with the possibility of an ugly mother.

"Well, maybe when she was a girl. After she got married...and then...well..."

I found it difficult to talk about Ma in those days. Even now, it brings a lump to my throat.

"I never knew my Mum," she said quietly. "It's my fault she died; that's what my Dad thinks. And now your Mum is...so, it's just the two of us, isn't it?"

"Yes. It wasn't your fault, Kathy. I'm sure your Dad doesn't really think that. A baby can't be held responsible in the proper sense of the word."

"Mmm, I don't know what you mean, again. We can be together to make up for not having our Mums," she chuckled, as if it was an enormous joke rather than something of a tragedy.

She continued to look at me but it wasn't a look that was waiting for a reply to her last comment.

Somewhere on the other side of the cemetery wall I could hear a woman singing in a lilting, beautifully clear voice, the way you might sing to a baby. Beyond that was the huffing and puffing of a railway engine hauling itself towards Stepney East and Fenchurch Street.

Little Kathleen Soper was kneeling in the grass, offering balm, looking at me, smiling, wondering. She hadn't looked at me that way before. Doves' eyes.

She moved her head a little closer to mine. Her mouth was just open, the moist, pink tip of her tongue visible between her teeth.

Of course, I had kissed Kathy before, many times, like kids do. For fun in some playground game of kiss-chase; to say goodbye; to cement a birthday wish; at all the usual occasions where one had to observe social niceties and requirements. But looked at another way, I'd never kissed her at all. I wasn't sure whether I ought to kiss her now. I mean, I wanted to; something was driving me forward to do so but at the same time I knew that we shouldn't because we were children; well...thirteen. Just briefly I wondered whether we were bad if we behaved that way; that's what adults would probably say.

Minutes had elapsed. Neither of us had spoken or moved very much. I lifted my hand, cupped her chin and drew her towards me very gently. Just for a moment, she resisted my pull and seemed to look even further inside me, her pupils dilating like ink dropped in a dish of milk. I shivered, despite the afternoon's languid torpor.

I put my mouth on hers and let it rest there. I knew that's what you're supposed to do but I was far from sure I was doing it right. I could feel her teeth against my lip and could taste peppermint in her mouth and smell something that seemed like vanilla in her hair.

It takes time and practice before you can kiss properly. Kids have to find out the best they can; I never heard of a parent teaching his kid to kiss.

"We've been thrown in at the deep end and we're out of our depth! Help, Dad's let go of the back of the bike! Jump forward and grab the rope; it's easy!"

You have to begin to learn and you have to begin to finish and some things don't need to be taught. They just happen.

That afternoon in the graveyard, roasting in the presence of the dead, Kathy and I heard no tutoring voices and didn't say a word to one another; and yet volumes were spoken. She had her hand on the back of my neck and was making little murmuring noises as her mouth began to move against mine. And then, suddenly, it was over and she pulled away from me, grinning. A pink blush spread across her cheeks.

"That was lovely, Freddie," she whispered.

"I..."

Quite simply, I couldn't speak. It was lovely; what else was there to say?

We didn't kiss again. To do so would have seemed pre-meditated and therefore wrong; immoral, somehow. Nevertheless, what had happened was natural, spontaneous, without guile or gross sexuality. Kids kissing; but kids on the cusp of maturity, aware of their emerging feelings. Maybe neither of us wanted to lose that moment.

We sat in silence for a while, just holding hands, being together, giggling. Every now and then I looked at her doves' eyes and she smiled.

My headache had gone completely. The woman had stopped crooning to the baby. Another train was hooting and jetting steam as it pulled into a station somewhere ahead of us. A little later, an aircraft with military markings lumbered its way belligerently across the duck-egg blue sky.

NAKED SHINGLE
July 1938

Kathleen Soper sits at the carriage window, watching the fields slide by and hoping to see brown and white cows grazing in the meadows beneath the castle. There is a book at school with a picture of brown and white cows. Every now and then, she lifts her head a little and, with her finger tip, traces on the window glass the outline of the smoke clouds being left in a billowing, fat ribbon by the panting steam engine ahead of them. Where the track curves a little to the left, she can see it, labouring and blowing under its heavy load. When it huffs into view, she emits a little squeak of delight.

"Ooh, look, the engine!"

Sitting beside her, close but not inappropriately close, Freddie Tanner is buried in a book. He likes to read. Not even the proximity of Kathleen, her breath smelling of butterscotch as she turns once again to beseech him to share in the view, can deflect him for long. Not even the undoubted delights of a train journey or the prospect of a picnic by the river can displace the fantasy in his head.

Benjamin Soper is irritated by his friend's absorption in a book. How can what happens in a book be so consuming? What world has Freddie found in there?

"Whadja reading, Freddie?"

Freddie sighs audibly and looks up. "It's called *Treasure Island* by Robert Louis Stevenson. The same as when you asked me a while ago when we were pulling out of Shenfield."

"Orlright, then," snaps Benny testily, his shoes kicking the floor in irritation. "I'm only askin'. Whassit about?"

"One of the best adventure stories in the English language. The best way of finding out the answer to your question would be to read it for yourself, wouldn't it, Benny?" says Archie Soper, adjusting his glasses and looking up from his newspaper. "I'm sure Freddie would lend it to you when he's finished, wouldn't you, Freddie?"

"Of course, Mr. Soper."

"Bum-licker!" mouths Benny, obscenely. Freddie makes a face.

"We'll be getting out soon, I think," says Archie. "Old Horace Keeble should be there to meet us."

He had written to the old man a fortnight previously asking for a favour in transporting him and three children to the river at Paglesham. Horace, whom Archie had known as a child when he visited his Uncle and Aunt at Stambridge Rectory, replied briefly that he was happy to oblige. For a consideration, naturally.

"Dad, where's the castle? I want to see the castle," squeals Kathleen.

"It's on the other line," replies Archie, rather abruptly, before returning to his newspaper. Kathleen looks disappointed and puzzled.

"There are two railway lines going into Southend," says Freddie quietly, reaching across the seat to touch Kathleen's hand. "This is the Liverpool Street line; you can see the castle only from the other line, you see, not this one."

"Oh," says Kathleen, smiling at Freddie. "I like castles."

"A pile of old stones, historical monuments or romantic edifices. Once a place to live in; now a place for a picnic. Or more. We can take our pick," says Archie from behind his newspaper.

"Are there any cows?" asks Kathleen. "I like cows as well."

"A few," says Freddie. "Not many really, Kathy. Mostly crops here, not cattle, isn't that right, Mr. Soper?"

Archie lowers his paper again.

"Yes."

"What do you mean by a romantic edifice, Mr. Soper?"

Archie grins to himself. "Oh, well, sometimes we invest history with romantic notions; you know, daring deeds at Culloden, valiant knights on their chargers. When actually it was just blood, sweat and tears. On the surface, bravery; under the surface, carnage. Men killed senselessly; women defiled and children orphaned."

Freddie looks out of the window at the blurred landscape. *"Mowing like grass your fresh fair virgins and your flow'ring infants,* you mean, Mr. Soper?"

Benny chortles. "Whassat, then, about virgins?"

40

Archie scowls at his son. "Why don't you just listen, Benny? You might learn something. You never know. Very good, Freddie. Shakespeare, is that?"

"Henry the Fifth. We read some stuff by Shakespeare last term and I got that out of the library."

"Really? Good for you!"

He looks at the little boy opposite him who has turned his attention once again to the exploits of Jim Hawkins. He has known Freddie Tanner since he was born; knows him well and yet every day the lad surprises him. There is no doubt he is extremely clever, bookish even, at times. He is not remote or entirely self-possessed as the bookish often are and yet he has moments of strange, blank-eyed disassociation. He is curious. Archie is aware that he manages to communicate with Kathleen in a way that others cannot; in a way that he certainly cannot himself. Or chooses not to, perhaps, for he has acknowledged recently that despite his every effort, he harbours deep within himself a resentment that his beautiful Grace died because the girl lives. She even begins to look like Grace. It feels unfair and unreasonable and yet bitterness serves no useful purpose, he knows, but it seems he cannot help it...but he will try; he will try harder.

And the boy too has no mother now. Archie, attuned to this particular form of domestic tragedy and in some way compensating for his distance with Kathleen, is happy to step in from time to time to give the boy some normality and some space to breathe. And some food for the imagination, which he knows is important. So, some thought-provoking remarks to sharpen the boy's mind. A picnic by the river to get the children out of the coarseness and muck of the East End for a while and, in Freddie's case, away from the pernicious influence of his father and brother.

Archie reflects that Vincent Tanner seems well on the road to a criminal record, or at least a deserved reputation for nefarious activities, so Freddie will find no succour there. And his father; well! Sid Tanner was hardly a paragon of virtue when his wife was alive, but now that she's gone – in Mr. Soper's head, the words "died", "fell to her death" and "murdered" all struggle for supremacy – he considers the man's behaviour nothing short of sinful. He knows that Tanner is blind drunk most nights and that he shares his filthy, soiled bed with any female who is willing, including some who are reputed to be very young.

With sudden, sharp apprehension, Archie realises that, if the gossip is correct, and it probably is, some of the girls said to make their way up Tanner's staircase as he slaps their behinds, are probably only a couple of years older than Kathleen. The thought makes him feel sick.

He will have to be vigilant. Mrs Johnson, for whose neighbourly assistance he is eternally grateful, particularly where Kathleen is concerned, has advised him that the girl has already started her times. He is surprised, as father's often are, but then she is developing fast. He has recently seen the way that men have begun to look at her: to his horror and disgust, even men in his own office when he took Kathleen there one afternoon. He recognises that she has inherited his wife's ethereal beauty. Dear God! Perhaps it won't be long before Sid Tanner's lustful gaze falls upon her.

"What's that?" says Kathleen, pointing through the window and peering into the smoke.

"It's a tractor, Kathleen," says Archie. "Ploughing, ready for sowing. Farmers have to plan ahead. We must do the same if we are to get on in this world."

Benny shifts uneasily at his father's apparent pomposity, wondering whether one of his little homilies is on the cards. He hopes not and he wonders whether "getting on" is all it's cracked up to be.

The chuffing of the engine alters slightly and there is a grinding and screeching as brakes are applied to slow the train.

"Hockley," says Archie. "Rochford is the next stop; that's where we get out." He stands up to slide down the window in the door and peers out, immediately retracting his head as a smut of soot lodges in his eye. Benny grins.

"There's one in the eye fer you, Mr. Soper!" he mouths and mimes to Freddie. Freddie grins back.

§

The ride out into open country in Mr. Keeble's trap entrances the children and especially Kathleen who watches the pony's tail flicking skittishly as they clatter into West Street. They are initially fascinated by the old cottages in Rochford: their white painted, clap-board walls leaning at times precariously into the street. In Market Square, old men lounge by the stone horse trough and a small boy watches the trap pass, his finger firmly in his nose.

As they pull away from the town, Mr. Keeble's pony trotting spiritedly ahead of them, Freddie drinks in the open spaces and the almost tangible tastes of farms and fresh air. Benny is surprised by the "bloomin' tiny" little schools at Stambridge and Paglesham and compares them with the towering Victorian institutions they attend in the East End. Kathleen coos at the flowers in the hedgerows and the flocks of birds in the fields but is a little intimidated by the dark spaces under the groping branches of the enormous elms that line the road.

"Like it in the sunshine," she says, shivering with the sudden chill of the ominous shade.

"Can you take us down the back road by the Smugglers' Elms, Horace? We'll get out just by Well House, if that suits?"

Freddie wants to ask about the Smugglers' Elms but decides he'll wait until later.

"What about thet hemper? It's heavy, boy!"

"We'll manage, Horace. Freddie and Benny can carry it between them. In fact, Benny could probably carry it by himself; he is built like the proverbial brick outhouse, I fear!"

The boys are happy to act as porters; indeed, Archie has to shout to them to slow down as they race ahead of him, the hamper swinging between them, so eager are they to embark upon the next stage of this adventure.

"Come on, Kathleen, keep up! I want to keep the boys in sight; they don't know where they're going when we get to the end there."

Kathleen is in no hurry. She wants to look at the wild flowers, to marvel at the towering prickles of blackberry bushes and the creamy profusion of elder. As they get down from the trap, she sees the bobbing tail of a rabbit disappearing into the bank of a ditch. She hangs back in the hope of seeing more.

The track winds its way enticingly between bushes to the river. Archie pauses for a minute to get his bearings, gradually recalled from years previously, and then directs them to the right. They walk a few hundred yards to a spit of shingle backed by lush green grass. To one side are oyster pits, a couple of men working in them. Further off to the right is a low shed with a clutter of boats around it. Ahead and to the left is a wide channel of water with mud banks on the far side, glistening now in the soft light. The water is remarkably still; just a few serrated wavelets etched on a sheet of silvered glass.

"Here we are; this'll do."

The hamper is set down on a small rug.

"It's beautiful," says Freddie, turning this way and that to take in the saltings, the rivers, the mudflats and some white painted buildings in the far distance. "It's so quiet and peaceful, isn't it? Not like Bamford Road! Just birds calling and the wind whispering in the grass. And a weedy, salty, muddy smell? Phew!"

He thinks that although they have travelled only about thirty miles, it seems like a different country. A country he feels he'd quite like to live in, if at all possible.

"The bird you can hear is way up there, see?" Archie points up into the hazy blue. "Skylark. She's probably seen us and she'll drop down into the field behind us shortly. You'll think that's where her nest is, but it'll be somewhere altogether different. It's a clever trick – a decoy, in a manner of speaking – for such a little bird. In nature, things are not always as they seem."

A few minutes later the bird does indeed drop into the long grass of the field and Freddie and Kathleen trot off, hoping to find a nest full of fledglings. Once out of sight of her father, Kathleen takes hold of Freddie's hand, giggling. Archie is right, however, and they return eventually with nothing to report.

"I was certain I saw where it came down!" says Freddie, a tone of exasperation in his voice.

"Wanted to see the baby birds," grumbles Kathleen, pulling grass seeds from her socks.

"I did warn you! Sometimes what we think we see isn't what we see at all. Never mind, Kathleen," says Archie. "Shall we go and have a look at the oyster beds? You two won't mind guarding the hamper, will you?"

Freddie is both surprised and pleased that Mr. Soper has walked off with Kathleen trotting beside him; pleased that he's giving her his undivided attention.

Benny is leafing through *Treasure Island* which Freddie has left on the grass. He flicks at the pages randomly, his eyes skittling up and down the print without any proper comprehension.

" 'Ere," he says, "thought you said this was an adventure? A proper posh story, like?"

"What do you mean?" asks Freddie.

"It ain't! Look, whassall this about tossing off?" Benny's finger traces the print and he reads painfully slowly, *this had nearly tossed me off into the sea,* it says. Page 121, look. An' on page 116 it says *when I awoke I found myself tossing at the south-west of Treasure Island.* I reckon it's a bit of a dirty book, innit?"

"Don't be stupid," Freddie replies.

"Bloke here's rubbed hisself off twice in five pages and you reckon it ain't a dirty story?"

Freddie grabs the book and looks at the page Benny has open.

"You're mis-reading it. That's not what it means. He's talking about the movement of the sea," Freddie says, a tone of patronising exasperation creeping into his voice. "He's in a coracle being tossed about by the sea."

"Oh, yeah? I know what it says. Plain as day, innit?"

"No. Well, yes. I mean, it's plain what the writer means from the overall context. You're taking it out of context and super-imposing your own thoughts," snaps Freddie.

"Context? Whassat? You know wot? You sound just like Mr. Bloomin' Browning, you do, sometimes. I know what it says. It's about this bloke tossin' off."

"No, it's not! You know, Benny, sometimes you can be so stupid? Words can mean different things depending how they're used. And sometimes they can mean the opposite of what they seem to mean. If you see...no, I don't suppose you do."

"Well, they bloody shouldn't! Whassa point of that? Ridiculous, that is! 'Ow are you supposed to know what you've read if it means the cockin' opposite of what it says? 'Ow do we get on in the world if everything's all arse-about-face? It's mad, is that! No wonder things is in a mess, innit?" Benny begins to shout, drawing the attention of Archie Soper, further off along the low, sea wall.

"Quite," says Freddie. "What Hitler said or almost said isn't what he meant. And sometimes what's mad is sane and vice versa. See?"

"Balls!" whispers Benny, so his father cannot hear.

"Not arguing, you two, I hope?" says Archie.

"Just a difference of linguistic interpretation, Mr. Soper, that's all," Freddie replies.

"Yeah, an' I'm in prefects' detention," snarls Benny.

Archie ignores the squabble and stands with his hands on his hips, gazing at the scene before him.

"It's a unique landscape, this. I knew it well as a child. Ha! And that seems a very long time ago! Dearie me! Did you ever read any Charles Dickens, Freddie? *Ours was the marsh country, down by the river, within, as the river wound, twenty miles of the sea.* "

Archie draws his hand in a slow arc across the water and the muddy banks as he speaks. "That comes from the beginning of *Great Expectations*. The very beginning, I think. It's a marvellous story. Starts in a graveyard, of all places! He was probably writing about an area on the other side of the Thames near the Medway and Rochester, but it could just as easily be here. Did you know that?"

"No, Mr. Soper, I didn't." Freddie looks now in awe at the landscape Dickens has described and wonders also about a tax collector who reads and who talks just like a teacher.

"But don't tell me, when he's on about the marshes, he's really talkin' about the mountains, is that it?" Benny grumbles.

Archie gives Benny a withering look. "Being angry and sarcastic when you don't understand will not get you anywhere. Ask. You have a sensible question to ask?"

Benny shakes his head. Archie sighs irritably and then draws a map from his pocket. He spreads it before him on the ground.

"Would you all like to see where we are?" he asks.

Benny yawns. "Nah. I might get confused, thinkin' it's just a place by a river, Dad, when really it's the Tower of London."

Archie ignores Benny's remarks. "I believe we ought to take an interest in our bearings; where we are in the landscape. Otherwise we are no more than the beasts of the field who know not where the field is. Nor do they care."

Benny grunts and gets to his feet. He begins charging up and down the sea wall like a small bullock. Kathleen too has wandered off; having removed her shoes, she is paddling gingerly at the murky water's edge.

"What's got into him?" asks Archie, when Benny is out of ear-shot.

"I don't really know, Mr. Soper."

"Be careful, Kathleen! You don't want to cut your feet on the shells down there," Archie calls.

Kathleen looks down at her feet and then bends to search for the shells. In her mind, she forms a picture of a South China Sea conch shell, seen in another school book.

"Yes, I would like to know where we are, please," says Freddie, looking down at Archie's map.

Archie smiles at him, wishing that his own children had the same intelligent curiosity. Of course, sweet as she is, Kathleen cannot help being slow and Benny; well, it seems he positively relishes a kind of belligerent disinterest.

"I think this is Paglesham Pool," says Archie slowly, tracing the waterway with his finger on the map and looking up at the landscape before him. "That must be the River Roach; Rochford down that way through Paglesham Reach and that's Potton Island...and then, over there, where you see the tops of the sails, is the River Crouch, leading out into the North Sea. Burnham-on-Crouch over there; the buildings."

Freddie follows Archie's pointing finger at each statement, dropping his head down periodically to relate what he sees to the map.

"Yes, I see."

He stares out across the near water, shading his eyes, for he feels a stabbing pain in his forehead.

"And out into the North Sea, Mr. Soper, what's there? I mean, if you sail away from here, what will you find? Right across the sea; away altogether, not just up the coast."

Archie laughs. "The idea appeals, does it? Well, not treasure or pirates like in your book, I don't think. Sand banks – ships run aground on this coast, you know; lives are lost – cold, grey water and then Holland. Germany too, of course."

"Germany? Gosh!" Freddie continues to look to the far horizon; his senses drinking in the scene, his mind wondering about lives lived far from these shores.

"But you can't actually see another country from here?" He thinks of different languages, different houses, different clothes. Different expectations, presumably. German children standing on their beaches, looking west, wondering the same way, just as he is.

"No, not really," says Archie. "You'd have to go to the south coast to do that. Dover, maybe; then you could see France. On a clear day, of course!"

Freddie takes the fish-paste sandwich offered to him from the hamper. Its edges are already curling in the heat.

"What do you want to be when you leave school, Freddie?" Archie enquires suddenly.

"I'm not really sure, Sir," comes the reply. "Mr. Browning says I must work hard and aim high. He thinks I should go to university to do about the law, he said. To be a solicitor."

"That's what you want?"

Freddie pushes his glasses up his nose. "I don't really know...I'm not really sure what a solicitor does. It sounds quite grand and so maybe it's something I ought to try to be...but it also sounds a bit...well...boring. In an office all day? I'd rather be..."

His voice trails away and he looks out across the water again, trying to bring his future and the rest of the world into focus.

"It's good to have an aim, Freddie. Very good; it's a fine ambition. But, well, grown-ups aren't really supposed to say this, but I think you're clever enough to understand. You see, sometimes things don't always turn out quite how you expect or in accordance with your plans. I wanted to be a teacher, once upon my lifetime, a long time ago, only..."

Freddie senses that Mr. Soper wants to say more, but is not sure whether he should ask him what he means. Instead, he merely raises his eyebrows and waits. Mr. Soper stares across towards Potton Island and rubs at his chin.

"Life has a habit of throwing things at you; I mean, events you can do nothing about," he says. "Or you go and do something daft and it queers everything for the rest of your life."

"You mean like this war that everyone says is coming, Mr. Soper?"

"Yes, if it does. When it does, I suppose. We'll all be affected one way or another and, yes, there's not much that we can do about that. External events, you know, like being struck by lightning. Or accidents: you might be a talented athlete and have high hopes of representing your country in the Olympics and then you break a leg; it doesn't mend properly and you have a limp for the remainder of your days. No Olympics."

"But we all have to carry on anyway, don't we Mr. Soper? Because if we worried about these external events or accidents all the time, we'd do nothing," says Freddie, quite pleased with his reply and proud that he's keeping up.

"Indeed. Quite so. Good lad! I think your Mr. Browning may be on to something! No, that's right, we can't hide away or give up before we start. But I didn't just mean that, Freddie. Sometimes – often – we are to blame ourselves for messing things up. You must think before you act; don't be impetuous. Our emotions can get the better of us: one hasty decision; a road crossed at the wrong moment, your mind preoccupied with other matters; carelessness with a burning match. A conception you didn't intend to happen. Little things, sometimes apparently insignificant things, can turn your plans to dust."

Freddie doesn't fully understand the reference to conception, but assumes that Mr. Soper is referring to Kathleen and Benny. He is too embarrassed to make any reply, but in any case, a shrill call attracts their attention and the conversation is ended.

"Dad! Please, please can I go in the water?" Kathleen is already hitching at her dress to undo the buttons at the back. "Oh, please!?"

Archie looks at his daughter. He is concerned about the dangers – the tide seems to be running fast just here, although it's shallow enough – but at the same time he doesn't want to restrict his children, perhaps especially Kathleen, for her horizons must perforce be limited. As he has just said to Freddie, one cannot hide away or fail to try new things. Despite the inevitable dangers or the risk of the unexpected, he feels that children should learn from direct experience rather than always being pinned to a hard, wooden desk.

"Well, alright, but just up to your knees, I think. And be careful; the water is running fast just here, look," he says. He points to where the river is swirling around the spit.

Kathleen continues to unbutton her dress.

"Kathleen! Are you...have you...are you properly dressed under there?" Archie adds, a note of warning sounding in his voice.

He is aware of his daughter's tendency to wear nothing much, if anything at all, under her outer garments. Even though he has always seen to it that clean underwear is in her chest of drawers and he reminds her to put it on, he knows that she pulls it off again as soon as he's out of sight. She told him once that it felt nicer without any on because otherwise she got too hot and itchy. He is unable to talk to her easily about propriety or the dangers implicit in unintended exposure in a public place. When she was just a little girl, it didn't matter that he might investigate, but now that she's approaching womanhood, he has to respect her right to female modesty, even though she herself, in her innocence, does not ask for it or, indeed, seem aware of her own changing shape. Mrs Johnson has spoken to her about it all but she cannot always be on hand. Not for the first time, Archie wonders whether he should have found himself another wife after Grace died.

Kathleen laughs. "Yes, Dad, don't worry! I've got my vest and bloomers on!"

"Mmm. Well, I suppose that'll have to do then."

Archie reflects that Freddie Tanner is a good, clever and honest lad and he reminds himself that they are both still children; but nevertheless, in recent weeks he's noticed the two of them taking long, sideways looks at one another.

Archie's concerns are partly justified. As Kathleen pulls the dress over her head, Freddie is not sure whether to look – which he desperately wants to do – or to pretend to be engrossed in the view, in case Mr. Soper is angry. He decides upon the latter, after a fashion. So, although his head is pointing up the river, his eyes are swivelled towards Kathleen who is now slowly edging into the water, her dress dropped carelessly on the dry shingle behind her. There is not much to see, however, except bony white knees and elbows, for her vest and bloomers are baggy, slack cotton.

Benny shouts, "Hey, Freddie, look! The 'orrible monster from the deep!"

"Shut up, Benny. Don't be so nasty," calls Kathleen. "Anyway, what would you look like? Quasimodo at the seaside?"

"Do you want to have a paddle too, Freddie?"

"No, Mr. Soper, thank you, I don't think so," says Freddie.

Kathleen edges slowly, a few unsteady steps at a time, into the water until it is just below her knees. She looks up and grins at Freddie. A few minutes later, after she has kicked at the greasy suds and bent to dibble her fingers in the water sluicing around her feet, she takes another cautious movement forward. Her left leg suddenly seems to disappear as her foot sinks into soft, yielding mud. She shrieks in alarm. Losing her balance, she falls sideways into the water.

"Help!"

"Jesus! Keep still!" shouts Archie as he jumps to his feet and makes towards her, levering off his shoes. Kathleen is flailing about in the shallows, the water splashing her hair and slopping up to her chin as she tries to stand again. Before Archie gets to her, she succeeds in doing so, steadying herself and finding a secure footing. She turns and measures the distance to the shingle.

"Hold onto me!" says Archie, extending his arm in her direction.

Freddie, who is standing a short distance off on the low sea wall, looks towards them, uncertain whether he should also rush to Kathleen's aid. The girl's underwear is heavy with slime and sea-water. It clings to her body as Archie helps her from the cloying mud. This is a novelty indeed: Freddie is surprised by the curving shape of her bottom and intrigued by the prominent, plump swellings, each with a hard, dark tip, under the sodden folds of her vest. Unwittingly, his gaze rests at a point somewhere a few inches beneath her collar bone where the swellings seem to hold steady despite the awkward, lurching movements that Kathleen makes as she stumbles towards the hard shingle.

He is suddenly embarrassed and surprised to find that he is aroused as well as intrigued. He turns his back on the scene so that Kathleen's modesty is preserved and lest his excitement is obvious.

Benny is not so considerate. " 'Ere comes a muddy old duck!" he shouts coarsely.

"Be quiet, Benny and come and give me a hand with your sister," snaps Archie.

Benny grunts in annoyance but lumbers down the sea wall to do his father's bidding.

Between them they manage to steer her towards the shingle, although she continues to stagger and squeal as the broken shells dig into her feet.

Somewhere to Freddie's right there is a sudden, insistent beating sound in the air. He looks up to see four swans lifting off from a pool of water in a further field. They curl slowly around over the elms on the lane to the village and then swing back towards the shingle spit, making their way, he thinks, for Potton Island.

He follows their graceful progress in wonderment, watching the creamy, white wings as they massage and press the air under them. Momentarily, he has forgotten Kathleen's plight.

The birds pass almost directly over her head as she is bending to the shallows, trying to splash mud from the thin cotton which continues to cling to the contours of her shivering body. As they pass, she looks up and then cries out in surprised delight.

NIGHT-WIND
9th September 1940

Benny gave me a sharp nudge in the middle of my back as I stumbled clumsily into the shelter, knocking my glasses half off my face. The siren sounded just as we were about to share a couple of bits of old bread smeared with some honey we found in the back of the cupboard.

"Look what you're doing, you great oaf," I complained. "It's like being in a box with a horse! Now I can't see a damned thing!"

"Push off, four eyes! Anyway, there's none so blind as them can see, or sunnink."

He and Kathy wormed their way past the flap of tarpaulin that served as a door to the Anderson Shelter in their back garden.

"Just a minute! Let me find my specs!" I wailed.

"They're here," said Kathy, quietly, squeezing my hand gently as she returned them to me.

As usual, I was at their house. Pa was at work and Vinny was off doing his basic training. He'd had his call-up papers just a few days after his eighteenth birthday. It was the best present he could have expected; he was overjoyed. It's just as well that I was at their place. The materials for our Anderson Shelter had been delivered but, of course, Pa had yet to get around to digging a hole and installing the thing. The holes he was digging were of a different variety.

"Sieg Heil!" Benny shouted, his right arm raised and his left index finger on the top of his lip like a moustache, "You kraut bastard! You invade Holland und Belgium und see vot you get!"

He tried to march, stiff-legged, in the small space but caught his foot in the duckboard.

"Ow!"

He then bent to light the paraffin lamp that was on the floor in readiness. "Don't you worry; Winnie'll sort it out," he chuckled. "Thass what Dad says anyway, now they've dumped that daft old sod Chamberlain."

"I don't see what's so comical," I said. "This is the third day in a row and the second time today. It's damned inconsiderate."

"Oh, I say! Inconsiderate, what?" responded Benny in his Alvar Lidell voice.

"It smells of wee in here," said Kathy. It did, she was right. It was also damp. There were crude wooden duckboards under our feet but they were laid over the bare earth. Moisture dribbled down the sides of the shelter. Something scuttled in the corner as Benny managed to get some flickering light from the lamp.

"Thass 'cos you knocked the pot over last night," he snorted, flopping down onto one of the wooden bunks. "If you need to go tonight, yer better go'n squat in the yard! But keep yer little white bum covered, or else the Warden'll be after yer for showin' a light!"

"You're rude, Benny," protested Kathleen.

"She only just noticed! Oi, where's yer gas mask, Sis?"

Kathy looked mortified and put her hand to her mouth. "Oh, no! Oh, no!" she wailed. "I left it in the lavvy!" With that, she made a dart for the tarpaulin flap. Benny and I both grabbed her.

"Now then, young lady, you can't go out there now; don't you know there's a raid on?" warbled Alvar Lidell. "Didn't you hear the siren?"

"But, Benny..."

"Have mine," I said, "the ruddy thing makes me claustrophobic anyway." In fact, I was already beginning to feel decidedly light-headed about being in the Sopers' shelter overnight, Kathy or no Kathy.

"No, what if...?" Kathleen began, but her protest was overwhelmed by the roaring of engines overhead.

"Dorniers," said Benny, who was becoming an expert on the sounds made by bombers, "big, murdering bastards! German bastards!"

There was a hissing, whining sound somewhere above us. Kathy hesitated and looked at both of us. Benny knew as well as I did that at moments of conflict with her, the best thing to do was to try to change the subject. Same technique you use for toddlers.

"Shame we didn't finish the honey sandwiches..." Benny said mournfully.

He was interrupted by a loud explosion that could not have been more than a couple of streets away. There was another shrill whine and then a sudden rush of air through the shelter. Our ears popped; earth fell down into our hair through the small spaces between the overlapping tin sheets of the roof. Kathy screamed and buried her head in my chest. Her screaming was echoed by someone else's in the distance and then a man's voice shouting, repeatedly.

"Get in the bloody shelter, woman! Whassa matter with you? Get in the shelter!"

There was another thunderous crack and a flash of bright orange light.

Benny dusted earth from his hair again. "That bleeder 'Itler is layin' on a firework display tonight. Bit early for Bonfire Night, Adolf, you onanist!"

I laughed. Benny had been teaching himself all the words for self-abuse.

There were several reverberating crumps in the distance and the sound of collapsing masonry closer at hand. A child screamed and called for its mother. A fire engine's bell was clanging somewhere over towards Wentworth Road.

"Sounds like they're hammering the docks again," I said, "like last night. It's alright, Kathy, we're alright in here."

"We 'ope," added Benny, for we both knew that an Anderson Shelter taking a direct hit offered not much more protection than an umbrella. "Yeah, sounds like it, dunnit? 'Swat the bloke on the wireless said about Hitler tryin' to paralyse the com...commercial life of the capital city, n'that, an' to de..de..sunnink the confidence of the pop...?"

"De-stabilise the confidence of the populace," I provided.

"Yeah, thassit, dictionary."

"Well, you do have to wonder how much of this kind of hammering the East End can take," I muttered, hoping that Kathy would have her fingers in her ears again.

The previous night the whole of the sky to the south had been an orange glow, punctuated by volcanic spurts of flame and fire as a paint warehouse was hit by a bomb strapped to an oil drum. The tyre factory was also struck, the fumes from the blazing rubber combining with dozens of other infernos to lay a choking cloud across the East End. It seemed that if they didn't blow you to small pieces with bombs they would suffocate you with acrid smoke.

"Britons never, never, never shall be slaves!" Benny was singing loudly. "We'll go and fight for our country and kill some Huns when we're old enough. So you can f-off, Mr. Hitler!"

I didn't say anything and Benny looked at me. "Won't we?"

"I don't know, Benny. I'm not sure I agree..."

"Do what?"

"It's legalised murder, Benny."

"Whadja on about, murder?"

"Killing people because the war gives you permission. It's wrong."

"But it's not...well, killing people...I mean, it's...well, it's fightin' fer yer country, innit? If the enemy gets killed, it's too bad."

"Certainly too bad for him. And his wife. And his kids. No, it's madness."

"Hey! Kathleen! We've got a bleedin' conshi in 'ere with us! Wait 'til I tell the others about you, Tanner," sneered Benny.

"You keep swearing. You mustn't swear, Benny. Dad said."

"Yeah, Kathleen, but Dad's not 'ere, is he? It's just you, me, the conshi and the piss-pot."

"Oh!" she cried, suddenly awoken to the fact of her father's absence. "Where is he, Benny? Is he alright? I want Dad!"

"Calm down," he said. "Whassa time now?"

"About eight, I should think," I said.

"Mmm. Bit late, but, well, I 'spect 'e was on 'is way – all delays an' chaos now, innit – and then the raid started so he'll be in the Underground somewhere. 'E'll be alright, Kathleen. Dad ain't daft."

He was right. Mr. Soper was a long way from being daft and it wasn't him who was in trouble that night, but Pa.

As I said, it's odd how those events that spin your life on a different trajectory are so unexpected. But then, that's a stupid thing to say because by definition they are likely to be unexpected and in this instance, we were in the middle of an air raid when life and death are very much in the balance.

Anyway, Pa normally worked at Bow Road station but they'd shifted him over to Marble Arch for a few days. The war was creating all sorts of emergencies and gaps that had to be filled. Pa probably didn't mind: he'd just about exhausted all the available women and their daughters at Bow, so to have had a fresh supply on tap at Marble Arch must have been appealing.

He didn't get to sample the new delights, however, because that night the station was struck by a bomb; or rather, one landed in the street above, the force of the explosion penetrating deep into the womb of tunnels beneath. People flocked to the stations during a raid because they thought that the Underground was safe, but some of those high explosive bombs could smash their way through fifty feet of solid ground. Tiles lining the curving walls of one of the platforms – the one where Pa was leaning on his broom – were blown off, shattering into thousands of ceramic shards. These missiles sliced through the air and the flesh of the people down there. It was just Pa's luck that one stabbed him deep in the neck, severing a vein.

In the confusion and panic – he wasn't the only one to be injured, of course – there was no help to be had. He probably bled to death within minutes, lying where he'd been discarded by the blast, a ragged mess of broken humanity amid brick rubble, dust, bits of newspaper, rat droppings and the mutilated remains of the others who had also been on that platform. He was not a father to be proud of; far from it, but I might have wished him a more dignified death than that.

Aunty Vi came up from Southend more or less straight away to deal with everything: the undertakers, the registrar, the funeral, the landlord of the house in Bamford Road and what to do with Ma's old clothing, the drawer full of twisted cutlery and the cupboard of chipped plates. She didn't hang about, Aunty Vi; she was like a whirlwind. Not that there was much to hang about for: we owned practically nothing and what was ours was worthless.

There were only about five of us at the funeral. Vinny didn't attend. I imagine that compassionate leave would have been possible during basic training, but I doubt that he'd asked for it. I don't think I ever forgave him for that. How can you not attend your own father's funeral?

I thought that if all the dozens of women with whom Pa had ever consorted had the good grace to pay their last respects, then rather than five of us rattling about in the church, we might have needed to hire the town hall for the wake. In fact, more space than that, if they'd all been in a horizontal position, as once he had known them. But "respect" was not something that either Pa or those women knew much about.

"You're an orphan now," announced Aunty Vi with a degree of finality that seemed more suited to the reprimand of an errant tradesman. "It's very hard, I'm sure, but there are many worse off than you, you know. Not all children whose parents have died have an Aunt prepared to take them in."

I must have looked surprised.

"It's the least I can do for my sister's little boy! You see, Freddie, dear," crooned Aunty Vi, her tone shifting seamlessly from vinegar to sugar, "you'll be coming to live with me in Southend. Well, us, really!"

She gave an embarrassed laugh. This was because my Uncle Henry had died some years ago; after an almost decent interval, Aunty Vi had cemented her relationship with a certain Bernard Potter who worked on the pier and, the cementing done, he'd moved in to her place in Pleasant Road, just back from the seafront and round the corner from The Kursaal Amusement Palace. They called themselves man and wife but they did not ever marry. That always surprised me, because Aunty Vi was someone who liked things to be above-board and correct.

"Couldn't I stay here?" I muttered. I shouldn't be ungrateful, I thought, because Aunty Vi doesn't have to do this, but I didn't really want to leave Bow or be away from Kathy. The prospect of being parted from her was far more painful than the fact of Pa's ugly death.

"Where? How would you pay the rent, you silly boy? Yes, I know what you're thinking," said Aunty Vi, "and the answer is no, I'm afraid. I spoke to Mr. Soper at the funeral and it's just not possible, or practical, much as he'd like to help."

"Oh, I see." There was a strange lump forming in my throat.

"Well, now," Aunty Vi continued, moving over to the window and peering between the tapes on its grimy panes, "as you know, they're already evacuating people from London and the south of the country, so you wouldn't be here anyway; you probably won't even be able to stay in Southend for the duration. You passed the exams here, so I'm hoping that on the strength of that we can get you into Westcliff High School – but all the boys there were evacuated at the beginning of June."

"So I have to go away somewhere?" I asked, swallowing valiantly and feeling suddenly that I was about to be cast adrift in a storm, alone in an open boat. Jim Hawkins in the coracle, spun by the currents off Treasure Island.

"You'll be fine," said Aunty Vi. "Whoever decided on evacuation the first weekend in June knew what he was doing. About a week later the other boys' school in the town, Southend High, was hit by a bomb! So there you are, you see! I think they sent them somewhere up north; Derbyshire or one of those places. We'll have to see about it all when we get home. Now, I've packed your things so we can be off in the morning. You'd better just check that I've got everything you want."

"I suppose you're right, then, Aunty. Thank you," I said quietly, politely. There was no point in arguing.

I turned and made my way slowly up the stairs to sleep at Bamford Road for the last time, wondering whether the morning would provide enough time for me to say goodbye to Kathy and, if not, when and where I would see her again.

RETREATING
mid-September 1940

Violet Salthouse is a woman who likes to get things done. She is an organiser, a decision-maker and a person who stands for no nonsense. This is not to say that she is without heart or sentiment, although those who do not know her well might be forgiven for reaching that conclusion. Her neighbours, perhaps, who see her bustling from her pin-clean house each morning with a shopping basket gripped purposefully in a neatly-gloved hand, might believe that she is a proud and officious creature.

Her decision to take in her nephew has been made for the right reasons; she has felt sorry and concerned for the boy for many years, especially, of course, since her sister fell to her death and the lad was left in the hands of her odious, fornicating brother-in-law. He seems a strangely sensitive boy, given to sudden headaches and periods of quiet introspection. He is undeniably very bright; it is difficult to see from whom he has inherited that trait, or his sensitivity. It certainly was not from his father and, truth to tell, although Isobel was pretty as a girl, she was rather cold and slow.

She has not consulted with Bernard about Freddie's future but there is nothing unusual in that. Bernard does not enjoy consultation about many things, but he is an easy-going man who is happy to be told which socks he is wearing today and what newspaper he should read. He knows that Vi offers delicious compensations – the neighbours would be dumbstruck to learn – after the curtains are drawn at night. He is in his fifties; fifteen years older than Vi and at his age he is prepared to put up with being bossed about because the pay-off after dark is worth the occasional humiliation.

Perhaps his equanimity results from his work with the Southend Lifeboat at the end of the pier. He knows that nine o'clock's robust, healthy yachtsman can be nine thirty's floating corpse: seeing sudden death at close hand can give a sense of perspective. A few months previously, Bernard was reaching over the side of the "Greater London" with a grappling hook, pulling terrified soldiers from the bloodied, boiling waters off Dunkirk. He watched as men were driven relentlessly into the sea. Staggering under the weight of their equipment, sliding on mud and pebbles, the water filling their lungs, they had to pray that one of our "little ships" would haul them to safety before it was too late. Many never made it home and Bernard is thankful each time he does, even if the woman he returns to can be a bit of a nag.

"Orlright, then, son?" he says as Vi and Freddie arrive, exhausted, at Pleasant Road. "I'm sorry to 'ear about your Dad. But we'll look after you now, don't worry."

"Thank you, Uncle Bernard."

Vi flops down into a chair in the crowded back parlour which serves as both a living and a dining space. Off to the rear is what she refers to as the "scullery" and beyond that, a tiny bathroom. Bernard paid for its construction when he moved in. Vi was appreciative and pleased that it gave her a status above that of her neighbours with their outside privies and tin baths, although she remarked that most men would surely buy their lady a piece of jewellery, not a toilet bowl and a gas geyser. Bernard had responded by saying that he was a down-to-earth fellow and anyway, with his "condition", he didn't want to traipse out into the yard six times a night or get out of bed every morning and step into an over-flowing chamber pot. Vi feels that Bernard's fascination with his nocturnal bodily functions is not one of his more endearing qualities. She lifts a finger and points vaguely towards the scullery.

"Phew! Make us a cuppa, love? It's a short walk down the High Street from the station if you've nothing to carry...whatever have you got in that case, Freddie?"

"Books, Aunty Vi. I couldn't just leave them behind at Bamford Road and, anyway, I might need them," says Freddie.

"Quite the little scholar, ain'tcha?" grins Bernard, clattering about in the scullery.

"Yes, he is and we'll need to get that sorted out tomorrow," says Vi. "Make a visit to the offices there in Victoria Avenue and see what we can do. But for now, you can unpack your things and settle into your room. We've put you in the one at the front. Nice and snug in there."

The house is one of a terrace and all its rooms are small. Vi and Bernard occupy the room at the back so as to leave the front bedroom available for paying guests, not that there'll be many of those now. The whole length of the seafront has been lined with concrete anti-tank blocks and barbed wire. Buildings are being sand-bagged against the imminently expected visits of the Luftwaffe; many hotels have been requisitioned for military use, including the grand and imposing Palace Hotel. None of this is really conducive to the holiday trade.

Later, Freddie smiles to himself at his Aunt's use of the word "snug" as he battles to find enough space to swing his empty case onto the top of the wardrobe. He has already discovered that its door refuses to open fully because of the bed. "Poky" might be a better description, he thinks, but at least it's his own room; that's a first. And, if he presses his face against the window, he can see the estuary.

Downstairs, Vi whispers to Bernard that the boy seems very withdrawn; very oddly silent. A couple of times on the train, she thought he had tears in his eyes, although it was difficult to tell because he kept his face to the window through the whole journey.

"Grievin' for his Dad, perhaps?" offers Bernard.

"Don't talk rot! Good riddance to bad rubbish, that is. For his orphaned circumstances, maybe. Must be a shock, mustn't it? I wonder what's going through his mind, poor thing. But no, there's something else. I think it's the Soper girl."

"Ey?"

"People down the road in Bow. Freddie's friendly with the twins – a boy and a girl. The boy's a lumbering great oaf but the girl, Kathleen, I think she's called, is terribly pretty. They're obviously not identical twins. She's not quite all there; a bit slow, you know, but she's very sweet and she's going to be a real beauty; well, she already is, I suppose. He wanted to go down there this morning, to say goodbye to her, I think, although he didn't actually say so. You know what boys are like at that age. But there wasn't time; I thought he was going to burst into floods of tears! I think our Freddie is grieving for the girl, not his father."

"Good Gawd! He's a bit young for all that, ain't he?"

"I should say. Let's hope he doesn't moon about too much; maybe he'll forget all about her when he gets back to his studies."

"Oh, yeah, I forgot to say. Pete popped in earlier. Like you thought, the school's been evacuated up to...er...Belper, is it? Derbyshire. So the poor little sod'll be on the move again, by the sounds of it. 'Scuse my language. Pete says he can meet us up at Westcliff High on Sunday. Be no one around then, he says."

§

Pete fiddles with the old key and eventually the wooden door creaks open, giving onto a short, dusty, red-tiled corridor with, Freddie can see, stairs at the far end going both up and down.

"They call this the East Entrance," says Pete. "Them stairs go up to the East Quad. Quadrangle, see?"

Freddie thinks it sounds like a castle. It doesn't look like one but the damp smell, coupled with an odour of drains and old urine could be about right, he thinks, for an ancient castle.

"Is this the main way in, Pete?" asks Vi, holding her hand to her nose. "It's a bit, well, scruffy, isn't it? And what's that smell? Very...well, pungent."

"Nah, the main entrance is at the front, but it's all sandbagged. Yeah, does whiff a bit. Bogs over there...oh, pardon me...and no matter how much disinfectant you throw at 'em, they still pong the same. Like a stable full of incontinent horses, I always says. Even though it's been empty for a few months, it's still the same...and that's why it also smells a bit musty, like. Boys themselves stink, o'course; you know, their feet and undergarments; I'm sure most of 'em never wash, being the sons of gentlefolk an' the like, an' I 'spose they've left some of it behind. That'll be the pungent yer on about. Bit like dogs too, in certain weathers."

"How revolting," says Vi. "Thank you so much for the detailed information."

"You're the caretaker, Pete!" chimes in Bernard, winking at Vi. "Don't you have to do a bit of friggin' cleanin', now 'n then? 'Scuse my French."

"Not in front of the boy," commands Vi, but Freddie is already lost in his own reverie.

Pete shrugs his shoulders. He is, of course, supposed to do a bit of cleaning, friggin' or otherwise, but it doesn't seem to make much difference and, anyway, there's no one around to check too often, so why bother? In fact, until his cousin Vi contacted him to ask for a favour in opening the door so that her nephew could have a squint at the place he might one day return to, he hasn't been inside the main building for over a week. There's been talk of the school being used as a military hospital. Pete can see the sense in that, because it's designed like a sanatorium, each room with a door to the open air, but until someone tells him that's what's happening, he's enjoying sitting in the late summer sunshine.

"You can 'ave a wander round, son," says Pete. "You'll get a better feel on yer own. We'll have a look in Mr. Williams' study, Vi – the 'Eadmaster, like – I gotta key! Very grand; got 'is own little fireplace in there!"

"Ooh!" trills Vi.

Freddie walks up the staircase at the end of the corridor and arrives in a quadrangle. On three sides are classrooms serviced by red-tiled cloisters, open to the elements. In the middle are overgrown grass and weeds. A tabby cat is asleep in the long grass. The regurgitated remains of a mouse or a rat fester on the edge of the tiles, flies clamping to the mess.

Freddie turns to the right and sees a series of heavy-looking, panelled doors. They are locked. He tries to peer into one of the rooms, number 10, but he cannot easily see over the frosted panes at the bottoms of the windows. He jumps up several times to look through the clear glass at the top. By levering himself onto the brick window sills for a few seconds, he is afforded a series of very brief glimpses of the world he might one day occupy, should the war ever end, which he supposes it must.

There are rows of wooden desks, some pushed out of alignment by their last occupants, who appear to have been in a terrific hurry to leave. One is on its side by the far wall. Cobwebs throttle the far windows. An exercise book lies open on the master's desk which is askew on its dais. On the blackboard, in a spidery script, are the words:

Move him into the sun –
Gently its touch awoke him once,
At home, whispering of fields unsown.

The rest appears to have been partially obliterated by someone's hand dragging rapidly across the surface of the board, as if the writer was carried off suddenly by The Grim Reaper. The room seems very dark and uninviting. Although it must have once been a place of noise and productive activity, it looks and feels now like a mausoleum. He thinks he can hear voices, whispering somewhere.

He walks a little further down the corridor and sees that, in fact, one door is open. Unlike the other rooms, it is necessary with this one to enter and turn to the right. All Freddie can see as he approaches is a brick wall, painted a dull cream and scuffed by the passage of hundreds of swinging satchels.

Room 7 is a laboratory. Freddie inspects with interest the stained benches, the gas taps, a box of dirty spatulas and the glass beakers in a corner cupboard. On the master's bench, a lone Bunsen burner stands sentry. A grubby lab coat is hanging on a nail at the side of a door on the left. He opens it and looks in. It is a preparation room, its shelves and cupboards still occupied by glass bottles of chemicals and acids. Stoppers are wedged confidently into the bottles' necks. There is an odour of formaldehyde and sulphuric acid used in the experiments and many other smells that he cannot identify. There is an undercurrent of decay there too, somewhere. Perhaps the cat has dragged a rodent's corpse under a bench and then wandered off?

He begins to see the laboratory full of small boys, poring over the dissection of a frog or discovering what happens when you drop phosphorous into a beaker of water. The elderly master, his clothing protected by the white lab coat which bears testimony to many drops of acid spilled, fusses around them, cautioning here; explaining a fine detail there. The boys are being taught the component parts of explosives, so that they may efficiently blow themselves into small pieces in some corner of a foreign field in a few years' time. Maybe they already have, thinks Freddie, for the school, he is told, has been teaching boys these things for at least twenty years.

He closes his eyes and listens. Something moves lumpenly in the preparation room and then there is a pained gasp, as if someone had been punched in the solar plexus. There is a wet, gurgling exhalation, followed by barely audible words.

"Christ! Help me, mother!"

Freddie is too frightened even to move and yet is uncertain that the voice was real. Could he have imagined it?

No! Now there are other voices; louder than before: the voices of boys as they go about their work in the chemistry class in front of him; the gruff voice of a master further down the cloister, chiding someone for carelessness; in the far distance, thin, reedy voices singing in the music room; then another master's voice droning his way through Latin verse and others yet again, perhaps out on the cricket square, urging one another to take a run. Above them all, in the cloister outside, there is a dominant, authoritarian voice, raised in anger, or mock anger perhaps.

"What do you mean, boy, you don't know why Mr. Webber has put you outside the room? Are you unable to fathom a reason, you cretinous individual? What sort of future in life do you imagine you'll have if you spend all your time standing out here? Unless you pay attention in class, you'll end up on the scrap-heap, boy! Now get to my study, you idle loafer; wait for me there!"

Freddie has another headache; he rubs at his forehead, raises his spectacles and presses his eyes. He hears voices, but there is nobody here, is there? There is nobody, surely, except Aunty Vi, Bernard and Pete and they have gone the other way, along the other side of the quadrangle, towards the hall. Haven't they?

Perhaps he should try to find them? Suddenly the laboratory feels cold.

He hurries along another stretch of tiled cloister. Ahead of him are windows and doors of a different type from those of the classrooms he has just passed. This must be the hall. There are shadowy figures inside the cavernous space and he presumes they are Aunty Vi, Bernard and Pete, although they seem too small and they are not moving. He presses his nose to a window; Aunty Vi is not there. He shivers; his head is thumping.

The figures are not clear, but seem draped in gauze or drawn with a white pencil in the air somehow. Perhaps the windows are dirty? He peers even more intently and sees that the hall is full of boys...or the outlines of boys...all in blue blazers. They stand motionless, facing the stage at the front on which the gowned figure of the headmaster stands erect. He flickers in and out of Freddie's vision. There is a darker shape behind him, moving almost stealthily.

The plangent notes of a piano sound suddenly and the boys begin to sing a hymn – not heartily or confidently but, as before, in reedy, wavering notes:

There is a green hill far away,
Without a city wall,
Where our dear Lord was crucified,
Who died to save us all.

He jumps back from the window. A chill lays its hand on his neck. Surely the voices are just his imagination? They must be, he reasons. How could he know otherwise, never having been to this place before? Perhaps they are the voices of boys displaced to Belper...or those churned into the mire of some other hill far away in France, its soil not green, but crimson with blood?

He runs from the scene and heads quickly in the direction of the grown-ups. As he turns into the corridor where he thinks the headmaster's study could be, the red tiles begin to swim under his feet. He manages to grab at the side of a cupboard to slow his swoon to the floor. Aunty Vi comes running to his aid.

STOLEN JUICES
Thursday 10th October 1940

My dearest Kathy,

I hope you can read this alright. Get little Norah to help you if it's too hard. I don't mind. That's if Norah is still next door, of course. I am greatly troubled to realise that I'm not sure where you are. You didn't put any address on the last letter and I couldn't read the postmark! I wonder if you have been evacuated too? I shall post this to 16 Bamford Road in the hope that somehow it will find you.

I am sorry I did not manage to see you to say goodbye last month. Please don't think I went away without a care. You know that is not true. I cried most of the way to Southend. On that morning, Aunty Vi said there was no time, but actually we had to wait for ages for a train. And then it went very slowly and they checked our papers every five minutes, it seemed. What a big panic! Anyway, I am sorry, Kathy.

Also I'm sorry not to have written or anything for so long. Don't get the wrong idea. It's just been so difficult and busy. I think of you every day and I think of you every night! (No more comment necessary!)

I have a place at Westcliff High School for Boys in Southend. Because I passed the exam in London, Aunty Vi managed to pull some strings. It's a very good school, apparently, but at the moment we are evacuated to a place called Belper in Derbyshire. That is where I am now. We have to share buildings that belong to the Herbert Strutt School here. The local boys don't like us much and we don't like them. They speak in a funny way!

I have been taken in by Mr. and Mrs Shaw. It's the rule that people have to give a home to evacuees. I am not living in the town. The Shaws' farm is some distance out of the town in a place called Belper Lane End. It's nothing like the East End! Here it's all fields and farms and it's very quiet. Yes, like Paglesham before this blasted war. Remember? What a lovely time we had that day! I remember someone who fell in the water!

I have to help with the farm work. In the mornings I have to get up early and feed the hens. You would like them. They are very large and have speckled feathers.

I have to write this under the blankets because it's quite late and Mrs Shaw has already told me twice to put the light out. She seems to think I'm only ten years old! It's freezing cold up here. I had a lot of homework to do but I really wanted to write to you tonight so I can post it when we go into Belper on Saturday.

I am alright here. It's hard work at school and the masters are very strict but most realise that it's difficult for us boys away from home. Wherever that is!? I suppose none of us expected to be in Derbyshire. It's difficult to know what to believe, Kathy. Some are already saying that there's no need for this mass evacuation because there is no real danger for us in Westcliff. But Uncle Bernard told me that they have ack-ack guns on Southend Pier! All along the sea-front there are concrete things to stop Hitler's tanks getting ashore and they say that bombs drop every night in Southend as the bombers head back to Germany, anxious to dump the load they haven't found a place for in London. So I don't know what to think. Please let me know what's going on where you are, if you can. Are you still getting bombs there?

We had some fun yesterday! The playing fields for the Herbert Strutt School are on the other side of the Belper Road. In some gardens next to the playing fields there are some fruit trees. Apples, pears. Lovely, eh? Well, we could see some pears still on the branches, so Peter Floate and I decided to see if we could climb up and scrump some.

It was lunch time and we reckoned most of the masters would be in the staff room smoking their pipes (the fug!) but Peter kept watch, just in case, while I shinned up the tree. You have to be careful! The Old Man (that's what we call the headmaster, Mr. Williams) sometimes has a bit of a walk round then. I managed to get about six big ripe ones before I almost fell down. I was feeling dizzy, you know, like I do sometimes. I think I was nervous about getting caught, so I was shaking a bit as well! What a feeble wreck!

Peter and I ate two each, there and then. Delicious! I had pear juice all down my blazer and it was quite difficult to get it off before afternoon lessons started. I didn't care when I was scoffing the pears because you forget just how hungry you are sometimes! Mrs Shaw is very kind but food is short what with the rationing and everything and sometimes all we have is just an Oxo cube in hot water or some soup made of something revolting that I won't mention because I know some things make you spew!

Kathy, I miss you so very much. Thank you for your little letter I got last week. Do I remember that evening in the cemetery? I should say so! Such a romantic spot, wasn't it?

I really want to see you. Nothing else seems to matter. I know we're not supposed to feel like that because we're too young but I do think about you all the time. I mean it, I'm not just saying it to make you feel better. I am going to try to get to London just after Christmas. I don't know how. Yes, I know it's quite crazy but I don't care. Aunty Vi says I have to concentrate on my studies and forget all about girls. She says it's too early for girls and it's not proper. She means you, of course. I cannot concentrate or forget about you, Kathy. You are now the most important person in my life. Did you realise that?

I will write again. Please let me know where you are. You can write to me at the address at the top of this letter which is the Shaws' farm.

One day, Kathy, we will be together again, forever. After the war, I suppose. Believe me, I mean it, I promise you.

From,

Freddie

xx

WHISPERING OF FIELDS UNSOWN
29th December 1940

In the very early hours of Sunday morning, Freddie slithers down a drainpipe adjacent to his bedroom window at the Shaws' farm and makes off towards the lane. His feet crunch on ice and snow underfoot; he tries to tiptoe for he is fearful of waking the dogs in the old barn. It is so cold that his breath is frozen stalactites in the air around him; he trusts that the shabby old coat that Mrs Shaw has bequeathed him will be warm enough.

He has left a note on his bed, explaining to Mrs Shaw that he hopes to get down to London to see a girl called Kathleen. He tells her the truth; he writes all about Kathleen; he tells her that he'll be alright, that he'll be back on the Monday or Tuesday but he just has to see the girl, for she is his childhood sweetheart. He cannot get her from his mind; he thinks he will settle better when he's seen her. He apologises for being such a trouble and causing her worry but hopes she will understand the reason for what he is sure she will regard as erratic, unseemly behaviour. He has a feeling she will.

He is not sure how he is going to get down to London. The government, in a state of panic about the likelihood of German hordes crossing the Channel, has put in place a whole series of measures designed to confuse an invader and to enable the military and civil authorities to monitor all movement within an exclusion zone stretching from The Wash to Lyme Regis in Dorset. Checks are made at road blocks, on buses and trains. Those without official permits or who are not residents or who do not have a good enough reason for their journey can be turned back or even prosecuted. Road signs and anything else giving or implying geographical location have all been removed. He could not make it on his own for the way would be impossible to find once he got closer to the city.

Aunty Vi gave him some money before he left Southend that he was supposed to give to the Shaws, but they would not hear of it. He intends to use this for the journey and prays it will be enough; if not, he'll get as far as he can and then hope to hitch a lift with someone who knows the road; if there is anyone, of course. He has never done such a thing before and is ignorant of the procedures and etiquette, but needs must.

There are long delays on the train; sometimes it stops for ages among fields for no apparent reason. Two soldiers in battledress get on at Leicester heaving their kitbags noisily into the luggage racks.

"Alright, lad?" says one, lighting a Woodbine and dropping with a sigh onto the seat. "Blow me, though, those bags are heavy. Where'ya off to?"

"London," says Freddie, wondering immediately about the wisdom of revealing his destination to a stranger.

"On ya own?" says the other man, licking the paper of his roll-up. "You off your rocker, lad?"

"Well, I...I'll be alright," stutters Freddie, wondering whether he will and remembering something Mr. Soper said about guarding against impetuosity.

"Ah hope you've got your papers; they're checking, you know. Off to see your girl, is it?" laughs the first, blowing a plume of smoke upwards. "Wish Ah bloody was. Don't know whether Ah'll ever see her again in this Life. Still, Ah saw quite a bit of her back o' the old stables last night; bits Ah ent seen before, ey, Bill?"

Bill chuckles knowingly and pulls at the trousers of his creased battledress.

The soldier's remark is fortuitous, for it gives Freddie a chance to rehearse a story, should he be asked. Sure enough, there are police waiting on the platform at Bedford. They open all the carriage doors and begin methodically to question the occupants of each carriage.

"Let me see your Identity card, Sonny-Jim," grunts a surly young police officer. He passes a hand across his nose and dislodges a small glob of mucus which hangs there pendulously for a moment before dropping onto his jacket. He opens the dun-brown document and studies it carefully.

"Says you live in Southend-on-Sea. What are you doing here?"

"On my way back there. Have to go through London, officer," says Freddie nervously. "My school is evacuated to Belper in Derbyshire."

The soldier with the Woodbine looks up, recollecting that the boy had said nothing about Southend-on-Sea earlier. He wonders whether to say so and thinks better of it. Let the lad have some fun with his girl.

"So why aren't you staying there? It's dangerous in London, son. Why are you travelling alone?" The police officer looks intently at the boy.

"My Aunt in Southend is seriously ill. I live with her. I'm an orphan. I got a message to come at once," Freddie says, rather too fast and with his fingers crossed under the ragged coat.

"Let me see the message, please."

Freddie coughs nervously. His plan could founder here and now and put him in big trouble. "I'm...very sorry, Officer," he stutters, "I'm afraid I don't have a written message. I was told by my headmaster."

"He could confirm that no doubt?" says the officer.

Freddie is not normally a liar and he knows he is digging an enormous pit for himself, but has to see Kathleen. It's worth the risk.

"Well, I suppose so, if you could contact him on a Sunday morning," he bluffs.

The police officer pauses, considering the probable difficulty of making that contact and the improbability of the little lad in front of him being a saboteur or a German infiltrator. He hands back the identity card.

"It's a bit unusual, but I'll let it pass. Next time, make sure you have everything possible to support your story. A note from your teacher on the school letter paper, for example," snaps the officer. "There's a blessed war on, you know."

"Yes, Officer."

There are no more incidents; luck is on Freddie's side for the rest of the journey. He makes it to London by late afternoon. Already it is getting dark as he picks his way through the shattered streets of Bow towards the cemetery; for it is there that he has suggested they meet. He wonders if Kathy has received his last letter. There was no reply. Perhaps he is insane to travel south when he doesn't even know that she'll be there. He wonders too whether she would just wait, perhaps hour after hour in these temperatures, a chill wind strengthening by the hour, not knowing whether he was coming or not. Both of us, he thinks, have placed a blind trust in the other.

He picks his way between the graves, heading for the yew trees. He sees movement.

"Freddie! Oh, Freddie! You did it!" From behind the furthest tree where she has been sheltering from the biting wind, Kathleen comes running towards him, throwing herself into his arms, burying her face in his neck.

His heart seems to ricochet against his ribs like a caged animal. He puts a hand to her head.

"Kathy, Kathy! I wondered...I didn't know...please, let me look at you!"

But the girl is not going to let go of him so soon; she has dreamed of this moment for weeks; he has promised it to her and now that it's here, she will hold him close, forever if possible. And anyway, she is crying tears of absolute joy and is too embarrassed to let him see just yet.

After a while, they pull apart a little and look at one another. She has grown. Even though she is wearing thick clothing, he can see that her shape has altered. He is sure that she is more beautiful than he remembers, even with red eyes and tears rolling down her cheeks. As she stares into his face, holding him tight by the hand, Kathleen feels calmer and more whole than she has for weeks; as if miraculously a part of her body that had been paralysed suddenly now has its sensations returned. They do not need to speak. Being together is more important than words.

Freddie is aware of another figure emerging from behind the tree.

"The wanderin' conshi returns, then, ey, mate?" Benny announces, a little sarcastically.

"Hello, Benny," says Freddie, trying not to show his surprise and irritation. But, as ever, Benny has read his mind.

" 'Salright, don't look so pissed off! I ain't intendin' to play goosegog, but I couldn't just leave 'er 'ere on 'er own, could I? You might not 'ave showed up. Anyway, Dad wouldn't have let 'er; he made enough noise about two of us, let alone 'er by hisself. I'll sod off in a bit, don't worry."

"Oh, I see, Benny, yes of course, I'm sorry. Ahem, um, so how are things? Merry Christmas, by the way. A bit late."

"Bugger Christmas, Freddie," says Benny caustically. "Don't see much to be merry about round 'ere. People's gettin' killed every blinkin' day."

"I suppose you're right. I live on a farm up there. We had chicken on Christmas Day."

"Bully fer you, mate! We 'ad a bit of scrag-end, but she had to queue fer bleedin' hours at Crossley's ter geddit."

Freddie looks at his friend, wondering about the bitterness that seems to have possessed him since they met last. He supposes it must be the ill-feeling about "conshis", given Benny's opening remark.

"Yes, they say it's really hard in London, now, because of the bombing every day."

"Too bloody right!"

Kathleen has her arm round his waist, squeezing hard.

"Kathy! Let me breathe!"

"Sorry! You're really here!"

"We listen to the BBC every night, where I am. It's very quiet up there, but not here, by the look of it. I can't believe how much damage has been done since September...I mean, whole streets gone, houses toppling into the gutter; fire damage, roads with craters the size of a cricket pitch...shouldn't you be, well, evacuated?"

Benny laughs. "Yeah, 'spose. But Dad won't have none of it. We manage. Britons will never be slaves an' all that; remember?"

"A bomb dropped on Arrow Road, Freddie," says Kathleen, her eyes widening. "Alice Jordan got killed."

"Really? Good grief!"

Benny laughs again, this time the dirty laugh that Freddie remembers so well.

"Yeah. She wos lyin' on her back wiv her legs open as usual and, you know wot? They say she didn't even notice Jerry's great big explosive thing bangin' into 'er until she realised one of 'er legs was missin'! Then she died; bled ter death, they say."

"Benny!" squeals Kathleen, "That's not very nice."

"Not really very funny, either Benny, even if Alice Jordan is, was a...well, you know."

"Bloody 'ell, Freddie, that school's givin' you some airs 'n graces, innit? Just a joke."

Freddie looks down at the ground, adjusts his glasses and pushes at a frozen tussock with his toe. Perhaps his old friend is right. Maybe it is him who has changed.

Benny coughs. "Anyway, I'm off; I'll leave you two love-birds alone! Just make sure you get 'er back to Bamford Road by about six, right? I'll be waitin' on the corner. And don't be late. And behave yerselves! No hanky-panky, right?"

As Benny trudges off towards the gates, Kathleen looks up at Freddie.

"Where are we going to go? It's cold here."

"I don't know. I'm sorry, Kathy, I didn't think of that. Well, I suppose we'll just have to walk about until it's time to take you back."

Freddie calculates that, at best, they have about an hour and a half together. He shuts from his mind the thought of having to say goodbye after such a short time and, worse than that, the worry of how to get back to Belper at night.

"There's people about everywhere," whispers Kathleen. "But not in here. No one can see us in here. I want to..."

She lifts her head and puts her hand around the back of his neck. As they kiss, for only the second time in their lives, Freddie feels his knees begin to give way under him. Whatever the difficulties he has faced to get here and will endure to get back, it's all worth it for this one moment. Moments are what he experiences now and not continuums.

He's not quite sure why or how, but as the honey sweetness of Kathy's mouth melts in his own, he divines that whatever he thought might unfold for him in the future, whatever plans he may have laid, whatever dreams he may have nurtured...they are all as dust in the night wind.

HE MAKETH ME DOWN TO LIE
29th December 1940

There wasn't much else we could do except walk about the smashed streets. All I knew when I set out that morning was that I had to see Kathy. I hadn't thought about where we might go or how I'd get back that night or, indeed, whether I could find somewhere to stay and go back the next day. Quite irrational, I suppose.

"Maybe Benny could find a way of getting you into our house," she suggested. "Without Dad knowing, I mean. Then I could see you tomorrow as well."

"Oh, what, like in the coal hole?" I laughed. "I don't know about that."

She looked at me as if she thought I was being defeatist, as if she expected me to come up with an answer. I couldn't. All my ingenuity and reserves of mental strength had been used up just getting there. I hadn't thought further than that.

So we wandered for a while, hand in hand, up Brokesley Street towards the Bow Road. Everywhere you looked there was destruction. The fronts of houses had collapsed; roofs were burned back to a few spars of charred timber; the roads were partly blocked with piles of rubble and permeating everything was a foul smell of broken sewers, ruptured gas mains and seared flesh. Kathy didn't ignore it all but she seemed less troubled than I was. I suppose that was because she'd lived through the decline into chaos whereas I'd been cosseted in Derbyshire. I began to feel guilty. If anything, the wind was even stronger and we huddled together for warmth, stopping every now and then in the shelter of a tree or behind a broken wall or a teetering fence to nuzzle at one another or steal a furtive kiss.

At about five o'clock, the sirens started to wail. Even as the unearthly sound began, we could hear the droning rumble of approaching bombers over the river and see the first flashes in the sky behind us as the docks began to take another pounding.

"Oh, no!" shrieked Kathy. "What are we going to do?"

We were too far from Bamford Road to make a run for it. In any case, what would Mr. Soper say if I fell into his Anderson Shelter, holding hands with his daughter? We stood in the street, a pair of lost sheep.

"Hey, you two!" yelled a warden, blowing furiously on his tin whistle to attract our attention. "What in God's name are you doing standing there like stuffed dummies? Move! Get into the Underground!"

I didn't need to be told twice. Grabbing Kathy's hand even more tightly, I dragged her into Bow Road and towards the station. We weren't the only ones to be making for the place. As we arrived at the entrance there was quite a jostle to get through and down onto the platforms.

"Look out!" yelled a voice. "Be careful! Let my mother through! She's eighty six!"

We moved slowly with the nervous crowd deeper into the bowels of the earth. I suppose if you'd been looking for a definition of Hell at that time, then worming underground into claustrophobic, crowded tunnels while high explosives detonated above; the threat of collapse and burial alive ever-present, then this would have been it. Humans made into rats. I tried not to think too much about where I was or what might happen, but rather to concentrate on helping Kathy down the stairs.

It was hot, airless and it stank. The station was being used daily by local people for protection. Some raids lasted for hours and so people had taken to bedding down for the night and relieving themselves in the tunnels. The stench of urine and faeces was overpowering, to say the least. Kathy gagged as we found our way onto a platform. She held her scarf over her nose.

"I suppose you get used to it," I shouted above the din. She shook her head.

People were standing about forlornly or were elbowing themselves a bit of space between those already sitting or lying on the cold platform. Some were clutching at blankets, thermos flasks, baskets of whatever food they had grabbed as they ran terrified from their homes. One family had a yapping mongrel dog tied with a piece of string to the leg of a bench. Children wailed and held on to grubby teddy bears, little toy cars or ragged comfort blankets. One group, further down the platform, appeared to be trying to put on a show for everyone else. They were trying to sing, "We're gonna hang out the washing on the Siegfried Line", conducted, after a fashion, by a fat, little fellow wearing a striped, sleeveless pullover. Behind him a small boy was leaning backwards slightly, urinating in a large arc onto the track.

"Watch out! We was 'ere first!" shouted a woman.

"So? You bought the bleedin' platform, didja?" said another. "Budge up a bit for us, ey, ducks?"

Grumbling, moaning, laughing, cajoling, shouting; gradually the crowds settled and groups coalesced into a mood of tolerant wariness, acknowledging deep-down that they had to co-exist in order to overcome the depredations forced upon them by the common enemy.

Of course, there was no telling whether this raid was to be ten minutes or ten hours and so I thought it best that we too should try to find a space to sit, in case it was a long one. As I was seeking a spot, someone shouted out that the docks were ablaze, that the wind was fanning the flames and parts of Canning Town and the factories along Bow Creek were already an inferno.

" 'Slike the Great Fire of London all over again!"

"It'll get rid of some of the bleedin' rats, then!" said someone else and others laughed ruefully.

"Oi, son! There's a bit of a space at the end, look. Take your sister dahn there!" A thin woman was calling out conspiratorially and pointing with a shaking finger towards the far end of the platform, near the gaping, black mouth of the tunnel. It wasn't obvious that there was a space but as we got closer, climbing over sleeping forms and stepping between squabbling children, I saw that in fact there was. At the end of the platform, someone had piled some barriers. There was also a big stack of burst sandbags. Between all this and the smudged, tiled wall of the end of the platform was a small space about eight feet long and two feet wide. Two or three of the barriers had toppled over against the wall to form a kind of roof. I couldn't believe our luck. We wriggled into the safety of this burrow and sat with our backs to the walls. We were still holding hands.

"It doesn't smell so bad now," said Kathleen, giggling.

"Mmm," I said hesitantly. "I think the air in here has changed direction, hasn't it? It was blowing out of that tunnel a minute ago. That's why it ponged. People are using it as a toilet. Now it seems to be sucking into the tunnel from this side; from outside, I mean, the way we came in."

Even as I spoke, the movement of air seemed to increase, bringing with it a different smell to replace the former one, but it was no more appealing. It was the horrible, choking stench of hundreds of fires blazing in the high winds all over the East End. After a while, we could smell something oddly spicy which began to irritate the backs of our throats. People were coughing and spluttering all around us.

"They must've hit the spice warehouses on the East India Dock," a choked voice managed to shout. "It's fuckin' pepper, that's what it is!"

"Ordinary pepper will do for me, thanks all the same! Will you be servin' the boiled eggs, shortly, then, mate?" quipped someone else, to much laughter.

A woman on the other side of the barrier let us have a splash of water from her jerry-can. We tried to wash the pepper from our throats and I soaked the ends of Kathy's scarf so that we could each put wet cloth over our noses and mouths until the pepper cloud abated. It took some time.

"Are you alright with staying in here for the night, then, sister?" I said later, the scarf put aside. I grinned at her, remembering the woman's remark earlier.

Certainly it looked as though the raid had solved my worry about where to go and, what's more, it looked as though I would be able to stay with Kathy all night! Alone in a restless crowd.

"Why did she think I was your sister?"

"Because we look so young and innocent and it didn't occur to her that we are really boy and girl and I've carried you off to have my wicked way with you. And because you don't look like that kind of girl."

I'm not sure why I said that. It wasn't the kind of thing I would normally say to Kathy. Benny would make that kind of remark, but not me, because she'd misunderstand or become frightened, not really registering the joking tone of one's voice. But I suppose we all underestimated her increased abilities as she grew up. We tended to treat her as if she was always only five. She wasn't; she changed.

"That's right; I'm not that kind of girl. But you can if you want," she whispered.

I didn't quite know how to react. It threw me for a bit. I just gave a bit of a non-committal chuckle. We both seemed to be saying things out of character! I suppose that what Kathy knew – or sensed – was that our relationship had changed with that first kiss in July. We were no longer little kids occasionally holding sticky hands. I wasn't too sure just what we were if it wasn't that, but Kathy had obviously come to her own conclusion. She'd had time to think about it while I was pre-occupied with Pa's death and the moves to Southend and Belper. I was a little embarrassed by her remark; maybe even a little anxious about what having my "wicked way" would actually entail now that she had, quite extraordinarily, given the green light. I busied myself pushing some rubbish out of our space and adjusting the barriers so that we had more privacy.

Kathy looked at me and smiled sweetly. "Who knows when we'll see each other again?"

"Carpe diem?" I grinned. "Seize the day, is it? Crikey, Kathy!"

After a while, it began to quieten down on the platform. People had to accept that they were there for the night and they settled to some kind of uncomfortable sleep. The lights flickered continuously and then, later, some were turned off. Those that were left on cast a ghostly yellow light on the bodies scattered untidily across the platform.

Occasionally we could hear the thumping and crunching of bombs detonating. Many of these, I think, were far off but the sounds and the puffs of air coming down the tunnels and shafts somehow made them seem closer than they were. Sometimes we could feel the ground shake beneath us as a high explosive charge drove into the earth somewhere fairly close. Muck would rain down on us then from high in the shadowy cavern of the station and people would scream or call out some imprecation or appeal to the Lord.

Every now and then someone would shout a report on events, gleaned one supposed from wardens on the surface or from a radio in a ticket office or something. It sounded pretty grim and I was glad we were tucked away in our burrow of sandbags and barriers. It was extraordinary, but once we were in there, no one else could see us. A man with a beard shuffled into the opening after we'd been there a couple of hours or so, but when he saw that it was occupied, he shuffled away again.

Eventually, through sheer exhaustion, we decided to try to sleep. We had been sitting up, Kathy leaning into my shoulder, but neither of us was really comfortable. My right arm was numb and Kathy said she had a crick in her neck. But how do you make a bed on a concrete platform? I decided to see if I could find something to help. Kathy was anxious about being left alone but I promised to be only a few minutes. I made my way along the platform, making sure not to tread on people, and then up the stairs to the ticket hall. To my surprise, no one challenged me. I was back in the burrow in probably less than five minutes.

"Here we are, Madam," I said. "I'll make up your bed now!"

I had found a small pile of newspapers, a couple of rather damp cardboard boxes and the remains of an old blanket.

"Not just for me," said Kathy. "We can share; it'll be warmer."

"But..."

"Yes, Freddie, please. I want to hold you. No one will see. No one will know. Please?"

"Alright."

We spread the papers and the cardboard onto the concrete and then I put my coat on top of them. Kathy's coat served as a very small eiderdown and the bit of old blanket we rolled into a makeshift pillow inside her scarf. It was hardly interior sprung, but it didn't matter.

"Snug as a bug in a rug," she said.

"I wouldn't be surprised," I laughed.

After a few moments, Kathy whispered into my ear. "Freddie, will it always be like this? Fighting and bombs and killing?"

I wasn't sure what to say for the best. I tried to be optimistic. "I hope not; I expect it'll be alright when we win the war."

"Are we going to win, then?"

"Of course. When it's over, you'll see. It'll be a different world then. And we'll be together. Happy."

And then we were quiet. We lay on our sides with our arms around one another. It was almost dark but there was just about enough light for me to see her face. She looked intently into my eyes, hardly blinking at all.

"Kathy...I don't think we ought to..."

"Ssh," she whispered, putting a finger onto my mouth.

We lay like that for some considerable time, just looking at one another. It's surprising what you can say without using language. And it's surprising what you can do if you let your instincts have their head!

She shifted towards me and put her lips to mine, her tongue flickering into my mouth, a shy fawn taking its first drink at the lake. Gently, clumsily, I ran my hand down her back and then around to the front. She had on a thick cardigan, buttoned almost to the throat. Expertly, with one hand, she unbuttoned that, the blouse beneath and then guided me inside. I had never touched a girl's breasts. Briefly, I remembered what I had seen when she fell in the water at Paglesham. She certainly had grown a bit since then! I was shaking like a man with palsy.

Of course, neither of us had been this way before at all. It should not have been happening. We were very young. We were not married – could not have been married, because of our age. Sexual contact between young people was a big taboo; still is; perhaps slightly less so now although that will change even more, I'm sure. What we were doing was tantamount to sin but it didn't seem to matter to us at the time. We didn't see it as sinful because, as mankind so often discovers, the heat of the passionate moment had more-or-less overcome conscience.

We helped one another with more buttons and belts, experimenting, assessing the route, murmuring our assent to one another as we began the climb. I recall the sensation of fine hairs on her upper calf and then the shock as I discovered that she was entirely naked under her skirt. I withdrew my hand suddenly, as if my fingers had been stung by flame. She giggled.

"I don't like drawers," she whispered into my ear. "Remember?"

She found my hand and drew it back under her skirt, between her loins. She shuddered and made a little whimpering noise.

"Ssh, Kathy! People will hear!" I muttered. She wasn't listening. "Anyway, look, maybe we ought to stop...you know, it's..."

She held my wrist to prevent me withdrawing my hand again and shook her head.

After a while, the caressing and stroking having become even more in earnest, if that was possible, I stopped worrying about the people on the other side of the barrier, or whether Mr. Soper would by now be calling the police; whether Aunty Vi knew what was going on, how I would get back to Belper to face Mrs Shaw or, more importantly, whether Kathy and I should be doing what we were doing. I gave in. For both of us, starved in one way or another of affection, there seemed to be no turning back.

Anyway, it was very quickly too late to worry about the morality of our actions.

"Good Lord above!" I whispered when we'd stopped wriggling. "No wonder grown-ups don't want you to know about it!"

She turned to me and put a hand behind my neck, pulling me towards her again.

"I love you, Freddie," she said simply. And it was true; I knew it.

"I've always loved you, Kathy," I replied. "You know that, don't you?"

"Yes."

I felt that I should pull away from her but she held on to me; not just with her arms but with her legs too. It even seemed that I was held tight inside her; not uncomfortably or against my will, but rather as if she was trying with her quivering muscles to pull me deeper into her womb.

There wasn't much noise out on the platform by this time: just the occasional voice or a child grizzling or the mongrel dog giving a cursory yap. Then a girl's voice – or perhaps a young boy's – began to sing. It was a lone voice, so unexpected in that place, so clear, so perfect and so resonant as it soared into the dark cavern above us that it sent a chill through us both.

The Lord's my Shepherd, I'll not want
He maketh me down to lie
In pastures green he leadeth me
The quiet waters by.

Kathy was weeping; not I think because she would necessarily have understood the full import of the words but simply because of the emotional force of that beautiful sound and what had happened between us; and all in such an ugly place.

Some minutes after the singing finished, Kathy began to move against me once more and I felt myself respond immediately and with urgency, as if we had not already made love. I was breathless, not just with the effort of keeping my exertions quiet but also with surprise at Kathy. For years we had seen her as silly, simple and therefore incompetent. She wasn't that night!

Afterwards, we lay there for several minutes, each coming to terms, I suppose, with the significance of our actions.

"Freddie?"

"Mmm?"

"Did we make a baby?"

"Oh, Lord!" I whispered again. The thought that such a thing was possible had not even entered my mind. I was horrified at my thoughtlessness, irresponsibility and impetuosity. So much for a fine English education! Was this, I wondered, one of those moments that Mr. Soper had talked of that day at Paglesham? A moment that affects your plans forever? I decided it was highly likely to be; I hoped I was wrong although at that moment I didn't really care.

A LIGHT GLEAMS AND IS GONE
5th May 1941

"Tanner!" barks Mr. Midgley.

"Present, Sir."

"Tanner, you are to report to the headmaster's study after break. You are excused period three. Go to period four as normal. Ah, Tompkins?"

"Present, Sir."

"Turnbull?"

"Present, Sir."

Freddie bravely and gingerly raises his hand. Mr. Midgley is a good teacher and he can be a kind man to the boys in his form, but he can also be sarcastic and he has a bite like a mad dog.

"What's the matter, Tanner? Not a weak bladder, I trust, so soon in the day?"

"Sir, er, no, Sir, but please, Sir, why do I have to go to Mr. Williams' study, Sir?"

"Tanner," says Mr. Midgley, dropping his pen with a clatter, "what do you think we are engaged upon here this bright, summer's morning? A parlour game? I have not the vaguest notion, dear boy. I am but an humble English teacher, not a clairvoyant. In this instance, I am a form master too and thus merely a conduit, a messenger, a carrier of information and tidings the significance of which is not mine to know. Now, I do concede that it is an unorthodox decree from On High, Tanner, for it requires that you should be untimely ripped from Mr. Smith's chemistry lesson. Accordingly, even though we must soon return to the business of registration, we may indulge in a little whimsy and speculation."

Mr. Midgley strokes his chin affectedly and gazes to the heavens.

"Let's see: you have been called to an audience with the headmaster either because you have sinned in extremis, or, you are about to have a great honour conferred upon you publicly and Mr. Williams, being the upright and thoughtful headmaster that he is, has decided to advise you of the fact before the public announcement, lest that splendid ceremony, including gun salutes and jolly bunting, should take you unawares and embarrass you. Now, which do you think is more likely, boy?"

Freddie swallows loudly. The other boys titter, laughing at their form master's deliberately verbose performance. They are grateful that his renowned sarcasm is not directed at them.

"I don't know, Sir."

"You have no idea, Tanner?"

"No, Sir."

"Dear, oh, dear. No doubt illumination shall follow." Mr. Midgley holds up a slip of paper. "Herewith my instructions, conveyed to you as they are written for me and inserted by an unknown hand into this register of your names. So, Tanner: *Theirs not to reason why, Theirs but to do and die.* Find out where that comes from by registration tomorrow, Goadsby, and stop fiddling with your satchel. End of break, Tanner, the headmaster's study. Understood?"

"Yes, Sir."

"Yes, Sir," says Goadsby, his acne flushing a bright red.

"Turvey?"

"Present, Sir."

§

Freddie makes his way to the corridor where the secretary's office and the headmaster's study are located. He has never been in trouble before; this is a puzzle. To the best of his knowledge, apart from the scrumping in October last year, he has never done anything wrong in school. He thinks it unlikely that Mr. Williams would have waited seven months before dealing with the matter of a few stolen pears; even more unlikely that it would be dealt with by extracting him from class. Have the Shaws complained about something? Surely not? Unlike some boys, he has behaved himself in his foster home; indeed, he has mucked in and helped on the farm, much to the Shaws' approval.

It's true that Mr. and Mrs Shaw were angry with him over his deception at Christmas, but the school was not made aware of this because Mrs Shaw extracted a promise from Freddie that nothing like it would ever happen again. In any case, she thinks him a charming, handsome boy and is not surprised that some lass has pinned her heart to her sleeve for him. Certainly, he seems more settled having seen the girl; no doubt they have come to some understanding or pledged their troth.

Freddie has paid attention in class and always completed his homework on time. His masters indicate that he is a very clever boy and is making excellent progress with a promising academic future ahead of him, the war always permitting, of course, so what could the matter be?

He takes a deep breath, adjusts his school tie and taps gently on the headmaster's imposing, oak-panelled door.

"Enter!" booms a voice.

Freddie turns the brass handle and enters the study. The headmaster is sitting behind his highly polished desk, in front of long windows that look out over playing fields, stone walls enclosing flocks of grazing sheep and then, far beyond, mauve hills. Fleetingly, Freddie registers their enticing folds and wishes he could be among them rather than where he is.

Sitting to the headmaster's right are Archie Soper, Kathleen and Aunty Vi. Freddie stops just inside the doorway, frozen for a moment in surprise and apprehension. Mr. Soper and his aunt look at him rather coldly, he thinks. Kathleen will not meet his gaze. She looks down at her hands in her lap, fidgeting with her fingernails. She seems to have put on some weight.

"Sit down, Tanner," says Mr. Williams, rather sharply.

"Yes, Sir," he manages to whisper hoarsely, his mind racing to make sense of this extraordinary situation. There can be only one answer and he begins to shake as he deduces what it must be. They must know about the night on the platform; they made Kathy tell and that's why she won't look up. But she wouldn't tell! Maybe she's been ill and a Doctor's examination has revealed...something?

But Freddie is not sure what that something might be

because the curriculum does not include a consideration of the hymen.

"I see that some slow dawning is occurring, Tanner?" pronounces Mr. Williams. "But before we begin, I do think you should have the good manners to greet the people in front of you, don't you?"

Freddie sits, staring into space, a rabbit caught in the glare of headlights.

"Tanner? Did you hear what I said?"

Freddie squirms. "Yes, Sir, sorry. Good morning, Mr. Soper, Aunty Vi." He pauses. "Hello, Kathy."

"Oh, Freddie," says Vi reproachfully. Mr. Soper nods curtly and Kathleen lifts her head for a second and gives a brief, bashful grin.

" 'Lo," she manages, barely audibly.

Aunty Vi's tone seems to confirm his worst suspicions. Freddie can see that Kathleen has been crying, although she looks otherwise very well. In fact, she is so beautiful, her skin so flawless, he wants to abandon all his schoolboy woes and carry her off to some little cottage in the slumbering mauve hills that he sees through the window. He's pretty sure she'd jump into his arms if he tried it. If they were quick, the grown-ups might never catch them. Maybe never, forever. Briefly, fantastically, it offers an appealing future; more appealing, at any rate, than the one that he fears may now be set before him.

"I'm not going to waste time asking you what you think this is all about, Tanner. I shall come to the point because we are all busy people and I have things requiring my urgent attention after this brief meeting," says Mr. Williams, wishing to make it abundantly clear that he's allocated five minutes to this difficult business and no more.

"Yes, Sir."

"It is not our usual custom to become involved in these kinds of issues where our boys are concerned, Mrs Salthouse. Our function is to educate, not to offer complex moral guidance. But this wretched war is creating unusual circumstances for all of us and I recognise that in those circumstances some boys' studies may be compromised. I fear that here, Tanner, if what I am told is true, your own very promising future will be cut short by your intemperate actions some months ago. I must say, I'm surprised at you, boy."

Freddie feels a sudden contraction of fear in his stomach, as if the headmaster had plunged a knife through his abdomen.

"Mr. Williams," says Archie Soper a little impatiently, feeling that they are becoming mired in verbiage, "I apologise for the interruption but I would simply like my daughter to tell Freddie what she told me two weeks ago. Perhaps we can then hear what he has to say. Then we can see where we go."

Mr. Williams looks a little annoyed. He is not accustomed to being interrupted, especially not by a tax collector.

"I was just coming to that, Mr. Soper, thank you. Please be good enough, Miss Soper, to comply with your father's suggestion."

Kathleen blushes as she looks up. She is confused by the man in the strange, black cloak. All eyes are on her.

"He means you are to tell Freddie what you told me; come on, Kathleen," says her father.

A clock is ticking on top of the headmaster's school trophy cabinet. Time passes; the mauve hills slumber. They all look at Kathleen. She draws a long, shuddering breath. Tears begin to trickle down her cheeks.

"Freddie, I...I...I'm expecting a baby. Our baby. In September. Or October. I...it's..."

She seems unable to say more. The room swims in front of Freddie's eyes and he wonders whether he's going to pass out. He feels acutely ashamed and embarrassed that these grown-ups know what he has done. They know of the insistent movements his body has made to facilitate intercourse and conception. It is as though he has exposed a part of himself to them; demonstrated to them beyond any doubt that he is a human animal too and no longer an innocent. He is surprised to find that it makes him feel dirty. And terrified to think that others will have to know too, sooner or later.

"Kathleen is expecting a baby in about five months, Freddie," says Mr. Soper sternly, his mouth a tight line. "That's been confirmed by the Doctor. I assume that you...that the...when you ran off from here to London just after last Christmas and were forced to spend a night in the Underground...that's when it happened, according to Kathleen. Of all places! A filthy station platform in public view! I must say I had hoped for better for my daughter and better from you, young man. You behaved like dogs."

Mr. Williams adjusts the folds of his gown and runs his finger around the top of his wing collar. He is not used to this kind of debate in his study.

"It wasn't like that, Mr. Soper, in full view and everything but I can see why you think it was. I'm very sorry."

"It's difficult to see it otherwise from my perspective, Freddie. It happened at the station, Kathleen? Is that correct? Not that it really matters now, I suppose," says Mr. Soper, seeming to ignore Freddie's apology.

"Yes, the station. I'm sorry too, Dad, really. But...but Freddie didn't make me. We wanted to...both of us...I asked him to...to...because I..."

"You asked him to?" says Vi, her voice rising in amazement.

"Yes."

Vi snorts and shakes her shoulders in a gesture of displeasure. "Good Lord! You should both be utterly ashamed of yourselves, the pair of you. It's...it's disgusting. I thought you were a nice girl, young lady. The shame for all of us! How are we going to keep this from the neighbours?"

"Tanner?" interrupts Mr. Williams, his eyebrows raised, feeling that he must somehow bring this uncomfortable scene to a conclusion. "You accept what is being said here?"

"Yes, Sir. If Kathy is expecting a baby, I, well..." He shakes his head in disbelief that period three is unexpectedly concerned with his impending paternity rather than Boyle's Law. "If Kathy is...in that condition, then I am the father. Sir. I do feel ashamed. I'm sorry; it's...well...yes, it happened in Bow Station; that was the only time we...and it's kind of Kathy to try to take the blame, Sir, but, well, it was me as much as her."

He looks sideways at Kathleen, trying to communicate his affection. The adults in the room look at one another, wondering whether the world has entirely lost sight of its moral compass since they were young.

"It must be the war," mutters Vi. "How can we expect children to behave if their elders and betters are blowing each other to smithereens and setting fire to the Bible...well...but, Good Lord! You're just children!"

Freddie takes a deep breath to say something which he would rather not have to articulate in this forum, for it is very personal and very embarrassing, but say it he has to, for otherwise these adults will assume, perhaps, that his actions were those of a Lothario. Or worse, a dog.

"I know we are very young, but I love her, Aunty," says Freddie. "I always have. It wasn't...what you think. Like dogs. And we are very sorry for causing this trouble."

"You are both under the age of legal consent," says Mr. Williams.

There is a long silence.

"But surely...I mean, I find it very difficult to...understand how you could know..." commences Vi, before closing her mouth and waving her hand in a hopeless way.

"Consent means agreeing?" asks Katherine quietly.

Everyone looks at her.

"Yes," says her father.

"I con...consented with Freddie and so did he. I love him too; that's why it happened," says Kathleen.

"There's rather more to it than that, young lady," snaps Mr. Williams. "You are both under-age, so it's against the law."

Kathleen shrugs her shoulders and looks at Freddie.

"I don't know much about the law. I know that making love is making a baby," she responds, folding her hands neatly in her lap, as if to indicate that nothing else needs to be said and what's all the fuss about?

Simple as that. Simple as Kathleen.

THE GRATING ROAR OF PEBBLES
May 1941

"Kathy, I don't know what we're going to do," I said somewhat lamely. "I feel ashamed. We've behaved badly."

We were sitting uncomfortably in Mr.Williams' secretary's office, given a few minutes alone by the adults at the end of the conversation in the study. At the head master's command, the secretary begrudgingly stomped out into the corridor to give us a modicum of privacy.

"I don't feel ashamed; why should we? We'll have the baby," said Kathy. "It's our baby. Like I said in there."

"You want to do that?"

She looked at me as if I'd asked the most stupid question imaginable.

"I mean, well, you heard what Aunty Vi said. We could have it adopted. You know, so it'll be with grown-ups who can love it and who know what they're doing. Who can look after it properly. What do you think?"

"We can love it and look after it properly. We can find out how. We made love and it's our baby, Freddie," Kathy said. It wasn't loud or confrontational, just determined, decided, straightforward.

"I know, Kathy. And we're just kids ourselves, really. I don't see how we can do it. Anyway, I expect the grown-ups will decide for us."

Kathy's eyes began to mist. "No. No! We should decide. It's our baby. You don't want to look after it? But, Freddie, I thought..."

"Well, you know. It's not that...you heard what Mr. Williams said; I mean about my promising future being cut short and everything? I'm supposed to be working to be a solicitor or something. How can I do that if...well...you see?"

"This baby is all I know about, Freddie. We made love. Not like dogs. We made love and we made a baby. So now we have to look after it, not get rid of it. That's our duty. Getting rid of it's not right, is it?"

I couldn't argue with her. I wasn't at all convinced about the practicalities and I suppose I was already feeling resentful that my starry future was being wrenched away from me before it had even begun, but to start to say such things seemed immoderate, cruel and selfish.

"Well, alright, Kathy. We'll just have to hope that they will help us somehow," I mumbled rather feebly.

That was more or less all we managed to say because Kathy threw herself at me and began wailing in such a weird way that I thought she'd lost control of her senses. Then the secretary came in and said we had to go back into the head master's study.

Mr. Soper and Aunty Vi asked Mr. Williams for special permission for me to miss the rest of the morning's lessons so that they could talk properly to Kathy and me. Mr. Williams very grudgingly gave it. I was surprised. I thought we would be given their decision which would probably involve our permanent separation and the adoption of the baby. I found I was surprised and faintly relieved to be proved wrong.

As we made our way down the corridor to the main entrance, the bell rang for period four. Within seconds, doors were flung open and boys began to emerge from classrooms, chattering noisily as they hurried to the next lesson. Soon we were engulfed in a choppy sea of blue blazers; I was used to this, of course, but the others looked a little perturbed, especially Kathy.

As one group scurried past us, I heard a voice say, "I bet that's Tanner's girl!"

"Shouldn't think so; more likely his sister."

"Bet it isn't. I don't look at my sister like that."

"Cor! Lucky blighter then! But what's she doing here?"

The rest of their conversation was drowned by the noise of hundreds of pairs of clattering shoes, doors banging and masters shouting for boys to keep to the left. I realised that later I would be quizzed over why I was missing from chemistry, why I'd been summoned to see the Old Man and who was the beautiful girl with the tearful and terrified expression.

"Go on, tell us; you been a naughty boy, Tanner?" I could hear them saying.

Mr. Soper strode ahead of us once we were out of the building and kept going at a fearful pace until he came to Market Street in the town. He found what he was looking for and directed us into a tea shop. Aunty Vi ordered refreshments as we settled into a corner table. Of course, I wanted to sit next to Kathy but we were made to sit opposite one another. She rubbed her shin against my leg for the next half an hour, unseen beneath the gingham cloth.

"Well," said Aunty Vi as she put down the tea-pot with a thump, "I'm sure we don't know what to say to the pair of you, do we, Mr. Soper? Fancy behaving like that and the two of you only children. I've never heard of such a thing in all my life."

"You'd better call me Archie since we are about to be related," he responded, sipping at the scalding tea. "They're fifteen; not adults, I agree, but not really children either, are they? Not physically, anyway. And I think I should assert that Kathleen is a nice girl, whatever current circumstances may suggest."

Aunty Vi seemed to think about this for a few seconds, for it was not the answer she expected. Then she gave a nod. "Very well; call me Vi, then. And maybe they're not children in a way; I don't know. Under the age of consent, though, like that Mr. Williams said. No denying that."

"I'm not one to indulge in recrimination, Vi," he said suddenly. "What's done is done. We all make mistakes. Let he who is without sin, cast the first stone. I've made mistakes in the past; so have you, I'm sure."

"Um, well, yes, very true, er...Archie," said Aunty Vi, her tone seeming to be a little more conciliatory. I wondered, briefly, what the mistakes were that Aunty Vi was conceding. As Mr. Soper's observation sank in, I recalled what I had heard back in Bow about him and Kathy's mother. And Aunty Vi and Bernard were definitely not married either and yet they shared a bed! The adage about pots calling the kettle black came to mind.

"But since Grace died – the children's mother, you understand – perhaps I have indulged in recrimination where Kathleen is concerned. Blamed her, I mean, for her mother's death. But it's not her fault. I have been wrong."

Aunty Vi shifted a little uncomfortably in her chair. Kathy looked at her father with that expression that indicated that she was struggling to follow.

"I have not given her the love she craves and so she has found it in your nephew's arms, Vi. Do you see? And Freddie has no parents, so maybe he too...well...I don't want to make any more mistakes where my children are concerned," he said, "so that the future is nothing but pain and misery."

"Well," said Aunty Vi, "very laudable, I'm sure. None of us wants pain and misery, Archie. So what are you suggesting, may I ask? We have to consider practical issues too, you know; money, for a start, as well as...pardon me...emotional ones. And there's a war on, don't forget."

"Kathleen is carrying a child, Vi. Right or wrong; legal or not; sensible or irresponsible; war or peace; rich or poor – we can argue it all day. No point; it's happening. She's several months gone. So, we could hide it away; dispose of it, in a manner of speaking, or we can try to accept facts and consider our responsibilities."

Each time he opened his mouth, Mr. Soper went up in my estimation. How different he was from Pa!

"Responsibilities?"

"Towards Freddie, towards Kathleen and, now, towards an unborn child. My grand-child and your grand-niece or nephew. He or she also deserves our consideration."

Aunty Vi opened and closed her mouth a few times, a goldfish in a hat.

"Well, yes, I see," she eventually managed to stutter. "But if you're suggesting what I think you're suggesting...well...what about Freddie's education? He has a fine future ahead of him, they say at the school. Very good at the sciences."

"Particularly human biology, it seems," said Mr. Soper rather tartly. "He had a fine future ahead of him but now things have changed. Pragmatism, Vi. Anyway, I'm not suggesting anything yet.

We must ask Freddie and Kathleen in a minute. But whatever happens, there will be sacrifices somewhere. That's inevitable."

"You only get one chance in life, Archie, don't you? Qualifications are important. You know, for the future."

"What future is that, Vi? It's difficult to say what's important these days, in my view. You said it yourself, back there, in a manner of speaking: the old values are on fire all across the world. In fact, they've been smouldering since 1914, really. Education? Yes, of course; but he could come back to it later. Many do." He took another sip of his tea. "Kathleen, I think I know what your feelings are. You've told me often enough in the last couple of weeks. But perhaps today's conversations have changed your mind, so I have to ask again. What do you want to do about the baby?"

"I want to keep my baby and look after it. With Freddie."

"Well, that's clear enough, then," said Mr. Soper, squeezing Kathy's hand. "And you, Freddie?"

"I don't want the baby adopted, Mr. Soper. I'd like to get my exams and all that but I'd like to be with Kathy too, but, well, I realise that may not be allowed. I'm not sure what's best or possible."

"You can't have it all, young man," snapped Aunty Vi.

"I suppose not," I muttered.

There wasn't much more I could say. Kathy and I were minors without rights or any income and so we were very much in the hands of Mr. Soper and Aunty Vi. In those days, illegitimate children were very often snatched from their young mothers by the kind hand of authority, their identities effectively changed and their true origins disguised or deliberately erased. They got dumped in orphanages or sent off to Australia and things like that. I'd even heard that unmarried mothers used to be sent to mental asylums; I suppose because their behaviour was seen as an aberration. I wasn't sure whether that still happened and I was frightened that someone could do something like that to Kathy.

"What are your views, Vi? We're both involved," said Mr. Soper.

Before she could reply, Kathy began to cry. I put my hand across the table and held hers.

"I don't like this talking," she sobbed. "Everyone thinks I'm stupid. Never mind about Kathleen; she's a bit simple. That's why she's in the family way. Didn't understand what she was doing. That's what you all think, isn't it? But it's me that's got the baby inside me. I know what some girls are like with boys. But this is not like that. I knew what I was doing. It's a love baby...tell them, Freddie."

I looked at Kathy with amazement and pride. I couldn't recall a time when she'd ever said as much in one go. Of course, I knew what she meant. I did my best to explain.

When I'd finished, Mr. Soper stood up and went over to the window. He remained there for some minutes, staring down the street. Aunty Vi poured the rest of the tea but she too seemed lost in thought.

"I'll do what I can, Archie. To help, I mean," she said as Mr. Soper settled himself back into his chair. "I surprise myself in a way, but perhaps these two deserve to be treated with some sympathy – although I still disapprove, mind! – and you have spoken persuasively. I hope I don't live to regret it! So what do you suggest?"

Mr. Soper looked at us all and cleared his throat. "It's dangerous in London at the moment. Too dangerous for a girl in the family way. I have a distant cousin living in North Essex; a place called Thaxted. I think she might help; take Kathleen in for her confinement. Save any embarrassment for her back at Bow, what's more. We can just say she's been evacuated."

Aunty Vi looked surprised. "Won't she want paying, for Kathleen's upkeep and so on?"

"Let's just say I'd be calling in an old family favour."

"Oh, I see. I'd like Freddie to stay at school, Archie, at least until he's sixteen – next April – so he can take his School Certificate," Aunty Vi announced.

"I agree. It gives everyone time. The baby will be born by then. At sixteen they could marry if they want and if we sign the papers. Freddie could perhaps find work to support his family. Better chance if he's got the exams. You'd be very young, Freddie, and I suppose you won't be going on to take your Highers, but, like I say, there are sacrifices in life for all of us. Of course, we haven't taken account of the war in all this but at least it's a path we can hope to tread. What do you say?"

"It's a lot to take in, Mr. Soper. Not quite what I thought my future was to be, but, yes, I see I have to make a sacrifice."

"Too late for spilt milk, Freddie," said Aunty Vi. "You should have thought about what you wanted for your future before you...well, you know what I mean. You're lucky it's going to work out this way. On the way up here, I thought we'd be discussing adoption by now."

"I want to be with Freddie, Dad," Kathy murmured.

"No, not yet. But we know how you feel, Kathleen, that's why I'm suggesting what I am. But you are still very young. Both of you have to prove yourselves for the next year or so. Show us you can work hard, Freddie; show us you are capable of looking after the child, Kathleen and both of you show us you can be patient and, above all, adult. You've jumped into the adult world ahead of your time; now we need to see that you're both deserving of being treated as adults."

With thousands being slaughtered on battlefields, at sea and in the air even while we sipped tea, I thought that perhaps there were some aspects of the adults' world we might care not to be treated to, but, of course, it wasn't the time to say so.

"And," said Mr. Soper, tapping the table with his finger, "just because we all plan that this will be so, it doesn't mean it's bound to happen. *The best laid schemes o' mice an' men gang aft a-gley*. Things go wrong. Sometimes there's nothing we can do about it, but at other times, it behoves us to think before we do something we'll live to regret. Do you understand what I'm getting at, Kathleen? Freddie?"

"I think so, Dad," whispered Kathy.

"Yes, Sir, I understand. And I know you've told me that before and I'm sorry I seem not to have listened. Shall I be able to see Kathy sometimes? And the baby?" I asked.

"We'll see," said Aunty Vi, snapping shut the clasp of her handbag with a sound like a pistol shot.

A DARKLING PLAIN
May 1941

When I'd arrived back at Belper Lane End, my head was full of the discussions that had taken place during the day. One thing's for sure: when I'd woken that morning, I hadn't expected the day to turn out as it did. And then, as if the news of Kathy's condition wasn't already enough to be going on with, there was a great commotion at the farm because one of Mr. Shaw's men had caught his hand in a machine. Mrs Shaw hurried me indoors and would say only that he'd suffered some extensive injury to his fingers which had been sliced by the cutting blade. She thought it unlikely the man would be able to do the same work ever again.

It was no wonder I had trouble getting to sleep! When I did, rather predictably the events of the previous few hours were scrambled into a bizarre dream. Nightmare, perhaps.

Repeatedly I found myself in a flat, dark landscape. Enormous, heavy-bellied, pewter-grey clouds were hanging like black-out curtains above me. On the horizon there were flashes of orange light and I could hear bombs and anti-aircraft fire. I was frightened and worse than that, I was as naked as the day I was born. I looked down towards my feet and saw that I was holding my severed penis in my right hand, out in front of me at about navel height.

It was large and semi-tumescent, clean and smooth like the body of a grass snake, except that it did not move. The eye of the circumcised helmet pointed speculatively ahead of me; the other end, where I might have expected to see gore and torn flesh; teeth marks, even, I speculated; was unmarked and entirely whole, like a mutilated finger long ago sewn up and healed over.

Strangely, although I was alarmed by the distant explosions and distraught in my nakedness, I was not especially shocked by the mutilation. It seemed completely normal. I recognised my own organ. I could feel myself in my own hand; that familiar and pleasing sensation. And yet how could that be, if it was a separate entity? I caressed its form in the usual way with my thumb, felt the sensation and watched as it was engorged with more blood. I held it at arm's length but there was no discernible change; still the thing felt a part of me. It was connected and yet it was not.

I had a sense that it could, if required, somehow be temporarily re-attached, snapped into its correct place as if it had a press-stud, to allow me to urinate; for indeed, a pressure in my bladder was intruding upon my troubled sleep. And then I became increasingly aware that it had to be permanently re-attached soon for it could not live long on its own without rotting and thus being lost to me forever. I knew I would need help with this but I was not sure who to ask. A feeling of helpless panic overcame me. I heard voices and then mocking laughter somewhere close at hand, although I could see nobody for a while. I felt threatened; pursued.

Then I saw that the head master was in his study, a forbidding, tall building standing alone on a windswept and bleak landscape. Although I knocked urgently on his door, he would not open it.

"Go away, you despicable child!" he bellowed.

I knew that Aunty Vi was busy baking bread somewhere but how could I talk to her about my damaged private parts? I thought that my best option would be to try to enlist Mr. Soper's help. I found myself running down Bamford Road in that slow-motion way of dreams, my legs refusing to work properly and my feet seemingly in the grip of quicksand. There were holes all over the place where bombs had lifted the paving slabs. There were scampering rats; a vile smell of human filth. My feet slipped into spongy fissures and then the hands of the dead began to grab at my ankles. I recognised one of the hands as Ma's, for she had a distinctive scar on her wrist.

"I need to speak to you, son," she gurgled through something sticky in her throat.

"I need to say goodbye, Ma," I managed to say before she fell back under the slabs.

Kathy appeared in the dream, dancing nimbly across the unevenly pitched stones. She was clad as on the day at Paglesham, her body voluptuous and revealed by a clinging, wet vest. Later, she was dressed in torn rags, her hair pulled back carelessly and tied with a strip of material. She seemed much older; an old woman, almost. Some of the rags looked as though they had been burned.

Yet, she was even more beautiful than in real life. Somewhere behind her shoulders there was a soft, yellow light. She walked towards me, smiling, holding out her hand.

"We can get it mended. Come on!"

As she touched me and lifted my part from my own hand, I pulled back instinctively, conscious that I was about to lose control of myself. I felt her palm close around me. She grinned.

And of course, I then awoke suddenly, aware that yet again I had messed myself in the most embarrassing way possible for a young boy.

STRUGGLE AND FIGHT
Echoes of July 1936

It is a Saturday morning in Pleasant Road. Although it is quite late, Bernard and Vi are still in bed, snuffling contentedly under the blankets. Bernard is swimming in the dregs of last night's many pints of beer at "The Minerva". They had been followed by one of Vi's bouts of energetic, nocturnal enthusiasm. Now he has one hand on her generously proportioned buttocks. He caresses them languorously. One never knows; occasionally Friday's enthusiasms are re-visited on Saturday mornings. But in this and almost every other respect, Bernard has learned to bide his time. Vi has to think it is her idea. Today, however, Bernard is doomed to be disappointed. There is a knocking at the door downstairs.

"Now who on Earth is that at this time of the morning?" grumbles Vi.

"It has gone nine, my dear. I'll go and see," says Bernard, pulling on a dressing gown and running his fingers through the straggling remainder of what was once a fine head of curly hair.

Moaning to herself, Vi levers her body into a sitting position. She can hear voices in the hall beneath her: Bernard's and another's that she does not recognise. Bernard sounds surprised. A few moments later he comes back into the bedroom.

"Someone from up Bow way wants to speak to you. I think you'd better come down."

Half an hour later, when she has made herself respectable, Vi goes into the front room where the stranger and Bernard sit in an uncomfortable silence, any kind of conversation between them having dried up twenty minutes previously. The man is small, clad in a greasy suit and has dust on his shoes. There is a smell of fish in the room.

"Good morning," says Vi, wrinkling her nose. "I am Violet Salthouse. May I know who I am speaking to?"

The stranger stands up and proffers his hand.

"Good mornin', Mrs Salthouse. I'm sorry fer the unannounced visit, like. Me name's Herbert Morgan – thass Bert to me friends –

an' I lives in Arrow Road, just around the corner from Bamforth Road. Morgan's Fishmongers. I was Sid Tanner's mate 'fore he died."

Vi's eyes narrow. The name is vaguely familiar. Isobel must have mentioned him as one of a group of men with whom Sid would spend every spare hour drinking in "The Railway Tavern".

"I see. I assume that something very important has brought you all the way down to Southend to disrupt our morning? How did you manage to travel? You don't have a permit; you're not a resident."

Bernard looks at Vi with surprise. It is not like her to be quite so rude to strangers.

"Well, let's just say papers an' dokkiments are easy to get from some quarters. An' I'm sorry fer the incon...wossname, like, but there's something you have to know, now that yer brother-in-law is, well, no longer with us. Gawd rest 'is soul."

"I doubt that the Almighty will look upon that request with much favour, Mr. Morgan. How did you know where to find me?"

"Archie Soper. I know 'ow his girl an' yer nephew are...well, friendly," says Bert, with just a hint of sarcasm.

Vi makes a mental note to let Archie Soper know in her next letter that it would appear that his ruse of "evacuating" Kathleen to Thaxted to avoid gossip has not been as successful as they had hoped.

"Do have a seat, Mr. Morgan," says Bernard, coming to the rescue and hoping to move things forward. He has a mind to play bowls later and before that; well, he hasn't entirely lost hope of a little canoodling with Vi before lunch.

"This ain't easy, Mrs Salthouse. What I 'ave to tell you is goin' to come as quite a shock an' I've been in two minds about whether to come dahn and tell yer at all, if I'm honest. But it's playin' on me mind, like, an' I can't settle ter me business. I need to get it off me chest. Is it alright to speak..?" He nods in Bernard's direction.

"Yes. This is my...husband."

Vi feels a pang of apprehension and a sensation of nausea, for she already has more than an inkling of what this malodorous man is going to tell her. It might be more a case of a suspicion confirmed than a shock.

"This is about my sister's death?"

"Yeah, it is. Well, Sid always said she fell dahn them stairs. She could 'ave done; I mean ter say, they're bloody lethal, but she didn't. Well, not in the way Sid wanted us all ter believe."

"Spit it out, man," says Bernard.

"One night in "The Railway", he'd had far too many; not that there was anythin' unusual 'bout that! An' he told me and swore me to secrecy 'cos otherwise he'd slit me throat. An' he would have too. He says he was on late turn an' still in bed after the boys went ter school. He shouts ter Isobel ter come upstairs cos he wants...well, you know 'ow he was. She's choppin' firewood, he says. He can 'ear her out in the yard, splittin' sticks. He bellows again an' eventually she comes upstairs, still wiv the axe in 'er 'and, although Sid says he never sees it 'cos she's got it behind her back. Well, I'm sorry, Mrs Salthouse, but this is a bit, you know, crude like an' I 'ope you'll forgive me. Sid says he's standing by the side of the bed, stark naked..."

Bernard gives a little cough as if to warn this man to be careful what he says.

"...and he's, you know, showin' his goods, like. On the display stand, so ter speak, if yer would forgive me. He tells her to come closer, he points dahn at hisself..."

Vi waves her hand in front of her face. "Spare me the sordid details, Mr. Morgan. I'm a woman of a delicate constitution. A summary will suffice."

"Yes, sorry, ma'am, I'm sure. So, she calls 'im a filthy so-and-so and says she'll fix 'im forever and takes a swing at his...his...Cockfosters. He reckoned he jumped back jussin time to save his manhood, so to speak. He grabbed the axe and then pushed 'er backwards. She falls and knocks 'erself out, bangin' 'er 'ead on the fireplace or summat, according to Sid's story. I 'spose the lump on 'er bonce must've just seemed one of many, poor woman, otherwise the coroner would've worked it out, wouldn't 'ee? Anyway, he's furious an' he grabs her bodily, like, an' shoves her an' kicks 'er dahn the apples'n'pears 'ead first, throwin' the axe after 'er. I 'spect thass what caused the gouge in the wall. Well, yer know the rest, 'cos the force of the fall when she's out cold snaps 'er neck. He puts the axe back in the coal 'ole and scarpers."

Vi falls backwards in her chair, her face grey with shock.

§

Half an hour later, Bernard having opened the windows to dispel the stench of fish and unwashed clothing; and made several cups of sweet tea laced with brandy; Vi stops trembling.

"My God! My poor sister, my poor, poor sister! I knew it, Bernard, I just knew it but there was no proof. But why didn't that horrible little man come forward at the time?"

"You heard what he said, Vi. Fear. Not telling on your mates, all that sort of thing."

"Oh, Bernard! What am I to do?"

Bernard sucks in his cheeks. "I dunno, Vi. Isobel wouldn't have known too much about it if she was out cold, you see. But, well, is there any point in doing anything? They're dead now, both of them, so it's, well...it's too late, isn't it? Not goin' to change anything or bring 'er back, is it?"

"Her soul's not at rest, Bernard, that's what I mean. And what about Freddie? Or Vincent come to that. Have I to tell them what I know about their mother's death?"

"Bloody hell! I dunno. That wants a bit of thinking about, don't it?"

LIFE'S PENDING PLAN
Summer 1941

"Tanner," said Mr. Midgley, flicking the sleeve of his gown after he'd wiped the blackboard with it, "kindly enlighten us with your best rendition of stanza four."

Mr. Midgley took a couple of paces towards the door and away from the cloud of chalk dust he had created moments before. Particles swirled in the rays of sunlight coming through the windows and settled in the hair of the boys in the front desks.

"Yes, Sir," I said reluctantly. There were one or two stifled guffaws from the back of the room. I had been trying to keep my head down; to make myself invisible, for the poem which Mr. Midgley had selected for us was Thomas Hardy's *To An Unborn Pauper Child.* I was acutely embarrassed. Some of the others had been pestering me with questions about Kathy and, of course, because I was unable plausibly to deny some of their accusations or to be genuinely dismissive of their intrusions, the shrewder ones in the form knew they were on to something. Rumours were fuelled primarily by the oaf Goadsby. I'm not sure to this day whether his interpretation of Kathy's presence at school was cleverly intuitive or just guesswork and bombast.

"That blinkin' lovely girl you were with the other day in The Old Man's office, Tanner? What was all that about, ey? Pretty girls on the premises? Most unusual, dear boy," he chuckled. "I was walking along the corridor towards you all. Surprised you didn't give her a kiss and a cuddle there and then, the way the pair of you were mooning!" He adjusted his lumpy crotch rather showily.

"And then, as the lovely lass turned the corner over there, I thought to myself, Goadsby, my boy, that pretty silhouette is of a girl expecting something she ought not to be expecting at her age! I can always tell, you see; it's the swelling bosom too large for the frock; the way they walk: the hand on the growing stomach; the arched back. I come from a family where all my aunts are variously and permanently with child. I know the signs, dear boy. So perhaps she's not quite the lovely, innocent lass she appears to be, my friend. Now, am I right or am I correct?"

"Don't talk rot, Goadsby," I said, but probably very unconvincingly. Or maybe I blushed. What he'd spotted, or thought he had, I hadn't noticed myself until we were about to leave the tea rooms that day. When Kathy stood up to go, she leaned back a little and it was true that there was a bit of a bump on her front. How on Earth Goadsby had noticed from a distance I don't know.

"Blimey, Goadsby, you should read medicine and become a blithering gynaecologist," said Hawkins. The others all laughed.

Mr. Midgley swung his attention to the back of the room. "Is something amusing you, Goadsby? I thought we'd established that Hardy's tone here is unrelentingly pessimistic. What's funny, boy?"

"Nothing, Sir. Sorry, Sir."

"One of these days, Goadsby, you'll be laughing on the other side of your face. Very well, Tanner, we await. Proceed."

It was an odd choice of poem, when I think about it now. Hardy at that time was too modern and his unorthodox views kept his work out of classrooms for many years. Perhaps, like Goadsby, Mr. Midgley was having a joke at my expense, although I would not have thought it likely. It's more likely that I was just over-sensitive about the whole business.

"Come on, Tanner, what's the reason for the delay?"

"Sir, it's a pregnant pause, Sir," said Goadsby and the whole room convulsed with laughter. Even Mr. Midgley, not known for clowning, saw the funny side of the remark and gave a little smile.

"Very droll, Goadsby. Now come on, Tanner."

"Sir," I muttered and began, trying to give my voice a neutral and detached tone.

Vain vow! No hint of mine may hence
To theeward fly: to thy locked sense
Explain none can
Life's pending plan:
Thy wilt thy ignorant entry make
Though skies spout fire and blood and nations quake.

"Not bad, Tanner; perhaps a little hesitant at the beginning, but not bad. Now, let's see...yes, yes, very well, Bates, I can see you waving; please give us the benefit of your understanding of the stanza, would you?"

"Yes, Sir," said Bates, our resident Poet Laureate. He was one of those too-clever-by-half, priggish boys that were Westcliff High School's speciality. Rather predictably, we called him Master Bates. He stood up.

"Bates," sighed Mr. Midgley, "I'm sure we'll all hear you perfectly well if you remain seated. You are not on the stage of The Albert Hall. Sit down, boy."

"Yes, Sir. Well, I think Hardy means that the child will be ignorant when it's born, Sir, because, well, because it knows nothing and can be told nothing of what's in store for it: the *plan* is misery, Sir, I think. Hardy says it has a *locked sense*. Locked away inside the mother. As we already said earlier, Sir, the suggestion is that Life will be awful and the child would be better staying where it is. But it'll be born whatever the poet does or says to try to dissuade it and even though the world is tearing itself to pieces. *Nations quake,* Sir. Like now, Sir, in this war. Although Hardy wrote this decades ago, of course, Sir."

Mr. Midgley looked at Bates and gave a wry smile. "Indeed, Bates. Very good. Maybe I was wrong just now; I think perhaps I should sit down while you stand up and wear the gown."

There were one or two laughs around the room at Mr. Midgley's scathing humour: by seeming to compliment Master Bates on his abilities he was at the same time suggesting he was a precocious upstart. Classic Midgley.

At morning break, I managed to find a sunny spot round by the school garden where I hoped to be able to sit quietly for a few minutes, watching someone hoe the radishes or Shovel Manure for Victory. I wanted to be away from the likes of Goadsby. I was out of luck, though. Barlow tracked me down and came sidling over to where I was leaning against a wall.

"Hey, Tanner," he said, picking at his pimples.

"What do you want, Barlow?" I said with a groan. "Can't a fellow have a moment's quiet?"

"Well, it's just that I've been wondering...I mean...what's it like? Doing it with a girl? What does it feel like? You know, what do you do with...when it's hard...is she...well...what happens, exactly?"

I gave him a withering look and he shifted his attention to a boil on the back of his neck.

"I almost did it last Christmas with my cousin. She was keen and I was gasping; it was practically pushing out of my collar. But in the end she wouldn't because we're related. She said it would be incest. And she said she wasn't the kind of girl who would be taken advantage of before she got married; you know. Maybe I should find a different class of girl, like you did? You know, I mean, one that's willing to let you do it. But how do you get to know a girl like that? Is it easy to tell the ones who will? Did you just ask her and she let you?"

"You know, Barlow, sometimes you really are a grubby guttersnipe and a bore," I said pompously and walked back towards the main buildings.

§

At the beginning of the summer, people began to drift back to their homes from evacuation, if they'd ever gone away in the first place, that is. Hitler had turned his attention to the Russian Front and although raids on our big cities and docks continued, it was not with the same relentless ferocity as during the Blitz on London. Operation Barbarossa was bad news for Russia but better news for us.

Most of those returning didn't know what they'd find; whether their old home was still standing. Many weren't of course, especially in London. Some folk were in for a shock: Aunty Vi told me about some people in Chadwick Road who'd locked up their place and evacuated to Bromley, of all stupid places to go. When they returned to Westcliff, they found their house had been broken into and stripped of everything of value, including the wood panelling in the hall. That's not quite the "Wonderful war spirit where everyone pulled together" that you hear so much about these days. But then, a lot of what you hear about those times is total nonsense. It seems to me we're already tidying away the horrors and investing it all with glamour. I expect that one day they'll start making tea-towels and mugs with the names of all the big battles on them. Commemorative crap, like you get at coronations and things.

Lots of people never came back at all in 1945. Five years is a long time, especially during a war. Things change: people die; bullets and bombs find their mark. Suddenly, futures became pasts. The idea that Southend and the Estuary generally were dangerous places, ripe for invasion, took root. You could buy enormous houses in Chalkwell Avenue for a song in 1946.

Anyway, Aunty Vi wrote to me to say that although they still had to be very watchful down on the Thames Estuary and that the Pier – "HMS Leigh" as it was called for the duration – was bristling with even more defences, nevertheless she wanted me to come home for the holidays in August. That was fine by me; at least Southend was closer to Thaxted than Belper and I dreamed that somehow I might be allowed to see Kathy.

I wasn't, but strangely, I did catch a glimpse of her one afternoon.

In the last couple of months of her pregnancy, she experienced discomfort and anaemia. The doctor suggested that sea air would do her good and so a visit to Southend was planned. No doubt Kathy herself suggested the location. Her people in Thaxted booked into a guest house somewhere up on Westcliff Parade for a few days. Kathy knew Aunty Vi's address but didn't really have any idea about where Pleasant Road was, except that it was by "The Kursaal", and neither could she be sure I was there and not still in Belper. She wrote to me at the Shaws' to say she hoped to be in Southend but, of course, I didn't see the letter until many weeks later.

But she didn't allow herself to become too mired in the if-and-buts. She never did. She trusted to luck and simply hoped that somehow, somewhere, she would see me. Even on days when she really didn't want to be bothered to move, she made herself go out and willed me to do likewise.

Perhaps telepathy works. Or coincidence. Anyway, one lovely afternoon that August I suddenly had a strange feeling that I should put down my book and go for a walk. The seafront itself was pretty well entirely cordoned off by the military so I cut around behind Pleasant Road and up through Cromer Road, across the High Street and towards Clifftown. I was ambling through Prittlewell Square when I saw her, with her people, walking slowly along the parade. She was really very large and I was surprised by her shape; a shape that spoke of a new life that we had created. It was difficult for me to comprehend properly. She was lugging it around every day, but I was still in the classroom.

I was about to shout out to her and already had my hand raised to wave, but I thought better of it. I didn't want to cause trouble for her. She must have seen me, though, or sensed my presence. She slowed and stopped, taking the arm of the elderly man who was accompanying her and nodding towards a bench under the trees. The old man guided her there, helped her sit and then stood off a little to look down on the Estuary. An older woman, presumably his wife, joined him. They looked over towards the pier on their left and then right up the river towards Canvey, pointing out things of interest to one another.

When she was sure that they were not watching, Kathy looked up, directly towards where I was standing by the railings of the Square. She raised her hand to wave and then held it palm outwards, to indicate that I should not approach. I had already taken a step forward. She shook her head.

So near and yet so far! She was no more than fifty yards from me, but it might as well have been fifty miles. For some time, I just stood motionless, looking at her. I didn't know what to do. She raised her fingers to her lips and mimed.

"I love you too," I semaphored back and then made a writing movement with one hand upon the palm of the other. She nodded.

The elderly couple moved back towards the bench to help her continue her constitutional walk. I returned to Pleasant Road, elated to know that the bond between us held good, not that I ever doubted that, I suppose. Absence makes the heart grow fonder, they say and that's true but it also makes you, at the same time, profoundly sad.

A BRIGHT GIRDLE FURL'D
October 1941

My dearest Freddie,

Mrs Scott is writing this for me. I hope you don't mind too much, but you know what my writing is like and how long it takes me. I thought this was best.

I am so happy that the baby was born last week. It is a girl. She is very pretty and she has your eyes. Maybe you already know because I think Dad writes to your Aunty every now and then. I would be much happier and easier in my mind if you were with me.

It was a difficult labour for me. The midwife said it was because I have small hips and the baby was large. Nearly 8lbs! No wonder I looked like one of those barrage balloons, especially in the colder weather now with coats and pullovers wrapped around my waist. I am glad it's over because I have been very uncomfortable for the last two months. Now I can try to be my proper size again. I was remembering as well what Dad has told me about my Mum and how she was so small she died having me. So I am happy and sad at the same time.

I would like to call her Grace Isobel. I hope that you agree with this? She can carry the names of both our Mums. Of course, the papers will have to give her surname as Soper because we are not married. I want us to be married as soon as possible, Freddie. Can we? We will soon be sixteen.

Mr. and Mrs Scott are being very kind to me but I cannot stay here forever, especially now there is the baby. It is only a small cottage. We should have our own place somewhere one day, like you said ages ago.

I hope that everything is alright for you at school up there? Is there snow yet? I suppose you must be working very hard for your exams this year.

Please write to me when you can. Mrs Scott says it's alright to do that now. Please let me know what your plans are for us.

I think about you all the time, all my love,

Kathy (and Grace Isobel!)

IGNORANT ARMIES CLASH BY NIGHT
December 1941

Like most families in the land, the Shaws listened to the BBC News on the radio every evening. One night the main item was about the Japanese surprise attack on the American base of Pearl Harbour in Hawaii. Once more, we heard about unprovoked hostilities, the outrage amongst Americans and the customary reference to injuries and loss of life. It was profoundly depressing news for it showed that the contagion unleashed in Europe was spreading inexorably around the globe.

It was announced that America was entering the war, news which I found was greeted with a mixed reaction. Mr. Shaw observed that the "Yanks were happy enough to watch us getting blown to blazes until their own people are killed!" At school fellows like Goadsby and Hawkins took the view that the Americans would soon bloody Hitler's nose because they had superior firepower and weaponry. They seemed quite excited about it all.

I suppose I was too preoccupied with my own problems to have a defensible view. I just felt that the Japanese attack and its implications merely added to my sense of despair and seemed to cement my feeling that violence just could not be the answer.

I did, of course, reply to Kathy's letter but I confess that I left it for some time because I told myself I was very busy at school with various Christmas functions, not to mention the never-ending mountains of homework which the masters continued to set, despite the so-called festive season.

But the real reason had nothing to do with school. I had been troubled by what had happened on Westcliff Parade – or, rather, by what had not happened – for some considerable time. I had been unable to speak to Kathy then or subsequently, to have a few private moments with her and I think that this lack of proper communication, coupled with her imminent motherhood – a fact which I had not had the opportunity to accustom myself to in the flesh as it were – made me feel that in some way she had become a stranger to me. I believe that in the years that followed, this had an effect on our relationship.

Her letter reported that she had given birth to my child and yet I felt that I had no part in that process or a familiarity with its ups and downs at all. I don't mean that I didn't accept responsibility for my part in Grace's arrival, not at all; it's just that sometimes it was as though it was happening to a friend with whom I had no biological involvement. These days they'd give my feelings a label: I didn't have "ownership" of the issue, or something bloody daft like that.

Furthermore, the tone of Kathy's letter rankled a little. I suppose I was aware that this might in some way have been influenced, or even caused by Mrs Scott but I felt that I was being put under pressure about a marriage and a family home. If I thought about it objectively, I could see that this was probably not really so and that it was perfectly reasonable and understandable that Kathy should want some reassurance about the situation. But I wasn't with her every day to see how things were for her and to talk through what was happening. I was divorced from all that and, what's more, I was many miles away at school where my work and the masters' comments suggested that I could have done well for myself, perhaps going on to get a degree and eventually a good, professional career. I remembered some of the things that Mr. Soper had said to me at Paglesham, by the river, that day.

In short, although it was as much my fault as hers that we were where we were, I was resentful. I expect that feeling conveyed itself in my reply which I finally wrote and sent with a Christmas card just before the end of term and my return to Pleasant Road for the holiday.

Kathy's card was waiting for me when I got there and inside it she had enclosed two or three photographs of her with Grace. They both looked so contented and beautiful that I immediately felt guilty about my earlier feelings.

"So, have you 'eard from your girl about the baby and all that?" asked Bernard one evening just before Christmas.

I showed him the photographs and summarised Kathy's views. She had repeated them in a note with the card, presumably because I had been non-committal or evasive in my reply to her letter. Bernard, who was nobody's fool, noted my glum tone.

"So what's eating at you, then, son?" he said, although I'm sure it was obvious. He plonked himself down in the battered old armchair that was one of two placed on either side of the fireplace in the back parlour. It groaned under his weight and one or two pieces of horse-hair stuffing attempted to jump out from under his sudden descent.

I grunted. "My future. Or lack of it."

"Let me tell you somethin', Freddie," said Bernard, reaching down into the scuttle to snatch a piece of coal with the tongs. "There's plenty who have no future at all, good or bad and yet only a while ago they thought they did 'ave." He lobbed the coal into the fire, sending a column of orange sparks up the chimney. "They've been blown to blazes and they ain't comin' back. Things might not be quite what you 'ad in mind, son, but at least you're still 'ere, ain'tcha?"

"You mean all those people killed in Pearl Harbour?" I said. "I know, I've been thinking about all that. Now the Americans are caught up in the mess."

Bernard laughed ruefully. "Over-paid, over-sexed and over 'ere! That's what they're saying already about the Yanks, you know."

"Some of the boys at school reckon the Americans will turn the tide."

"Maybe. I'm not so sure about that. Anyway, I didn't just mean Pearl Harbour, you see. No; Pearl Harbour, London, Liverpool, North Africa, Dunkirk; even off the end of the pier, son. People fall off pleasure steamers and drown, you know. They don't usually mean to do it; wasn't plannin' to do it at breakfast."

I got up from the table where I was slouching irritably and went to sit opposite Bernard by the fire. Aunty Vi stuck her head through the scullery doorway.

"Tea, anyone?"

"Yes please, love. Freddie and I are just 'aving a little chat so there's no hurry."

He might just as well have said for her to keep out of the bloody way. That's what he meant. He had the poker in his hand and was prodding at the coals to shift some ash. But he wasn't really thinking about the fire; or at least, not that one. I could tell from the expression on his face and the slightly glazed look in his eyes that he was probably out at sea again, wrestling with the elements to save a life.

"I never really told you about what 'appened at Dunkirk, did I?"

I shook my head.

"You know, in years to come, they'll make out like it was some glorious bloody thing that all those ragged, patched and holed little boats did, pluckin' the valiant tommies out of the water. It wasn't a glorious thing we did, Freddie. It was bloody, grim desperation. Thousands of men, trapped on those bleedin' beaches, deserted by their officers and betrayed by the politicians and the generals. It was a shambles; a disgrace. And it wasn't pretty either. I saw men who'd been walkin' for days to try to escape Jerry's Panzers. Days! Exhausted; hysterical; weeping; bleedin' from untreated wounds. Men stumblin' along carryin' others whose limbs had been blown away. Drunk, some of them. What else was there to do? They didn't know what the fuck was going on – 'scuse my language – and thought they were goin' to die on those beaches or get ground into a French field by a tank. Or get sliced into ribbons of bacon by an airborne machine gunner. No hope, no guidance, no chance of makin' it home, so far as they knew. What would you do? Sing The National Bleeding Anthem?

And then, there we all were, doddery old men in knackered old wrecks, bobbin' about on the sea like toy ducks in a soddin' bath; tryin' to get them off with no bleedin' harbour and no piers or jetties worth the name. Men got strafed just as they were about to escape; cut into pieces like lumps of cheese. I saw some poor bastard's head – no body, you unnerstand – its eyes wide open in horror, bangin' against the hull of the lifeboat like a bleedin' apple in a barrel. It was in the way, so someone gave it a bloody good jab with a boat-hook to shift it. Christ, can you imagine that? Some of those poor buggers just slid under the water and drowned quietly, pulled under by exhaustion and the weight of their fuckin' kit bags — 'scuse my indelicacy — at the last minute. And the others waited more-or-less patiently on the beaches, bloody great snakin' lines of thousands of men like they was waitin' for a bus or in a ration queue for bread rather than a chance to get away from Hell and back to their missus an' kids."

Bernard was quiet then for quite a while, watching drowning men in his mind's eye.

"Not all those boats got back, you know. The "Renown" from Leigh was lost and the "Crested Eagle". So even if you got off the beach and into a boat, there was no guarantee that Jerry wasn't going to blast you to buggery – sorry, I get like this when I think of it – an' small lumps before the bloody craft got under way. It wasn't glorious, Freddie, boy. It was carnage, like all war."

Bernard kicked at the scuttle contemptuously and spat into the fire. I looked at him with a new understanding and even greater respect than before.

"*The old Lie: Dulce et decorum est, Pro patria mori,*" I said.

"Do what? What language is that, son?"

"Latin. It's from a poem by a man called Wilfred Owen. About the Great War. We did it at school. It means it's a lie to tell children that it's a sweet and glorious thing to die for your country." I said.

"You're a clever lad. Let's hope your generation can use some of this education to stop any more wars."

"I'm not sure they'll ever stop, Uncle Bernard," I began hesitantly. "And I don't believe in the war and fighting. I object."

"Friggin' hell, son! Pardon my Flemish. You mean, when the time comes, if it comes, you're a conscientious objector?"

"Yes, I think I am."

"Mother of God! Well, in confidence, I can't say I blame you, son; probably agree with you if I'm honest but I should keep quiet about it for now, if I was you. Alright? Just between us, see?"

"Here's the tea," said Vi, elbowing her way through the door, a tray in her hands.

"Anyway," Bernard began again suddenly, "the point I'm tryin' to make, son, is that at least you have a future, with a bit o' luck. Those poor sods is dead and gorn forever, as the song says."

"Bernard! Mind your language in front of the boy."

"Oh, yeah, sorry, son. Bit late for that, though, I'm afraid. I 'ave been effin' and blindin' some. Makes me angry to think about it all. You should count your blessings, Freddie; that's all I'm sayin'."

Aunty Vi poured the tea. I got up to let her sit by the fire and pulled a dining chair over to sit between them. The fire crackled enthusiastically. Our legs were toasted wonderfully; our backs were iced solid by the draught sucking under the hall door and into the scullery.

Bernard slurped at his tea, winning a censorious glower from Aunty Vi.

"Sorry, dear," he said mechanically. "Freddie's worryin' about his future. The girl wants to know when they're gettin' married and so on. She's 'ad enough of Thaxted, by the sound of it."

"Humph! There's some as would pay a fortune to live there, I hear. Well," said Aunty Vi, putting down her teacup very deliberately. "I've been in communication with Archie Soper, as you know. He's a good man, Freddie; you're also lucky to have him as a future father-in-law. I think we're agreed that you must concentrate on your exams until next June. Six months."

"You mean I can't see Kathy or the baby; Grace?"

"We understand your feelings, Freddie. But like we said a while ago, it's a case of slowly does it; let's be sure you really do feel like you think you do."

"I know I do. I'd like to see my child and my...well...my intended?"

"Hear your Aunty out, son," said Bernard, throwing another lump of coal on the fire.

"Go steady with that coal, Bernard," admonished Aunty Vi. "There's a war on and it doesn't grow on trees."

I was about to make some facetious remark about the fact that it does grow on trees, sort of, but I decided against it.

"We have to think about whether you and the girl are to marry and, of course, that's up to the two of you. If you decide to do that then we next have to decide where you're going to live and, most importantly, how you're going to support them. Work, in other words."

"We want to be married, Aunty," I almost whispered. Bernard looked at me and patted my knee.

"No one's goin' to stop you, son, if that's what you really want," he said kindly.

"What work can I do?" I asked.

Aunty Vi fidgeted with her dress. "Well, your Uncle Bernard might be able to find you something on the pier. There are some civilians working there, even though it's in the hands of the military. I suppose you'd have to live with us for a while in that case but, well, I'm not too sure about that. May not be in any of our best interests. Mr. Soper writes to say there could be a job on a farm out at Paglesham; he knows the people. Not much money; hard work but a cottage thrown in. Of course, it wouldn't normally be available to someone so young but, well, Mr. Soper says he thinks he could swing it. So, you'd have your own place and some income. And of course farming is a reserved occupation if you stick with it."

"What does that mean, exactly?" I asked.

"You don't get called up, son. You don't 'ave to go an' fight," said Bernard with a grimace and a wink as he tipped the dregs of his tea-leaves into the fire. They spluttered in the embers.

PART TWO

A LAND
OF DREAMS

1943 - 1945

HARROWING CLODS
3rd February 1943

It is late afternoon and already opaque darkness threatens. Flat clouds the colour of lead coffins skim in relentlessly from the North Sea. It is bitingly cold in the wind, although not quite frozen. For this, the men on the farms and in Shuttlewood's rickety boatshed on the saltings are grateful. Working in the open – or as good as, where Shuttlewood's men are concerned – is a delight in summer. But in February, a different story is told.

In a field between muddy Waterside Lane and the straggling line of the low sea wall, a young man stumbles amongst bulrushes and elder shoots in a glutinous ditch. A thin skein of rain, a gossamer of chilled liquid threads, slides over his back, into his collar and through every fibre of his rough jacket. It soaks him to his core. Shivering involuntarily, he bangs his arms together across his chest. He wears an old hat with a wide brim; something he found in an outhouse at the cottage behind The Chase. It keeps some rain out of his eyes, but it is too large and falls across his forehead so that he must from time to time, with irritation, shove it back onto his head. Now, the water sluicing from the brim falls onto his chapped hands. It splashes the handle of the old spade he uses to chop at roots and dig out the ditch.

He pauses, standing to straighten his aching back. He looks towards the cluster of little cottages that is the village: a gouache of matt browns dotted, here and there, with the filthy yellow of decayed thatch. An oily pigtail of smoke slithers from a chimney over by the pub and he can see rooks jousting in and out of the elms and horse chestnut trees that surround The Chase. A lone seagull, cruising in from the river in hope of a worm or a slug in the ditch, alights on a tussock of sedge and observes the young man with a flickering but curiously lifeless eye. The young man is certain that he hears the seagull speak, telling a story of a journey south across the grey seas from a rocky island way off the coast.

"Why did you come here?" he asks.

The seagull looks at him, its head tilted to one side, as if pondering the question.

"Why did you?" it croaks rudely.

The young man shrugs and then bends his back to the task with a grunt and a sigh. The spade shudders into the sodden, brown earth. He levers up a clod and hurls it onto the side of the ditch. It is hard labour for which he is paid very little. But this, says Farmer Boardman, is because he is provided with a place to live and, not infrequently, a chicken, a sack of potatoes or some cabbages.

"I am not a bloody charity," says the farmer. "There is a war on, so we all have to make sacrifices. And there is an allotment available, if you wish to grow your own vegetables. Or you could keep your own hens at the back of the cottage. And don't forget, at this time of the year, there is pretty well bugger-all else to do except ditching so count your blessings that I keep you in work as a favour to my old chum Archie."

The young man nods his acquiescence, at the same time realising that it has not even occurred to him to keep hens. He is a townie.

"Thank you very much, Mr. Boardman," he observes.

The seagull says that he ought to be grateful and keeping hens is a good idea. They taste better than seagulls. Everyone knows that.

Of course, he helped with the hens at Belper, but he didn't ever wring their necks or pluck feathers from their slack, old lady's skins. He shudders at the memory. He wonders whether Kathy would be less squeamish and then smiles to himself: of course she would; beautiful, dependable, pragmatic Kathy. With another sigh, he adjusts his hat once more. Digging ditches; harrowing the fields with a stubborn old horse; pulling potatoes by hand; hacking Brussels sprouts; shovelling slimy filth from the pig-sties; re-placing tiles on the old barn in a snow-storm – all this and more he has done and expects to do, for this is now his lot. He knows that he pays with all this for a few minutes of sensuous delight and loving bliss on a station platform a few days after Christmas in 1940.

"C'est la vie; c'est la guerre, c'est l'amour," says the seagull ironically. It must be a bird from France.

Sometimes he wonders whether, given that time again, he would do the same. And then, recognising his own human weakness, he smiles knowingly; of course, he would. We are what we are. Mr. Soper was right about impetuosity and emotions.

Now stepping gingerly between the puddles in the lane comes a young woman carrying a child. She is slender and startlingly pretty. Even with an old cape wrapped around her and hooding her head, she is an arresting sight. Her natural curls refuse to be constrained by the garment; as she walks, the gentle curves of her body are somehow evident within the heavy, damp cloth. The child, a little girl of angelic appearance, is tucked into the folds of the old cape, her face peeking out just under her mother's. As the young woman passes the Home Guard hut behind the pub in Waterside Lane, Lol Bradley looks up from desultorily polishing an old American carbine. He breathes appreciatively through his trumpet of a nose.

"Thet's the newcomer, ain't it? A pretty young lass," he says.

"Ha! She is and thet's fer sure. They're finding it hard going, so I hear," replies his companion.

The woman rounds the bend in the lane, past the old village pump and then the stern façade of Milton Villa as she hurries towards the gun-metal slick of Paglesham's waterways. As she approaches Waterside Cottages, she sees her husband in the field to her left. The child sets up a keening wail as its little face is pinched unkindly by the sharp, salty fingers of the North Sea. The woman strokes the infant's head before pushing her way through the scrub elm, onto the clay of the ridges at the edge of the field.

"Freddie! Freddie!" she shouts into the gloaming. The rain, increasing now in force, lashes at her face.

"Da-da!" echoes a small, reedy voice.

A spade lifts into the fading light, as if tossed from the underworld. A head follows and then a body, hauling itself from the mud of the ditch.

"Freddie? It's so cold; you'll catch your death," calls the young woman, but without rancour because her husband's temper is short these days. "It's almost dark. Surely you can stop now?"

"Huh! I'll have to come back at day break; when the shadows have flown away; remember? Jesus, they probably never will. They've only just arrived! I have to bloody work, Kathy, otherwise we starve," he says bitterly as he tramps over the sticky furrows.

"Kissy Da-da," whispers the little voice from within Kathleen's cape.

"I know, Freddie, but if you're dead of the pneumonia, you can't work. Please?" says Kathleen, cold tears runnelling her cheeks.

"I don't know about pneumonia," he snaps, "but my head feels like it's being squeezed in a bloody vice."

Freddie looks at Kathleen, his love for her dissipating his anger. He reaches towards her and takes the child from within her cape into his arms.

"Hello, Grace," he says, "and how's my little piece of Bow Station platform?"

Kathleen smiles and giggles. "Oh, be careful, Freddie, she'll get cold."

"Da-da!" says the child, as Freddie hands her back to the warmth of the cape.

Together, they plod back down the lane, past the lights of the Plough and Sail public house. A lamp is burning in the window of Chaseway Cottage. As they near it, there is a sharp knocking on the window that fronts Lane End.

"There's Miss Harris, look!" says Kathleen.

A small, thin woman with her hair coiled in "headphones" appears from the back of the cottage, a shawl thrown over her head. She has a bowl in her hands.

"Mrs Tanner!" she calls. "Would you like this stew? I cooked too much; Mother is unwell and off her food. Athelstan has sent a message that he'll not be home until Sunday. Please, you'd be very welcome."

"Miss Harris, yes, thank you. You are very kind," says Kathleen.

"Not so bad last night, was it? Only one siren at about two. Did you hear Jerry overhead?"

"Yes. We were up anyway, with Grace," says Freddie. "The noise seems to wake her up. We saw the searchlights too, over by Stannetts somewhere, aren't they? Blessed nuisance, isn't it?"

"Yes, of course it is! I take some food up for those poor men at the searchlight sometimes. Poor fellows; so cold. There were some bombs dropped on houses in Westcliff, I hear and one just the other side of Church Farm," Zillah replies, tickling Grace under the chin.

"Is that close?" Kathleen looks alarmed.

"Well, yes, quite near, dear. But we must all try not to worry. I always say to Mother, if one's going to land on our heads, there's not much we can do to stop it, is there? What's coming is coming."

"I suppose not," says Kathleen, unconvinced.

"Unless we all move right away but even then, you can't be sure, can you? Anyway, I'm not going anywhere. I've been here since 1911. I'm staying put, Jerry or no Jerry."

"Good for you," says Freddie, glancing impatiently towards their own cottage.

Zillah Harris looks at the young couple in front of her. The young man seems uneasy; the woman beautiful yet somehow adrift and the child; well, the child cannot understand its circumstances but it must be fed. Sometimes the couple seem strangely at odds with their world, even allowing for the fact that the war creates domestic upset. The young man speaks well; she feels he must be quite a bright lad and she wonders why he is working on the land.

"If you need anything, you have only to ask," says Zillah, softly. "Pop down anytime for a chat if you like; or ask my Aunty Minnie next door to you if there's an emergency. She says she sees you out in the garden sometimes; although not so much now it's so cold, I suppose. We all try to help here in Paglesham, you know. Doing our bit! The Show must go on!"

Freddie wonders how much Aunty Minnie has said about what she saw in the garden. Momentarily he has a strange vision of his neighbour seated in a theatre's balcony, watching the two of them writhing on a grassy stage. Quite a show for a spinster.

"Thank you, Miss Harris," says Kathleen, giving the little woman a broad smile.

Freddie smiles too. "Er, yes. Thanks ever so much, Miss Harris. We do appreciate your thoughtfulness."

The young couple enters their cottage. It is basic, but it is enough. There were a few sticks of furniture left in it when they arrived; nothing fancy, but it'll do for now, Kathleen observed. For a while they sleep on the floor but then old Mr. Whimpery in Barn Row says they can have his double bed. He hasn't been up the stairs for over a year, because of his arthritis. He is happy sleeping in the chair by the fire or curled up on his ancient sofa. The bed is almost as old as he is, thinks Kathleen, and as dirty. They have a job getting it out of the cottage and carrying it around to Lane End. Its mattress is stained and mildewed with the Juices of Ages. But after a good airing and some soap and water, it just about passes muster; beggars cannot be choosers. They christen it that night; gingerly, for they are worried that any over-enthusiastic wriggling could break its back.

Freddie puts Grace into the cot that he has fashioned for her. He kicks at the fire. He tramps out to the back where there is a pile of roughly-chopped timber he has collected from the field edges and down the lanes. Coal may be rationed but logs and branches are not. He returns to the one room they heat and throws small logs into the grate. They hiss and spit as the flames attempt to take hold.

"Miss Harris's stew and some potatoes," says Kathleen, bringing in two plates.

"Thanks," says Freddie, spooning the food into his mouth. "So, without Miss Harris's stew, it'd be just potatoes?"

"Yes. I have some bread, though."

Freddie grunts his annoyance and wipes a dribble of gravy from his chin.

"I'm sorry, Freddie. But there is no more money until you are paid."

"I know. I know. It's not your fault. I'm sorry. It's just that...oh, I don't know. It all seems so bloody hard and depressing, that's all."

"Yes. We're together though. All three of us. That's all that matters to me," says Kathleen quietly.

"Mmm. I was wondering; what about keeping some hens and growing some vegetables out the back there; you know, dig it over when it warms up in the Spring?"

"Can we do that? Do you know how?"

"We'll have to find out. Mr. Boardman will help, I'm sure. He's a bit gruff, but he's not unkind. And Mr. Loader at the pub keeps chickens, so he'd know. I know a bit from when I was at the Shaws' place."

There is a pause. Grace snuffles in her cot and a mouse scuttles somewhere in the ceiling above them. Kathleen pushes her plate aside. She picks up a bundle of sewing and begins laboriously stitching. Archie has sent them some of his old shirts. She is making a nightgown for Grace and some blouses for herself. Miss Harris has been instructing her in the principles of "make do and mend".

"A letter came from Benny. He wants to visit us next week."

Freddie bangs his tin plate down with a clatter. "God Almighty! How are we going to feed him? I hope he likes potatoes because if he doesn't, he'll starve to death."

"It'll be alright. Anyway, I'd like to see him. It gets lonely here, Freddie."

"We've only got ourselves to blame for the whole bloody situation, I suppose."

Kathleen looks at her husband. He is not usually so crude and abrupt; certainly, he did not used to be before...before they had to marry and he chose to hide them here. She knows that people think she is simple and stupid; but she understands her husband's growing anger and frustration. Freddie needs something to aim for. He needs a dream and she wonders whether it's to be found among the salty swatchways and wind-blown fields of this desolate place.

COUCH GRASS
23rd July 1942

We were married at Southend Registry Office in July of 1942, just a few weeks after I'd taken my School Certificate at Belper. I suppose it's no wonder I didn't seem to know my arse from my elbow for some months, if not years after that: jumping from being a blazered schoolboy to a married man with a family in such a short space of time. It was mainly a sense of disconnection that I experienced – that somehow I was in the wrong place or I was the wrong person in the right place. Odd.

After the conversation I had with Aunty Vi and Uncle Bernard about my future, just before Christmas in 1941, I had to decide whether it was best to try for the farming job at Paglesham or Uncle Bernard's suggestion of work on the pier. The latter seemed like quite a good idea because it would mean we'd be somewhere familiar and close to the town for shopping and so on. Aunty Vi had seemed reluctant to have us at Pleasant Road but in the Spring, she wrote to me to say that she had talked to Bernard about it again and that, once we were married, we could have the front room and Grace could have the little room next to it. But we'd have to agree on some sort of rent, she said, because if we were living there, she'd lose her B&B income.

The only thing was, the pier was not the pier, it was HMS Leigh. (I was never sure why it wasn't HMS Southend since it's nowhere near Leigh, but there we are.) It was equipped as a war machine with guns and the like. It played a predominantly military role. I wasn't at all sure that I could stomach that because my feelings about what we were doing to one another as human beings had turned from distress and disbelief to utter revulsion. When news about what the Germans were doing to the Jews in Auschwitz began to filter through in late 1942, after we were married, I felt that my decision to take the farming job was the right one. Of course, the full horror of the gas chambers was not totally clear until the end of the war, but nevertheless, the implications of what one heard in 1942 were enough to confirm me in my views. Any kind of war where children and innocents are slaughtered is an abomination. And there is no other kind, is there?

...why, in a moment look to see
The blind and bloody soldier with foul hand
Defile the locks of your shrill-shrieking daughters;
Your fathers taken by the silver beards,
And their most reverd heads dashed to the walls,
Your naked infants spitted upon pikes...

Shakespeare, as always, says it all, really. And what amazes me now and was beginning to amaze and appal me then was that after the unrelenting carnage of history, let alone the Great War, the country picked up the bayonet only twenty years later and started gouging eyes and spilling blood all over again. We never learn.

Apart from all that, I remembered the glory of that day at Paglesham in 1938 and although I realised that it was many years previously, when I was a good deal younger, nevertheless the occasion affected my decision. I had often thought about the village and had always thought it would be a fine place to live. So, that's what I told Aunty Vi. She relayed the decision to Mr. Soper and the arrangements were made for the summer.

Even our wedding was accompanied by the wail of air-raid sirens! It was a Thursday, the 23rd July, in the morning. Mr. Soper was there, Benny, Aunty Vi and Uncle Bernard. Much to my surprise and delight, Mr. and Mrs Shaw somehow managed to wangle a permit and they attended too. Vinny wrote to say he might attend, but of course, he didn't. I wasn't surprised and, to be honest, I didn't care. I hadn't seen him for years.

Kathy looked absolutely gorgeous. She'd saved her clothing coupons and, with a little help from Aunty Vi and her sewing machine, she managed a very pretty, pale yellow dress with a matching hat and gloves. All very swish at the time. Of course, we didn't have a white wedding in a church; apart from the expense, most people didn't do that in those days if a child had already been born. It just wasn't the done thing; even revealing that you "had to get married" or that you were marrying to give a child legitimacy could be enough to make you social pariahs.

Anyway, just as we were saying our vows, the siren went off.

The Registrar, a short man with buck teeth, a lisp and spittle, broke off in the middle of "Kathleen, do you take this man...?"

"Oh, dearie me," he said. "We ought to go into the shelter, you know."

"Blimey!" said Benny, who was acting as best man, "Now yer see it; now yer don't!"

"Is it really necessary?" interjected Aunty Vi from somewhere behind me. "Anyway, you'll have to start all over again from the beginning, won't you? I'm sure the vows have to be a complete thing and not all in bits."

I grinned to myself. I'd heard of coitus interruptus but I wasn't sure what the phrase would be for an interrupted wedding. Pompous interruptus, perhaps.

"Very well, if we must, we must," said the Registrar, spraying Kathy's dress with small globules. He began where he'd left off and the ceremony was completed in double-quick time. There was barely space for us to say, "I do" but, of course, we already had and Grace, the proof, was grizzling somewhere at the back of the room. As we were signing the register, the all-clear sounded. All symbolically very appropriate, I thought. I was about to explain the irony to Benny and then thought better of it, because of course he wouldn't have understood what was funny.

"Whadja bleedin' on about, mate?" would have been his most probable response.

We had some celebratory cakes and tea in Garons in the High Street and that was more-or-less it. Our "honeymoon" was spent at Marsh Cottage in Lane End, into which we moved that afternoon, my employment with Mr. Boardman due to commence the following Monday.

It was a beautiful, hot afternoon; the kind of weather that Paglesham likes best. We could hear some voices calling to one another down on the sea wall and there was a donkey braying somewhere over towards Church End. Otherwise there was silence.

The grass in the back garden was so high that it was possible to play hide and seek in it. Kathy put Grace into a large cardboard box (it served as a play-pen for some weeks) and then crawled on all fours into the grass.

"Bet you can't find me!" she called over to where I was sluicing my head and chest in the crystal clear, freezing water I was pumping from the well.

I flicked water from my eyes and turned to where her voice had come from. She was nowhere to be seen. Grace looked at me, blinked and pointed her chubby finger towards the grass.

"Mama," she squeaked.

"I know!" I whispered, and then more loudly, "I bet I blooming can! Entering from stage left!"

We hadn't seen each other, apart from the unsatisfactory occasion on Westcliff Parade, since we'd been together in the tea-shop twelve months before. And prior to that it was the station platform. I was so charged with desire for her, I could hardly see straight. It took me less than a minute to track her through the grass. As she had done, I went on my hands and knees.

"A dirty old dog is coming to find you!" I growled.

But she was a cat. She'd padded around deep in the middle of the thicket to make a nest. She was completely naked, her wedding dress folded neatly and placed to one side. Of course, I'd never seen her that way before. I'd never seen any girl that way before. To say that I was awe-struck at her perfect form and beauty or that I was speechless and breathless would be a series of inadequate clichés and understatements. She smiled cheekily and held out her arms.

"I don't see any underwear," I managed to croak, indicating the pile of clothing as I crawled towards her.

"I don't wear any," she chuckled. "You know that."

"Not even on your wedding day?"

"Especially not on my wedding day," she whispered, pulling me down on top of her and sliding her hand under my belt all in one go.

"Goodness me!" she exclaimed.

Afterwards – probably only two minutes or so, if truth is told; maybe not even that – we lay side by side in the grass, watching the sky. High above, some fighter planes were circling and diving in a dog-fight to the death. Then we noticed that in an upstairs window of the cottage adjoining ours, a woman was looking down at us: two kids wet and stark-naked in the grass.

"Mama!" shrilled Grace.

Kathy grabbed her dress and slipped it over her head before crawling out of the grass to retrieve Grace in her box. She brought her back to the love-nest where she promptly fell asleep.

Apart from a foray back into the cottage to get something to eat and drink, we stayed out in the warmth of the garden, lying in the grass, making love, all though the afternoon and into the evening. It was a clear night and soon the sky was littered with thousands of stars. We lay and watched them, twinkling. Just like all young lovers under the stars, we thought it could never change.

NOR CERTITUDE
November 1942

Dear Tanner,

I hope this finds you alright. I found out you live in Pleasant Road but I don't know the number or whether your name is the same as your Aunt's. I have never been to Pleasant Road but I understand it's down by The Kursaal. One wonders therefore if it is very pleasant!? My people have a house in Crosby Road. My pater says he thinks it's tawdry at The Kursaal, but he's a JP and also says there's some rough types down there. No offence, of course.

We're back at school now in our own buildings in Kenilworth Gardens, thank Heavens. I expect you know that anyway. First day back was after the half term holiday so everyone had time to get their things back to Southend. I think we'd all had enough of being stuck up in Derbyshire!

Old Midgley told us you had the best results of any of us in the Certificate exams. Top grades across the board, he said, giving a bit of a sniff like he does, as if he thought it was bad form or something. So well done, Tanner. Seems a shame you are not here now to start on the Highers. Can't you wangle something? I did almost as well as you with top grades except in Chemistry. Blessed subject! I just could not get the hang of all those peculiar formulae and stuff. Just doesn't seem to have much to do with the real world. I mean, I know it does because we're all chemicals (and Goadsby with his vile flatulence more than others!) but there is no feeling in any of it. I think you understand what I mean by that. We intelligent people have to stick together in my opinion; there are so many fools in the world.

You will never guess what happened earlier this year, before we left Belper! Maybe you already know, but maybe not? The Old Man died! He got pneumonia and although he rallied for a few days, it got worse and he died on 14th February. Not much of a Valentine's present, was it? Gone, just like that. Poor old bloke. He was a good sort, really. Some of the masters have been saying that it was the stress of being up here and not back at Westcliff that did for him. Sapped his strength and resolve, they say. It makes you think, though, doesn't it? None of us is certain we're going to be here from one minute to the next.

We knew he was ill, but when we got the news, everybody was really shocked; some of the tiddlers were even crying. Daddy Smith has to take over until they have time to find a new head master, apparently. I expect he's wondering whether he's going to drop dead as well. Some of the chaps reckon he already is, of course.

They say you got married to that girl in the summer! Is that right? Seems hard to believe but if all those rumours last year were true, I suppose maybe you are! Funny old life, isn't it?

I'm hoping to be able to read Law when the time comes. What on Earth will you do with yourself? I expect you must be feeling pretty rotten about everything, having made such a mess of it so early on.

Perhaps we can meet up sometime for a bit of a chin-wag if you feel like it?

I'll sign off now with that nickname everybody uses but which I don't like, as you know, but just to show good will.

Your friend,

(Master) Bates

NOR LIGHT
February 1943

On the Sunday when we were expecting Benny, there was a knock at the door quite early. I'd only just got out of bed, reluctant to leave Kathy's whispering caresses and enfolding loins. It was colder than Charity; I was struggling to get the fire alight and to boil some water for tea.

"Hello, young fella-me-lad," said Lol Bradley as I opened the door. I looked at him with some surprise. I'd passed the time of day with him a couple of times in Waterside Lane, but no more. I'd seen him with several others one time cutting sprouts in Clements' Field next to Milton Villa. He'd waved at me cheerily. He seemed a good sort.

"Oh, hello," I said. "Um, I'd offer you some tea, but I haven't even got a fire going yet!"

"Don't you worry, boy. Just wonderin' whether you want ta earn a little extra today? There's a stackie to be emptied over et the creek. Wal usually helps but he's laid-up sick. It ain't very nice work but, well, one and six is the pay. You interested in thet?"

"Yes, I am," I said immediately. "We're, well, a little short just now."

"I thought as much," said Lol. "Not that I'm pryin', mind."

I met him an hour later by the path to Well House and we walked across the fields from Back Road towards Church Hall and the little quay. It was a gloomy, cold morning with a thick mist curling off the fields as we trudged along the road. Lol explained that we'd be unloading the hold of a barge – what he referred to as a "stackie" – with stuff to spread on the land. We'd have to shovel it into baskets and then haul it out and heave it into a waiting cart. He said it was dirty work. He was right.

When we arrived at the quay there were two or three other men there, mostly from Church End, I supposed, because I didn't recognise them. Each of them was wearing an odd assortment of old clothing with a hood tied under the chin. Their coat shoulders were padded with paper or rags and they had waders or heavy boots on their feet. Two men were wrapping old scarves or cloths over the lower parts of their faces. I must have looked perplexed. Lol pointed out a collapsing shed and told me I'd find some similar gear in there.

"What we're shovelling ain't nice, boy. Git yassilf covered up!"

I did as I was told, returning from the hut after a few minutes. One of the Church End men looked at me and laughed.

"You'll want sumpin' on yer face 'cos 'o the stink, boy. Don't 'spose you shovelled any ol' shit before, have ya?"

The other men joined him in laughter. I wrapped something round my head quickly, not because of any smell but rather to hide my embarrassment.

There was a smell, it was true, but we were right next to Church Farm. There were some pigs grunting and squealing somewhere so I assumed that's what accounted for it. Well, I daresay I could smell the pigs, but the stench coming from the hold of the stackie was far worse. In fact, I don't think I've ever smelled anything as bad before or since. It wasn't just the smell of ordure. There was another stench in there too, but I didn't know what it was, although it reminded me of the aftermath of those air-raids in the Blitz in Bow. I should have guessed, I suppose.

There were a couple of ladders leading down into the hold and I followed Lol into the subterranean gloom. The smell was so revolting that it seemed almost palpable; it made me gag a few times. I felt dizzy and heard buzzing in my ears. I hoped with all my might that I wouldn't embarrass myself by toppling into whatever was below the ladder.

"You alright, boy?" said Lol as he heard me spluttering.

"I'll be alright in a minute," I said, hoping that I would, "when I get used to it." I looked back up through the hold's opening, at a square of grey, misty sky. I had a sudden, terrible feeling that I might pass out, fall into the stench of darkness and never see the light of day again.

"You never git used to it," he replied through his scarf. He grabbed at his shovel viciously. I wondered whether he felt that if he were too half-hearted, he might change his mind and go home. I don't think anyone would have blamed him if he had.

"What in God's name is it?" I took a step forward from the ladder, my boots sinking into a slimy morass, a puff of foul gas rising up around me.

"River sludge; bits o' fish, street sludge, human sewage, dead cats and dogs. Rats. Whatever they scoop off the streets of London or from the backs of privies, boy. Lovely, eh? Good manure. Right, let's get to it."

So, the other smell I'd noticed was putrefaction. Indeed, it wasn't long before our shovels unearthed the partly decomposed remains of a small dog, its teeth bared in a yellow grin; its little identity collar still around what was left of its neck.

"Oh, dear God!" I muttered, lifting the vile object into a basket.

"Save your breath," grunted Lol, "we'll be done quicker that way. We gits paid when we're done."

It was almost pitch-black in the further recesses of the hold but it didn't seem to matter that much. We worked to some degree by the feel of the shovel in the mire, simply bending, scooping and tipping into the baskets. When these were full, we had to lift them onto our shoulders – then I understood the need for the packing – and carry them up the ladder. That was almost worse than the shovelling: not only was it back-breaking, but the vileness was right next to your face, sliding sometimes in green rivulets down your back.

We stopped for something to eat after a few hours but I had little appetite for the sandwich that Kathy had hurriedly made for me that morning. In the afternoon, back in the hold, we heard the sirens whining, explosions in the distance and then, very close at hand, the sound of the ack-ack gun behind The Punch Bowl.

"Thassit, lads, shoot the bastard out of the sky!" shouted someone from the other end of the hold.

To keep my mind from dwelling too much on the grim task in hand, I tried to remember another of Owen's poems that we'd done in school the previous term, *The Sentry*. It seemed appropriate to the circumstances I found myself in. I have to confess that I was feeling very sorry for myself. I worked at remembering the words, concentrating on them, rather than what I was obliged to do.

Rain, guttering down in waterfalls of slime,
Kept slush waist-high and rising hour by hour,
And choked the steps too thick with clay to climb.
What murk of air remained stank old, and sour
With fumes of whiz-bangs and the smell of men
Who'd lived there years, and left their curses in the den,
If not their corpses....

"Nearly there, son," said Lol. I had stopped looking or trying to measure how much more there was for us to shovel. I just kept my sights to a small space around me.

"Then it's home for a good scrub and after that, a couple of pints in The Plough," he said. "You want ta join us?"

"Well, I'm not seventeen 'til April," I said.

"Incha? I'd hed thought you wuz least eighteen. You've done a man's work; don't see why you can't hev a man's drink. Mum's the word, ey?"

"Well, I'll have to see, but thanks."

"Leave the clothing here and don't go nowhere public. You don't know how much you stink! Ol' Mark Brown got asked to leave Woolies, 'coz o' the stink, when he wuz daft enough to go along in there without washin'!"

When I got home, it was dark and a thin drizzle had replaced the morning's mist. The cottage window had a lovely warm glow coming from it as I trudged up Lane End. I looked in and saw that Benny was sitting by the fire, toasting his feet. I'd forgotten all about his visit.

"'Ere he is!" he chortled as I came through the door. "Phew, bugger me, Freddie! What 'appened? You shat yerself?"

"Good evening, Benny," I said, "I see your language hasn't improved any, then? Although it does appear that you have mastered the past tense."

"Yeah, I'm a crude little sod, it's true enough. 'Ow you doin? Blimey, mate! Died, gorn to 'eaven and then come back again, by the smell of it!"

"Could be," I said.

"Here's one for yer! Remember that *Treasure Island*?"

"What do you mean?" He was obviously busting to tell me some witticism but, of course, I wasn't really in the mood.

"It's a joke, right? Now...where's yer buccaneers?" grinned Benny.

"I don't know. Where are my buccaneers?" Of course, I fell right into it.

"On the side of yer buckin' head!" chortled Benny, slapping his thighs in amusement.

"Oh, yes, very droll, Soper, as my form master Mr. Midgley used to say. Most entertaining, but spare me the encore."

"So 'ave you found Treasure Island out 'ere at Paglesham, then?" asked Benny, oblivious as ever to my sarcasm.

I frowned. "Mmm. Not sure about that. I think I'm still at the stage of being caught in the rigging while Israel Hands is throwing dirks at me."

"Friggin' in the riggin', ey? Yeah! I'll tell yer about that later; look out, here comes the missus!"

Kathy came through from the kitchen. She was about to give me a welcoming kiss, but reeled back instead.

"Pooh!"

"Alright, alright, I'll go and douse myself."

Kathy offered to boil some water but I played hurt, saying that I was sure they wouldn't want me standing about, reeking like an elephant house, while water was boiled.

"Too right," said Benny, "go an' stand under the bloody pump."

"Don't be daft, Freddie, it's far too cold to wash under the pump."

So I waited, stinking the place out, until eventually there was enough hot water to put in the tin bath.

§

Benny had brought some food with him from London. He said not to ask how he'd come by the pork chops, so we didn't and ate them greedily. Then he wanted to go down to The Plough for a couple of pints. I was worried that I had only the one and sixpence and that I ought not to spend it on beer. And, of course, we were not old enough anyway. But I remembered what Lol had said; there'd be no difficulty there. What's more, Benny looked about twenty: he had developed heavy, broad shoulders and impressive stubble on his chin. In fact, the rather unbecoming features he'd had as a boy were less noticeable now; I suppose he'd had a man's frame too early.

"It's on me, come on," he said, grabbing his coat.

The door to the public bar creaked on its hinges. Inside the long, narrow room, lined with wooden, pew seats built into the panelling of the walls, there was a pleasant fug of tobacco smoke, old clothing and stale beer. The floor was liberally covered with sawdust; probably not a bad idea in view of the fact that Whopper Staines, who was sitting with Bill Robinson, a cribbage board between them, was kicking brown gouts of manure off his boots every time he shuffled his bony backside. Bill was sucking noisily on a clay pipe, breaking off from the cribbage every now and then to spit fulsomely into the spittoon by his elbow.

Vic Cardy and another man were playing darts. Dapper Wally Wood, dressed neatly in his Sunday best, sat in the opposite corner to Whopper, where the air was cleanest, supping his pint with measured restraint. There was no sign of Lol. Maybe we were too early or maybe, as one of the other men in the barge had implied, he'd failed to get a pass for the evening from his wife.

"Good evening, lads," Wally said as we came through the door. The other occupants of the bar made similar observations and Bill expectorated again into the spittoon. I wondered briefly whose job it was to empty that; it would be almost as bad as shovelling out the stackie.

"Good evening," I said, a little nervously. I hadn't been in there before and I felt that we were interlopers, as you so often do in a small "local". I didn't know how to conduct myself, what to drink or how to ask for it. Of course, I need not have worried.

"Two pints of brown and mild, please, love," said Benny.

Benny hadn't asked me what I wanted, no doubt shrewdly realising that my probable difficulty in answering the question would give the game away. The woman behind the small, mahogany-topped bar looked at us suspiciously and frowned. I assumed this was the legendary Mrs Loader, the landlady, whom I had never met, or seen, although we lived only yards apart. I'd heard that she was very strict about under-age boys trying to buy beer. But it seemed she didn't want to be troubled that evening or she thought that the great hulk in front of her was old enough. Anyway, she reached down to find two bottles of brown ale.

"I'm not your love," she said to Benny. "Mrs Loader's the name."

"Sorry, I'm sure, Mrs Loader. No offence meant."

I thought for a second he was going to add "love" but, of course, Benny didn't have the wit for such a thing. She frowned again and then, to make her point, she very deliberately and slowly pulled two separate halves of mild, tipping them into pint glasses before decapitating the brown ales and adding some of them too.

"That'll be two shillings, please."

Benny counted out the money. "It'd be one and ten pence in Bow."

"You pay extra for country air," said Mrs Loader, with just the hint of a laconic smile.

"Yeah, I smelt some o' that as I was comin' on the bus. Well, down the 'atch!" he said and took a long gulp of his beer. He seemed quite accomplished.

"Er, yes, um...cheers," I responded and took a cautious sip of the murky liquid. It tasted quite sweet and did not have the sharp sting I had been lead to expect.

"That's 'cos it ain't bitter," explained Benny. "Blimey, you are the innocent still, aintcha?"

I grinned. "So, are you working? Kathy said something about the Underground?"

"Yeah. Engine sheds. You know, greasin' 'em and mending the buggers when they conk out. Which they do all the bleedin' time. 'Salright, though. Money's not bad."

"And your Dad?" I asked. "Kathy doesn't seem to know."

Benny laughed and took another swallow of his beer. "Well, she never did, did she? Bless 'er! He's alright. Same office; same routines. Says he wants to get a transfer down to Southend when the war's over, to be closer to you an' his grand-daughter, so watch out!"

"What about you? Got a girl?"

"Nah, not really. 'Ad me end away a couple a times round the back o' the engine sheds but nothing serious, like. I got a list, though," Benny chuckled into his glass.

"A list? Of what?"

He leaned towards me and whispered. "Women I want to 'ave it off wiv. I want to 'ave a virgin schoolgirl, a married woman with kids, a woman in a uniform – there's this clippie on the number fourteen wot I could really go for – then a red-head, a negress and a nun."

I snorted loudly into my beer. "When's all this, then, before next Wednesday, is it?"

"Nah, nah, give it a couple a months, son," he grinned. "You made it with the virgin well ahead of me, anyhow. Got any nuns 'ere?" He looked around him as if he expected one to pop her wimpled head out of the door to the snug.

"Oh, well, look, I'm sorry about that, but..." He waved a dismissive hand before I could continue.

"Forgeddit. Was always goin' to 'appen wiv you two. You might of thought of givin' it a bit longer, but, well, too bloody late now for worryin' about spilt milk. Or somethin' else the same colour. Anyway, I thought I'd ticked a virgin off the list an' all, but turns out I ain't." He finished his beer with one long swallow and clonked the glass down onto the bar. I raised an interrogative eyebrow.

"Yeah. Margie Jordan, Alice's little sister. You remember?'

"But she's only...oh, well, no, I suppose she isn't now," I said.

"Let's just say she's nearly sixteen. Went down the canal towpath wiv 'er. Bit of a kiss'n'cuddle and she drops her knickers, just like that! Just like Alice, I 'spose. Lovely; like a slinky ferret. But it turns out I wasn't the first. Or even the bleedin' second, come to that. Little tart. Two more, please, lo...Mrs Loader."

Realising that I was falling behind, I closed my eyes and swallowed the rest of my beer in one go. Already my head was spinning.

"Anyway, that's enough about my love-life. What about you? 'Ow long you goin' to shovel shit and dig ditches, then?"

"Language, if you don't mind," said Mrs Loader.

"Oh, sorry. Forgot I paid extra fer the clean air, like," said Benny. I laughed; it was quite a witty remark for him.

"Well, it's not all like that, you know. Winter's hard, it seems, but it was really much better in the summer, when I started." I heard a defensive tone in my voice.

"Kathleen says you're tired most of the time an' pissed off all the time. Well, she didn't say pissed off but that's what she meant. Whassup?"

I took another drink of the beer. I was getting used to it; decided I quite liked it.

"Well, Benny, I suppose it's just that it's not quite what I thought I'd be doing with my life, you see. I mean, it's keeping us alive and I'm feeding my family, so when I look in the mirror in the morning, I can do so with self-respect...but...well...there's no stimulation, that's the nub of it. No developing future; it's never going to be much different and I don't have to...well, use my brain. It's a bit deadening, I suppose. I don't know; it's not what I thought my life would be...but I can't say I wasn't warned; your Dad told me all about it years ago."

"Did 'e? How's that?"

"That day we came here for the picnic just before the war started; you remember? When Kathy fell in the water?"

"Oh, yeah! An' you couldn't keep yer eyes off her little chest tryin' to pop out of her wet vest. All mapped out, wannit, even then?"

"Looks like it! Couldn't help myself! And now...well, it seems like I have to pay for that by having no future, I suppose."

"Depends wot yer mean by future. We all got a future of one sort or another until we're under the slab. And then, whassa difference? Anyway, there ain't what you mean by a future fer lots o' blokes, Freddie. You should see some of the sad old sods I work with; been lying under engines of one kind or another for bloody years. Day in, day out."

"And I thought we'd be happy out here in the country. Fresh air and so on! But actually, I think Kathy's finding it difficult, especially now, in the winter. No one about. Maybe we should be in the town. We're townies, after all."

Benny belched. Whopper looked across from his game. "I think the Vicar 'ed like another cup o' tea, wouldn't ya, Vicar?" he guffawed, licking a damp stub of cigarette from one side of his mouth to the other.

Benny acknowledged the joke by belching again.

"That's enough of that. Manners maketh Man!"

"Sorry, Mrs Loader."

"Kathy's been talking?" I said after a while. "I mean, you said she says I'm fed up all the time?"

"Relax, son. Nah, not really, you know how she is; rambles on summin' shockin' sometimes."

"She's not daft, Benny, not a bit of it. Really marvellous with the baby. Never puts a foot wrong."

"I ain't surprised. Turned out a real beauty too, ain't she? You'll 'ave to keep 'er locked up."

"Mmm. Well, maybe that's why we're tucked away out here, Benny. Not too much to worry about with these old fellows! I hope."

"You never can tell. It don't stop getting' stiff just 'cos yer over fifty. So I'm told, like. 'Spose we'll find out one day."

"I don't know what I'd do if another man...well...you know..." I said, frowning into my beer.

"Bloody hell, Freddie! Stop worryin' about stuff you can't do nuffin' about, son. Blokes is gonna give 'er the eye, aren't they? She's a big girl, ain't she? You know, like that Jane Russell. Bound to 'appen."

"I suppose so," I said. I didn't really want to talk about it. We just stared around us at the others in the bar for a while. Benny sucked at his beer and then gave a little cough.

"Somethin' I wanted to ask you about. We'll both be eighteen before all that long, Freddie. Whadja gonna do when yer gets yer call-up papers, ey? I'm hopin' fer the Royal Signals; you know, wot wiv the electrics work on the trains an' that; or maybe the Armoured Division. Quite fancy squashin' shit outa Jerry wiv a tank."

"I'm working on the land, Benny. Farming is a reserved occupation. And I'm short-sighted, don't forget." I adjusted my glasses, to make the point.

Benny squared his shoulders and looked at me intently. "Bloody excuses. You don't have to stay on the farm. You can still enlist. Can't you? Take yer soddin' specs off!"

I drank some of my beer, put down my glass carefully and looked back at him. "I could, but I'm not going to."

"I don't see why not?"

"I didn't expect you to, Benny. It's a matter of principle. And I'm not the only one who thinks that way, you know," I said.

"Principle? Whadja on about, principle?"

"My principles. I don't believe in armed conflict. It doesn't achieve anything in the long run except death, misery and then, later, more armed conflict and so on."

He looked at me with a sneer and threw the remaining half a pint of beer down his throat.

"Bollocks!" he snarled. It seemed as if he was about to say something else but he changed his mind. Instead, he turned and stomped out of the bar, the locals looking after him with surprise. I shrugged as if I didn't understand what was happening and followed him through the door.

"I never thought that you of all people could be so bloody useless!" he barked. "Christ, it's fuckin' embarrassin' even to be seen with yer, let alone to be yer brother-in-law. Conshi!" He spat forcefully in my direction.

There was a bus waiting. Benny turned on his heel and went to speak to the driver.

"Give us five minutes, mate," he said. "I wanna get outa this place. The stink's makin' me sick."

Despite her obvious disappointment and despite my efforts to reason with him, he told Kathy loudly that he didn't want to spend the night in the same house as a conshi. He gave her a hasty peck on the cheek, grabbed his bits and pieces and was gone without a backward glance or any word to me. I didn't see him again until after the war.

BEGIN, AND CEASE, AND THEN AGAIN BEGIN
8th September 1943

On the day that Italy surrendered to the Allied Forces, we surrendered Aunty Vi's coffin to a damp grave under some overhanging branches in a corner of Sutton Cemetery. Rain dripped down my neck throughout the interment. I don't think I've ever been to a funeral when the sun was shining and the birds were singing jauntily among the apple blossom. This one was no exception: it was horsing it down.

There was quite a crowd there because she was well known in the area, so the neighbours rallied round. People always turn out, in my experience, when someone dies young or unexpectedly. Poor old Bernard took it quite hard and wasn't able to come to terms with it all for several months.

Nobody had known that anything was wrong until a couple of days before she died. Aunty Vi herself must have known that she was ill but she didn't say anything to anyone until it was too late and she could bear the pain no longer. The doctor told me that some cancers are very aggressive and very quick.

I managed to speak to her before she died but only because Brian Horsfall, her immediate neighbour in the terrace at Pleasant Road, took the trouble to get a bus out to Paglesham. He arrived there mid-afternoon on a Saturday and Miss Harris, who was doing some clearing up in the Garden Field, saw him get off the bus, looking a bit lost. She directed him down the lane to us and kept the bus waiting while I changed my shirt.

"We'll have to hurry," said Brian, rather unnecessarily. "She's really bad and she keeps asking for you. Bernard asked me to come and fetch you."

Of course, it took an age to get into Southend. Aunty Vi was in the back bedroom. She was a terrible colour, like damp alabaster. Her breath smelt like rotten meat and the whole room was enveloped in the odour. Her face was creased with pain even though the doctor had given her something. I suppose it was morphine because she was sliding in and out of consciousness all the time. Once she knew I was there she pulled at my hand and started talking, with difficulty, straight away. Bernard was on the other side of the bed and she made it plain that he had to fill in the gaps.

She kept losing her thread, but with occasional prompts from Bernard, she told me that some time ago, she'd had a visit from Bert Morgan, one of Pa's one-time drinking friends. Pa had told him that, as we had suspected all along, he had pushed Ma down the stairs at Bamford Road in a fit of rage when she wouldn't do his sexual bidding. To suspect something awful like that is bad enough, but to have it confirmed, especially under such circumstances, is truly terrible.

Aunty Vi died three hours later.

I could have stayed at Pleasant Road but it didn't feel like the right thing to do. I wanted to be at home with Kathy so that I could talk through what I had heard and what had happened in front of my eyes. I didn't want to talk to Bernard about it, although he did elaborate on the exact nature of Pa's sexual expectations, according to Bert.

Anyway, Bernard quite properly had a closer and more recent death to grieve over. So I assured him of my preparedness to help in the coming days and took my leave. I managed to get a bus to Rochford and then walked from there to Paglesham. It was very late by the time I got home. Grace was snuffling in her cot but Kathy was waiting up for me, sitting on the big chair the people at The Chase had given us. It was quite a chilly night and she had a blanket wrapped around her. As I came through the door, she looked up at me. She could tell from my face what news I had to impart.

"Oh, no," she whispered, bringing her hands to her face. "I'm so sorry, Freddie. She was kind to us."

I slumped down into the other chair and we sat looking at one another for a few moments. "Yes. She was a bit of a battle-axe at times but you knew where you were with her and you're right; she didn't have to take me in like she did."

"My Dad said she had her head screwed on."

"She did, it's true. She told me something terrible before she died, Kathy. I think that's why she sent for me." My breath was coming in shuddering gasps.

Later, lying close together in bed, I finally gave way to my feelings and cried like a baby for some time into Kathy's hair and across her neck. She just held me close throughout and listened as I talked of the grotesque obscenity of knowing that your father has killed your mother; of the unfairness of a life that wipes out the good and the innocent and gives more room for evil; of the seemingly callous indifference of Vinny; of the iniquity of a society that prohibits a point of view at odds with convention and of the vile horrors of a war that is sanctioned by those whose responsibility is surely to know better. And then, inevitably, in the early hours of the morning, I arrived at self-pity's door and bemoaned my lot as a farm labourer wading in mire instead of a future as a graduate professional in a white shirt.

"Are you very unhappy with your life, Freddie?" asked Kathy. She kissed my forehead.

"Sometimes," I whined.

"It's not easy for me either, you know. No electricity. Pumping water from the well. Damp walls and floors. No company that I can really feel comfortable with. I don't see my Dad hardly at all. My brother comes and then gets angry and goes away."

Despite my misery, I smiled to myself in recognition of Kathy's outlook. She didn't generally concern herself with world events or philosophical arguments. Life for Kathy was about the simple practical issues of day-to-day living and the proximity of those she cared about. There was nothing else and who is to say she was wrong?

"Mmm. We have each other and, what's more, we made the bed, so we have to lie on it; is that what you're going to say?"

She giggled. "Not a very soft bed, though, was it, on the platform? Yes, I was going to say that. But more than that. I don't know how to say it. All the bits together are more to me than the bits one at a time. Something like that. We are here together and we have a beautiful daughter, who is healthy. A family. And I love you."

"I love you too. I'm sorry for being such a miserable sod. I suppose I've been bottling it up for some time."

We lay in silence for a while and I began to stroke the firm flatness of her belly.

"We can if you like," she whispered coyly. "It looks like it won't make any odds. Stupid rhythm method!"

I didn't grasp what she was saying for a moment.

"I'm three weeks late. I'm pretty sure I'm expecting again, Freddie."

"Jesus!"

As the dawn broke and in the short time we knew we had before Grace woke up, we made love loudly and energetically. Old Mr. Whimpery's bed jumped and squeaked like a box of chicks. It lurched on its rusty castors against the party wall, thumping so hard that poor Miss Wiseman next door must have thought that the invasion, long anticipated, had finally begun.

THE MOON LIES FAIR
November 1943

I was very surprised to discover that Aunty Vi was a woman of some means because she was always complaining about the cost of everything. But perhaps I shouldn't have been, because I was vaguely aware that Uncle Henry had run a very successful business in Hamlet Court Road for many years and that when he died, he left her "very well provided for" as they used to say in those days. Bernard came to the relationship with Aunty Vi with his own assets and a regular income, so she didn't need to spend her inheritance and managed, more or less, to live on the interest from her investments.

I was her only close relative, apart from Vinny, and in her will, she bequeathed me a quite substantial sum of money and the freehold of the house in Pleasant Road. There were some caveats about the house being held in trust with some of the money until I was twenty-one but I would receive a sum immediately and could draw on the fund, up to a certain limit, each month. Some distant cousins received modest sums each and the considerable remainder was left to Bernard. With an appropriate touch, Aunty Vi left a large, leather-bound set of the classics to Archie Soper. It included all the works of Dickens; he was delighted. Vinny was not entirely forgotten, although Aunty Vi's waspish sense of humour left him merely a sampler that had been done by Ma in her childhood: a faded image of a child in front of a cottage, beneath which were the words, "Bless this House". He never received it, of course.

"Kathy, you know, not for the first time, my life has altered overnight. Throw of a dice. Swing of the pendulum and all that."

Kathy looked up from her mending and took in the room with its bowed ceiling, faded wallpaper, rusty grate and ill-fitting windows. There was a cold draught coming through them as well as under the door; the ragged curtains moved ceaselessly and a cobweb in the corner flexed like a bellows. We were sitting on either side of the fire; every now and then the draught would suck a puff of wood smoke back down the chimney.

"It all looks the same to me," she said, an amused grin on her face.

"We have money and an income. We could put tenants in the house in Pleasant Road and have even more income, don't you see?"

"How much?"

I laughed. "Women of a certain class are not supposed to ask their husbands that kind of question."

"I'm not of a...type or class," she said, hesitantly, for she was not sure of the words, "I'm just me. Kathleen Tanner; Soper Class, perhaps! Is it wrong to ask, then?"

"No," I said. "I've always liked your spirit." I told her approximately what income we would have and how much rent we might expect. I'd done my homework, like a good boy.

"Crumbs! What about Uncle Bernard?"

"I asked him after the reading of the will. He won't be staying there. Doesn't want to any longer than necessary, he says. Apparently he has a place in Genesta Road in Westcliff – I had no idea – and as soon as it's vacant, he's going to live there."

"So when would he move out?"

"He's not sure. His tenants have been there for years so I don't think he wants to push them out but on the other hand, he said he's going to find Pleasant Road, well, unpleasant because of the memories. I reckon he'll give the people until after Christmas; so maybe next year sometime."

"We could live at Pleasant Road, then," Kathy said after a while, putting one mended item aside and looking for others in her basket. She looked up at me, smiling, as if to say, "You see, I'm not stupid; you didn't think of that, did you?"

"Us?"

I threw another lump of coal onto the fire and added a log from the basket. Woodlice, like men under attack, scurried in a futile attempt to avoid the flames.

"Yes. Without the rent, we'd still have enough to live on because it's more than now. I expect you could find some work too. I wouldn't want to live there if Uncle Bernard was still around because, well, you know. It wouldn't be private," she grinned.

"You mean you wouldn't be able to squeal in that engaging way you've developed when the lamps are out?"

"I haven't the faintest idea what you're talking about Freddie Tanner," she said.

"Not much!" I laughed and then after a pause during which we were both turning over the possibilities, I asked, "Well, you're not really happy here, are you?"

"I have to be where you are, Freddie; that's my life and I'm happy with it. If you have to be here, that's fine. But now, you don't have to be. Before, we had no choice. Now, we do. It's like...well, it's a kind of second chance, isn't it?"

"Is it?"

"Yes. You're always saying we're trapped and we should have waited before we...you know. Well, now we're not trapped. You could get the higher exams, couldn't you?"

I was the one everyone thought was clever and she was the one who was supposed to be simple. But, as so often, she was there first. A mind uncluttered by education, prevarications, calculations, judgments, balances and checks can sometimes be razor sharp!

"Do you like the farming life, Freddie?" she asked.

I sighed. "Well, sometimes...but no, not really. I suppose I feel demeaned by it. Sorry, I mean, it makes me feel worthless, somehow."

"You're not. It's what Dad calls honest toil, I think."

I laughed. "He would! But what about you? You'd be happier in the town, wouldn't you?'

"Yes. All of us together, of course."

"Of course. It goes without saying."

"The baby's due in May, I think, so could we move there before that?" she asked quietly.

"Ah! Nest building, is it?"

"Yes, I think it is. That's how expectant mothers feel, you see."

"There is another thing we have to think about, Kathy. If we move there and I give up the job on the farm, then when my call-up papers come, probably in April, I won't any longer be in a reserved occupation, so..."

So, I could stop hiding in a remote village; I could stop avoiding arguments with the likes of Benny or just alluding to my principles and opinions in discussions with Bernard. I could apply to go before a Military Tribunal when the papers came and ask to be exempted from service on the grounds of conscientious objection. I could stand up and say what I felt out loud. Unexpectedly, it was suddenly clear what I should do.

Kathy looked up from her sewing because I'd stopped talking without finishing my sentence. She smiled at me encouragingly. I don't know to this day whether she knew what I was thinking, but it wouldn't have surprised me.

WAR'S ANNALS WILL CLOUD INTO NIGHT
May 1944

The room seems far too large for the long table and chairs placed awkwardly within it. They have not been arranged, but simply placed randomly. Now the individual items seem to be searching the chamber for others of their kind to which they might somehow cleave: bookcases, clock cases, sideboards, chiffoniers or escritoires perhaps, but there are none. The mahogany table with its pie-crust edge and the ladder-backed chairs are waiting, alone, in front of two, long windows of a kind frequently found in buildings of this period and this mock-Gothic style. Afternoon sunlight beams as best it can through the blast-taped and grimy panes, uncleaned since 1939. Outside, the London traffic, such as it is now, grumbles and honks. Occasionally, a fire engine's bell is heard or the shouts of vendors in the market opposite.

Motes of dust float aimlessly in the shafts of sunlight. There is a stale smell of other, older dust that has already, over many years, settled and solidified in distant, uncharted corners or on the tops of the fluted columns that frame the doorway, or on the architraves high over the windows. There is also a smell of polish, for the table and the chairs have been given a cursory shine commensurate with the importance of the drama to be acted out in this gilded hall.

A clock ticks sonorously. Then there are voices outside in the corridor. The space echoes to the footsteps of four men who enter through heavy, panelled, oak doors, their shoes rapping crisply on the marbled floor. One of the men, obviously the one in charge, stops in front of the furniture, looking a little bemused. He grunts irritably, places his folders on one of the chairs and begins to shunt the table this way and that, hoping to find a position that seems to give the thing some purpose and authority in the cavernous space. After a while, he aligns it with the windows. One of the other men puts four chairs behind the table and a fifth chair, on its own, unmoored to anything at all, facing the table some ten feet away. The stage is set.

Pens are unscrewed; papers are shuffled; chairs scraped to and fro.

"Orderly!" says the man in charge to a weasel-faced individual loitering by the doors. "Send in Mr. Frederick Tanner, if you will?"

"Yessir," says the fellow, turning sharply to withdraw.

"We'll have to crack on this afternoon, gentlemen. Got ten to see, I'm afraid."

The members of the tribunal grunt, breathe heavily through their noses, smooth their double chins and flick through their papers.

The orderly's heels sound staccato clicks on the tiles of the labyrinthine corridors as he walks to fetch Freddie from the waiting room.

"Curtain up, Mr. Tanner, you're on. Fixed your make-up, I hope?" he says. "They're all fired up and waiting. Now, when you get in there, you'll see a chair on its own in front of the desk. Bunch of toffs behind the desk. Stand to one side of the chair until you're told to sit. Get it?"

"Yes," says Freddie.

"Come on then. Mind you, they might ask you to pick it up and spin it round, balancing one leg on the end of your finger, like a firkin' circus act," he whispers confidentially as they clatter back towards the chamber. "Nothin' would bleedin' surprise me. It's all a farce! Fred Karno's Army's got nothing on this lot!"

Freddie tries to grin, but his nervousness makes his mouth appear to have a tic. The orderly hums to himself and then begins to sing, very quietly:

We are Fred Karno's army,
Fred Karno's infantry;
We cannot fight, we cannot shoot,
So what damn good are we?
But when we get to Berlin
Old Hitler he will say
Hoch, hoch, mein Gott
Vot a bloody fine lot
Fred Karno's infantry.

He swings open the door and gives Freddie a sharp prod in the small of his back to propel him into the room.

"Mr. Tanner, Sah!"

"Thank you, Orderly."

The man in charge verifies Freddie's name, age and address and then asks him to be seated. Freddie sits but is unsure whether to lean back in the chair, a posture that seems too casual, or to sit forward which probably makes it look as if he's about to make a dash for the nearest lavatory. Certainly, his bowels are squeezing and gurgling like the gas geyser in the bathroom at Pleasant Road.

He has spent a long time thinking about this day; a long time preparing his case and many hours talking it through with Bernard, who has been surprisingly helpful and supportive. They have written out things he might say and then honed the phrases; they have discussed how he might answer certain predictable questions. He wants to get it right.

"I wouldn't mind betting there's millions who object to this war, Freddie," Bernard says, "but precious bleedin' few – 'scuse me once more – will stand up and say so. Good for you for being prepared to do that, right? All power to your elbow, my son and if I can be of 'elp, on the quiet like, then I will."

The man in charge gives a peremptory cough.

"Good afternoon, Mr. Tanner. I will introduce the members of the tribunal. My name is Gregory Marchbanks. I am a County Court Judge but, of course, this is not a trial so you should call me Mr. Marchbanks or Sir. Either will suffice. On my left is Mr. David Henderson, a trade union branch secretary, in accordance with the requirements laid down for membership of the tribunal. On my right is, firstly, Mr. Arnold Mackenzie who is a member of the local Chamber of Commerce and on my far right, Dr. William Fry, a medical practitioner and lay preacher. Also in accordance with the legislation under which we operate, you will note that there is no representative here from the Armed Services. I repeat, this is not a trial and the intention is not to intimidate you, but to hear your views. Is that clear?"

"Yes, Sir," says Freddie, keeping his head up as Bernard has suggested during their rehearsals.

"Very well," says Marchbanks, pulling at an ear-lobe. "Please be advised that we can allocate no more than about fifteen minutes to your case. Be as expansive and persuasive as you can, Mr. Tanner. We had a young man before us yesterday who was able to say only that he, "didn't believe in it". He had nothing else to say and, candidly, that won't do. You understand?"

"Yes, Sir, I understand."

"Good. Well, then, please begin by telling us what your objection is to taking up arms in defence of your country," says Marchbanks.

"Before war was even declared, Sir, one of our Ministers wrote that, "War cannot be ended by war or any situation improved by it". I believe that to be a succinct summary of my own views, but I might also have added that in the pointless pursuit of war, millions die who had a right to life, rather than to be cannon fodder. Millions died in the Great War and here we are again. What was the point of all that slaughter, Sir? *What passing-bells for these who die as cattle? Only the monstrous anger of the guns.* We have to do something to stop the cycle of human destruction, Sir. My refusal to take up arms will make no difference on its own, but if hundreds and hundreds of thousands of English, Germans, Japanese, Russians – ordinary people who just want to live peacefully; people who have no particular grievance against their neighbours unless they are incited by war-mongering politicians or meddlesome priests – if these ordinary people all do the same, then it might." Freddie hopes that an obviously intelligent opening will stop the tribunal from falling asleep in the sunshine warming their backs through the high windows.

"What do you think was meant by "War cannot be ended by war", Mr. Tanner?" asks Mackenzie. "It caused that Minister a good deal of trouble, not least with the Church."

"I know, Sir. But just because the Establishment, including the Church, slaps you down, you should not feel that it's prohibited for you to express your views. Our country is a democracy."

"Yes, Mr. Tanner, but let's not stray too far from the point here, shall we? I'd like to know what you think the politician meant by those words. It may help to expand on your own view, which is what we're interested in, you see, not other people's views," says Mackenzie again.

"I don't think we are straying from the point, Mr. Mackenzie, if we consider a man's democratic right to object to what his political masters are doing, if I may say so. I think that the phrase in question means that conflict begets conflict, Sir. Someone beaten or hurt, whether it's an individual or a nation, will seek revenge. They blitz London; we blitz Berlin. The end result of that is that more little, innocent children are killed and greater anger and resentment is fuelled. Wars usually lead to entrenched positions: culturally; spiritually; geographically. More fighting and death. Legitimised murder. It's wrong. Sir."

"If one country invades and subdues by force another country, then we should sit back and do nothing in case people are killed? Allow democracy, to which you refer, to be swallowed whole?" asks Fry.

Freddie looks Fry directly in the eye. "Sir, respectfully and if I may, I suggest that you are making the mistake of assuming that a conscientious objector – a pacifist, perhaps – is blind and inert. Or that he has no objection to something like Nazism. I object to Nazism most vociferously because at its core it is evil and aggressive, assuming that one kind of human is superior to another. It seeks to destroy completely those people it vilifies. It is based on hatred, not love. I don't accept Nazism, but I would prefer that we try to deal with it in ways other than by descending to its own murderous levels. The Bible suggests a different course. Killing is not the answer and I object on that basic principle. I do not wish to be involved in killing another human being."

Marchbanks looks at Freddie with surprise. Clearly, this is a very thoughtful and intelligent young man.

"Well now, the Bible also says "eye for eye; tooth for tooth", does it not?" says Fry.

"Yes, Sir. Exodus, Chapter 20, I think," responds Freddie, "but the New Testament, in which we read about Christ's ministry, teaches peace, respect and love. But war doesn't enable us to get very far with any of that, Sir. At school, I learned to love Thomas Hardy's poetry, Sir, and in his little poem called Christmas, 1924, he says,

> Peace upon Earth!' was said. We sing it,
> And pay a million priests to bring it.
> After two thousand years of mass
> We've got as far as poison-gas.

That's my view too, Sir. It seems to me obvious that peace on earth cannot be achieved through military aggression."

"How is it achieved, then?" asks Marchbanks.

"I don't know, Sir. I am not a politician, a diplomat or a strategist. But there has to be another way. Where people from all countries sit around a table and discuss things and try to resolve their differences before they begin murdering," says Freddie firmly.

"What do you say to those who have accused you, or shall accuse you of cowardice and a lack of patriotism, son?" asks Henderson the trade union man, whom Freddie had decided was going to remain silent.

"Patriotism and jingoism are different things, Sir. I'm as patriotic as the next man but I do not agree with blind obedience to the cause as the jingoists would have it. I listen to my principles, Sir. And cowardice? Well, I've read many things about men committing suicide in the trenches during the Great War. Perhaps this was because these young men – boys, really – saw, smelled and heard terrible, inhuman things they didn't tell them about before they left home in their misguided patriotism. Fear and absolute terror do strange things. Some might call it cowardice, Sir, but I wouldn't. You hear people say that soldiers are brave and prepared to die for their country. But maybe it's resignation and a grim acceptance of the inevitable. They're trapped on the battlefield by the enemy and by orders, expectations and convention. They have no choice and it makes the rest of us feel better to call it brave."

Marchbanks fidgets a little in his chair and spins the top of his fountain pen against his lips.

"Isn't that a little cynical, Mr. Tanner? The survivors of the last war might say that their colleagues gave bravely of their lives that we might be free. What do you say to that?" he says.

"Well, as I say, Sir, my opinion is that most didn't give their lives willingly, they had their lives wrenched away from them. Pawns in a game they don't really understand. *As flies to wanton boys, are we to the Gods; They kill us for their sport*. No choice, Sir; no control, no destiny; just hopeless cannon fodder to appease a military diagram somewhere. And millions dead is a high price to pay for just over twenty years' freedom, surely? Less than that in Spain! The current madness, on that basis, will need to be repeated in 1965 or thereabouts. There has to be an alternative way of dealing with differences; I want no part in a process that regards human life so cheaply."

The only sound in the room for a while is the imperturbable ticking of the clock. The men behind the desk look at Freddie, wondering whether his is the face of a new generation.

"If you are exempted – if, I say – you might be required to do other work regarded as supportive of the war effort or be given non-combatant duties in the army, for instance. What's your view on that? Are you a purist conscientious objector?" asks Fry.

"I suppose I'd like to be able to say that I was, but I think Bertrand Russell may be right to say we have to take a pragmatic view, Sir. I'm not prepared to pull the trigger because I think it's morally indefensible, but some other support role would be alright."

"Such as?"

"Well, Sir, my uncle works on Southend Pier, Sir; HMS Leigh, that is; on the lifeboat, and I hear that the RAF has a unit there responsible for kite balloons. He says they need a civilian to assist with the helium bottles and with some administrative duties. I did well in the Sciences."

Freddie thinks it worth making a bid, although he's been warned that tribunals do not generally want to be seen to be too compliant; in fact, they prefer to recommend allocations away from the applicant's home on the basis that everyone should suffer some sacrifice in war.

"I'll note your comments, Mr. Tanner. I think we have now heard all we need to. But before you go, let me make an observation. Clearly, you are a very articulate and intelligent young man. What were you doing as a farm worker? Shouldn't you be studying?"

"It's a long story, Sir!"

Marchbanks glances back down at Freddie's papers and then smiles. "I think I understand. Take my advice: when the war is over, complete your education. You should study the law, young man. Or politics. Do something with your life."

"Thank you, Sir. As you see, I have a family to support. But it has been suggested before. Thank you for the encouragement, Sir."

"Very well. Now please wait outside for a few minutes, just in case we need you again."

"Yes, Sir. Thank you," says Freddie.

After he has left the chamber, the tribunal's members put down their pens and lean back in their chairs.

"Good Lord!" says one. "That's a brain and no mistake!"

"Mmm. Maybe too clever with his bits of poetry and so on. Feels like he's just read me his essay on the poets of the Great War. Does he believe what he's saying or is it just an academic exercise? Prepared phrases; a bit too off-pat, wasn't it?" says Mackenzie. "I see he wears glasses and the report says he's very short-sighted. In which case, he'd probably be exempt on medical grounds anyway. So why is he here?"

"You think he's just exercising an argument to make himself feel better?" asks Marchbanks.

"In short, yes. It was a rehearsed performance."

"I don't think so," says Henderson. "He believes it alright. He's read his subject; prepared his case, but doesn't that make him seem all the more earnest about it? You won't hear many who can put it like that."

"Agreed," says Fry.

§

A few days later, a brown envelope arrives in the post at Pleasant Road. Kathy, on her way back from a panicky visit to the bathroom in the last week of her pregnancy, picks it up with difficulty from the doormat and takes it up the stairs to the front bedroom where Freddie is bouncing Grace up and down on the mattress.

"I think this must be what you're waiting for," says Kathy, puffing at the exertion of the climb and holding onto her abdomen.

Grace tries to snatch the letter from her hand as she reaches across the bed. Freddie opens it with nervous fingers, reads briefly and then gives a little nod of satisfaction.

"Good! They believed me, Kathy!"

"Grace play bounce! Grace play bounce with Daddy!" shouts the little girl.

"That's very good news, Freddie. And I think the baby agrees; I've started, Freddie, my waters have just broken! You'd better send for the midwife! Ow! Quick, Freddie!"

"Oh, God! Why didn't you say straight away?"

"I thought you'd want to look at that first. Please hurry, Freddie!"

Typical Kathy, thinks Freddie as he rushes downstairs to alert the Horsfalls next door who have agreed to run for the midwife when the time comes.

SKIES SPOUT FIRE AND BLOOD AND NATIONS QUAKE
1945

Kathy had our second daughter without any complications – in fact, the midwife made it to Pleasant Road just in the nick of time – a few minutes after midday on the 20th May, 1944. Because she was an early summer baby, associated always in our minds with fresh sunshine, and because she was born in the house that Aunty Vi left us, we called her Violet May.

Grace took one look at her new sister and said, "Ooh! Yukky baby!" and indeed, it is true to say that the little mite had not inherited her mother's beauty or perhaps even her father's adequate visage. She looked like a miniature of Benny. We both laughed at Grace's perspicacity, for even doting Kathy had to agree that the child was not the pretty little thing that Grace was.

"I'm sure she'll change," I said. "All babies do."

"Well, as long as she doesn't swear like Benny, I don't mind," cooed Kathy, holding the baby to her magnificently swollen breast.

"Or chase after monks, married men, ginger-tops and schoolgirls in their gym-slips," I replied.

Kathy looked at me as if I was crazy, but I didn't bother to explain.

So, I spent the rest of the war on HMS Leigh, although most of us living locally still referred to it as the pier, but quietly, because the military personnel didn't like to think that they were stationed in a former amusement palace and jetty rather than on a real ship. Gloss is everything these days – and then too.

Cheekily, I had dropped a hint to the Military Tribunal that I would be prepared to work on the kite balloons. I did so because I thought that the chairman, Mr. Marchbanks, was giving me a more than sympathetic hearing and I wondered whether he might be able to pull some strings. Whether he did or not I shall never know, but I was granted exemption from combatant duties on the condition that I carried out acceptable civilian work. I was stationed on the pier from late May 1944.

But it wasn't the kite balloons I found myself inflating with helium. Initially, I was allocated to work with the pier railway staff, more-or-less as a porter. So, in a manner of speaking, I was inflating egos, because men working in a lowly role will always need to be told how indispensable they are. Not that such a task was my official responsibility, for, of course, I had none, but because I was able to string together more than two sentences, for some reason it fell to me to tell them how the war could not manage without them. What absolute tripe!

The trains were in use pretty well twenty four hours a day: ferrying service personnel; the sick, wounded and survivors who were brought off ships at the pier head; and all manner of other things such as the helium bottles for the balloons, ammunition, food and other stores.

It was hard work, especially at night when things, or people, had to be lugged about during the blackout but, of course, there was a terrific camaraderie on the pier as there is under any difficult circumstance and where people are operating in a specific location. I wouldn't say that it was enjoyable but after the lonely life in the fields on the Paglesham marshes, it sometimes seemed like a party, although there were a number of incidents that made me realise just how close the war was. We heard the noises of war all the time at Paglesham, but Paglesham wasn't a military target; HMS Leigh was.

In June 1944 about 130,000 Allied troops landed on Normandy's beaches in an operation called Overlord. It took the Germans by surprise and was one of the turning points of the war. The number killed and wounded was far fewer than had been predicted, but some of those who were stretcher cases found themselves bound for HMS Leigh. I was responsible at that time to a fellow called Stan Purkiss and he alerted us, one evening, that there was a panic on. He stuck his head into the little hut that we porters had managed to commandeer at the far end of the shore station.

"Oi! Look lively, you buggers!" he yelled in his odd, squeaky voice. "There's a ship bringing stretcher cases from France in half an hour. Hands off cocks, on socks!"

Stan was not known for his subtlety. He had a collection of vulgar phrases and words that peppered almost everything he said. As men of a certain type will, with younger men or boys, he took me under his wing when I arrived, obviously deciding that I was a delicate and sheltered flower who needed some breaking in. One lunch-time, when it was quiet and it looked as though we might be able to slip away for an hour or so, he said he was taking me to The Minerva for a pint. Or six.

It was an old pub, almost next to The Kursaal, only a few hundred yards from Pleasant Road. It had a bad reputation, being frequented by criminals and prostitutes. Or so I'd heard. He barged in through the main door as if he owned the place and shouted his order for two beers before we got anywhere near the bar. As we walked across the room, he bent down to where a rather over-weight woman with blonde hair, like a hayrick, was sitting at a table. He squeezed her buttocks; she had a generous backside and her cheeks were hanging over the seat of the chair.

"Oi! What the..?" she began. "Oh, it's you, Corky. I might of bloody known!"

"Fancy a quick one, Doreen?" he said. "I got fifteen minutes!" His voice rose to a little squeal and his eyebrows danced suggestively.

"It's never anything else with you, is it, dear? Fifteen minutes? You must be bloody joking! Fifteen seconds, more like," she replied with heavy sarcasm. Stan laughed like the proverbial emptying drain and attempted to slip his hand into The Hayrick's ample cleavage. She swatted him away as if he was a wasp. Stan chuckled once more and we took our beer to a corner table.

"Corky?" I said. "I thought you were called Stan?"

"I am, but in here I'm Corky."

"Does one dare ask why?" I said.

"Oh, I say, Squire Tanner, one does! It's because in here I'm always poppin' me cork."

I looked at him quizzically over the top of my beer glass.

"Bloody Norah! You know, havin' it away? Exploding corks; jets of white bubbles? I've bin with 'er loads of times," he said, cocking his finger towards The Hayrick. "They got a couple a rooms. She's easy but she smells something bloody awful of whelks. But then, it's Southend, so maybe I shouldn't expect the roses of friggin' Picardie!"

I almost choked on my mouthful of bitter. "Sounds lovely," I said. "Anyway, isn't she, well, a bit flabby and...um, ugly?"

"Bloody choosy, eh? Well, you're young; you can afford to be. At my age, yer don't worry too much about the mantelpiece when yer stoking the fire. You're just grateful yer poker's still man enough for the job and there's a fire you can stoke." He took a swig of his beer. "Well, alright, I see yer point. I suppose I could always put a bag over 'er head."

"Yes. I must confess, Stan, I would rather make love to an attractive woman and one I can respect," I said.

Stan laughed again. "Holy Moses! That's Officer stuff, son. And you mark my words, when this lot's over, there'll be lovely women – lovely, not just the trollops – desperate to do it. Bloody desperate; and keen as mustard. And the officers can go and toss themselves off. And money, my boy, for those of us sharp enough to grapple it aboard. Things is gonna change, I can see it. All that you-have-to-meet-mother-first stuff will be out of the window."

"How do you work that out, then?" I asked.

"Stands ter reason. Look what happened after the last lot – Grandma's Victorian attitudes chucked out the window; the toffs not 'avin such an easy time of it. Rise o' the Labour movement. Same kind of thing'll happen again, right? Social revolution, son. All the ropes holdin' down the ordinary man will be cut through. Women'll start on about how they want a bit o' the action an' all, if you ask me," he said.

"Action?"

"Where've you been, son? You know – what we were on about; stoking the fire. Except in the future, the women'll be grabbin' the poker, so to speak!" He guffawed at his own wit.

"*Oh, Brave New World, that has such people in't,*" I muttered.

"Do what, Professor?"

And so it went on for another fifty minutes until, three more pints down the line, Stan decided it was time to go.

"I'll just nip into the bog and water me cocks," he grunted, levering himself unsteadily into a standing position. He belched repeatedly, like an ack-ack gun in slow-motion. "An' then we'll go and win the war. On HMS Leigh. Nah, sod it, on the pier...oh, Gawd! I think I've had one too many."

"Cocks? Plural?" I grinned. "Sounds like a bunch of bananas. How many have you got?"

"I dunno, son," he said. "I haven't seen them for years; under me gut there somewhere. I have to feel around for them like eels in a bucket. All I know is, they spray like a watering can."

I continued laughing all the while he was off in the gents.

But if he seemed like a sozzled reprobate after a few pints in The Minerva, he was a different man when there was an emergency.

"C'mon, grab those stretchers! Double quick, all of you!"

We did as we were instructed and made our way, on the rumbling train, to the Pier Head and thus to the Prince George extension where the troop ship was just tying up.

It would have been reasonably easy to take off the nine stretcher cases but for the fact that Jerry decided this was just the time for a little target practice. As we were carrying the injured down the gangplanks, a lone Messerschmitt dropped out of the low cloud base somewhere over the Nore to the east. There was no warning; no siren; no period of grace. One moment there was nothing and the next, the killing machine fell upon us, as if under the force of gravity, guns spurting ragged streaks of fire from its wings.

At times like that, especially in war, you are forced to recognise that we all hang onto life's high window-sill by our finger-tips. The slightest thing can dislodge us and send us hurtling into the endless abyss. Once you're falling, there's no going back for another try, like kids on a climbing frame.

There was no time to do anything. I was on one end of a stretcher with Mark Smith on the other. We'd just got to the bottom of the gangplank when the aircraft fell upon us. Stan was halfway down with the second stretcher, Patrick Baxter on the other end. As the noise of the aircraft's guns suddenly assaulted our ears, Pat looked off to his right. It was the last voluntary movement he made in this life, for as he did so, the trace of bullets ripped along the planks under our feet and then up and across his abdomen and chest. It would have been less messy if he'd thrown himself on a chain saw. The force of the impact spun him round and off the gangplank so that he fell onto the pier's deck below. His hands were locked on the stretcher, of course and that followed him, its occupant screaming horribly. Stan was pulled off-balance but managed to stay where he was.

Pat lay twitching very slightly, his body oddly arranged like discarded gunny sacks. As the bullets had struck him, blood and pieces of flesh had jetted some distance into the air; now that his heart had stopped, blood leaked stickily from him, dripping through the deck's planks and into the slippery, grey troughs of the Thames below. One moment he was a healthy, family man with a future, helping someone senselessly maimed in Normandy; the next moment he was ribboned meat, pointlessly slaughtered while "doing his bit".

The fighter had gone. The whole episode had probably occupied less than thirty seconds. The after-shock, for the Baxter family, would probably last for more than thirty years.

"Come on, you lot! Don't just stand there gawping! Get the rest of 'em into the trains before that bastard comes back!" said Stan as he jumped down onto the deck to check on Pat and the poor fellow who had been on the stretcher.

§

A few weeks after that, a supply ship fouled a mine somewhere off the Ness. Luftkorps aircraft carrying two acoustic mines apiece had been across the Thames and over our heads many times. Many of the mines fell on land, but about a quarter of them fell inside a protective boom of forts sunk in the Estuary to deter invaders.

Many of these mines had time-delay devices. Mine-sweeping exercises did not recover all those dropped. They lay unsuspected for days until their mechanisms were triggered by the vibrations from a passing ship's propellers.

This ship had called at HMS Leigh to take on board its kite balloons and then cast off to continue its voyage. About twenty minutes later, there was an explosion over on the Foulness Sands that shook the pier's old cast-iron piles as if they were mere driftwood. As it happened, I was enjoying a quick cup of tea with Bernard in the Solarium tea-room; he was about to go on duty with the lifeboat. The whole place seemed to flap like a tin roof in the wind. Some pictures fell from the walls and dozens of glass tumblers were thrown from their shelves.

"Bloody hell!" he shouted, practically throwing his cup and saucer to one side. Tea dribbled down the front of the counter. "Sounds like something nasty, Freddie; you blokes 'ad better get ready for lotsa wounded!"

With that, he ran out of the door.

According to Bernard's account, the port bow of the ship had been blown open and, of course, she began to take on water rapidly. Many of her crew had been killed or fatally wounded in the detonation of the mine; others met their fate as the ship's boilers exploded and her fuel ignited. The sea around the ship was a lake of burning oil, debris and screaming men. Whatever drills had been instilled in the crew about launching lifeboats were either forgotten in the holocaust or impossible to carry out because of the ship's rapid list.

Out of a crew of sixty nine, only two survived. Twenty three of the crew were never accounted for; it was thought they were mostly men working in the forward part of the ship at the time and it was assumed that they were blown asunder by the explosions, their unidentifiable remnants dropping to the sands below or drifting aimlessly with the currents.

Forty four corpses or parts of corpses were brought to shore via HMS Leigh over a period of some two days. We had to requisition more body bags. The soft, dead weight of each of them passed through the hands of those of us working the stretcher train at that time.

The awful lumpiness of those bags, their smell, the sounds they made as we heaved them as respectfully as we could into the trains, and the drawn, strained faces of those I worked with through those forty-eight hours haunt me still. Sometimes I wake in the night, drenched in sweat, certain that I am covered in blood and that the body bags are piling up around me faster than they can be loaded onto the trains.

§

Other images from that period were no less sickening. In the early part of the year, the Russians liberated Auschwitz, followed by other death camps. The awful truth about the manner in which Jews had been exterminated like rats – actually, worse than the treatment meted out to rats – confirmed the rumours of earlier years. Kathy listened to the news with incomprehension.

"But why would people do that to other human beings?" she asked.

"Will you let me read you something?" I said. I went to my bookcases – for over the years, I had been buying books whenever I could afford them – and withdrew a volume.

"I know you like to do that," she replied. "I don't always understand, though."

"This is from Joseph Conrad's novel The Heart of Darkness," I said. "Written in 1902, long before the Great War, let alone this one."

"Oh."

"*It was just robbery with violence, aggravated murder on a great scale and men going at it blind – as is very proper for those who tackle a darkness. The conquest of the earth, which mostly means taking it away from those who have a different complexion or slightly flatter noses than ourselves, is not a pretty thing when you look into it too much.*"

"I don't really know all those words, but I kind of understand what it says," said Kathy, chewing her lip. "People hurt other people because they don't look the same?"

"In essence, yes. Or because they believe in a different God."

"But God is about love, isn't He?" she responded.

"You might have thought so, if you weren't caught up in History," I said.

A few weeks later, on April 30th, we were told that Hitler had killed himself in his Berlin bunker. Kathy said, "Good riddance to bad rubbish," which, I suppose, put it as well as anything, although I read to her again to show that Conrad had something to say about these things too.

"*The wilderness had found him out early, and had taken on him a terrible vengeance for the fantastic invasion. I think it whispered to him things about himself which he did not know...it echoed loudly within him because he was hollow at the core.*"

"What does that mean, that he was hollow at the core?" she asked.

"Well, inhuman, I suppose. No feelings, no conscience, no morality. Nothing. Just hate personified. It's not about Hitler, of course, it's about Conrad's character in his story, but it fits the bill."

And then, God forgive us all our multitudinous trespasses and heresies, the Allies dropped atomic bombs on Hiroshima and Nagasaki in August, immolating those peoples into surrender a few days later.

I read just recently that fifty million people died during the war, six million of whom were Jews. I remembered that afternoon in London at the Military Tribunal, years ago now, where I'd been asked about those who gave bravely of their lives that we might be free. Fifty million "gave bravely"? I don't think so. They were degraded and gassed like vermin; they were drowned in the icy waters of Scapa Flow, the cold snatching the life from their lungs; they were blown to wet atoms in the terraces of Bow while they were doing the week's washing; they were shot to sliced meat in the jungles of the Pacific and they were butchered and thrown into the air by a fighter plane's staccato guns on the end of Southend Pier.

Gave bravely of their lives? Utter tripe. Bravery didn't come into it for most of those millions. They were not consulted; they had no choice.

> Was it for this the clay grew tall?
> – O what made fatuous sunbeams toil
> To break earth's sleep at all?

NOR LOVE
1945

About a week after the events on the pier described above, I awoke suddenly in the early hours of the morning, excited and troubled by a strange dream.

I have always experienced peculiar dreams (more peculiar than dreams are anyway, I mean) and especially after my parents' deaths. At that time I would dream about them fighting; I would dream about Ma toppling from buildings and cliffs; I would dream about Pa violating young girls.

Often I would dream about that last morning: in these dreams I am not in so much of a hurry to leave the house; I have a sense of foreboding and I want to tell Ma but, of course, I do not have the words or, indeed, a reason to explain. I just look at her but she is impatient for us to be gone and shoos us out of the house so that, no matter what I do each time I dream this dream, I cannot alter it so that I can say goodbye to her properly.

These dreams and many others like them came with regularity, perhaps once a week when I was at school, but they increased in frequency and severity, if that's the right word, during the war years and especially after. The headaches that preceded or followed them increased too. And, furthermore, I was aware that I was also day-dreaming — literally. Some people call that having hallucinations, but I don't like the word.

If dreams are rightly defined as indicators of subconscious conflicts and their resolutions, one might have thought that with the end of the war and with my continued contentment with Kathy and the girls, they would have declined. But not so.

In the particular dream to which I refer, I was travelling at great speed in a train. I do not know where I was going or where I had come from. That in itself was disturbing —no known origin or destination. The compartment was not at all like those on either of the two Southend lines; that is, essentially a box with two hinged doors and padded bench seats; one facing, and one with its back to the engine.

In my dream, the compartment was larger, like a room. On one side there was a bed; opposite that a small table and chairs and I think, a couple of easy chairs. There was a smaller ante-room, connected to the main room by a door.

The train was travelling at some considerable speed; our compartment was swaying with the movement, sometimes quite violently. The sound of the wheels rhythmically striking the joints in the rails was considerable. I say "our" compartment, because I was not alone. Vinny was there too, sitting on one of the chairs, his legs crossed jauntily. He looked at me with a knowing smile. He was wearing a Navy uniform and he was nursing a glass of whisky.

"Long time, no see, you see?" he said.

"At sea," I responded in the daft way that dream-conversations proceed.

"Oh, yes," he said, lifting the tumbler to his lips. "I've been with salty mermaids in the Mediterranean. And girls in Sicily tasting of black olives, see?"

Written down now, that seems plainly absurd, but within the dream, it was an unremarkable comment. Not that there was any time to respond, for we were interrupted. There was a scrabbling noise on the other side of the partition that separated our compartment from, I assumed, the next compartment or perhaps a corridor or some such. In real trains the partition is solid from floor to ceiling but in this case, it was not. It was solid up to a height of about six feet and then above that there was an open space with just a few stud timbers visible. Into this space appeared the hands, face and shoulders of a pretty young woman. Clearly, she was pulling herself up the other side of the partition with some difficulty. I had the feeling that she was trying to escape some awful persecution. Once she had her forearms and some weight on the top of the structure, she paused. She shook her head as if to be rid of annoying insects. The motion released coiled tresses of lustrous dark hair that fell onto our side of the wall.

It was difficult at that stage to be sure of her age because most of her body was out of sight and her face — or, rather, the upper part of her face — was covered. She was wearing one of those brightly-coloured masks that cover the eyes and nose; the sort favoured by the aristocracy when they attend a masked ball. Nevertheless, then and later, I estimated her to be in her late teens or, perhaps, twenty years of age.

"Help me!" she said. "I want you to...help me!"

She was looking at and speaking to me, not Vinny, there was no question. I lifted my arms towards her and she seemed to slither effortlessly over the partition into my grasp. As we stood thus together, she put her mouth to mine and very gently bit on my lower lip.

Vinny stood up, put down his whisky glass and disappeared somewhere behind me into a third room that until that moment I had not noticed before. I was aware that he did so in order to afford us privacy, for it seemed he knew what was to follow.

The girl was slender and had extraordinarily soft and silky skin. She gave off an intoxicating odour of jasmine and recently-washed hair.

"Come on, now," she muttered. We pulled one another down onto the bed. In dreams, practicalities are conveniently made to vanish: we had no clothing. I ran my hands up her abdomen to her ribs.

"Come on!" she whispered seductively.

It is extraordinary how in dreams sometimes, one can seem to experience all the sensations of wakefulness. So, I could taste this girl's mouth as if it was real; I could smell the freshness of her hair. Perhaps the dream had been prompted by Stan's frequent allusions to stoking fires and not looking at mantelpieces; I don't know. But we were not"making love". That would be a ridiculous euphemism. This was not "love" – this was unabashed, fevered copulation.

As we writhed and wriggled, I was aware of Vinny's hovering presence somewhere behind me. And then at other moments it seemed to be Pa. Whoever it was, I turned and glared at him over my shoulder and he shuffled off into the ante-room.

The girl was nothing if not enthusiastic. Her energy was matched by the rhythmic lurching of the train. It was quite a fairground ride, with something of the urgency, speed and swooping lack of control typified by roller coasters. Except that, although we had been locked together for some time, I could not finish. My head began to pulse.

Vinny was now standing to one side, his arms folded across his chest, a sneer flickering across his lips.

"Come on, you useless sod, just get on with it!" he said.

"Oh! Come on, come on!" she wailed repeatedly.

But I could not, so the ride seemed destined to continue indefinitely or until I fell to one side, reduced to a shuddering husk by the girl's voracious appetite and my own ultimate failure.

I awoke, almost trembling. My frustration and my lust for the girl in the dream had not abated as I returned to consciousness, or a kind of consciousness. It was still dark and I reached across the bed for Kathy. As my hand touched her back, she stirred; I pulled her towards me and lifted myself onto her, without much sensitivity or finesse.

She murmured something and put an arm round my neck. But my response, I'm ashamed to say, was not as tender because I used her with no concern for her feelings, either physical or emotional. I suppose at that moment she was not Kathy: I closed my eyes and saw once more the dream-girl, the glinting mask making her face seem like a statue's; her hair wriggling under me like a basket of snakes as we thrashed on the train carriage's bed. She removed the mask and turned towards the light. Her face was one I had seen many times in a photograph that used to sit on the mantelpiece in Bow. It was a photograph taken of Ma when she was a girl – or at least that's how it seemed in that perplexing dream. Later, I decided it was not Ma at all; that was my mind playing cruel jokes.

I opened my eyes. Kathy was looking at me with a pained expression. I pulled away from her, avoiding her gaze.

"Freddie? Whatever...?"

The absolute horror of what I had experienced rendered me speechless. I was shaking like a man with palsy.

"I do love you," she said, "you know that, but that wasn't nice at all, Freddie. You hurt me because you used me. You were like a dog in the road. I don't want you to do that again. Ever. Do you understand?"

Her remark about dogs made me remember the things we were accused of in the Old Man's office in Belper, that time during the war when Kathy was obliged to reveal her pregnancy. She threw back the blankets angrily and got out of the bed. I heard her go downstairs to the bathroom and then, some while later, I heard her feet coming back up the stairs. She went to the back bedroom and wriggled into bed with Grace.

I lay in the dark, disgusted at my violent, sickening behaviour. I knew that most of it wasn't real, but the fact that my mind could have created it and made it happen meant that it was real, in a way. We can sit in a theatre and be appalled, cry, feel sick and have to run from the place even though we know that we watch actors in a play. In this case, I was still trying to separate reality from sick fantasy.

It seemed to me, as the colourless, grey dawn leached across the sky, that I had behaved no better than my father. In fact because in the dream, the masked girl had almost become Ma, it suggested that I was my father. Or worse than that. The thought that I could be capable of his kind of vicious, animal promiscuity – indeed, that I might have inherited the trait; become the trait, so to speak – was a notion that I was unable to dispel. And the realisation that my half-awake mind, if that's what I should call it, had encouraged me to subject Kathy to such physical debasement, a process that I had enjoyed and found satisfying, was the worst horror of all.

PIECES OF EIGHT
June 1945

The pier was decommissioned almost as soon as the war in Europe was over. It was re-opened to the public on the 17th May 1945. People were still being shot to blazes in the Pacific and the Japanese still had several weeks more to learn what inhuman horror President Truman had in mind to drop upon them. But here in Southend, the trippers were back, linking arms as they strolled down the pier, laughing in the early Summer sunshine.

"Where are you going to, Daddy?" asked Grace on the Saturday evening of that weekend, clutching at my leg as I began pulling on my jacket.

"Daddy's just going to say hello to Great Uncle Bernard and Stan," I said.

"Ah, really?" asked Kathy. "And that will involve beer at The Minerva, will it?"

"I expect so. But it's supposed to be business; that's what Stan said, anyway."

"Business? What business?"

"I don't know until I go and find out, do I?"

"Don't drink too much, Freddie, please?" she said, putting her arm around me.

Kathy was becoming critical of my fondness for beer because, she said, it made me thoughtless in bed; that I was only thinking about myself and not her and why did I sometimes have my eyes shut? Since the railway carriage dream, we'd had words about it several times. My feeling was that the beer made me less inhibited, rather than more aggressive, but Kathy didn't agree. Of course, I didn't really want to discuss it at all because it reminded me of Ma and Pa.

"Don't worry. I'll just have a couple, alright?" I said.

"Does Gubby like beer, Daddy?" said Grace. She was not able to get her tongue around "Great Uncle Bernard" so she'd invented "Gubby" as a shortened form.

"Yes, he does," I replied, tickling her under the chin.

"I don't like beer. It smells very...smells very sewer," she squeaked, still clutching my leg.

"Sour, do you mean?"

"Sewer is about right, Freddie," said Kathy. "Beery breath; not nice – drains. *Out of the mouths of...of babes and sucklings*, isn't it?"

"I thought I was the one with the quotations? You blinking women are ganging up on me," I laughed. "I'll see you later."

Bernard was already in the bar and Stan appeared after a couple of minutes.

"Wotcha, Corky!" said The Hayrick, her voice rasping like a saw. "I thought you'd 'ad enough this morning?"

"Hello, Doreen," said Stan, giving her a leer and a slap on the behind. "A man can never 'ave enough! But I've come in fer a drink and a chin-wag, haven't I? Chin-wag, not a quick shag!" He laughed and nodded towards the table in the corner where Bernard and I were seated. Bernard had already bought Stan's pint which was waiting for him in a pool of ullage on the table.

"Well, I can fit you in," she wiggled her hips provocatively, "about nine, if you change your mind."

Stan snorted. "You could fit a bloody shire horse in; and the cart!"

"Cheeky sod!" rasped The Hayrick, punching Stan good-naturedly on the arm.

"What a hussy!" said Stan, collapsing into the spare chair at our table. "Cheers!"

"Down the 'atch!"

Stan took two or three long pulls at his beer and then set the almost drained mug on the table, wiping his mouth with the back of his sleeve.

"Not a bad pint. Better than at The Hope, anyway. He never cleans 'is pipes."

"Not like you, then, ey, Stan?" I quipped.

"Now, don't you start gettin' vulgar, Prof! You know what? I might take her up on that appointment," he said, adjusting the eels in his basket and looking over at The Hayrick and her friends. "Or that other one, maybe, with the rubbery lips. Imagine those..."

"So what's this all about, Stan?" interrupted Bernard, who could see that Stan was going to ramble lecherously as usual and then slope off to the back room. "You said you wanted to talk business? Tell you what, why don't you come and sit over 'ere and then you won't be able to look at them tarts? They're obviously distractin' you."

Stan smiled. "Alright, son. Keep yer 'air on. I'll just get another round in."

He did and to my surprise, on his return, he sat in the place that Bernard had suggested.

"So," he said, "hostilities with the Hun 'avin ceased, as they say, what you geezers goin' to do with the rest of yer lives? What about you, Prof? Off ter college an' that, is it?"

"In all honesty, I don't know, Stan," I replied.

"In all honesty, he doesn't know!" Stan said, mimicking my voice. "Well, if you ain't gonna do that, you'll have to think o' summat else."

"You should, Freddie," said Bernard. "You're a bright lad and you're still young. You could 'ave a shinin' professional career, son."

Stan was watching me carefully and at the same time, running his forefinger through the puddles of beer on the mahogany table-top. "He's right, o' course."

"Well, I know he is. I always said I would and part of me wants to do that but...it seems like time's moved on, Bernard. I don't know; when you're at school, you continue being at school and then, I imagine, you go to university. Progression. But I got diverted, so to speak. And now it doesn't seem quite so important. I can read at home; visit the library at Victoria Circus."

"That's true, Freddie, but it ain't the same as a good, inspirin' teacher, now, is it? Someone to point you in the right direction, you know, rather than that you just 'ope you're going that way," replied Bernard.

"I expect your right, Bernard. But, well, what for? I don't need qualifications to earn money now. Self-improvement, I suppose?

Yes, I can see the point but you have to want to do it and I don't want it badly enough, I think. My brother-in-law, when we were kids playing in the graveyard, said that in the end, it makes no difference what you do, because you're dead. I mean, I know that mankind cannot think that way, otherwise we'd still be in caves, but it's strange – his words have stuck with me for some reason. Anyway, I've got two kids to clothe and feed. Not to mention a wife!" I laughed ruefully.

"The wages of sin is an empty wallet," chuckled Stan. "An' I should bloody know!"

"You could look at it another way; you can support the family without earning, Freddie, so there'd be no hardship financially like there is for lots of students, I hear. You know, I'm sure that's why your Aunty Vi...well, you know what I'm on about," Bernard said, obviously having decided not to refer to the legacy in front of Stan. He needn't have worried because Stan had worked it out for himself some considerable time previously and I hadn't denied it when he'd asked.

"Well, I'll think about it, but I'll take some convincing. I took a left turn some years ago; it's too late now to go back to the junction. That's how it feels, anyway. And Stan knows about the money," I said.

"I don't know all the details, like, Bernard," Stan said hurriedly, "but the Prof here did let me into 'is confidence some while back. Actually, it's partly that what's on me mind."

"What do you mean?" asked Bernard sharply.

Stan told Bernard not to be so touchy and then began to talk about the pier and how popular it had been with trippers before the war and how it looked already as if that popularity was set to return.

"Stands ter reason, don't it? People has 'ad bloody nearly six years of misery an' hidin' under the stairs, not knowin' from one minute to the next whether they was goin' to get their arses blown off. So now they wants some fun. 'S obvious."

His contention was that because money would still be short for many people, expensive fun would largely be out of the question.

But, he thought, for Londoners, a quick trip to Southend on the train, an ice cream for the kids, a cuppa somewhere where you could sit in the sun and look at the boats, a silly hat for Aunty Mary and a bit of a flutter on the machines in the arcade would fit the bill. The pier, he argued, was the magnet. People had flocked to it in the thirties and they would again.

"Anyone offerin' cheap fun could clean up, no question," he concluded, clonking his beer mug down to emphasise his point. "You'll see; entertainment is going to be very big business. Your round, Prof."

I took the empty mugs to the bar. I was concerned that the evening was young but already we were on the third pint, although I'd promised Kathy I'd have only two. I made a mental note to myself that when I got home, I should brush my teeth vigorously and not be in too much of a hurry under the eiderdown.

"The soddin' tax man will probably 'ave at least a 'alf of it, if that miserable, bloody Chancellor has 'is way," grumbled Bernard.

"There's a lease up for grabs at the pier head. Not cheap but a big space on the lower deck," said Stan. "Amusement arcade, boys, that's the name of the game. But it needs funds for the equipment and the premium on the lease, o' course."

Bernard sucked in his lower lip. "You're suggestin' some sort of partnership?"

"Yup. Three way equal split on the investment; three way equal divvy on the profits."

I was naïve about all this kind of thing and had to ask Stan for more information; primarily, of course, what he meant by "investment". He'd done all the sums, he said; worked it all out to the nearest penny.

"That's a lot of money, Stan!" I exclaimed.

"Bloody hell!" said Bernard. "You are jokin', ain't ya?'

"Nah. It's a cast-iron certainty. Of course it's a lot of money. But I'm sure we'll get it all back in a year and from then on it's plain sailin'. I tell yer, that pier is goin' to be visited by millions, all with coins jinglin' in their pockets. Some with just a few bob and some others who 'ave got money to spend and nothin' to spend it on, right? I mean, we're busy makin' stuff like refrigerators and then exportin' 'em to the bleedin' Yanks to pay off our debts, aren't we? For export only, an' all that stuff. So, either way, we win. You see, we don't need to persuade people to spend or give 'em a hard-sell or offer a money-back service. Just provide machines and rides or summat and they'll throw the money at us. Bound to."

"And if it goes wrong?" I said.

"How? I told yer, the war's over. 'Ow many more times 'ave I got ter say it? It's a new world out there. People are fed up to the back teeth with rationing, restraint and friggin' utility this and utility that. It'll all go, given time, you'll see. Give 'em a little bit of escape; a happy dream, see? Cheap fun, thrills, bright lights and candy floss and they'll be screamin' for more, like tarts on a tandem. Talkin' of which..."

"But if you're wrong, our funds are down the toilet, right?" said Bernard, stabbing at the table with his finger.

"O' course. That's the nature of a bleedin' gamble, innit? But it won't go wrong. Trust me. I can feel it in me waters. All of 'em. Now, what do you say?"

Bernard said that he was getting on a bit and didn't know whether he wanted to risk his hard-earned cash at his time of life. Stan suggested that in five years he could have more cash to retire on than most people earn in a lifetime. Bernard flopped back in his chair, thinking about that one. I said I didn't know anything about amusement arcades or selling candy floss and Stan laughed.

"Typical bloody schoolteacher-type remark, Prof! What's to know, son? We find out. Probably take us all of fifteen minutes."

"Why are you askin' us?" said Bernard.

"You've both got some money. Or so I reckon. And so 'ave I, as it 'appens. That's the first thing; never begin with loans. Second-off, the operation needs brass neck an' bullshit, right? That's me. It needs a steady hand...or maybe a lead weight or a brake to pull me up when I gets too bleedin' cocky – that's you, Bernie boy. An' the Prof here contributes some brain power to do the accounts, deal with the paperwork and speak politely to the bank manager. Only thing none of us is any good at is mechanics an' that. We'll need someone to be on 'and to mend things when they pack up; grease the nipples, so ter speak. And I'm talkin' machines, not tits. I can 'andle them meself!"

"I know someone," I said. "My brother-in-law Benny that I mentioned a while ago. Train mechanic. And he likes nipples; both sorts."

"Speak to 'im, Prof. Then it's what they calls a winnin' team. If we're gonna do it, we have to sign the lease by the end of next week."

"Next week? Do me with a barge-pole!" exclaimed Bernard.

"Nice of you to offer, old fella, but no thanks," replied Stan. "But I might give Rubber Lips a quick stretch. Why don't you boys 'ave a chat an' I'll be back shortly? In less than a minute, accordin' to Doreen!"

"*Keep thy foot out of brothels, thy hand out of plackets, thy pen from lender's books and defy the foul fiend,*" I said, laughing. "Looks like you got it right on only one, Stan - avoiding the money-lender."

"What's a placket?" grinned Bernard.

"A woman's petticoat," I said.

"Ho, ho! I wasn't thinking of just putting my hand in her petticoat, but I'll let you know and see you later," Stan announced.

§

We signed the lease the following week. Bernard had done some asking around the town and on the pier and had to admit that it looked as if Stan could be on to something. I talked it through with Kathy, if only because it involved spending some of our money. I was unable to decide whether the risk was too great, but Kathy saw through to the heart of the matter.

"The East End's a mess now, Freddie. You remember what Dad said in his last letter? That's why he's coming down here. All that bomb damage. People's lives smashed as well. A day by the seaside or on the pier? Yes, I think they will. People will come. Let's do it. Let's both do it."

As simple as that. As simple as Kathleen no longer was.

The next time I met with my new partners, one evening at Pleasant Road, I suggested that we could appeal to the sense of fun and adventure that Stan had talked about by calling the place Treasure Island.

"Bloody good idea, Prof!" chortled Stan, slapping me on the back.

"Well, there could be a kind of running idea there, you see. We can put "Pieces of Eight" over the kiosk where people come to get their change; we can have a café called "The Admiral Benbow"; we could get some of the old dummies from the waxworks and dress them up as Blind Pew, Jim Hawkins, Ben Gunn or Long John Silver; maybe we could get some sort of ride made for kids which is in the shape of a galleon – the "Hispaniola"; we could have a big slide or tree-house construction called "Spy-glass Hill"; some sort of creepy, dark place for them to go into; you know, with rubber skulls, dangling bits of cobweb and what-have-you that's called "Skeleton Island"; do you see? It gives the whole place a kind of magical quality for children and they'll drag their Mums and Dads in to spend their money."

Stan and Bernard looked at me, both with their mouths open.

"Well, stuff me with a tart's laddered nylons!" Stan announced. "You're a firkin' genius!"

"Language!" snapped Kathy, censoriously.

"Very inventive, son, very imaginative. Sounds like a winner to me," said Bernard.

"Of course it is," said Kathy. "That's what you get when you ask someone with brains, isn't it? And when Grace is off my hands at school, I'll run the café. Mrs Horsfall says she'd be happy to look after Violet May for a few bob. I want to be involved too."

I hadn't really taken too much note of what Kathy had said in our first discussion, but at that moment, I remembered she'd said, "Let's both do it". For years, indeed, for most of my life, I had been accustomed to regarding her role as secondary and her observations as often oddly apposite but nevertheless, somehow locked in childhood. I suppose that sounds dismissive and patronising and I don't mean it to be. It's true that I was finding our private life a little jaded and when I tried to spice it up or give it more energy, Kathy accused me of being aggressive, but nevertheless, I loved her dearly, was continuously in awe of her beauty, which seemed to develop further with every year, and I was proud of her undoubted capabilities as a wife and mother. But I suppose I never saw her being anything else.

Stan laughed. "Of course you can, my dear! You'd bring in the crowds just standin' there on yer own, wouldn't she, Bernard? There you are, Prof, didn't I say that the women would soon be in charge?"

For some minutes I was not able to say very much and just looked at Kathy in amazement. She sat quietly, giving me a winsome smile from time to time.

BOOK THREE

TREASURE ISLAND

1947 - 1950

SO VARIOUS, SO BEAUTIFUL, SO NEW
Summer 1949

The two or three years that followed the end of the war were probably the best time of all for Kathy, me and the girls. There was, of course, a mood of relief and optimism about the future across the whole country, despite the fact that many hardships and shortages remained. Everyone hoped that rationing would finish but it didn't for some years. In fact, the meat ration was reduced in 1950 because we were having an argy-bargy with the Argentine. Bernard's "miserable" Chancellor, Stafford Cripps, expected everyone to endure further sacrifice. It was alright for him; he was a vegetarian! Nevertheless, many people felt more confident about their personal circumstances than they had done and with the dangers of war over, they settled down, as the saying used to be, and began to procreate. Men came home from the war – those who survived – and got their kit off. There was a phenomenal surge in the birth rate in 1947 and 1948, a sure indicator of the mood of the country.

I suppose that most married couples, as they progress through life, can look back and identify a time when things were at their happiest. I mean, even if you're poor or one of your children is not too healthy or something, there'll nevertheless be a period when it seemed you were pulling together. For us, it was during those optimistic years. We stayed at Pleasant Road. In 1948, with things going well for us, I did suggest to Kathy that she might like to sell up and buy a place in one of those rather grand roads south of Chalkwell Park, like Mount Avenue or Chadwick Road.

"There's a lovely place on the market in The Leasway," said Archie Soper one afternoon, supporting my suggestion. "Then you'd be just round the corner from me." He had managed to obtain his work transfer and had bought a large house in Chalkwell Avenue in 1946. It had been empty throughout the war, had been broken into and had suffered some bomb damage to the roof so that the weather had got in, but Archie was nothing daunted and drove a very hard bargain on the price.

"Mark my words," he said at the time, "there's going to be money in property. Especially big places with good addresses. I'll do it up and sell it on when the time's right; after all, I don't need six bedrooms, not even with Benny loafing about there when he's not ogling girls on that pier! I wish he'd find himself a nice girl and settle down."

"He finds quite a few girls, but none of them is what you'd call nice," Kathy remarked sagely.

"The Leasway's a lovely road, Kathy," I said, hurriedly. We both knew what kind of girls Benny lured on the pier.

"We couldn't afford that," she replied.

"Yes, we can, I think. How much is it, Mr. Soper?"

"Freddie, for Heaven's sake, you should be calling me "Dad", or "Archie" if you prefer! You've been my son-in-law for some years now, you know. And I don't know the price but I'll find out."

"Well, no harm in asking, I suppose," said Kathy, conciliatory as ever, "but no big ideas. It's too posh for us over there. Great big houses; what do we want that for?"

"Look what's happening in America, Kathy, now that the war's over. Ordinary people are reaping the benefit. And a lot of the benefit is in property, what they call luxury goods, furniture, home-making and so on. It'll be the same here."

"I'm not interested in America, Dad. Anyway, it suits us here for the pier and with Mrs Horsfall on hand next door."

"We won't need Mrs Horsfall so much once Violet's at school, Kathy," I said. "She starts next year, don't forget. And if we were over that way, they'd be at Chalkwell Hall School – it's very good, I hear. And a big house? Well, it shows we're going up in the world, doesn't it, Mr...Archie?"

"That's right, Freddie. What do you say, Kathleen?" pressed Archie.

"I said, I'm not interested in America or about going up in the world," she said. "Toffee-nosed neighbours with Pekinese dogs! I'm quite happy here."

So we stayed where we were and left the money in the bank. In fact, we added to it very considerably during those years because Treasure Island was an instant success. During 1949, more than five million people visited the pier. Good Lord! Five million! Looking back now and considering the sad decline in trade, it seems almost impossible that during one day that summer, 55,000 people were carried up and down the pier on its brand-new, green trains! I'm not suggesting for one minute that everyone who came onto the pier visited our arcade but, of course, many thousands did and all we had to do was keep the machines working, the rides operational and The Admiral Benbow café permanently ready to dispense tea and cakes – and people just lobbed their money at us.

"Easy as fallin' off a blinkin' log!" said Stan. "What did I tell you all?"

He was right, although I had a feeling even then that something might go wrong or it might not last, or that we should be investing our money in other ventures; spreading ourselves, so to speak. Archie thought we should be buying up cheap property but Kathy didn't see the point – why did we need more than one house?

Stan, on the other hand, was convinced that foreign travel, perhaps by air, would increase in popularity over the following years because, he said, people would eventually become sick of candy floss on the pier and would seek out something more adventurous when they found they had some money in their pockets. He thought we should go into travel agency and forge a link with the airport just outside Rochford. Stan did seem to be able to read the mood of the nation at that time. He saw that people wanted fun and would pay for it; he saw that people would begin to buy luxuries and fripperies after the bleak austerity of the war years and he saw the likelihood of an increased popularity for foreign travel.

"You know what?" I said to Kathy one evening. "We're making enough money to mean that we can shut the place up completely during the winter months and put our feet up. In fact, we could go and sit by the sea somewhere else. Somewhere exotic, maybe?"

"Is it just about making money, Freddie?" Kathy replied. "I mean, I quite enjoy meeting people, organising everything. And the fresh sea air. Isn't that enough?"

"The point I'm making is that we can afford to do more than just work, day in; day out. Like I said before, we could afford better than this little terrace and we can afford a long winter holiday. Some people go to the South of France, you know; the Mediterranean, where it's warmer. Stan reckons it's going to be the thing in a few years."

"France? Abroad? Why would we want to go abroad? They eat frogs there, don't they? Anyway, it's only rich, stuck-up people who go to the Mediterranean."

"We are rich, Kathy," I said plaintively.

"Maybe, but we're not stuck-up. You can't come from Bow and be stuck-up, Freddie! Frogs' legs, isn't it? Disgusting! Anyway, what about the girls' schooling?"

"They can go to school in St. Tropez. Qu'ils mangent de la brioche," I said. "Let them eat cake."

"Sometimes, Freddie, you do talk a lot of rubbish, you know?"

Of course, I didn't think I was talking rubbish and later years proved that both Archie and Stan were correct and that my own intuitions were well-founded. But there we are; Kathy was content with what we had achieved and was quite implacable. Perhaps I should have just gone ahead and done what I thought we should do without her agreement or even without her knowledge, but I didn't. After all, it was true that a great deal of our success on Treasure Island was due to Kathy's management of the café and the attractions of her personality: to have deliberately gone against her wishes – or, perhaps, her limited horizons – when she was so pivotal to the operation would hardly have been playing cricket.

Of course, not everyone thought that she should be working on the pier; or working at all, come to that. Most women didn't in those days; they were expected to stay at home, look after the children and deal with the domestic chores. Going out to work was somehow to fail in your duty; it was not womanly or feminine for those who didn't need to work. Kathy didn't need to but she chose to because she wanted to help and she enjoyed being with people. Odd, really, because in this respect she was years ahead of her time and yet she wouldn't contemplate even a short trip to Boulogne!

She was surprisingly good at managing staff and ordering stock; the former was no surprise because Kathy was always able to communicate with people. Stock control required organisational skills that I simply did not know she possessed. She was also ahead of her time in recognising that there is more profit in food than almost anything else; and more profit in home-produced food such as cakes and pastries than items bought-in. So she had an army of people baking in their kitchens for the café and our own oven seemed permanently in use too. As I say, rationing remained a difficulty but with some ducking and diving, she seemed to cope.

But more than any of that it was her personality and, I suppose, her beauty that appealed to men and women alike – not to mention the children – so that they flocked to Treasure Island. She had that remarkable ability to make every customer feel special and welcome and to make every potential customer, hovering at the entrance to the arcade or the café, decide that this was the place to spend time and therefore money. She didn't shout to people like a market trader or entice them like the owner of the freak-show at the circus; she just smiled; ran her fingers through her curls in that wonderfully ordinary, unpretentious way she had; said hello; referred to the weather or engaged in genuinely interested chit-chat with their children. But it worked, every time. Not that it was a ploy; she was just being herself and that's why it worked. There was no artifice with Kathy.

She was not one of those women who appeal only to men and who manage somehow to antagonise their own sex with their physical charms. I suppose that's because there was no provocative, preening archness about her, so other women didn't see her as a competitive predator or someone obsessed with her own attractiveness. Naturally, men noticed her without fail. Old men, young men; sometimes, I think, even blind men, somehow seemed to spot her in the milling, laughing crowds at the pier head.

Men had noticed her since she was about thirteen because she developed rapidly at that time. In the late 1940's, when she was in her early twenties, she was at her most alluring. If you look at photographs now of Marilyn Monroe at the height of her fame, you might be quite surprised at the fullness of her figure: she had quite large hips, for example. These days beauty is deemed to be willowy: many models and film actresses have slender frames. They begin to panic when they put a few pounds on their thighs or their backsides and throw themselves mercilessly into starvation diets. A few pounds on the bust is alright, of course, but not if it slides further south. Kathy was very slender as a girl but later she became the shape that was fashionable at the time – the Marilyn Monroe shape. Everyone told me I was a lucky man. I was, there is no doubt, but it didn't stop me behaving like a complete idiot.

Men would sometimes nudge one another and stare at her, wolf-whistle even; fathers would sneak a peek while pretending to keep an eye on their kids; young boys would whistle quietly, laughing and adjusting their trousers; old men would smile, lick their lips and become misty-eyed. Mostly, it wasn't a problem then because convention prohibited any behaviour that was too unseemly and anyway, Kathy herself didn't invite crudity. Although you acknowledged her undoubted physical assets, said Stan – and we all knew what he meant by that – she was just like your sister.

I'd be lying if I said that there were never occasions when men over-stepped the mark, but there were fewer than there had been when Kathy was younger. When she was sixteen or so, perhaps she lacked the confidence and the homely qualities she had in her twenties; Stan was probably right about that as he was about so much else. Of course, I would sometimes find myself angry at the way some men looked at her on the pier or whispered to one another, especially if I cared to speculate about what they were probably saying. But mostly I tried to ignore it, as Kathy did herself. It wasn't a bone of contention between us.

So, things were good for a while. Then, in the summer of 1950, two seemingly unrelated things happened, both of which had far-reaching effects. I was going to say "unexpected" but, actually, it was all probably entirely predictable. That's the gospel according to Mr. Vickery, anyway.

YO, HO, HO AND A BOTTLE OF RUM
5th August 1950

One of the wonderful things about working on the pier was that you were generally surrounded by people who were there to have a good time. They were on holiday for a week or so, or had escaped the muck and smoke of London for the day. Trippers! How we loved them! People smiled, laughed, joked, bought daft hats and took endless photographs of one another leaning against the railings, outside Treasure Island or over by the lifebelts with Dad putting his palms together as if about to dive into the foaming briny. No matter, and however silly or pointless, just for a while people tried to throw off their backs those things which otherwise bore down upon them: life's sack of rocks forever to be toted until Doomsday, for that, of course, will go onward the same, *Though Dynasties pass.*

Being always surrounded by laughter and good humour is infectious. Even on the wettest and windiest days, good old British stoicism prevented too many descents into pessimism and glumness. In fact, on rainy, blustery days we often sold more tea and cakes than on sunny days. People kept on coming. So for me, to be on the pier was to be where there were smiles. It sounds trite, but it was true.

It was also true, although I didn't fully appreciate it at the time, that the pier was in the vanguard. As the decades went by, people spent more and more on holidays, cars, houses, furnishings, entertainment, clothing, trinkets and who knows what else. Just after the war we were not very sophisticated as a nation and it would be some years before we learned to be consumers in an affluent society. But even in 1949, you could see the beginnings of it in people's desire to fritter, to gamble, to buy themselves a bit of fun and escape.

I didn't understand it that way at the time. As I say, I liked the laughter and, furthermore, being more than a mile out from the shore, one was able to enjoy the endless permutations of light playing on the sea and the glistening mud-banks; to breathe fresh air laced with salt and seaweed; to watch ships, laden to the waterline, threading their way cautiously through the Oaze Deep and the Princes Channel via the Girdler, hoping to avoid old wrecks, newer wrecks and the shifting, swallowing sands. Leaving London behind – London, the monstrous town...marked ominously in the sky, *a brooding gloom in sunshine*, as Conrad would have it – they headed for the alluring mystery of other, far-away lands. Or so it seemed to me.

But perhaps more than any of those things, it was the sense of being out in the space of the Estuary, the town shimmering behind me, the coast of Kent a yellow and green smudge in the other direction; I gloried in the vastness of the sky out over the distant North Sea; the majesty of nothing between me and those sepia horizons. Almost every day, I thanked my good fortune that I was not strapped to a desk somewhere in the gloom and stench of the city or pinioned on the rack of a factory's production line, deafened by relentless machinery. Although it's true that when the arcade was busy, it was certainly not quiet!

One humid Saturday afternoon that summer, I felt one of my headaches coming on and decided to get outside in the air, away from the clatter of plates and cups coming from The Admiral Benbow; away from the piercing shrieks of children clambering the rigging of the Hispaniola and to put behind me the ceaseless gyrations and whirrings of the amusement arcade machines. One of the children's favourites was The Laughing Policeman: you put a penny in the slot and the little puppet rocked about, laughing in an inane, hooting manner.

Sometimes it made me laugh too and at other times I wanted to put a pick-axe through the bloody thing. I confess to having had periods of such extreme irritability around that time, coupled with the headaches and dizzy spells. Mostly, I kept this to myself, but when it became obvious, Kathy put it down to my increasing fondness for beer. Naturally I told her that she was talking complete twaddle. In fact, she probably wasn't, for it was true that my consumption had slowly but inexorably increased to the point where I was beginning to conceal from her – and perhaps myself too – my frequent visits to one of the pubs on The Golden Mile.

It was usually enough to get away from the arcade's noise and have ten minutes communion with the Thames. I ambled into the sunshine, around to the quieter side of the building where I leaned against the railings and looked down at the choppy waves. There were a number of small boys there, arguing about their fishing.

"What you usin'?" said one.

"Well, s'just a bit o' bacon fat an' that from breakfast," said another.

"You daft cock," said the first. "Bacon fat? Lugworm's what you need for whiting or dabs! Don't you know nothin'? You'll be suggesting cornflakes next!"

"Well, I ain't got cockin' lugworm, 'ave I? You never know. They might be browned off with that and fancy a bit o' bacon an' egg."

The first boy laughed and threw his line back into the sea. "And you need your hook on the bottom, not flappin' about just under the waves," he said. "They're bottom feeders, you idiot! Just like your Uncle Brian," he added for good measure.

I grinned at them and relaxed against the rail, taking long breaths of the air and reflecting that, although I was anchored to terra firma a mile away, I was nevertheless breathing the kind of air breathed by sailors en route for The Orient.

Some little sailing dinghies were running with the offshore breeze, parallel with the pier stem and about half a mile off to the east. There were about fifteen of them, all very similar. As they jostled across the waves, their putty-coloured sails billowing in the wind, they looked like ducks racing for scraps of bread. I supposed that they must have come from one of the yacht clubs; it being a Saturday morning, no doubt youngsters were being taught the rudiments of sailing.

I looked over and between their sails, further back to the town, just making out the masts of the replica Golden Hind at the shore and watching the sun glint in the windows of The Palace Hotel, sitting high and proud on what, a hundred years ago, must have been the edge of a small cliff.

After some minutes of letting my eyes idly scan the shore, the beach and the water, I noticed a couple about twenty yards from where I was lounging, doing much the same thing themselves. The man was pointing out across the waters, indicating something for the woman's benefit. She threw back her head, laughing and the man ran his hand down her shoulders to her waist and let it come to rest on her rear for a few moments. They had their backs to me, so I could not see their faces. There was nothing especially unusual in the sight: leaning on the railings was what countless hundreds of people did every day. But there was something about the man's stance; the way he held his head and his shoulders; the way he had one leg hooked behind the other; the way he had dropped his arm down to the woman's behind, that made my stomach dip and roll alarmingly. It seemed I was looking at Pa.

Even as I was staring at them, the man turned in my direction so that his body would provide a shield against the wind, allowing him to light a cigarette. He cupped his hands, blew smoke and then flicked the match into the waves. As he did so, he looked up towards me. He took a long draw on the cigarette and squinted against the sun. He raised his free hand to shade his eyes, looking directly at me. He stood that way for perhaps twenty seconds, said something to the woman and then began to cross the space between us. The woman looked annoyed and raised her hand as if to object, but it was too late.

As he came close to me, he slowed and then stopped, unsure that his first instincts were correct. He shaded his eyes once more, flicked the cigarette over the side, took a couple of steps forward and spoke.

"Freddie? It is, isn't it?"

"Yes," I responded. "Hello, Vinny."

"Well, what about that?"

I wasn't sure whether to throw my arms around him or push him backwards over the rail into the sea. He was my brother and yet he hadn't been there when I needed him; he was my own flesh and blood and yet he was also Pa come back to life, the pig, bringing sacks full of vile memories with him. I felt a surge of filial emotion and terrible hatred, simultaneously.

We just stood looking at one another for some time. We said nothing. For all I know, his thoughts were like mine. It's possible. His woman had come trotting over to where we were and now she too, sensing the tension between us, stood silently, a few paces off, watching us curiously.

I felt an odd spinning sensation and staggered forwards. I heard a thumping and whirring in my ears as if a spool tape had run out of control. The present and the past began to run together and I was watching them both, as if they were being played out in front of me on a stage.

DRAMATIS PERSONAE
1936 and August 1950

The stage is bare except for a café table and some chairs down left; a door in a frame in the centre, upstage; some pier railings down right. There is no wall on either side of the door: it stands alone. The main stage is gloomy; perhaps some dim lights off to suggest street lamps in the distance. There is a red light coming from behind the door. Shadows are cast on the cyclorama, but not precise shapes. We see movement – what appear to be a girl's legs in silhouette come into focus; it must seem that she is lying down. We sense only the legs and another, darker shape moving between them. We hear a man's gruff voice and a woman's squeals of sexual pleasure. We hear the voice of Nat King Cole singing 'Mona Lisa' for a few moments and then this fades and is overlaid by brassy, big band music: quiet at first, so that the other sounds are not drowned and then louder as TWO BOYS ENTER gingerly from stage left. VINNY is almost 14, quite tall and angular; FREDDIE is about ten, shorter than his brother and altogether neater. They are dressed in night-wear. They approach the door. VINNY bends to its keyhole which we now see has a sharp, bright light shining through it.

VINNY
(Holding his finger to his lips.)
Keep quiet, you daft sod, otherwise they'll 'ear us, won't they? Get out the way!
There is a pause while he looks. Freddie stands, waiting. His hands are pulling nervously at his pyjama cords.

FREDDIE
What are they doing? What's that squeaking noise?

After a short while, Vinny stands up and moves downstage a little, leaving the keyhole for Freddie, who bends for his turn. Vinny is tugging uncomfortably at the front of his pyjamas. It should be obvious that he is distressed by whatever he has seen...and yet. He looks back at Freddie who, after a while, joins him downstage.

FREDDIE

What's Pa doing with Alice? I don't understand.

VINNY

(Angrily)

Doing to Alice, you mean.

FREDDIE

Alright, then, what's he doing to Alice?

VINNY

He's like a dog! And Ma's still cold over at Micklewhite's. I'll get him for this, one day, you bloody see if I don't. Stinking, stinking pig!

FREDDIE

(Considering the remark with care).

Pig? Dog? Like dogs? Dogs sniff one another's...well, you know. That's disgusting. Anyway, what for? Does she like that?

VINNY

Sounds like it, don't it? Bit more than sniffing. He is a filthy dog; they're both filthy. A dog and a bitch.

Suddenly the music stops. The red light is extinguished behind the door. There is a shout off right and the slam of a different, much heavier door. Brighter light on stage centre.

VINNY

Look out! It's Pa!

Both boys scurry to hide behind the upstage door; we see their faces, peeking out occasionally, during the following action. PA, a large, dirty-looking man, unshaven and wearing a greasy cap, clumps in from the right, pushing MA ahead of him. He is drunk. She is thin, wearing a tired housecoat. She was probably once very pretty. Her hair, presumably earlier scraped into a bun, falls untidily around her shoulders.

PA
(Loudly, coarsely)
Come on, woman, you heard wot I said. Get up the ruddy stairs and get yerself undressed. Stripped.

MA
(Tearfully; frightened)
Oh, no, Sid, please? Not tonight, please? I'm still bleeding from...

PA
(Striking her a blow across her face; it sends her stumbling downstage.)
Don't answer me back, you slattern! You 'eard me – get up the stairs and get ready!

MA
(Clutching at her cheek.)
Sid, please, you'll wake the boys...the neighbours...please, maybe if I just...

She is unable to finish her sentence. PA unbuckles his belt and strikes her forcefully across her back with it. She falls to the floor. He strikes her again and kicks her in the groin. She screams.

PA
(Yelling, almost incoherently.)
Whassa matter with yer? Don't you understand wot I'm sayin'? Get...up...the...f ---- stairs!

FREDDIE

(Appearing from behind the door.)
Pa! Stop it! Please stop it! You'll hurt her!

PA

What? Yer little toe-rag! Mind yer own business! You should be in bleedin' bed, anyway!

PA grabs FREDDIE with one hand and strikes him with the belt using the other. The blow lands on FREDDIE'S legs and he falls to the ground, crying in pain.

FREDDIE

Pa! Please...don't...aah!

PA strikes him again with the belt and then kicks at his head two or three times. More screaming. We are aware of VINNY'S face behind the door but he does not move to intervene.

MA

(Trying to get to her feet and put herself between PA and FREDDIE.)
Sid, for pity's sake, leave the boy alone. Stop kicking his head, will you? What do you want to do, kill him? Leave him. I'll go upstairs... and do whatever you want... but leave him alone!

PA

Go on then, woman! And you, yer little runt, I'll learn yer to interfere...!

PA gives FREDDIE another sharp kick and then pushes MA offstage left. Lights dim except for a spot on FREDDIE, still lying on the floor, sobbing.

FREDDIE
Feebly.
Ma? Mummy? Vinny? Help me; I can't stand up. He kicked my head, Ma. I can't see properly. (*Loudly; wailing.*) There's funny lights and noises in my head.

Momentary blackout. Lights up on the pier railings, close to which FREDDIE and VINNY, now men, are standing, facing one another. Sounds of the sea, seagulls and children shrieking with enjoyment, the latter emerging from Freddie's crying and whimpering.

VINNY
Freddie? It is, isn't it?

FREDDIE
Yes. Hello, Vinny.

(The illogicality of some of the following conversation should be clear to the audience but not to the characters.)

VINNY
Well, what about that? I'll be jiggered. I reckon I haven't seen you for ten years.

FREDDIE
Yes; we noticed that. We carried on regardless. And what did you do in the war, Daddy?

VINNY
What? Killed some of the enemy. Screwed a lot more of the enemy's wives. And their daughters. My God, the daughters!

FREDDIE

That's nice, Vinny. An old soldier remembers, eh? Maybe they'll give you a moment to reminisce in front of the Cenotaph in November? I have daughters. Two of them.

VINNY

Yeah? Terrific. I remember September 1943, when the Ities were about to switch sides! You shoulda seen some of those girls!

FREDDIE

I was digging ditches and burying Aunty Vi in September 1943. Where were you? Come to that, where were you at Pa's funeral or my wedding? How can you not attend your own father's funeral? What excuse for that have you got, valiant old soldier?

VINNY

(Lighting a cigarette and sucking on it rather vulgarly).

He was a bastard. And I was on active service, brother. Fighting for King and Country. Yeah, keen to show which side they were going to be on, those Itie tarts. You shoulda seen the melons on those girls in Salerno when we was on shore leave. Amazing bodies, those Itie girls. Tits like you wouldn't believe. I 'ad some, I can tell yer.

FREDDIE

Is that all it was about then? The war? Screwing Italian girls? I'm all right, Jack, never mind about the horrors of Belsen?

VINNY

'Course not, you pompous prick. What do you know, anyway? Machine guns; bodies torn apart; terrible food; crazy orders; gut-wrenching fear; jock itch; blood in the sea. But, then again, when you ain't had shore leave or a woman for weeks, yes, that's what it's about. Well, what else is there for a sailor a long way from home?

FREDDIE

No, nothing else, Vinny. Silly of me to ask. Whatever it might have been...now I only hear its melancholy, long, withdrawing roar. Nothing left but melons.

VINNY

Still talkin' rubbish, then? And what did you do in the war, little brother? Bleedin' conshi, last I heard. That right?

FREDDIE

That's right. But I wasn't bleeding; indeed, that's what I was hoping to avoid on my part and that of thousands of others. Principles.

VINNY

Bull! Always reading the wrong bloody script, you are, you feeble sod.

FREDDIE

Principles; but you wouldn't understand that. Feeble? Who tried to stop Ma being kicked to death by Pa? You? Or me?

VINNY

Yeah, yeah.

FREDDIE

I get these headaches now.

VINNY

Yeah? Least you still got your head. Lots of my muckers got their heads blown off; brains all down their nice tunics. Spaghetti.

Pause. He drags on the cigarette and then speaks wistfully.

You know, there was this one girl in Agropoli; couldn't believe the size of her hooters, let alone her age. Unbelievable. They were all starving, the family; well, you know. I gave 'er father a few lira and he left us alone. Never known anything like it. She smelled of honeysuckle. I'm thinkin' of goin' back to find her. But I expect she's fat and has six kids by now.

FREDDIE

The Child is father of the Man. One of them might be yours. In which case, God help the water melon girl.

A woman appears down right, by the railings. She is obviously annoyed.

WOMAN

What's going on? I thought you was buying me some lunch an' that?

VINNY

Ah! This is me long lost brother, Freddie. Freddie this is...er...Maggie.

WOMAN

Marjorie. Hello, Freddie. Vinny, I heard you talkin' about women's breasts. Again.

VINNY

So wot? I can talk to me own brother about what I like, can't I? What's it to do with you?

WOMAN

I don't like it. It's not respectful. You keep on doin' it.

FREDDIE

Ah, ha, boys! What brave men walking the plank blindfold, what shot of cannon, what shame and lies and cruelty, perhaps no man alive could tell.

WOMAN

Ey? Is he alright?

VINNY

Dunno. Maybe not. Tell you what, why don't you nip back to the boardin' house? Yeah? I'll be there soon as you can say afternoon nookie?

FREDDIE

Ah, ha! That's his business, is it? Licking like dogs. Overhung with ferns, probably.

WOMAN

You ought to think about getting him seen to. His mind is like a cess-pit.

VINNY

Yeah? So see you later? Here you are; here's a quid. Get yourself some perfume or something.

WOMAN

Push off, Vinny. I'm not taking your bribes or hanging about in some flea-hole while you talk breasts with your loopy brother. I'm going to find some real company.

(She exits stage left, huffing.)

FREDDIE

Exit stage left, pursued by a bear! I thought she was your wife.

VINNY

Very funny. I don't even know her name for sure. Maggie? Mary? Millie? Met her at The Kursaal last night. Goes like a rabbit; I'll say that for 'er. Wife? No, thanks. Bloody liability, they are. Let her go; good riddance. 'Ere, can we get a cuppa round 'ere somewhere?

FREDDIE

Be my guest.

He directs Vinny to the table down left. They sit. A waitress appears.

VINNY

Teapot for two, please, gorgeous. An' some toast or something?

FREDDIE

Ask Kathy to add some strawberry jam or whatever she's got, would you, Mary?

WAITRESS

Alright, Mr. Tanner.

(She exits).

VINNY

Nice little backside. I like a neat rear.

FREDDIE

(Singing.)

They scraped him off the tarmac like a dollop of strawberry jam and he ain't gonna fight no more! Glory, glory Hallelujah...

VINNY

(Ignoring the singing).

What's with this gaff, then? Admiral Benbow?

FREDDIE

It's a café. Part of Treasure Island. My business. Well, our business. Partnership.

We hear the distinctive sound of The Laughing Policeman.

VINNY

Yeah? Straight up? Well, that must be earnin' some and that's for sure.

FREDDIE

You have a job?

VINNY

Watchin' and waitin'. Talkin' of watchin' — who's that in the back? (*He is pointing upstage to where we see Kathy engaged in some café business.*) And talkin' of balloons, which I believe we were – get an eyeful of those!

Loud, angry trumpet. Lights dim suddenly stage left and come up stage right. KATHLEEN is leaning against the railings, alone. Nat King Cole is singing again. VINNY enters stage left, still smoking. He sees KATHLEEN and walks over to her. FREDDIE is watching the following from behind the upstage 'keyhole' door.

VINNY

Well, hello, beautiful!

KATHLEEN
(*Sighing; she's heard it all before.*)

Good morning. You'll have to excuse me, I have a business to run.

VINNY
(*Sotto voce*)

Terrific melons!

KATHLEEN

We don't sell fruit. Do you want a pot of tea? (*She looks at him more carefully.*) Don't I know you from somewhere?

VINNY

A dark night in Portsmouth Docks, maybe...

KATHLEEN

I beg your pardon? Ah, now, yes, I recognise you as a roving, wild dog from the streets of Bow. Vinny! My handsome brother-in-law! Or so they used to say!

VINNY

Am I? Well, what d'you know? I missed the wedding; sorry about that; let's dance now to make up for lost time. Once you've lost it, you can't get it back.

The brassy music begins again, suddenly, with the raucous trumpet. VINNY takes hold of KATHLEEN, one hand behind her waist and the other just under her breast. KATHLEEN laughs and they dance provocatively for a few moments. Their grotesque shapes are thrown in silhouette on the wall behind the door. FREDDIE steps out centre stage, watching, as VINNY presses KATHLEEN against the railings. He pushes his knee between her thighs; her dress rides up. He starts to kiss her and fumble at her breasts. He lifts her skirt and puts his hand inside. She does not seem to resist.

FREDDIE

(Pulling Vinny from Kathleen violently.)
Let go of my wife, you filthy swine! You're just the same as Pa!

VINNY

So it's true! She is your wife, you lucky sailor! Shares with your brother, then?

FREDDIE

Over my dead body! Blood and sorrow!

FREDDIE succeeds in separating VINNY from KATHLEEN, spinning him round so that he faces downstage. But it is PA we see, or seem to see, not VINNY. FREDDIE staggers backwards, clutches at his forehead and then brings both his hands up in a rabbit punch which he lands on PA/ VINNY'S neck. Cut lights to total darkness. KATHLEEN screams.

Once more, we hear the distinctive sound of The Laughing Policeman; it gradually slows as if a mechanism is winding down.

THE THING THAT'S DEAD BUT WON'T LIE DOWN
13th August 1950

A little girl with curly, auburn hair holds her handsome Daddy's hand as they walk from the station towards the arcade. Her little sister trots along beside them, clutching her favourite teddy. It is early on a Sunday morning in August and it is their Daddy's turn this week to open the shutters and to make the place ready for business. Daddy, Grumpy Gubby and funny old Stan take it in turns to do what Daddy calls the seventh day, although he keeps saying that on the seventh day he's supposed to rest. "And so is every other blighter in Christendom," he says. Grace doesn't understand, if that's the case, why Daddy and Mummy keep on working.

The sun is shining and already trippers are riding the trains and ambling around in the balmy air, looking for somewhere for a cup of tea. Fishermen are setting up their rods in the most favoured places, hoping to catch whiting, dabs or pouting on the incoming tide. As the sun rises higher in the sky, it silvers the Estuary as if someone has thrown a bucket of glittering fish scales across the tops of the waves.

Violet looks at her feet and their passage across the thick, wooden planks of the pier head. She likes to look down through the gaps to see the soapy, grey water of the Thames sloshing about against the barnacled piles in the gloom below. Her Mummy says that people are forever dropping their coins in Treasure Island and that sometimes the money rolls away from them and before they can retrieve it, it slips through the gaps where the caulking has fallen away. The coins drop into the sea.

"People stand and stare at the planks, as if it hasn't happened! There must be a small fortune down there," chuckles Kathleen.

There is a hooting sound as The Royal Daffodil approaches the pier, ready to tie up and then, later, to take hundreds of folk across the Channel to Boulogne.

"Daddy?" says Grace.

"Yes?"

"When can we go to France?"

Freddie laughs. "Well, your Mummy's not keen on that idea because they eat frogs' legs in France, don't they, dear?"

"Yes; horrible thought! Come on, Grace," says Kathleen, "I want to get the kettles on for tea. People want refreshments from two minutes after we open. Look, they're hanging about already. Looks as if Benny's here too; I think the door's ajar."

"When is a door not a door, Grace?"

Grace understands her Daddy's fun with words, but even so, she's puzzled.

"I don't know, Daddy."

"When it's a jar!"

"Very amusing, Freddie," sighs Kathy.

"Just trying to amuse the girls. Umm...there were one or two maintenance problems yesterday afternoon. I don't think Benny finished, so looks like he's got in early. I'm pleased to see such dedication to duty!" says Freddie whose view is that Benny is doing his job properly if all the machines are taking money and Benny is sitting doing nothing. He closes the little access door which Benny has left open by a few inches and then pushes the shutters aside, grunting with the effort of making them slide in their runners.

"Have to get Benny to oil these again," he pants.

Freddie has barely pushed the shutters aside when people begin entering the arcade, chattering with excitement. A group of small boys, shoving at one another in their anxiety to be first, scuttle towards Skeleton Island. Freddie throws a few switches just inside the entrance and coloured ceiling lights come on, as well as the large Treasure Island sign in the middle of the arcade.

"Give us a few minutes, folks!" he calls. "Some of the machines take a while to wake up on a Sunday!"

"Is it different in France, Daddy?" asks Grace, looking at The Royal Daffodil mooring up.

"That's what they say, Grace," replies Freddie, a similar conversation with Archie, at Paglesham, before the war, coming suddenly to mind. "But I don't know, because I've never been. Not even to Boulogne. Mummy doesn't like the idea of abroad; so here we stay."

Recollecting their rather indifferent love-making the night before, he thinks, not for the first time, that Mummy doesn't seem to like lots of things these days, especially in the bedroom. He wonders then about Vinny. He is not sure whether he really saw Vinny and Kathy kissing or whether it was just one of his dreams. Either way, the actuality or the possibility makes him sad, angry and confused.

He bends down behind the Roll-a-Penny and switches it on. It flickers unconvincingly and Freddie slaps the case irritably with the flat of his hand.

"I like the idea of abroad," says Grace, emphatically, "because the sun shines and there's no ice on your windows in the morning. But Patsy says they don't have proper toilets. You have to squat down or something; there's no seat? That sounds horrid. And in my school book it says people ride elephants. I want to ride on an elephant, Daddy."

"And me too," says Violet in her shrill voice.

"Oh, dear. I think you must have turned several pages at once in your book! I don't think there are wild elephants in Boulogne, or even in Paris. And we gave away India a couple of years ago, so we'll have to think of another place you can go."

"Alright," says Grace, not really listening now. "Can I put some pennies in The Laughing Policeman?"

This machine is Grace's favourite. It requires no skill; it is not necessary to manipulate a clumsy crane towards a heap of tawdry prizes; it does not involve flashing lights and odds stacked against the player; it is simple, unashamed fun and silliness. Of course, she'd like to put pennies in What the Butler Saw but Daddy says it's for grown-ups only and anyway, what the butler saw is not worth even a halfpenny. He saw nothing. Probably rather less than you can see in the shelters halfway down the pier stem after dark on a Saturday night. And certainly less than he and Vinny saw through a key-hole eons ago. Or he thinks he saw until a few days ago; now he cannot be so sure. It feels as if his mind is playing tricks.

"I should think so. If Uncle Benny has mended it," says Freddie. "It started misbehaving on Friday. The poor old Laughing Policeman sounded as if he was going to be violently sick. And I think he was breaking wind."

"Daddy!" squeals Grace, scandalised.

"What's breaking wind?" asks Violet.

Freddie makes a wet, flubbering sound with his lips. Both girls shriek with laughter.

"Freddie!" says Kathleen. "Don't teach them to be crude. That's Stan's influence, that is."

As Kathleen makes her way towards the cafe, Freddie digs into his pockets to find some coins. He looks around for the machine, but sees that it's not in its usual place.

"Oh! He's not here. He must still be in Uncle Benny's workshop," says Freddie. "So, I think the best thing is for you to go and help Mummy wipe the tables and things while I go and see what Benny is doing to PC Big Tummy. Off you go. Maybe we can make him laugh later?"

"Alright, Daddy," says Grace. She takes Violet by the hand and drags her reluctantly towards The Admiral Benbow where they can hear the clattering of tea cups and saucers.

Freddie makes his way between the rows of machines, flipping switches here and there to turn them on. More lights flicker; mechanisms whirr as they warm up. He unlocks the door to the pay kiosks for the Hispaniola and Skeleton Island. The spooky interior of the latter with its spongy floor, its distorting mirrors, rattling bones and ghostly shrieks and hoots is very popular, especially with little boys. The jostling group he saw earlier is waiting excitedly at the kiosk.

"Is it open now, Mister?" asks one. He is wearing a pair of tattered shorts that appear to be several sizes too large. He is clutching at himself in the way that little boys do when they need to answer a call of nature urgently.

"In a minute, son. Just waiting for the man who takes the money. Why don't you pop along to the toilet – over there, look – so that you don't wet yourself when the skeletons jump up out of their graves? You have to watch out for a really gruesome one called Josiah Maltby," says Freddie, adopting his best, spooky voice. "You'll know you're nearly there when you see a great big, crumbling gravestone leaning towards you, the moss and ivy hanging off it in wet bunches. On it are the words "*At rest until the day break and the shadows flee away*". Mysterious, ey? I'm sure this boy will save your place for you. If you still want to go."

The boy in the baggy shorts looks up, his eyes widening in anticipation of horrors to come. His hand is clutching hard at his nether regions.

"Really? Not sure wot you're on about, Mister, but alright, then," he says and dashes for the toilet. "Save my place, Tommy!" he bellows over his shoulder.

"Morning, Mr. Tanner," says a voice. "Sorry I'm a bit late. Overslept."

"Hello, Sam. Mmm, well, only a couple of minutes. You've got customers already. Going to be another busy day, by the looks of it."

"So I see! Right, boys, we'll have you in there in two shakes of a lamb's tail," says Sam, settling himself in the kiosk and installing his cash tray. "Prepare to be terrified out of your wits!"

"See you later, Sam," says Freddie.

"Let's hope they don't wet themselves, ey, Mr. Tanner?" whispers Sam. "I had enough of mopping up last week!"

Freddie chuckles. "All part of the joys of the job, Sam."

Sam takes entrance fees from the little boys, occasionally glancing at Freddie as he continues on his way towards the rear of the arcade where a couple of store rooms, the Pieces of Eight change booth and the workshop are situated. Freddie is surprised to see the door to the workshop is closed. Benny normally keeps it open because it is a confined space and, although it has a window looking across the Estuary, it can be hot and claustrophobic otherwise.

"Benny?" he calls, opening the door. "Have you fixed The Laughing Policeman?"

He swings the door open, takes a step into the little room and then freezes in surprise and embarrassment. As he might have realised with a little forethought, Benny is fixing something else.

FIFTEEN MEN ON THE DEAD MAN'S CHEST
13th August 1950

I caught Benny and a girl called Sandra in flagrante delicto one Sunday morning as I threw open the door to the workshop. I assumed he was mending The Laughing Policeman but the officer stood idly in his glass case, his head collapsed on his faded uniform. It seemed he was asleep on duty. The only fellow wielding a truncheon was Benny.

"What the..?" said Benny, looking over his shoulder. "Why don't yer knock before you open a door?"

"Well, I..." I was unable to speak. I couldn't see the object of his attentions properly at that point because Benny was leaning across her, his back to me. I didn't know who it was, not that it mattered then or later. What happened mattered, but she didn't.

The room was rich with the smells of coitus, cheap perfume and the oily innards of various machines, of which there were several in the process of repair. Odd cog wheels, levers, coin chutes and coils of wire were piled in a corner. Tools and bits of rag lay strewn across just about every horizontal surface except the one that the girl was occupying. A table-football machine was braced against the far wall under the window and she was on her back on that, her hands gripping the edge of the toughened glass of the top. It was just as well it was toughened, given the enthusiasm that Benny had brought to his movements. He had one foot braced on the machine behind him. The table-football made little squeaking noises. So did she.

He stopped. It seemed that nothing happened for a long time. I could hear the sea smacking the iron piles beneath us and the shrieks of the little boys in Skeleton Island. I was just able to see the girl's face twisting around to find out what was going on. Presumably, in her reverie, she had not heard what Benny had just said.

"Whassup? Come on, Benny!" she grunted.

Benny remained motionless for a few more moments; I suppose he was deciding what to do and waiting for me to back out of the door so that he could finish. But I didn't. I was transfixed by the scene in front of me. It was disgusting and intensely compelling all at the same time. Benny gave an exasperated gasp, took a step back and then bent forward to grab at his trousers which were around his ankles. He hoisted them up, levered himself inside them, buttoned them and then turned, squeezing through the narrow space between two machines.

"You stupid pillock, Tanner!" he hissed venomously into my face before elbowing past me. He stamped out of the room, slamming the door behind him.

The girl sat up, looking at me. I recognised her then as the daughter of the people who ran a kiosk near the little station. She had a thick mane of ginger hair and was very pretty, in a rather Golden Mile kind of way. Not surprisingly, given the circumstances, she put me in mind of Alice Jordan, the girl Vinny and I had seen through the key-hole and who later was killed in an air-raid.

Her blouse was undone. Her skirt had hitched up around her waist and she was still wearing her suspender belt and nylons. She didn't bother to try to hide herself.

"Ooh!" she whispered.

I turned towards the door, thinking to leave so that she could get herself properly dressed. But I didn't leave; as I say, I was greatly disturbed by the scene that was so suddenly and graphically presented before me. I suppose the fact that she didn't bother to hide herself; that clearly she had no moral scruples, was partly what made me do what I did. I put my hand to the door knob and then hesitated. I thought that if Kathy could cavort provocatively with Vinny, I could have some fun too. It wasn't a reasonable or a logical thing to think, but that's what happened.

I was sure I could hear Pa laughing somewhere.

I moved my fingers towards the door bolt. I smiled to myself, thinking that Benny should have locked the door. I pushed the bolt home and turned back to face the girl.

"Ooh!" she said again.

"Sandra, isn't it?"

"Yes," she said, flicking the ginger hair back out of her eyes. "And before you ask, I'm nineteen."

"So you say!"

I moved towards her through the narrow gap that Benny had just barged through.

"Who cares what her name is?" whispered Pa. "Or 'ow old she is. She's ready."

"I won't tell, promise," she smiled. "Come on!"

"But...you don't even know my name!"

"Yes, I do. You're the one married to that beautiful Kathleen in the café," she murmured, laughing at my observation and adjusting her nylons. "Freddie Tanner, ain'tcha?"

"That's right," I said.

"Well, it don't matter much anyway, these days. Look at all those blokes in the war. Away from home and their wives; havin' it off with French girls in barns by the roadside, they reckon. You know, where they stopped for a rest. Standin' up, mostly, my Uncle reckons. Knee-tremblers, they called it! Winning the war; comin' home covered in glory. Covered in something, anyway. What a load of horse droppings, I say?"

I should have sent the little whore packing, but I didn't. I moved to stand in front of her, my legs between her splayed thighs. I remembered Alice through the key-hole, which, of course, is not quite the same as Alice through the Looking Glass. Then I saw Vinny trying to pull off Kathy's blouse. I heard Pa grunting his approval.

"You're probably right," I said, moving my hand inside her blouse. "Italian girls, according to my brother. But I'm not away from home or in the war."

"So what? Who cares? Don't ask me to sort out your conscience!" She paused, letting me run my fingers across the solid orbs of her chest for a while. She shuddered, as if someone had walked over her grave.

"Cor, have a heart, Mr. Tanner!" She giggled and put one arm around my neck and, with the other hand, unbuckled my belt with practised alacrity.

So she finished what she'd started with Benny, with my astounded but enthusiastic assistance, right there in that grubby little room on top of a table-football game! Stan had talked of ignoring the mantelpiece but I couldn't do that, no matter the circumstances, which were hardly uplifting that morning. I couldn't keep my eyes off her face. It took on a curiously ugly beauty: her lips parted occasionally, a snake's mouth snatching a bug-eyed frog; her eyelids fluttered in a dance with easeful death; and the creamy softness of her throat, as she threw her head back, looked like a swan in the ecstasy of flight or a torpid descent to a water-logged death in the reed beds. It was difficult to tell.

It was the dream in the railway carriage made real; the sensations I wanted with Kathy but which she wouldn't permit. This girl, a wriggling, slippery snake of a thing, felt nothing like Kathy at all. She was small, compact and urgent. Kathy was deliciously voluptuous but more leisurely. But "leisurely" was not what I wanted.

Breathlessly, Sandra began to sing a song popular at the time: "If I knew you were comin', I'd have baked a cake!"

I couldn't help laughing. The little footballers were clattering furiously underneath us. Stanley Matthews was lurching backwards and forwards on his pivot, no doubt trying to attract the referee's attention towards the foul being played on top of the glass, just over his head.

If later I regretted my actions, and I did, at the time I was only too happy to do as this hungry young woman required. I began to realise why so many men like to have different women; I began, for the first time, to have just some inkling of what was driving Vinny and what had driven my father.

§

"Oi, next time you barge in on me like that, turn round and frog off again, will ya? I can't do it wiv an audience. Whassyer game any'ow? Some kind of...wossname, are yer? Watchin' people doin' it?" growled Benny as he came back into the workshop.

I had opened the window wider to get rid of the smell in the room and was watching the heaving, grey sea beneath us, although it wasn't that which was making me feel sick.

"Voyeur," I supplied. "No, of course not. How was I to know what you were doing?"

Benny grunted irritably. "What else would I be doin' wiv the door closed? Stickin' Penny Blacks in me stamp album? I told yer years ago about me list, didn't I? I've managed 'em all 'cept the nun and the red-head. Not much chance of the nun, I s'pose, although never say die; but I've 'ad me eye on that little Sandra fer a couple 'o weeks and this mornin', there she was. Bright and early and lively. So, I 'ad me list out an' me pencil stub behind me ear. A red-hot red-head. Know wot I mean? What would you do? No need ter answer that; I can work it out for mesself; look at the state of you."

I opened my mouth to speak, but couldn't find the words to acknowledge my own sordid behaviour. In fact, I was already having difficulty believing what I had done.

"Come ter think of it, since I didn't, well, finish the business, I s'pose it don't really count as a strike off me list, does it? Whadja reckon? Not that it matters, 'cos she'll be back. Lovely though, ain't she? Talk about Sanderson's Rocket!"

"Stephenson's," I said.

"Sanderson's, Stephenson's; who gives a damn? She's got pistons, s'all I know. So, where is she? I'm still an eager boiler-stoker, mate!"

"She went about five minutes ago," I said.

"Shame. Oh, well. Like I say, next time."

"I'm not sure I'm really very happy about you using the workshop like that, Benny. Could be bad for the business, if it got out."

Benny looked at me with his mouth open. He dropped his spanner on the bench with a thud.

"Do what? You're 'avin' me on, aintcha? You're off yer nut, yer know that? Don't come the high an' mighty with me, old son! What was you doin' after I left? Canasta or playin' table football, was it?"

I ignored his question and began looking at his workbench and the open backs of the machines he was repairing.

"What are you doing with this?" I held up the gearing and leverage for the little crane-grab. It was popular because the tawdry prizes — little pink dolls, packs of marbles and the like — attracted attention and, on the face of it, manoeuvring the grab using the wheels on the outside of the glass case seemed easy enough. It wasn't, of course, because the thing had to be sufficiently difficult to ensure that we made a profit.

Benny looked a bit shifty. "Just makin' a few adjustments."

"Why? What adjustments? It's working all right, isn't it?"

"Well..."

"I don't want you altering the odds on anything, Benny, is that clear? We make a good profit; people come back because they don't have the feeling they're being cheated," I said, again sounding pompous.

"You're a fine one to talk about cheatin' an' alterin' the odds, aintcha? All honest an' above-board, was it, with that tart just now?" Benny spat threw the window.

"Look, Benny..."

"No, Freddie, you bloody look. Tryin' to make out like butter wouldn't melt! Goin' on about the machines when that ain't the real issue, like. Wot we're talkin' about ain't what we're really talkin' about, again, is it? Woss got into you just recently? It don't matter if you won't admit it, 'cos it's written all over yer face. An' the inside o' yer pants too, probably. Most blokes'd be crowin' about it, but not you. Always the same, you. I thought you was s'posed to be the one with the...wossname...principles? You look like yer lost a 'alf crown and found a tanner, Tanner. Anyway, I can always go an' ask Sandra, can't I? You fink she'll be all coy about it?"

"No, I don't suppose so," I said.

"Too bloody right, she won't. In fact, she's probably tellin' every other little tart wot gets off the train right now. They'll be queuin' up, shortly. 'Ad yer thought about that? You'll have ter open a new attraction. "Tossin' at the South West of Treasure Island" or summat like that. Remember that one? Or how about "Hot Hispanic Whores of Hispaniola"? That's got a ring to it, don't yer reckon?"

I sighed. "I suppose I've been a bit of an idiot."

"Yeah, just a bit. All of us blokes are idiots, though, ain't we? An' it's my sis wot's goin' to be hurt if she finds out. I thought you two was s'posed to be true love and trust for ever more? Childhood sweethearts my rear end, then, is it? She don't deserve any of this, Freddie, an' you know that better than wot I do. I mean, if yer goin' to put it about, well, I can't stop yer an' it's nuffin' to do wiv me really, but maybe yer shouldn't be doin' it on yer own doorstep, so ter speak. You know, wiv yer wife only a few yards away."

I just stood looking at him, a feeling of utter hopelessness and sticky guilt overwhelming me. Benny leaned his back against his workbench and folded his arms.

"So now you feel like crap, yeah? Only got yersilf ter blame, mate. I mean, I know that Sandra's gaspin' for it an' she's got a tidy little body, but yer didn't have ter drop yer trousers, did ya?"

I shook my head, pathetically.

"I could probably fix it for yer. I mean, keep her quiet."

"How's that?"

"Because I know somethin' about her wot she'd like to be kept a secret, right? Found out by accident. All information comes in 'andy sooner or later. But it'll cost yer," grinned Benny, tapping the side of his nose.

"Cost me? You mean money? Is that what you mean?"

Benny laughed. "And always the bloomin' innocent, aint'cha? Well, I don't mean shirt buttons, my old son, do I?"

"I see. So now I'm being black-mailed by my own brother-in-law, is that it?" I snarled defensively. "I don't believe it. It's turning out to be quite a morning!"

"Well, you better believe it; it's what they calls practicalities, innit? Needs must an' all that. Yeah, you shoulda stayed in bed wiv yer lovely wife and then gone ter church. There's plenty wouldn't see wot yer problem is; beautiful woman like Kathleen. Whadja want to go humpin' a bony little tart for? Don't make no sense, does that. An' don't let's call it blackmail, Freddie, mate, it's an ugly word. Payment for services rendered sounds better. Do yer an invoice if yer want, for the taxman, like. More professional, that way."

I gave Benny what I hoped was a withering look but, of course, there wasn't too much I could say and I knew I had to put up with his mockery and vulgar, caustic sense of humour. I remained slumped against one of the machines, wiping my hand across my aching forehead as if that might somehow erase the ugliness of my actions.

"You know wot? I hadn't got yer down as a man who likes a bit on the side. But then I s'pose we're all human. Like I say, when it comes down to it, all us blokes is lead by the old trouser snake. 'Specially out 'ere," Benny chuckled, picking up his tools again.

"What do you mean?"

"Well, dunno that I'm too sure. Seems like different rules apply on the pier, somehow. Girls'll do it out here over the waves when they wouldn't dream of it at 'ome. Thass my experience. P'raps it's the ozone? Maybe they think they're on 'oliday and no one'll know when they do gits 'ome. I dunno. Anyway, you want my assistance wiv this, or not? 'Cos if yer do, I need to go an' sort Sandra right now, before she starts blabbin' it around."

I kicked at The Laughing Policeman. His body jerked upwards and he gave me a baleful glance before his head flopped back on his chest.

"Doesn't look as if I've got much bloody choice, does it? How much?"

"Three 'undred," he said, as if it were a tram fare. "An' give over criticisin' me work."

"What? How much? You must be joking!" I retorted. "And I'm not criticising the work, I just have...well, my doubts about why you're making adjustments, as you put it."

"If I can make a few bob extra with a bit o' tweakin', wot's it ter you? And, no, I ain't jokin'. You can afford it several times over. Three 'undred a year, that is; take it or leave it, thassa price for peace in our time at Pleasant Road," he smiled.

"*The blood-dimmed tide is loosed, and everywhere the ceremony of innocence is drowned; the best lack all conviction, while the worst are full of passionate intensity,*" I said, mostly under my breath.

"I ain't got a clue wot yer on about, Prof," snapped Benny. "Posh words ain't gonna help ya out of this one. Education's no friggin' use to yer now, if it ever was. So is it a deal?"

"It's not a deal," I said bitterly, "it's a reluctant submission. Go on and speak to Sandra and we'll talk about the other business some other time. You blackmailing swine."

"No need to be offensive," he said, as he went to the door. "You sticky-fingered adulterer."

SHAME AND LIES AND CRUELTY
27th August 1950

Needless to say, facing Kathy and the girls later that morning and, I thought, for the rest of my life was far more difficult than dealing with Benny's remarks and his outrageous demand for money. I paid him because I had no real option; he promised me that Sandra would be silent but, of course, that was not the end of it for me.

As I'm sure most men in that situation discover, it's the guilt that is so corrosive. It didn't do any good to tell myself that it was merely a moment of stupid weakness or erratic human behaviour; that I gave in to temptation and would never do it again; that it was just an impetuous lapse (just as Archie had spoken of in 1938) and not a covert relationship; or that, as Benny would have it, the curiously detached geography of the pier was to blame.

Sometimes I just tried to blank it from my mind; occasionally this worked for a few hours. At those times, it didn't exist, or it was in the same place as all the other fantasies about women that I experienced, in common with most men. Sometimes I begin to justify it to myself by recollecting the incident with Vinny, when I saw Kathy submit willingly to his wandering hands. I was certain it had happened. So, what I had done with Sandra was just a matter of getting even, a form of retribution. That's how I explained it to myself.

But more often, every time that Kathy smiled at me or took my arm or one of the girls wanted to sit on my knee, my mind's eye was visited by images of Sandra wriggling under me. When Kathy and I made love – and at this time, it was usually Kathy who took the initiative – I found myself avoiding her gaze, holding back and making comparisons in which she came off badly. And then I felt even guiltier that I was able to make the comparisons in the first place. Later, I realised that she was testing me. How we lie, even with our bodies.

After a couple of weeks of this torture there were still times when I could force the memory out of my head, but there were far more occasions when I thought it would be best to make a clean breast of it and take whatever the consequences might be. I didn't know, but I doubted that Kathy would wave her hand dismissively and suggest that it was of no more significance than knocking over a bottle of milk.

"Is something wrong, Freddie?" she asked one Sunday night after we'd been in bed some time. The street light gave the bedroom a pallid glow; I could see that she was lying on her back, staring up at the ceiling.

I wondered about pretending to be asleep, but thought better of it. "What do you mean?"

"You know what I mean. You hardly talk to us and when you do, you seem angry all the time; you never sit still; wandering about for no reason or you're in The Minerva or off on the pier or somewhere every day when you don't need to be. I mean, when it's Bernard's day or Stan's."

I coughed nervously. Somewhere down on the seafront, a voice yelled coarsely. Another voice, in my head, was urging me to tell her the truth. But I couldn't. "Well, I'm a bit worried about the cash flow," I said. "I need to keep a very close eye on everything and everybody; that's why."

"What do you mean? You haven't said anything." She turned on her side to face me. The glimmering street light picked out her features as if she was graveyard statuary.

"I didn't want to worry you. I think someone's stealing from the tills. Or a till," I replied, trusting that this topic would divert her attention from the real issue, little realising that it was about to drop me in a pit. "And I think Benny's fixing the machines so he can siphon off some of the coins. He as good as admitted it the other day."

"What? My own brother is cheating us? I find that very hard to believe. Are you sure or is this just another of your fantasies?"

"Well, yes, reasonably sure. I'm sorry; that's why I've kept quiet, because he's your brother. I didn't want to upset you."

"If I'm upset, it's not because of that," she whispered.

I ignored the remark and kept talking. "Trouble is, I'm not a mechanic, so I can't quite pin down what engineering jiggery-pokery he's up to. You know, adjusting the levers or the time controls and things. That's why I have to watch every move."

"Mmm, I see," she murmured. "And the tills?"

"Well, actually, they're all alright, except Skeleton Island."

"Sam?"

"Yes, looks like it, although that's hard to believe as well. Only recently, though."

Kathy was silent for a while. "Maybe that's not so hard to believe," she said at last, very quietly.

"Why? I thought we could trust Sam," I said.

"I hope we can, Freddie." Kathy drew in a long shuddering breath. "He knows something; something you'd rather keep quiet...so he thinks he has a kind of...what is it? Immunity...is that the word? Now he thinks he can cheat us. Perhaps that's also the case with Benny?"

"What?" I said, my heart sinking as I recollected that morning when Sam had watched me going towards the workshop.

"Sam came to me two weeks ago to say he'd seen you go into the workshop; he saw Benny come out, adjusting his trousers and looking like thunder. Then a bit later, he saw that kid Sandra come out, looking like the cat that got the cream."

Icicles fell into my pyjama collar, even though it was August. "Oh? Ah, well, yes, I remember. When I opened the door, I saw them, well, you know, doing it. I was very angry. I gave Benny a piece of my mind and then, well...the girl got dressed and left as well."

"Mmm. The girl left as well? Immediately?"

"Yes."

"But this is very unusual, Freddie, isn't it? It's not a brothel we're running, even though we employ my brother. I mean, why didn't you come and tell me straight away, or perhaps later that night? Why would you say nothing at all about something like that?"

"Well, I suppose because we were busy, it must have slipped my mind," I said, knowing as I said it, that it sounded pathetic.

Kathy sat up in bed and punched at the eiderdown. "Slipped your mind? What, that Benny and some tart were f...fornicating in his workshop? That happens every morning, does it? I don't think so, Freddie!"

"Well..." I began, hopelessly.

Kathy's voice began to take on a shrill, accusatory tone. "And when he'd finished with her, you had a turn, is that it? Your own bit of...of...jiggery-pokery? Adjusting your levers? And then you gave the ginger cat the cream?"

"I think you're misinterpreting things," I said, more in hope than any expectation that my response would be believed, and amazed at Kathy's sudden apparent ability with metaphor.

"I don't think so, Freddie. She didn't leave immediately, according to Sam. Why would Sam lie? Oh, God! How could you? How could you, after all these years? There's never been anyone else since we were kids! What was it you said to me once? *Ah, love, let us be true to one another*? From one of your poems, I suppose. What kind of truth is this, then?"

"Well, what about you and Vinny?" I said.

"What? Vinny? What's he got to do with anything? Have you gone mad? What are you talking about?"

"I saw you with him on the pier. Kissing and fumbling."

"Are you serious? You're talking nonsense. More fantasy. You must know that? Oh, God! Freddie! How could you? You're not denying it?"

I took a deep breath. "No, I'm not denying it. I'm so sorry, Kathy, so sorry. I don't know what else to say. I just...well, you know, things have not been quite right for me in bed recently, and...and well, I saw you and Vinny. With my own eyes. So I suppose I thought..."

Kathy interrupted me, jumping out of bed, somehow shouting and sobbing at the same time.

"What kind of a fool do you think I am, Freddie? Simple Kathleen is it? It's alright, she won't know what's going on? Well, she knows this time, don't you worry. Vinny? Vinny! For Heaven's sake, Freddie, you must know you're talking complete rubbish? Crazy stuff? Maybe you should think about seeing Dr. Marshall?" And with that she began crying uncontrollably until eventually she stumbled out of the room and went downstairs.

Later the next day, when I was out, she took herself and the girls off to Archie's place in Chalkwell Avenue. She left a brief note – handwriting was never her forte, of course – to say that she intended to stay there until she had decided what was best. But she would not look after The Admiral Benbow any longer, since that would put us in close proximity, so the partners should find someone else to manage it. The note said I had to advise Stan and Bernard of her resignation from the job. She didn't care who her successor was, she wrote, as long as it did not involve the "ginger slut" Sandra.

I didn't know what to do. I couldn't seem to think clearly about events, except that I wouldn't need to give Benny any more money. Even more peculiar was that I felt numb; I should have been distraught, weeping and wailing in despair: I had been unfaithful to my wife in a disgraceful way and she had left our home with our two daughters. Some men commit suicide under such circumstances but I was unable to feel any real emotion at all. It was as if something inside me had been cut off; disconnected.

But that numbness soon went and was replaced with a terrifying anxiety. I felt afraid and ill at ease even in broad daylight. Darkness made things far, far worse. At night I had to lock all the doors, push chairs under door handles and I nailed up some windows. I hid under the bed.

THINGS FALL APART; THE CENTRE CANNOT HOLD
September 1950

"Bit of a mess, then, ain't it?" says Stan. "I don't understand what he was playin' at with that floozy. Now look what's 'appened."

"You of all people should know what he was playin' at," answers Bernard. "In fact, he probably got the idea from you."

"Don't be bloody daft! And don't try an' blame me. Anyway, I'm a free agent; I ain't married. He is." Stan bangs his glass down on the table for emphasis.

Bernard rubs his jaw thoughtfully. "True, I suppose. Well, I don't know what to think. He has been a bit odd these last few months, sometimes. Anyway, who are we goin' to find to replace Kathleen at the Benbow? I mean, she's the centre of attraction. People come back askin' after 'er; wantin' 'er to make their ferretin' pot of tea! 'Scuse my Swedish."

"I dunno, but I'll tell you who asked me yesterday if the job was available – the ginger floozy!"

"You are jokin'? Sandra or whatever she's called?" Bernard replied, a look of disbelief on his face.

"The very one. The carrot-topped tart. Terrific figure on 'er though, I'll give 'er that. She'd bring in the clientele alright, but it wouldn't be families lookin' fer a cuppa! No, no. I'll ask around. We'll find someone. I'm more worried about Freddie, though, to be honest. I ain't seen 'im fer days. What about you? I mean, maybe he's opted out of it an' all? Like he can't cope with life any more. So maybe it's not just Kathleen we 'ave to replace." Stan finishes his pint and begins fumbling in his jacket for money, for it is his round. "Same again?"

"Yes, thanks."

While Stan is buying another round, Bernard slumps back in his chair. He had wanted to tell his partners that he'd decided to step down; he's had enough and now that he's in his sixties, he'd like to retire and spend more time in his garden. But, as ever in life, events have overtaken his plans. He can hardly retire now, leaving Stan entirely in the lurch. He suspects that Stan may be right: that

Freddie too cannot any longer be relied upon to pull his weight in the business. He feels a wave of annoyance and resentment well up inside him.

"Here we are," says Stan. "Cheers. 'Ave you seen Freddie at all?"

"Thanks; cheers; 'appy days by the seaside! Well, I've bin to the house three times but he won't let me in. I know he's in there alright, the stupid little bugger – pardon my vulgarity – but he won't open the door. I was shoutin' through the letter box at him."

"What's 'is game, d'you reckon? Hidin'?"

"I don't know. Maybe."

"So I could be right, then?" Stan sucks at his beer pensively. "It's both of them gone A.W.O.L., not just her? Did yer manage to speak to 'im through the letter box?"

"No, but I know he's there. Definite. From what I can see, the place looks like a bomb's 'it it. Kathleen'd 'ave a fit," Bernard replies.

"Maybe not," grunts Stan. "Maybe she don't give a tinker's cuss no more; left 'im to stew in 'is own juice."

Bernard looks thoughtful. "Well, women are bloody funny creatures, we all know that, but I don't think so. Kathleen won't 'ave stopped lovin' 'im. But he's hurt her and she can't understand that; probably can't even begin to fathom it out, poor girl. I'm just wonderin' if..."

"Maybe I should go along there an' try to get him to open the door?" Stan says, but without much conviction.

"You could, but I don't think it'll do much good. We're his business partners – both of us – an' he knows he's causin' us aggravation, so he don't want to speak to either of us. But, well, he might speak to Archie Soper, especially if he thinks the bloke's got a message from Kathleen."

§

At first, Kathleen seems opposed to her father going to speak to Freddie, but when Archie points out firmly that some communication is probably better than none and that Grace and Violet also have to be considered, Kathleen reluctantly gives way.

"But don't go making any promises, Dad," she asserts. "I don't want to see him at the moment and I'm not ready to forgive."

"Meaning you might be one day?" asks Archie, going to fetch his cap and bicycle clips.

"Meaning I am not able just now to forgive him the terrible thing he has done to me. I don't know yet whether I ever can."

"I see," says Archie, fighting with his trouser turn-ups.

"It would be one thing if he really had found a different true love," Kathleen says, sniffling, "but he hasn't. He's been with a cheap slut. It's so humiliating."

"Yes," says Archie, looking Kathleen in the eye, "we all suffer humiliation in life. Sometimes we have to rise above it."

It takes Archie only fifteen minutes of brisk pedalling along the Esplanade to reach Pleasant Road. He leans his bicycle against the front wall and knocks briskly on the door, putting his face close to its panel of reeded glass. There is no response, although, as Bernard had said, he's sure Freddie is there because he senses movement against the light coming in at the back from the scullery window.

"Freddie? It's Archie! Open the door, there's a good chap?" Archie glances around him, certain that the neighbours are watching. On cue, Mrs Horsfall opens her front door a few inches.

"Mr. Soper! Good morning! Not interfering; but just to let you know he's there alright. I heard him banging about a while ago. Actually, I don't think he's been outside for several days – unless he goes at night."

"Thanks. I'll keep trying. I think it might be best if he didn't hear us talking about him, though," says Archie in his customary forthright manner.

"I see," says Mrs Horsfall, closing her door again, "just trying to be helpful, that's all."

"Freddie? Freddie?" Archie whispers loudly through the letter-box. "I'd like to talk to you about Kathleen. About...Kathy...and the girls too, of course. Please open the door?"

There is a pause during which Archie can hear distant squeals coming from the rides in The Kursaal. Suddenly, a bolt is shot and the door opens. Freddie steps back into the little hallway.

"You'd better come in, then, I suppose," he says quietly.

Archie steps across the threshold and closes the door behind him. A stale smell of unwashed clothing, sweat and rotting food assaults his nose. Freddie appears not to have washed or shaved for days. There is a large orange stain on the front of his shirt. He holds his right hand, which is wrapped carelessly in a grubby, bloodied tea-towel, across his chest.

"Good God, Freddie!" says Archie. "What the heck happened?"

"Oh, I think I...cut myself trying to open a tin of soup," says Freddie, sounding as if he's having difficulty remembering the event. "Yes, tomato soup." He points at the orange stain.

"Let me look at it."

Freddie takes a step backwards. Instinctively, Archie realises that his son-in-law is apprehensive and nervous; frightened even, like a trapped animal.

"It's alright, Freddie! I'm not going to hurt you, old man. Just let me look at the hand. Tell you what, let's go in the other room, where there's a bit more light?"

"Alright," mutters Freddie, allowing Archie to steer him by the elbow into the back parlour. Momentarily, Archie regrets his suggestion. The smell is far worse here than in the hall. There is hardly a clear surface but rather a chaos of clothing, encrusted crockery, old newspapers, a loaf of mouldy bread, unopened letters, children's toys and dozens of empty beer bottles.

Archie removes the tea-towel from Freddie's hand. He has cut one finger quite badly, but it's not a hospital case.

"When did this happen, Freddie?"

"Not sure. This morning, maybe? Sorry. Ha! Confused a bit," comes the reply.

"So I see," says Archie, affecting a chuckle. The wound does indeed appear to be fairly recent and is not septic. Archie washes it in the scullery sink and then roots around in the bathroom at the back. He finds a bottle of Dettol and some clean lint. He dresses the wound as best he can, taking the opportunity to try to demonstrate to Freddie that he's there to help, not to pass judgment.

"Are you eating, old fellow?"

Freddie smiles wanly. "When I can get the bloody tins open, Archie."

"And are you getting some rest alright? I mean, managing to sleep? Difficult time for all of us, Freddie. You need to sleep. I suppose you'll say you manage to sleep when you can find the bedroom?"

Archie intends his comment as a jocular remark, a kind of ice-breaker, but as he says it, he wonders whether it's closer to the truth than he supposes.

"Yes, something like that," says Freddie, wincing as Archie tries to secure his arm in a make-shift sling. "I usually sleep down here. Don't like the bedroom. I sleep a lot, actually. Easier that way."

"To sleep, perchance to dream?" responds Archie, not really meaning it as a question.

"I can do without the dreams, as a matter of fact," Freddie mutters.

Archie looks him in the eyes. "Troubling, are they?"

Freddie doesn't say anything, but looks about the room nervously, as if expecting to see something terrifying.

"What's the matter, old son? Something bothering you?"

"Of course. To start with I didn't seem to feel much, but now I can't stop crying. I miss Kathy; you know how much I care for her...and the girls too. And I keep seeing...well, I suppose I should offer you some tea?" says Freddie. "But, I don't know where it is...I don't know how..."

Archie finishes fiddling with the sling, gives Freddie a reassuring tweak of the shoulder and then returns the things he's used to the bathroom cupboard.

"That's alright, Freddie. Don't worry. I'll make some in a mo. Let's have a bit of a sit first, shall we?"

He encourages Freddie to sit in one of the armchairs by the fireplace. He sits in the other one. He decides to say nothing initially, to see whether Freddie will open the conversation which both of them know has to take place.

"How's...how's Kathy?" Freddie asks eventually. "And the girls? I do miss them...I...it's not right when they're not here."

Archie looks at Freddie again. His eyes look red, as if he has indeed been crying, as he says. Tears are appearing now, presumably at the mention of Kathleen's name.

"They're fine. Well, you know, like I say, it's difficult times but they are healthy if somewhat emotional. That's to be expected."

"Yes." Freddie covers his face with his free hand. "Oh, dear God in Heaven!"

Archie leans forward and pats him on his knee. "Look, Freddie, don't upset yourself. I'm sure we can sort this out, given time. You aren't the first husband to...well, you know...and you won't be the last. Time's a great healer."

"I hope so," sobs Freddie, "but Time has confounded me just now."

"Look, I'm not going to beat about the bush," Archie says, "that's not my way, as you know. I know that you care about Kathleen; you always have. I don't think that's in question. But you've hurt her badly, you understand that, don't you?"

"Of course."

"Good, well, that's a start. And I'm not here to tear you off a strip or something; I've strayed too in my time. Most men are bloody weak when it comes down to it, I'm afraid."

"I didn't think I was, but..."

"I didn't think you were either, Freddie, as a matter of fact. You and Kathleen have always had something special between you, so...well...apart from the obvious; I mean, the availability of the girl, I suppose...what happened? You see, I'd have thought that you'd swat any such offer or temptation aside with no difficulty at all. Has something gone wrong between you and Kathleen?"

Freddie sighs. "Not really, Archie. I...well, I suppose I'm a bit bored in the bedroom, you know, but...no. I love her as I always did."

"Bedroom boredom happens to most of us, Freddie," grins Archie. "Certain time of life, or time of marriage. But it's not necessarily a good enough reason for doing what you did."

"No, I know. And then...well, I was feeling angry with her too; jealous, I suppose would be a better word. She's not quite as holier-than-thou as she makes out, you see. I know what she's been up to. I saw."

Archie frowns, not certain how to respond to this odd twist in Freddie's remarks. "Jealous? You're jealous because of what? What are you saying? You're not making too much sense, old man; you mean she's done something she shouldn't? Is that what you mean?"

"I think so. You see, I saw her and Vinny kissing and, well, fumbling at each other. He was squeezing her...her breasts. He had his hand up her skirt. It was horrible!" He winces at the memory.

Archie says nothing for a few moments, his mouth open in astonishment.

"I can't quite...let me get this straight, Freddie. You're accusing Kathleen of...canoodling with Vinny?"

"Yes, I saw them. It could be more than canoodling, for all I know, Archie, don't you see? May have progressed by now."

"Progressed? But...when was this occasion; when you saw them, may I enquire?" asks Archie, rather stiffly.

"Not sure; you know, confused. Er, about three weeks ago, I think?"

"Three weeks ago? So quite recently then? This summer?"

"Oh, yes, quite recently. Just before I, well...consorted with Sandra; I think it's why I did it," Freddie murmurs.

Archie snorts. "Consorted? Well, it's an interesting word for it, Freddie. But, well, I still have great difficulty in rationalising what you seem to be suggesting. I'm sorry to keep repeating the question, but, well, you say you saw Vinny and Kathleen together, about three weeks ago? And that's why you...went with Sandra, or whatever she's called?"

"Yes! I'm not a fool, Archie, I know what I saw." Freddie bangs his left hand on the arm of his chair to make his point. "He was on about Italy; the girls in Salerno or somewhere like that."

Archie looks at the young man opposite him; takes in again the unkempt appearance, the rather wild eyes, the hand twisting the shirt-front; the indescribable mess; the nonsense he's talking. With sudden clarity, he understands that his son-in-law needs help.

"Freddie, I don't think so. Your brother Vinny was killed when two torpedoes hit his ship in the English Channel in 1943. HMS Charybdis, in October, I seem to recall. Seven years ago. Somewhere you have the official letter. We all attended his Memorial Service, didn't we? You know, because they never recovered his body; or hundreds of others, come to that. Terrible. He's been dead for years, Freddie. The last time Kathleen saw him, she'd have been about fourteen."

"Vinny's like Pa; they like them young..."

"Listen to me! Vinny's dead, Freddie. He's been dead a long time. You can't have seen him three weeks ago. Except, perhaps, in your head...?"

Freddie looks at Archie in stupefied disbelief and then begins crying; great, heaving sobs welling up from deep somewhere inside him.

BOOK FOUR

STRINGS OF BROKEN LYRES

1950 - 1953

THIS TEMPEST IN MY MIND
Late September 1950

As he cycles slowly back to Chalkwell Avenue along the Esplanade, the pavements and beaches thronged with trippers enjoying what could be the last fair day of the year, Archie Soper realises that he has quite a task ahead of him. All her life, his daughter Kathleen has been described as "simple": some people have employed the term pejoratively but most have meant that she is unaffected and straightforward. In a world increasingly given to hypocrisy, guile and various forms of illusion and deceit, in Archie's view, this has been a commendable characteristic.

"There's no side or pretence with Kathleen," one of Archie's work-colleagues had once said, pretending not to be looking at the girl's breasts straining the buttons on her school blouse. "You know where you are with her; she always says what she thinks. Quite alarming, in one so young," he had said, licking his lips.

It was true when she was a girl, thinks Archie and it remains true now. But that simplicity, that tendency to assess a situation intuitively, to make a decision or adopt a determined position might now be the very thing that will hinder any repair of her marriage, assuming that she wishes it repaired. Archie finds it hard to believe that she will not, sooner or later. He can see that Kathleen will have to be flexible; will have to accept something she'd rather not accept and shift her position. Compromise; forgiveness; understanding. Dogmatism will not work. Pragmatism might. Most difficult of all for Kathleen, she may have to try to understand that Freddie's actions were almost certainly not those of a sexual opportunist or a scheming adulterer. Archie's visit to his daughter's hovel of a marital home and his conversation with Freddie have brought him to the belief that the latter's erratic behaviour and his apparent inability to distinguish reality from fantasy all point to a slide into some kind of mental instability.

But whatever Kathleen may or may not be encouraged to embrace where her errant husband is concerned, there is little doubt that Freddie needs help immediately. Archie decides that he will phone his office and arrange some emergency compassionate leave and that he will return to Pleasant Road when he has spoken to Kathleen. Freddie ought not to be left alone. He tells Mrs Horsfall simply that Freddie is having a "bit of a problem coping on his own" and that he'll come back later. Mrs Horsfall purses her lips and remarks that it's the little girls she feels sorry for because, "They're always the ones who suffer in this situation".

Archie wonders whether he should call a doctor but he is aware that this could initiate action by other authorities that could result in Freddie being swept into some form of supervisory care. Archie doesn't feel that the circumstances merit that – or at least, not yet – and some instinct is telling him that Kathleen holds the key to Freddie's return to normality. As he has anticipated, however, she is not especially receptive to his observations later that afternoon.

"He's capable of picking up a broom or doing the washing up," she says when Archie refers to the squalor of the house in Pleasant Road.

"Yes, Kathleen, I know, but that's not quite what I mean. It's out of control; he's out of control, don't you see? The place is filthy. So is he; unwashed, unshaven and stinking. He won't leave the house. He won't answer the door. Now, that's not because he doesn't know how to deal with any of it or because he can't be bothered but because he seems to have lost track of time, of reality and the understanding that these things are necessary. I don't think he should be left on his own at the moment."

"I don't really know what you mean, Dad. Maybe he's just feeling sorry for himself? You know, wallowing in self-pity or something? And I'm not running over there as if everything's alright just because he's putting on an act; pretending to be off his trolley to get me back, is it?"

"No, Kathleen, I don't think that's it at all. Something's happened to him, don't you see? He's not making sense is he? All that twaddle about you and Vinny, for example."

"You think that's a sign of him losing his marbles, then? More likely he was drunk again."

"Well, it's possible; I'll not argue with you about that. And it's certainly true that there were a lot of empty bottles everywhere. Perhaps we need to get him off that."

Kathleen sniffs again. "There you are, then. I just think it's a man in a panic, trying to come up with an excuse for...for adultery!" Kathleen fumbles for her handkerchief and dabs at her eyes.

"If he was entirely stable, he'd have come up with a more plausible excuse than the one he did come up with, wouldn't he? Since we all know that Vinny is long gone?" says Archie.

Benny comes clumping into the kitchen where they are sitting. "Orlright?"

"Good day?" asks Kathleen, sniffing even louder than before.

"Usual. Stan's got some woman from The Minerva servin' at The Benbow but she's ugly and she's slow and she's bloody rude to the punters. Why doncha come back, Kathleen? We need yer!" He flops down with a sigh onto one of the kitchen chairs.

"I said what my feeling is at the moment," says Kathleen. "I resigned. That's that."

"Stan and Bernard will be 'appy to re-employ yer, guaranteed," says Benny.

"I've been to see Freddie, Benny," says Archie, determined to keep the central issue in the spotlight. "In my opinion, there's something wrong; he's not well. I'm just trying to explain that to Kathleen."

"He's made his bed, so he has to lie on it," she mutters, remembering ruefully a conversation at Paglesham some years ago – a lifetime ago.

"Whadja mean, Dad? 'Ere, any tea on the go?"

"I'll make some," says Kathleen, pleased to have the opportunity to have something to do. "There's hot water."

"I mean his behaviour seems to me to be irrational. He doesn't always make sense; he admits to troubling dreams and...well...I suppose we'd have to say hallucinations. Dreams are one thing; we all get those, but he told Kathleen he'd seen her kissing Vinny on the pier when we all know the man's been dead for seven years. He told me the same thing with great certainty this afternoon."

"Blimey," says Benny. "Well, I'm not that surprised. He has been a bit odd fer a while."

"Really?" asks Archie. "In what way?"

"I dunno. Difficult to pin down, like. He was definitely odd on that day...well, you know...when all this started. But before that, one afternoon he said he'd had a cuppa with his Ma in The Benbow. I thought he was jokin'; but he wasn't; he meant it."

"Excuses," says Kathleen, putting the teapot and some cups on the table. "Twaddle and pretending. And too much beer."

"I don't think so," responds Archie. "Well, maybe too much beer; I just said to Kathleen, Benny, that there were certainly a lot of empty bottles lying about over there."

"Well, then," Kathleen mutters. "First stages of alcoholism, perhaps."

Benny pours some tea. "You mean he's off his trolley?"

"I think he needs help," answers Archie.

"Look, Dad," Kathleen interjects, "he knows what he's done. Adultery; simple as that. So all this about Vinny and hallu...hallucinating and stuff is all just a smoke-screen, isn't it? I mean, what does he take me for? Take us for? Idiots?"

"I'm not sure he has the ability just at the moment, to take us for anything, Kathleen. To tidy the vernacular, the poor man doesn't know his rear-end from his elbow; or now from then from before the war."

Benny chuckles. Kathleen slaps her hand on the table. "If we're going to talk like that, Dad, then...well, pardon me, but he's talking crap. He always has, hasn't he? Mostly it's been educated crap so we haven't been too sure. You know, quoting this poem, that poem; on about this or that from bloody Shakespeare. It's all fog. Or...or...ice cream words that melt in front of your eyes. Or like meringue; you know, covering up the real thing. Perhaps he should have been a solicitor, like they used to say."

Archie and Benny look with amused surprise at Kathleen.

"Yes, really! He once told me solicitors make a good living from talking educated crap."

"It sounds funny when you say it, Sis," grins Benny.

Kathleen waves his comment aside. "I mean it. I'm sure he's making it up, all this about Vinny, rather then admitting to...having it away with that girl."

"No, Kathleen; just like Benny says, he's not making it up, he believes it; about Vinny, I mean. That's the problem, pure and simple. Or it's as complicated as you want to make it. So, he didn't admit it...about the girl...to you, you mean? Would it help if he did?"

Kathleen looks at her father. "It might be a start. He didn't deny it. Not quite the same as admitting it, is it?"

" 'Ere we go again with bloody words!" says Benny. "Didn't deny it is the same as admittin' it, ain't it? Whassa difference?"

"A lot of difference, so far as I'm concerned," retorts Kathleen.

"I don't see it. Same bloody thing, innit?" asks Benny, slurping his tea.

"Did he apologise?" asks Archie.

"Yes. He said he was sorry."

Benny gives a sigh of exasperation. "Well, if he said he was sorry, then he's admitted it, ain't he? What more d'ya want from him? You want 'im to grovel, say it all over and over again 'undreds of times an' then eat razor blades, eh?"

Kathleen manages a smile. "Something like that, I suppose. I'm a woman."

"We noticed. Anyway, what sorta help are you on about, Dad?" asks Benny.

"I'm no expert. Well, maybe psychiatric help, I suppose. But, in my opinion, we ought to be cautious about involving the authorities just yet, so I'm going to go over there and stay with him for a bit to see what's really what. Then we can decide. And I mean "we" Kathleen because I'd like to think you'll help with this. In fact, it's you who should be deciding anyway, not me. But if you won't help him, I will. He is sorry, very sorry and beside himself with remorse. If you want my opinion – maybe you don't, but I'm giving it anyway – he did what he did when he wasn't fully in control of his senses. Quite simply, his mind is not functioning properly. What's more, he still loves you as ever, he says, and now he needs our help. Your help, though, mostly."

Kathleen looks at her father, her brow furrowed with anger and anxiety. She screws at her pinafore with trembling fingers. "Fog," she snaps dismissively. "Meringue. Ice cream. Utter crap. I think he needs to look at himself in the mirror."

"Sounds like he 'as been," grunts Benny, "in Skeleton Island. All those distorting ones wot we've got."

"Quite so," says Archie. "That's the most sensible and perceptive thing you've said since about 1936."

"Thanks, Dad."

§

In the end, it is a conversation with Grace that prompts Kathleen to take a more sympathetic view.

"Girls?" she calls on the following Saturday afternoon. "It's a lovely day; just like summer, rather than autumn. Shall we go swimming?"

"Yes!"

"But the tide's right out, so, what do you want to do: the swimming pool along the front or a walk out on the hard to the Ray Sands to swim out there?"

"We don't like the swimming pool, Mummy," says Grace. "It smells funny. And some girls in my class say there are bits of razor blade in the shute."

"And by the changing rooms it's all mucky and boys get their willies out," adds Violet. "And they wave them about."

"Oh, dear," replies Kathleen casually, not wanting to say what she is thinking, which is that most boys seem to continue waving their willies about when they become men. "I think the smell you're talking about is the chlorine, Grace. To stop the germs. It is very strong, isn't it?"

"Because people wee-wee in the pool," asserts Violet gravely, "Pamela told me. So it must be true. Pamela knows about everything."

"Right, so, you'd prefer to go out to the Ray, then?"

"Yes," they chorus in unison. "Is Daddy coming too?"

"No."

"Oh, but why not?"

Half an hour later, they trot past the Crowstone and begin tip-toeing gingerly across the pebbles and shells at the beginning of the hard, a walkway running at right angles to the beach. Old railway sleepers have been set in the mud to make an edge for the path and to prevent the crushed cockle shells from being washed away by the tides.

There are dozens of people making their way out towards the channel of water they call Leigh Swatch, perhaps half a mile from the shore, for there it is possible to swim, even at low tide. Progress is slow for most, especially those with naked feet, for the sharp edges of the shells and the barnacles encrusting the old sleepers are vicious.

"Ouch!" squeals Grace. "Feels like razor blades here too! I wish I had my old plimsolls."

"And me too!" echoes Violet.

"Well, they're at Pleasant Road, I'm afraid. You'll just have to look where you're going and tread gently. Not far now," says Kathleen.

Grace considers this for a moment or two. "Why can't we go and get them, Mummy? Why are we at Grandad's? And why is Grandad at our house? We don't understand."

"And I want my other teddy," whines Violet.

Kathleen sighs. "Look, girls, perhaps we'll talk about it later. Not now. We can have a lovely swim, now, see?"

Coming off the end of the hard, all three of them lower themselves into the brown water, warmed as the incoming tide has sluiced it over the Estuary's mud-flats, basking in the afternoon sun. It is only a few feet deep but nevertheless, Kathleen grips Violet's hand. Grace doggy-paddles the few yards to the other side of the Swatch and pulls herself onto the Ray Sands, dripping and glistening like a small seal. Kathleen helps Violet to flounder and splash her way there too and they all sit on the damp sand, its surface still ridged by the last ebb tide.

"Now, we must watch the water there," says Kathleen, nodding towards the Swatch. "The tide is coming in fast; we don't want to be trapped on the wrong side. Otherwise Uncle Bernard will have to launch the lifeboat to come and rescue us."

"I want to go in the lifeboat!" shrieks Violet. She jumps up and down in excitement and then notices that her feet are sinking into the sand. She stamps around in a circle, watching as the previously firm sand seems to liquefy and turn to a wobbling jelly.

"Mummy! Look! Why is it doing that?"

"I don't know, dear; that is strange, isn't it? It was very hard just now," says Kathleen, looking puzzled.

"I think her jumping about is making the water come to the top," announces Grace, with the air of someone explaining a very obvious matter to a simpleton. "So now it's not what it was when she started. It changed; more water than sand or mud. Miss Freeman says that things aren't always what you think they are or what they seem to be. They start out one way and then they change."

Kathleen looks at her daughter and smiles to herself. The child sounds just like her father, years ago.

"Really?" asks Kathleen, thinking that Miss Freeman sounds like a right know-it-all. "I don't remember doing stuff like that when I was at school."

"Like the pier, Mummy, look," Grace points off to her right. The pier, a mile or so distant, is a tracery of black girders, set firmly in the mud at the shore end and seeming to dance on the shimmering water at the far end. "Because it's a long way away, it looks tiny and like matchsticks, doesn't it? And one end looks as if it's floating. But we know it's not really, so it's not what it seems to be from here."

"You're a clever little girl, Grace," smiles Kathleen. "Just like..."

"I like it on the pier," announces Violet, continuing to create quicksand under her feet. "It's big, not tiny. Not matchsticks!"

Kathleen wonders whether the pier and all that it has come to represent in her marriage and their lives could indeed now be regarded as matchsticks. From this perspective it certainly seems to be a flimsy, rickety construction on questionable foundations. And of course, as Freddie himself pointed out one day, the whole place is a palace of illusions, candy floss and temporary, crude pleasure, all bought with money.

"It has no serious purpose," he had said. "And when it did have, during the war, it was a conduit for the trappings of war and the corpses that war spews up. Now youths lean over the rail to spew up sour beer. Their freedom and right to vomit and fornicate in the shelters – that's what hundreds of thousands died for."

"Mummy," says Grace, cautiously. "Did you and Daddy have an argument?"

"Well, yes, I suppose so."

"Violet and I would like you to make it up, Mummy. We want to go home. It's a long way to go to school from Grandad's," says Grace.

"You could always change schools," replies Kathleen, although she knows that the girls are not likely easily to embrace that idea.

"No, thank you. Grandad says that Daddy is not very well. Is that why he's gone to our house?"

"Yes. That's what Grandad thinks."

"Is Daddy not very well?"

"I'm not sure about that, Grace," mutters Kathleen.

"But, Mummy, if Daddy's not very well, or even if he might not be very well, shouldn't we be there too? It's not Grandad's job to look after Daddy, is it?" Grace looks at Kathleen searchingly.

"Well...you see, I think Grandad may be mistaken."

"He isn't usually, Mummy, that's what you always say. And sometimes people need other people's help and stuff – that's why I want to be a doctor when I grow up – but mostly they need their husbands or their wives or their children to be with them if they feel rotten, don't they?"

Kathleen looks at her daughter, assimilating the astute observations of a mere child. "It's good to have an ambition, Grace. I'm sure you'll make a wonderful doctor one day. Come on, we need to get back," she announces, suddenly getting to her feet.

"To our house?" shrills Violet. "Oh, goody!"

"No, I mean back to the hard over there, look. The water's a lot deeper suddenly; quickly, now."

"It'll be alright, Mummy. You carry Violet and I'll hold onto your cossie. Sometimes it's more difficult going back than coming out in the first place, isn't it?" smiles Grace.

As they stagger together across the Swatch, the water at Kathleen's waist and Grace's shoulders, they can feel the force of the tide coming in from the North Sea, trying to pull their feet from under them. Kathleen leans into the current and notes that Grace has a determined expression on her face as she too fights the tugging water. Each step has to be taken carefully and deliberately, toes being curled into the sand below for purchase.

But it has to be done; they have to reach the safety of the hard or be swept away up the Swatch. As, finally, they stagger breathlessly onto the cutting shingle again, Kathleen realises that her father and her daughter are right. She must at least give Freddie the benefit of the doubt and try to help him, if that's what he needs. Giving up and allowing events to sweep away what they had makes no sense.

As Grace has implied, with the extraordinary insight of a child, it can be difficult to go back but sometimes that's what you have to do, even though life's passage is relentlessly an ebb tide.

SHUT OUT THAT STEALING MOON
October 1950

In late October of that year, Kathy and the girls returned to Pleasant Road. They hadn't really been away for that long, but it seemed like months to me, although I know now that it was my illness that caused me to think that way and perhaps even to do the terrible thing I did.

To begin with, Kathy was hesitant, stand-offish and cold. She didn't want to be near me and refused to sleep in the same room for many months. I couldn't blame her. Initially, she busied herself with clearing up the mess I'd made when I was there on my own. I wanted to help, for it seemed like a way of atoning, but she was having none of it.

"Just keep out of my way," she snapped, scrubbing at the kitchen floor or cleaning the parlour windows. I was left standing in doorways, pulling nervously at my pullover like a little boy who's just wet himself again. And that's precisely how she wanted it. The worst times, of course, were when the girls were at school and Archie was at work, for then I was on my own; I could find no safety behind others and was exposed to the full force of Kathy's indifference and contempt. It was a particularly painful and distressing time. I had known Kathy all my life and loved her with all my heart and yet I did not know her completely; did not know that she was capable of such icy resolve.

"And who has brought this coldness to the fore in the one he loves? Who has allowed the ice to settle in her heart and the fog to swirl around the once warm hearth of the family home?" I repeatedly asked myself such lofty questions and many others like them.

Kathy resumed her control of the domestic arrangements so that food was prepared and laundry was done, for example, but it was as if I was a rather unwelcome house guest; a guest who had done something unspeakably vile and who deserved to be spoken to only briefly and when absolutely essential. I was not allowed to help in any way. I tried to engage her in conversation but received little response. One afternoon, some several weeks after her return, I stood in the doorway of the parlour where she was finishing some ironing. I took a deep breath.

"Kathy," I mumbled. "Please stop punishing me this way. You know I am sorry for what I did. I wish it had never happened."

She didn't say anything.

"Kathy...I'm apologising. Again?"

"I heard. Would you mind out of the way?" she said. "I need to collect the girls from school."

"I love you, Kathy. I always have and I always will."

"Huh!"

I think that without Archie's help and understanding, things might never have gone beyond this stage.

"Freddie, you have to promise her one or two things, old son," he said gently one afternoon, a couple of days after she returned home.

"Why can't she tell me herself?" I asked, somewhat petulantly.

"She doesn't appear to be ready to talk to you in that way, just yet. I think you have to accept that and also accept that, for the time being, I may have to be a go-between. It's not a role I had anticipated but there we are; if I can help, I will, for all your sakes. Kathleen!" he said, raising his voice a little so that she would hear him from the scullery. "Would you come in here for a minute, please?"

Kathy came and stood in the doorway, broom in hand, her stance and the hunch of her shoulders making it evident that she was in no mood for too much conciliation, let alone chit-chat.

Archie looked at me, willing me to say the right thing and not become too controversial or, perhaps, patronising in my tone. He needn't have worried: I was ready to do almost anything to enable things to return to the way they had been. But, of course, rarely can we go backwards and, as if he'd read my thoughts, Archie began with a similar observation.

"Kathleen, I have no doubt that Freddie wants to make amends. He's listening. Now, you were childhood sweethearts; almost never out of one another's sights. You consummated your love very early and, well, because your Aunty Vi and I could both see that things were serious between you, we did what we did in order that you could have a future together. You had...you have, I hope...a loving marriage and two lovely children. Whether it's possible to go back to how your marriage was before...well, before this happened...is difficult to say, but the question is, do both of you want to try? Both of you; not just one of you. Freddie has done something unutterably stupid; I think he knows that. Don't you, Freddie?"

"Yes, of course." I looked at Kathy; it seemed the right moment to say it again. "I'm so sorry. I love you and I apologise." Kathy didn't grimace or grunt as she had before when I'd said this; she just held my gaze for a second or two and then looked down at the floor.

"Good," said Archie. "My view is that you're not well, Freddie. That's what's causing the erratic behaviour. But I'll come to that in a minute. So, Freddie wants to try to make amends; it has to be willingly undertaken by both of you. What about you, Kathleen? Are you prepared to allow Freddie time and space to show that he means what he just said?"

There was a long pause but eventually Kathy looked up again, glanced at her father and then looked at me.

"You did a terrible thing, Freddie. The worst thing you could have done to me. But, despite that, I still care. So, yes, alright, I'll try. But it won't be easy for me. And I want us to sleep in separate rooms until...well...until I feel alright about...you know. If I do."

Archie looked me in the eye. "That's quite a concession from a woman suffering the kind of pain you've inflicted, Freddie and given your past lives together. Do you see that? Are you agreeable to that?"

"Yes, if that's what she wants," I said. A tear rolled down my cheek. I couldn't help it.

"Good," said Archie once more. He'd have made a good teacher, I thought; not only is he educated, he'd be good at sorting out arguments between children.

"But there's more, Freddie. Firstly, something I've already talked to Kathleen about – you have to stop drinking so much.

Preferably, stop completely. It's not helping your mental stability and it's making you aggressive with Kathleen, she says, especially when...well, I think you know what I mean. Are you prepared to do that?"

Kathy was watching me carefully. I felt a stab of annoyance that I was being spoken to this way and that my ability to cope with a couple of pints was being questioned. Again, Archie seemed to be able to read my thoughts.

"Just a pint or two would probably not be a problem, Freddie, but if you're honest, you'll agree it's gone far beyond that, on a daily basis. Hasn't it? That's why I'm suggesting you give it up completely. So, are you prepared to agree to that? I think Kathleen would say that it's got to be a condition of her staying here. Kathy?"

"Yes, it is," she said.

"Very well," I said, perhaps a little truculently. "Kathy and the girls are more important to me than the beer."

"I'm pleased to hear it," said Kathy, softly. In other circumstances, it might have seemed a dismissive or sarcastic remark, but that afternoon, it was a positive comment that gave me some hope.

"So far, so good, then, Freddie. Now, the second one is a bit more difficult and you know what I'm going to say because I've already spoken to you about it a couple of times before."

"Yes, Archie," I said, "I know what you're going to say. I've thought about it as you suggested. You want me to go to the doctor and see whether he thinks that some psychiatric treatment is called for. I respect your view and I appreciate...well, I hope we both appreciate what you're doing for us and because I feel that way, as you said, well, I'm listening. I'm surprised that I'm not telling you to take a running jump but I want things to be alright between Kathy and me and so therefore I'm prepared, perhaps a little reluctantly and apprehensively, to agree to your suggestion."

"Good man. Well done."

There was another pause. Kathy looked as if she was going to cry. She told me many months later that Archie had talked to her several times about this, persuading her that I was not just being difficult or making things up to try to excuse what I'd done. Eventually, she saw what he was driving at but told him that she was certain I would never agree to any such intervention because I was proud and stubborn.

Kathy took a couple of steps towards me, hesitated, then put her hand on my head and kind of ruffled my hair. It lasted no more than a second or two and then she turned on her heel and returned to the back of the house. Needless to say, I wept like a baby. Archie sat with me until I finished snivelling, his hand resting firmly on my shuddering shoulders.

§

Not surprisingly, giving up the beer proved considerably easier than undertaking the psychiatric help, for the latter threw all manner of things at me that I found hard to assimilate at first. But there was no denying that both things helped. Without the alcohol in my system, my mind resumed a greater clarity and I felt far more positive about everything. I had been suffering with bouts of anxiety but with the cessation of alcohol, that disappeared totally at this time.

I made sure I didn't go anywhere near The Minerva or any of the other seafront pubs. I was certain that if I did, all would be lost. Archie was right, I'm sure: total abstinence was the key. Stan was in some respects my biggest problem because he was constantly trying to lead me astray. For him, sly, covert misbehaviour was the spice of life. Furthermore, he couldn't seem to comprehend that not drinking was not just a sop to what he envisaged as my nagging wife; it was my lifeline.

"Come on, Prof," he'd whisper. "Just a quick one. She won't know! Buy some peppermints and by the time yer gets 'ome tonight, she won't smell it on yer breath. Yeah? Just a quick half?"

It took all my resolve and will-power to resist him, but I knew that if I didn't, it wouldn't just be a "quick half" but pint after pint every day and I'd be back to where I was before, or worse. That much I sensed irrefutably.

So, I was able to return to Treasure Island quite quickly, for it seemed to me and Kathy that a resumption of that work and the purpose it gave, would be bound to be a positive influence. Certainly, being back in the thick of it and out in the sea air every day was curative in every sense. Definitely much better than being cooped up at Pleasant Road, watching Kathy do the housework. Then, at the beginning of 1951, with things between us on a far more stable footing, Kathy agreed to return to The Admiral Benbow ready for the 1951 season. Before that happened, Benny and Stan between them ensured that Sandra, the "ginger slut" as Kathy called her, was encouraged to find employment on Canvey Island. She drowned in the floods of 1953.

The summer of 1951 wasn't so good as far as the weather was concerned; it seemed to rain nearly every day and, naturally, that was a worry. We also wondered whether the Festival of Britain on the south bank of the Thames would provide Londoners with a reason not to come to Southend because it was meant to be, "fun, fantasy and colour" according to the organiser. It's true that our takings were down a little on the previous year, but whether that was due to the rain or the festival, it wasn't really possible to say. We managed to take the girls up to the south bank one afternoon during the school holidays and they had a wonderful time, particularly at the funfair. Kathy and I, like most people, were awestruck by the assault on the senses of the festival – its intention, of course – with sculptures, murals, fountains and all sorts of things to delight the eye.

I was particularly entranced by the Skylon, an enormous tower or mast shaped a bit like an exclamation mark that rose dozens of feet into the sky above the Dome of Discovery. It was held aloft by very thin cables but you couldn't see them, even quite close-up and so the thing appeared to hang in the air without any support. Kathy looked at it for some time, a finger twirling in her curls.

"Bit like us, isn't it?" she announced. "Seems steady enough but you can't see what's keeping it up."

"Love, Kathy," I whispered, "that's all that matters. Anyway, what's with you and all the symbolism?" But I didn't really want an argument and I didn't think the time was quite right for some cheeky remark about the Skylon's steady erection.

Every Tuesday I had to go to the hospital for a regular appointment with Mr.Vickery, a thin man with a greasy suit and even greasier hair. He sat with a small clipboard on his lap and asked me all manner of peculiar questions about my childhood. Every now and then, when he thought I wasn't watching, he'd rotate the end of his pencil in one of his ears, extracting little clumps of wax which he wiped onto the side of the chair.

He seemed particularly interested in Pa and my attitude towards him when I was a child and now, in adulthood. Did Pa ever cuddle us or show any affection? I laughed out loud at that one. He sent me for tests after I'd talked about the occasion when Pa had kicked me in the head.

"It seems the attack may have caused some permanent neurological damage. It could explain the headaches and much else besides," he said.

He wanted to know whether I'd witnessed Pa's brutality to Ma and whether I'd ever seen them, or heard them, having sexual intercourse. He looked a bit alarmed when I told him it was an almost daily occurrence. He wanted to know about my love life with Kathy and whether I was gentle with her or whether I wanted to dominate and punish her. I wasn't quite sure what that was all about, but I assume he was suggesting that Pa's sexual violence had been imprinted on me. Bloody psychiatrists! No wonder they call them trick cyclists. Well, I don't know; maybe he was right. Who can say?

"Punish her for what?" I retorted.

"What are your feelings about women generally?" he responded. "Young women, for example, that you see on the pier during your work?"

"The same as most healthy men feel, I expect," I said peevishly.

That didn't seem to satisfy him and he continued probing. Some lines from Shakespeare came to me, so I threw them at him.

Die for adultery? No.
The wren goes to it, and the small gilded fly
Does lecher in my sight.
Let copulation thrive...

"What is the significance of that, Mr. Tanner?"

"Fairly obvious, isn't it?" I said. "Let copulation thrive, yes? It's what makes the world go round, Mr. Vickery. So, when the young girls are on the pier in their summer dresses, showing their legs and who knows what else, I'm ogling them like everyone else."

"Ogling? Why did you choose that word?"

I hissed through my teeth with obvious annoyance. "Well, I suppose it could be because it's the appropriate word. I could have said "watching" or "observing" but those words wouldn't convey what I meant. Ogling: although originally it meant something like "looking at with amorous intent" it now has connotations of lust and desire. And that's what most men have when they see pretty girls scantily clad, which they usually are on the pier in warm weather. Whatever they say to their wives, most of whom, of course, will offer the usual matron's assessment of any pretty, flirtatious girl: she's a trollop because nice girls don't do that sort of thing."

"Why are you trying to hide from this issue behind your learning?" he replied.

"*Who is it that can tell me who I am*?" I said.

He smiled. "*King Lear*, Mr. Tanner. *To deal plainly, I fear I am not in my perfect mind.*"

"Touché," I snapped. "*When we are born, we cry that we are come to this great stage of fools.*"

I know he was only doing his job, but I couldn't resist the jibe. I then told him that I thought he was supposed to be teasing out the reasons for my allegedly off-beam behaviour, rather than hurling gratuitous insults. He should be sweetness and professional light, I suggested; it was his job to tolerate my rudeness and truculence. He smiled to himself and said nothing for about a minute while he scribbled furiously on his clipboard.

"Tell me a little more about the girl with the ginger hair. Sandra, I think you said? What was the special attraction?"

I wanted to tell him that the attraction was that she was practically a stranger so there was no commitment asked for or given; that it was obvious she would do it vigorously and without restraint; without asking for love and without asking for gentleness. She wasn't like most girls; she wasn't a "good girl" at all. She was like an animal and that aroused me beyond description. And she had a taut little body. That do for a start? But I thought perhaps I'd be playing into his hands so I just said something about her unexpected availability; that Benny had already warmed her up and what was a man to do in that situation? But I don't think that was the right answer; maybe it was the same answer? Anyway, he started scribbling again.

I suppose he had reason to scribble. I'd begun to wonder about my sexual preferences, I have to admit. Let's face it, even if Kathy had invited it and encouraged me, it was not then (or now?) usual for a boy so young to have intercourse with a girl on a railway platform; twice in a few minutes, with people all around. The dream I'd had that had culminated in me forcing myself on Kathy rather brutishly was still something I'd prefer to forget and, of course, the episode with Sandra, in which there is no doubt I had enjoyed a frantic coupling, also seemed to fit a pattern. So, not a very satisfactory assessment.

Of course, when we got onto Ma and how she'd died and how I felt I hadn't been able to say goodbye to her or properly grieve for her, Mr. Vickery had a field day. Naturally and very predictably, he eventually came around to all that Freudian stuff about the relationship between me and Ma. I didn't co-operate much with him about that. It felt too intrusive, even for a psychiatrist.

His conclusions seemed to be (if I interpreted the reasoning behind his questions correctly – and I'm sure that's not what you're supposed to do, but I did) that I had learned to be sexually dominant and violent from my father, that I was angry with all women just as I had been angry with Ma for failing to protect me and then dying, leaving me to Pa's fists. He seemed to imply that my dreams about my penis being severed and so on implied a reluctance to accept my own masculinity, for that early experience had shown me that masculinity meant hurt. Or maybe it was because I wanted to make love to Ma – I didn't; what an idiotic suggestion – and I was tormented by guilt. Basically, it was all down to maternal deprivation. Of course, the Victorians thought that psychological ill-health must result from masturbation.

In that case, as I once explained to sniffy Mr. Vickery, Benny would have to be locked away, for he'd started when he was about ten. He didn't think it was funny, needless to say.

In the 1950's, the absence of a mother or a dysfunctional mother-child relationship was the scapegoat. It would be bound to cause promiscuity, anxiety, guilt, instability and slow development in a child, they said.

As Benny would have remarked, "What a load of old horse manure!"

Having said that, I suppose that I would have to agree that having somebody force you to consider your childhood and the various circumstances and factors that shaped you will, perhaps, help you to understand why you think and behave as you do. And with that understanding comes an ability to control oneself? It's possible. And he prescribed some tablets. They gave me the trots.

Anyway, I found that I felt better. I was alright again. It took time and patience, but gradually Kathy and I returned to something like our old ways and one glorious summer evening in 1951, she invited me back into her bed. It was quite unexpected and I hadn't asked.

"Freddie," she giggled. We were sitting in the back yard, enjoying the last of the sunset. The girls were already in bed.

"Mmm?"

"I'm very hot out here. I had to take my underwear off earlier."

For a moment or two, I didn't twig what she was really saying. But when I did, it didn't take us long to scamper up the staircase! After such a long period of abstinence – well, enforced celibacy – I found it difficult to pace myself and take things as I knew Kathy preferred.

It was Vickery who suggested that I should sit down and write out my memories of the past – all of it, with candour and without omitting what he called the "difficult periods". I said it had all been pretty difficult and if I was going to write only about the easy stuff, then I'd need just one sheet of paper; in fact, I said, if he'd pass me his clipboard, I could do it there and then.

"Do you find that sarcasm helps you to deflect things that you don't want to have to deal with?" he asked, sucking on the waxy end of his pencil.

Nevertheless, I took him up on the suggestion and bought some little exercise books for the purpose. It wasn't easy; not just because one is testing one's powers of recall, but also because, as Vickery had no doubt intended, the process obliged me to confront once more some of the things that happened in Bow that I would rather forget.

MY WAY OF LIFE IS FALLEN INTO THE SERE
August 1952

With a grunt and a sigh of irritation, Doreen rolls heavily off Stan and sits on the side of the bed.

"It ain't no good, Corky."

"No," says Stan softly, almost tearfully. "I'm sorry. Maybe it's the beer. You know, brewer's droop, an' all that."

"Yeah, could be!" She pats Stan on his arm and smiles at him. "Never mind. I s'pose I should tell you not to take it so hard, but you might get the 'ump about that too, ey?"

"It's not funny, Doreen. And it's bloody frustratin' when you want to and you can't. Makes a man bad-tempered." Stan chews at his lip for a while. "It's a bit of a blow for a man, Doreen, when 'e gets old and 'e can't do it any more, when all along he's never even 'ad to think about it; you know, it was always there at the ready. Ain't the first time either, is it? 'Umiliating, like, see?"

Doreen turns back onto the bed and props herself against the headboard with a pillow. "It 'appens, Corky. None of us is gettin' any younger, are we? Most of us is goin' there, sooner or later." She reaches for her cigarettes.

"I read somethin' in the paper about that American bloke, you know, Kinsey, or whatever 'e's called. Seems he's doin' research on women now and how they like it as much as men and can keep on doin' it for longer. I mean, later in life or summat," says Stan mournfully.

"Is that news, then? I'll tell you something else an' all, Stan. I mean, I know I'm on the game, more or less, an' I'm different, but lots of women have affairs, you know. You blokes 'ave sometimes got the wrong idea about women being all innocent and not wantin' it."

"Oh, I know. I reckon it'll all change, Doreen. Time'll come when it'll be the women what's chasin' it, not the blokes. An' then the blokes'll be bloody terrified and runnin' the other way. There'll be even more limp ones then!"

Doreen laughs, the movement flicking cigarette ash across the already grimy bed-spread.

"Don't say nothin', though, Doreen? Do us a favour in front of the blokes?"

Doreen smiles at him indulgently. "Alright, Corky, don't upset yerself. Yer secret's safe with me! Anyway, maybe it's as much my fault as yours. I ain't exactly Ava Gardner, am I? All flab, thighs like an elephant's, no waist and me front sagging below me belt. No wonder it's gone ter sleep!"

"You're alright, Doreen. I'm the one who was always telling the Prof not to look at the mantelpiece an' all that. No, that's not it. It's me, conkin' out. I wish I could go back twenty five years, that's fer sure."

"Don't we all, darlin'? What was you doin' in 1925, then?" Doreen blows a long column of smoke up to the ceiling.

"Girl called Elisabeth. I was a handsome, healthy thirty eight; she was...well, she was still at school."

"Blimey! Really? I dunno; you blokes are always chasin' after young girls."

"Nearly eighteen. Sixth form at St. Bernard's; just got a place at university. Daughter of a bloke where I worked at the time. Fell for 'er the moment I saw her. Couldn't 'elp it. Crazy; bloody crazy. 'Er parents go potty when they find out. Well, you know; I'm too old an' I'm already married. All that. We run off together; up north. After a while she changes her mind, says she's sorry but it'll never work; 'er parents will never accept the situation and she don't want ter be cut off from 'er family forever. A favourite Aunt persuaded 'er it was all a big mistake. She says she still loves me but we'll both get over it and she goes 'ome."

"Did you get over it, then?"

"No. Took me about three years before I could even bloody smile again," Stan mutters.

Doreen pats Stan on the knee. "Did you ever hear from 'er or see 'er after that?"

272

"I tried to make contact; get 'er to change her mind, but it was no good. She's married with kids an' livin' up near Chelmsford. That's all I know. Ah, well; long time ago now, ain't it?"

"Oh, dear. Convent girls!" Doreen chuckles. "Why would you want ter go back to that pain, Corky?"

"I wouldn't. I ain't thinkin' of the pain. Although I'd suffer the pain again just for a few more nights with 'er. Jesus! No, it's the youthful energy of it I miss. All bloody gone now, worse luck but, like I say, I ain't never forgotten 'er. Think of 'er practically every day. I dream about 'er still. Quite a lot. I mean, what's that all about if you're dreamin' of some girl you haven't seen for a quarter of a century? Well, she ain't a girl no more, of course. Wonder what sort of life we might 'ave had if she'd stayed the course? Stupid old sod, ain't I? You can put it on me tombstone – here lies Stan Purkiss, still droolin' over a girl from the past," says Stan, wiping at his eyes with the back of his hand, "because droolin' is all 'e's got bloody left."

"No, Corky, that's not all that's left. We all 'ave memories and many of 'em hurt, that's fer sure, but it don't make you stupid. But, well, think about it. She'd be in 'er prime an' you'd be ready ter draw yer pension and… "

"Struggling to get it up?"

"Sorry, but, well, love, that's the truth and no mistake! Time marches on, Corky. Nothing's forever and you're a long time dead. But come on, now, buck up! Enjoy what we 'ave an' no backward glances, you see? Let's go an' 'ave a drink, shall we? Cheer us up?"

"Maybe you're right."

"Of course I am," says Doreen, heaving herself from the bed and beginning to get dressed. "You can't live in the past an' have that time again. Onward and upward!"

"Onward I 'ave no choice about," grunts Stan. "An' upward? Don't look like it, does it? Onward and downward; onward and drooping."

Doreen laughs. "Yes, it's a funny old world. A man's lucky if he gets out of it alive. I heard that somewhere."

"That bugger Kinsey, I expect."

A SHOW AT THE END OF THE PIER
Christmas 1952

Scene 1

The camera pans the crowded bar of The Minerva. The pub is decorated with tawdry gummed-loop paper chains and sprigs of tired holly. It is very seedy and very noisy. FREDDIE is leaning against the bar, nursing a drink. He is alone and despite the crowd, there is a space around him as if others are wary. It should be clear before any dialogue commences that he is drunk. STAN and BERNARD approach him.

STAN

Hello, stranger! What a turn-up for the festive books, ey? (*Freddie turns around unsteadily.*) Blimey, Prof, how many 'ave you 'ad? Two pints of best, please, Mary!

BERNARD

Dearie me. You look a bit the worse for wear. Does Kathleen know you're here?

FREDDIE
(Slurring throughout.)
'Lo, Stan. Uncle Bernard. Merry Christmas, my dear old friends. Um, well, quite a few. I don't know, to be exact. Five or six? No, she doesn't; too bad, ey? Naughty boy, Freddie. (*He smacks himself across the back of his hand and grins inanely.*)

STAN
(Looking at the empty glasses on the bar.)
An' whisky an' all? But aren't you supposed to be...well...on the wagon? What's going on?

FREDDIE

It's Christmas. Nearly. I felt like it. And, to be honest, we had a bit of a disgeement...disagreement.

STAN

Oh. Sorry to 'ear that, Prof. I thought you was doin' alright, the two of you? Thass what you told me a few weeks back.

FREDDIE

(Taking a long swig of his beer and motioning for the barmaid to replenish his glass.)

We were. We are. Mostly. But tonight, well, we're going out...you know, to the special show in the Pavilion. One night only; not recommended for minors. (*With heavy sarcasm.*) Chuckle at Christmas with Cheeky Chester and Mr. Jester. For crying out loud! What's the world coming to when we're all bloody children again?

BERNARD

Crikey! I wouldn't have thought that's Kathleen's cup of tea, is it?

STAN

That's right; his act's pretty blue from what I hear, so it's not fer kids or, well, someone like Kathleen. I mean, no offence intended, Freddie, but she ain't exactly quick at that kind of crude stuff, is she? Actually, I'm surprised the Council's agreed to havin' 'im in the town at all.

FREDDIE

Not my idea anyway. She's back there now, all of a fussation about what she's wearing and how I have to be on my best behaviour. On and bloody on, like she does. Front row seats, you see?

STAN

Very posh, Prof.

FREDDIE

Not really. We all know Harry in the box office, don't we? He's always leering at her and he persuaded her to take the tickets. Ing...er...ingratiating himself, the lecherous slug.

BERNARD

Come on, Freddie, he must be bloody eighty if he's a day.

FREDDIE

Doesn't stop him trying to peer down her dress. Like everyone else, it seems.

BERNARD
(Impatiently.)

"Seems" is about it, though, Freddie, isn't it? Maybe it's all in your bleedin' imagination, son; excuse my Swahili.

FREDDIE
(Aggressively.)

Look, Bernard, I know what I see! I know when men are trying to ogle her...breasts.

STAN

Calm down, Freddie.

FREDDIE

Alright, alright. Sorry, Bernard. I didn't mean...oh, shit.

BERNARD

Apology accepted. What was the argument about? Or don't we want to know?

FREDDIE

Women! Well, she starts on about how we'll be at the front so everyone will see if I do anything..."strange", she says. Strange! What does she mean by that? I'm a bloody freak show, now, am I? Is that what you all think? Just my bloody im...imagination, everyone says. Oh, I don't know, maybe I am getting it all out of pre...proportion again, but I feel I've had it up to here...you know; holding back in...in the bedroom, walking on broken glass, bloody

Vickery and his insidi...insinuations again when I thought I'd got rid of the greasy little toerag; drinking bloody water and orange juice.

STAN
Water's enough to drive a man to drink. Another one for the road?

BERNARD
(Looking concerned.)
Is that a good idea? You're not used to it anymore.

FREDDIE
(Draining his glass.)
Yes, please, Stan. Why not?

BERNARD
I can think of a thousand reasons.

FREDDIE
Oh, sod it. So I got all hurt and petulant and said I'd go and lock up and meet her at The Pavilion at seven thrity. Thirty.

STAN
I locked up hours ago, though. And it's twenty past now!

FREDDIE
I know you did. It was just an excuse to get out down here. Haven't been in here or anywhere else or had a beer for months and months. Bloody hell! Twenty past? (He clutches at his head.) Bugger! Bit of a headache. Not used to the beer.

BERNARD
Isn't that what I just said?

Scene 2

Outside The Pavilion. Cheerful theatre-goers queuing. It is a bright evening and the pier's illuminations and those on the foreshore twinkle enticingly, the coloured lights reflected in the waters of the high tide. The camera focuses on a poster advertising the evening's show. "You have not heard it any cheekier than this!" KATHLEEN is seen standing alone, looking anxious. She looks beautiful in expensive and fashionable clothing. FREDDIE is seen weaving his way through the crowds towards her.

KATHLEEN

There you are! Where on Earth have you been?

FREDDIE

(Trying hard to appear sober and making things worse.)
Sorry, Kathy. I...I bumped into Stan.

KATHLEEN

Freddie! You've been in the pub, I know it. You've been drinking! I can smell it! You agreed not to...

FREDDIE

Look, Kathy, just let me have some fun? It's Christmas. I only had one.

KATHLEEN

Only one what? One bottle of Scotch? You're not supposed to, Freddie, you know what it does to you.

FREDDIE

Alright, alright. And I'm sick of bickering, Kathy. It didn't used to be like this.

(He wipes his hand across his forehead. Despite the winter cold, he appears to be sweating.)

KATHLEEN

And whose fault is that? Look at the state of you! Really, Freddie! *(Sighing.)* Look, I want to see the show. There isn't time to take you home now, so we'll have to go in. *(Hissing forcefully.)* But...behave, will you?

FREDDIE

Yes, Mummy, I'll try to be a good little boy. I'll remember to speak only when I'm spoken to and I promise not to play with myself too obviously.
>*(He rubs his palm across the front of his trousers and grins lasciviously.)*

BY-STANDER

Is this man bothering you, Miss?

>*(FREDDIE reacts angrily, clenching his fist and drawing back his arm.)*

KATHLEEN

(Grabbing at FREDDIE'S arm before he can do anything, although he is so drunk that his staggering movements suggest he is more likely to fall over.)
Freddie! No, no, thank you. It's alright. He's my husband.

FREDDIE

(Loudly.)
Her husband is bothering her! What a filthy swine. But she didn't mind being bothered in the fields out at Paglesham, once upon a long time ago with no knickers! No bickering then, was there?

(The bystander walks off, shaking his head. KATHLEEN continues to grip hold of FREDDIE and seems unsure whether to continue with the evening or whether to take him home.)

KATHLEEN

Please, Freddie, for God's sake! People will hear! What a thing to say in public! Please don't ruin my evening. You know I've been looking forward to this for weeks.

FREDDIE

Alright, alright. Come on, let's go and chuckle with Farty Fester, or whatever he's called.

Scene 3

The inside of the theatre. The camera pans the auditorium which is packed. CHESTER is well into his act. He is a fat little man wearing a lurid green waistcoat, through which his stomach protrudes, and striped trousers that appear far too tight across his backside. On his knee or carried aloft is a ventriloquist's dummy dressed in a striped waistcoat and plain green trousers. He wears a jester's hat. MR. JESTER'S face is ugly and frightening: he has a hooked nose, thin lips and very red skin.

MR. JESTER

I hear you buried your wife?

CHESTER

I had too; she died.

(Some audience laughter, but it's an old joke. Camera cuts to KATHLEEN; she looks a little perplexed.)

MR. JESTER

That would explain it, then.

CHESTER

Yes, God rest her soul. She was a funny woman, my wife. A few years ago, she ran off to Indonesia with a second-hand car salesman.

MR. JESTER

Jakarta?

CHESTER

No, she went of her own accord.

(Laughter.)

MR. JESTER

What did a second-hand car salesman have that you didn't?

CHESTER

Upholstered seats and a walnut dashboard.

MR. JESTER

Ooh! Did your wife like walnuts, then?

CHESTER

She liked any kind of nuts.

MR. JESTER

I got married last month. My new wife's an angel.

CHESTER

You're lucky. Mine's still alive.

MR. JESTER

I thought you said she was dead?

CHESTER

Hard to tell, especially with the lights out. No signs of life, no matter what I do.

MR. JESTER

You should try poking her with a stick.

CHESTER

That's what I mean.

The camera cuts to KATHLEEN and FREDDIE. KATHLEEN is smiling in a bemused way and obviously trying to enjoy herself, although she casts occasional anxious glances in FREDDIE'S direction. He has his hand to his head and is frowning. He looks at the stage, but somehow it appears he does not see it. By whatever device, the film director should make it clear that what happens from now on is partly what KATHLEEN and the rest of the audience hear and see too; and part of it is seen and heard only by FREDDIE. So, there should be a change of lighting or, perhaps, an echo effect on the soundtrack.
For FREDDIE, CHESTER'S routine is now very bawdy Music Hall and is certainly "close to the knuckle". There is some shocked laughter. There are some who watch in an uncomfortable silence. Occasionally there is a covert hiss or cry of "Shame!" We should be aware of a sense of undefined menace. This could be conveyed by the dummy's face. The dummy now sports a large codpiece, out of all proportion with its body. Periodically CHESTER flicks it or waggles it at the front row. As with all stage Fools, MR. JESTER has a licence to clown beyond propriety.

MR. JESTER

What did a second-hand car salesman have that you didn't?

CHESTER

I think my big-ends were noisier than his.
    (He turns around and wiggles his capacious, striped rear at the audience and makes a farting noise with his lips. MR. JESTER lifts the codpiece into the air and waves it under his nose.
    Cut to KATHLEEN; she has her hand over her mouth in horrified surprise; FREDDIE looks angry.)

CHESTER

And he liked to boast that he had a hot-rod that he kept for weekend trips to Brighton. Or was it Southend?
(CHESTER grabs MR. JESTER'S codpiece and waves it at the front row. Some laughter, although it is uncertain. FREDDIE is looking thunderous.)

MR. JESTER

Oh! Do they have dirty weekends in Southend? I didn't know that. *(He laughs vulgarly.)*

CHESTER

So I've been told. I think it's this pier that does it.

MR. JESTER

Really?

CHESTER

Yes. Ozone, they say. Makes people frisky. I took a walk down to the end this afternoon. Beautiful young woman with luscious lips, striding purposefully towards me. I asked her if she'd like to join me in a cup of tea. *(MR. JESTER waves the codpiece.)* She said she doesn't like greasy spoons in her mouth!
(Shocked laughter from those who understand the ribaldry. Cut to FREDDIE who is mouthing something inaudible at the stage.)

CHESTER

Do you like it here on Southend Pier, Mr. Jester?

MR. JESTER

It sticks out a long way, doesn't it?

CHESTER
(Wiggling the codpiece provocatively.)
Oooh! It has to. It wouldn't be the longest pier in the world, otherwise, would it? My wife had a job in a pier kiosk once. But she had to give it up.

MR. JESTER
Why?

CHESTER
She got barnacles on her piles.
(Laughter.)

MR. JESTER
Did you go into that Amusement Arcade up there? Treasure Island?

CHESTER
I did. I played the machines. They've got one with film stars on the front.

MR. JESTER
On the front? The sea front?

CHESTER
Now you're being obtuse.

MR. JESTER
I saw your lips move then. It's that letter b. The word "awkward" is easier. The front of what?

CHESTER
The machine. It has pictures of film stars. Ava Gardner. Gregory Peck. I put my penny in Jane Russell's slot.
(Some tentative laughter.)

MR. JESTER

In broad daylight? Didn't she mind? *(More business with the codpiece.)* Perhaps she thought it was Gregory Peck.

CHESTER

No, no. You misunderstand me. It's just a game of chance.

MR. JESTER

So I believe. Of course, it got worse when the GI's were here and then again when all the Tommies came home from the front.

CHESTER

The sea front?

MR. JESTER

Now who's being...awkward? No, the fighting front. In France or wherever they were f...fronting. Everybody was putting his penny in the slot, they say.

CHESTER

I think we'll have to increase your medication.

MR. JESTER

Madness sometimes speaks the truth.
    (Cut to Freddie who is looking angry and perplexed.)

MR JESTER

We could always ask her if she minded. Jane Russell, I mean. *(He points into the audience.)* She's in the front row. I recognise her.

CHESTER

More fronts! Front row? How can you recognise her with these lights right in front of your eyes?

MR. JESTER

(It's clear this is a regular part of the routine; he begins to peer out, shading his eyes ostentatiously.)

Some parts of her are easier to see in the dark than other parts. Her front parts, in fact. They cast big shadows, you see.

CHESTER

(Also now peering through the glare of the stage lights out into the auditorium.)

Oh! I thought that was the dome on the Solarium...

Well, what do you know? I think it is Jane Russell down there in the front row!

MR. JESTER

Jane Russell back to front on the sea front with her front in the sunshine; you've got some front, Chester! And this is my frontispiece! *(Waves the codpiece.)*

Cut to KATHLEEN who is not really keeping up but is nevertheless beginning to realise that it seems that CHESTER is referring to her. Some audience members are craning to see.

CHESTER

Lights!? Let's see the lovely lady, if you please!

A spotlight swings across from the side to illuminate KATHLEEN. She is uncertain what to do and makes as if to stand up. Some applause and laughter. The audience can probably see that it is not Jane Russell, but it's certainly a buxom girl. FREDDIE grabs at her.

KATHLEEN

(Loud whisper.) Freddie! Let go! What are you doing?

FREDDIE

(Loud whisper.) Sit down, will you? You want every man in the place ogling you? It's a bloody disgrace!

CHESTER

Ah! Well, now I see you clearly, Miss, I see you're not Jane Russell, but I'm sure we can all see how a man blinded by the lights could make the mistake.

MR. JESTER

Yes, we can! Some parts of her look just like Jane Russsell!
(CHESTER smacks him on the codpiece.)

CHESTER

Will you be quiet? Is that your boyfriend in the front row with you?

KATHLEEN

My husband!

MR. JESTER

Ooh! Well, his name must be Rigor Mortis.
(Laughter.)

CHESTER

Would you tell us your name, Miss?

FREDDIE

Sit down! Tell him to shove off. Everybody's looking.

KATHLEEN

It's not Miss, it's Mrs. Mrs Kathleen Tanner.

MR. JESTER

Look out, Chester. I think her old man's going to thump you in the front.

CHESTER

Are you enjoying the show?

KATHLEEN

Well, oh, yes, it's lovely.

FREDDIE

Lovely? It's disgusting.

CHESTER

Let's have a big round of applause for Mrs Kathleen Tanner...

MR. JESTER

...and parts of Jayne Russell...
(Laughter.)

CHESTER

...from...Southend? (*Kathleen nods*) From sunny Southend!

Audience applause. Freddie looks around him at other people,
accusingly.

MR. JESTER

Such lovely fronts from the sea front! (*He elevates the codpiece.*)

FREDDIE has his hands on the arm-rests of his seat. It appears that
he is about to get to his feet.

CHESTER

Mrs Tanner, please do come backstage after the show, we'd love to
meet you properly. (*Camera focuses on his mouth. His grin becomes*
wider; his lips are moist.)

MR. JESTER

Yes! That's at the back not the front. Bring your fronts but leave the
old man on the sea-front!
(Laughter. KATHLEEN sits down.)

KATHLEEN

Yes, I will. Thank you.

FREDDIE lurches to his feet. He starts shouting. He is unsteady. Some theatre flunkeys begin to move towards him.

FREDDIE

No, she won't! No you bloody won't, Kathy! The man's a disgrace; a menace. He should be locked up. I'd rather let you sit alone in The Minerva than let you go backstage with this...dirty old man! Don't you know why he wants to get you there?

KATHLEEN

Freddie! Freddie! What are you doing? Sit down! Don't be ridiculous!

FREDDIE

(Screaming.) You think he just wants a cosy chat? It'll be just like Vinny, won't it? He'll be feeling you...

FREDDIE is clearly not going to sit down. His arms are waving wildly, his eyes are blazing. The camera should show him as someone apparently demented and out of control. Seeing the flunkeys advancing on him, he vaults over the rail into the orchestra pit and then, with surprising agility, levers himself into the foot-lights. He grabs at MR. JESTER, pulls him from CHESTER'S arm and then rips the codpiece from the dummy. He throws the codpiece to one side and drop-kicks the dummy's torso into the audience. He turns to CHESTER, who by now can see that it would appear that a madman is on the loose. He has begun to move towards the wings. FREDDIE is too quick for him, however, and grabs his waistcoat, spinning him round. He kicks CHESTER in the groin and then punches him in the head. We might be reminded by flash-back technique of the scene where PA kicks FREDDIE. CHESTER falls to the ground. Audience members are screaming, shouting and so on. Cut to KATHLEEN whose hands are over her face in absolute horror.

Black-out.

HERE'S A NIGHT PITIES NEITHER WISE MEN NOR FOOLS
Saturday 31st January 1953

The Meteorological Office first begins to send out warnings of rapidly deteriorating weather, especially for the East coast and the Thames Estuary, on Friday 30th January. A very low depression is moving south; strong, hurricane force winds are whipping the seas into monstrous walls of freezing water, twenty feet or more in height. Spring tides and very high levels of water running into the North Sea from swollen rivers add to the problem. Water begins to pile up in the southern, narrow reaches of the North Sea and then has nowhere to go but onto the marshy coastlines of East Anglia and the Low Countries. It is later described as a one-in-a-thousand-years combination of factors.

Freddie hears the weather forecasts and warnings but, like many people, he does not register their full import straight away. In his case, this is more because he is, "having one of his funny times", as Kathleen puts it, than that he does not understand meteorology.

Just before Christmas, he begins behaving oddly again. When they go to see the Christmas show at the Pavilion, he has been drinking, even though he is not supposed to do so. He has managed to stay clear of alcohol for a considerable time and the lapse disappoints Kathleen, for his actions threaten their cautious domestic stability, let alone that they might upset her evening out. It is clear he does not approve of the show, but before long he falls asleep – or into a drunken stupor – in his seat. There he thrashes around, kicks his legs, waves his arms about and shouts incoherently a couple of times, much to Kathleen's embarrassment, but otherwise he is mercifully quiet. He is not easily roused at the end of the evening. Fortunately, Bernard is on hand to help Kathleen. He has gone to the theatre to make sure everything is alright, having been worried by Freddie's appearance earlier in the evening. The two of them manage to get him home, although they have to drag him most of the way.

By the Saturday afternoon, there is widespread concern about flooding. The pier is closed as a safety measure, but Freddie, unknown to anyone, is still there and has been since very early morning. He has been hiding in Treasure Island where he has a stash of alcohol: bottles of beer and whisky are carefully smuggled there over many weeks. Between the roof of the Arcade and the top of the Pieces of Eight change booth, a space about four feet high, he has made a kind of nest. It is a snug, dark place. It is safe like the Anderson Shelters; enclosed like the burrow on the platform; gloomy like the space under the graveyard yew trees he remembers from his childhood and damp-smelling like the tunnels at Bow Station. It could also be comforting like the marriage bed or the womb but the terrible shrilling of the wind creates a nervous unease. He can hear waves breaking alarmingly loudly against the pier's piles, causing shock waves under his body. He draws his knees higher up into a foetal position and tries to block out the noises of the storm. Better to replace them with his distant memory of Ma singing nursery rhymes to him when he was little. He listens attentively, trying to focus on Ma's face. He cannot now remember her with any certainty. He has never had a photograph to help him remember. It is a source of great sadness to him.

That part of his mind that is not befuddled by drink or his mental confusions knows that he is lying in the cramped space above Pieces of Eight and that a terrible storm is brewing, but this little clarity is fast disappearing like the dull grey light over the Thames. Mostly, it is cold and frightening; not at all what he instinctively anticipated when creating his cave. Sometimes the whistling of the wind and the hissing or running seas sound like voices. They are not soothing or friendly voices either; rather they sneer, hector and denigrate.

Things are being blown about; doors are opening and closing; the sails on Hispaniola are flapping and the fading light is producing flickering shadows that look like people moving amongst the machines and booths. He is not sure and he wipes his glasses on his shirt in case smears are causing illusions. He lifts the whisky bottle to his mouth and takes several gulps. That will be sure to steady his nerves, he thinks.

Across the slippery deck, slicked with brown suds, the old pirate ship's mast is creaking and shuddering with the force of the storm. He can hear the seas smacking against the hull, making every plank groan, and he can hear the wind howling horribly through the rigging. He hopes that Hispaniola will not founder. Is that Long John Silver pacing the deck, lifting his crutch high in the air from time to time and casting imprecations at the unruly elements? Yes, for he is the only one known to have lost a leg. If a man with one leg can ride the storm, there is hope for the rest of us. It seems a good idea to have another ration of grog.

Now there is something scuttling down the mast? It is an odd creature that seems to have five arms and legs. Long John swipes at it with his crutch. There is some old sacking hanging across the opening to Freddie's burrow and he pulls this across his face hoping to conceal himself, as children do when they put their hands over their eyes. Of course, it does not deter the creature's movements towards him. It is Mr. Jester.

"*How that personage haunted my dreams, I need scarcely tell you,*" says little Freddie, reading from his copy of Treasure Island with a shaky voice. "*On stormy nights, when the wind shook the four corners of the house, and the surf roared along the cove and up the cliffs, I would see him in a thousand forms, and with a thousand diabolical expressions.*"

Mr. Jester stands in front of Freddie's hiding place, smoothing his codpiece languidly.

"What are you doing here? Don't you know there's a terrible storm? It's dangerous. There's already several inches of water on the sea front. And in Pleasant Road. What about your lovely young wife?" says Mr. Jester. "You should be looking after her. Otherwise somebody else might."

"My wife is no concern of yours, you leering brute," mumbles Freddie.

" Hispaniola will float, never fear."

"*Here's a night pities neither wise men nor fools,*" says Mr. Jester, pointing down at the deck where water is splashing up from below. "She's already listing to port. Going down, as sure as you."

Freddie wipes sea-water from his eyes. As his vision clears, he sees that Mr. Jester is swinging away through the rigging, an ungainly five-limbed monkey. But he is still not alone. He can just make out the door to Benny's workshop, swinging to and fro as the wind takes it. Inside the workshop is the girl with ginger hair, beckoning with her finger.

"Oh, oh, come on, Freddie," she calls. Her thighs are silvered with phosphorescence from the sea. She rubs them together like a praying mantis and Freddie leans forward, hoping to stroke their lissom smoothness, but of course he cannot reach.

"Give her one!" shout Pa and Vinny in unison. "Come on, what's the matter with you?"

Freddie looks around him but he cannot see his father or his brother. Suddenly, in one of those moments of absolute clarity which he experiences even in the depths of his hallucinations, he knows they have been dead, like Ma, like Aunty Vi, for a long time. And the girl with ginger hair and silver loins is not here either. He must be imagining all this then? He begins to weep and then swigs at the bottle again.

Now there is another voice, but seemingly not disembodied this time. A thin, emaciated figure shuffles towards Freddie. He taps with a stick on the wet deck or the metal stanchions to find his way. His damp hair is plastered to his furrowed brow; his free hand trembles.

"Who are you? Are you Death?" says Freddie, terrified, trying to push back further into the safety of his hole. "You see? I have my grave ready."

"Hah! I am a poor blind man," says Pew, "who has lost the precious sight of his eyes in the gracious defence of his native country, England, and God bless King George!"

"You're an old soldier? Go away!" screams Freddie, "leave me alone!"

"Too late for that. Ah, now, there you are!" says Blind Pew, coming to a halt in front of Freddie. "I can't see, but I can hear you stirring. I can smell the mouldering earth." He lurches forward, unerringly reaching for Freddie's hand. Freddie tries to withdraw it but he is too slow; the drink has numbed his reactions. The old man has a tight grip on his wrist. With his trembling, bony fingers, he presses something into Freddie's palm.

"Mark it well, boy!" he cackles, tapping his stick repeatedly, in time with the way the wind is clattering the ship's halyards.

Freddie opens his palm and sees that he has been given a corner from a page of one of his own journals. On one side of the damp scrap of paper there is a round, black spot, marked heavily in jet-black ink.

"The black spot! So...but...how...how long have I got?" asks Freddie, reaching for the whisky bottle.

"That's what we'd all like to find out, my lad," saws Pew. "But here's a word of advice from one who knows! Old Pew may be blind but he sees. Don't put too much store by that old gravestone you have propped up there ready, see? "At rest until the day break and the shadows flee away." You remember? Of course you do! Fine words, fine words, but let me tell you, the shadows stay with you, boy, they stay with you." With that, the old man turns and makes his way laboriously across the deck, its planks now awash with sea-water being forced up through the joints by the raging seas beneath.

Freddie looks down at the black spot and then screws it into a small ball before throwing it into the water slopping about in the bilges. He raises the whisky bottle to his lips once again and drains the contents. He feels faint; his head is thumping even more insistently than the swell kicking the structure beneath him. He falls into a stupor.

He lies unconscious for some time. Opening his eyes much later and looking down, he sees that the waters have risen several inches. Is the ship sinking? It is much darker but he can still see enough. Yes, Hispaniola has tipped several degrees to port. She's turning turtle!

Benny's workshop door is still moving, but now not with the wind. It is washing backwards and forwards with the movement of the flood. The girl with ginger hair, whose name he is struggling to recall, is now lying face down in the muddy water sluicing in the doorway. Her hair floats around her head, a strangely luminous mass of tangled, orange seaweed. She appears to be naked from the waist down. Pa is standing beside her, buttoning his fly. He smiles and licks his lips.

Someone is shaking his shoulder violently.

"Come on, Mr. Tanner, they're waiting. There isn't much time. Look lively!" snaps the orderly. "Stand to attention in front of the table."

Marchbanks looks at him, his half-moon glasses perched on the end of his nose. "What have you to say for yourself now?" he asks. "How much for your fine principles this evening?"

"Ah, there you are, boy!" booms the voice of Mr. Williams from the other end of the long table. His bellow is loud even over the howling of the wind. "What did I say? A fine future ruined by gross intemperance! Isn't that right?"

Mr. Vickery looks up from his papers and begins to pull an enormous lump of wax from one ear. It is the size of a stag beetle or a cockroach. He rolls it between his thumb and finger. "How do you feel about your life, Mr. Tanner? Do you feel that you have fulfilled the potential that others saw in you in your youth?"

"Ha!" exclaims the head master. "Boy could have read law or medicine, perhaps. Look at him, drunk in charge of a flooded amusement arcade. How tawdry! How superficial! But then, there we are: the country's going to the dogs!"

Freddie hangs his head, blubbering like a child, waiting for the head master's cane to lash his outstretched hand. Fleetingly, through the tears clogging his eyelashes, he sees Mr. Jester again, running across the deck, his codpiece riding high in front of him. "Meet me down on the platform!" he yells, chortling.

"Kathy...I don't think we ought to..." Freddie mutters.

"I'm not that kind of girl. But you can if you want," whispers a voice. Freddie peers into the darkness. Is it Kathy? Or someone else?

"These days," yells the head master, "everyone's that kind of girl. No moral fibre; no discipline; youths roaming the streets at night, drunk; polluted cities and polluted minds! What have you to say, Tanner?"

"If I should die, think only this of me: That there's some corner of a foreign field that is for ever England," intones Freddie lamely.

"You?" says Marchbanks. "Clever, maybe, but no soldier, were you? Conscientious objector. No glory or requiems for you, no reserved plot; just everlasting nothingness."

"For ever England? For ever polluted in every way. Mark my words," says the head master. "It's coming."

"...But you can if you want," whispers the little voice again.

"Kathy? Kathy! Where are you? I'm sorry, Kathy, I didn't mean to do it; any of it. Help me, Kathy! For God's sake help me!" he cries.

There is no answer other than the screaming wind, the waves jarring the piles and deck planks beneath him and the shattering of glass and crockery as the Thames hammers through the broken windows of The Admiral Benbow.

"She's going down!" shouts Long John Silver from somewhere on the poop deck. "Come on, boys! Abandon ship! You hear me? The old Hispaniola is going down to Davy Jones! Abandon ship!"

Freddie hears the warning shout and jumps towards the steps he has set against the booth. As he begins to slide down them, he sees a crumpled, lifeless body lying at the bottom, its head partly submerged in the rising waters. It is Ma. He wants to tell her that he knows she suffered in order to protect him. He bends to her but it is too late; he can see that her flesh is already decomposing. He opens his mouth to scream but nothing emerges except a trickle of yellow slime.

"Bloody lethal, those stairs," calls Pa as Freddie coughs, retches and stumbles out into the night. On the open deck the noise is deafening. The seas are breaking over the rails and the wind has the screaming intensity of a machine-shop. Pieces of wood, glass, tin and canvas that have been ripped from the super-structure are now being thrown through the air with all the force of shells from a gun. Hearing explosions, Freddie looks off to the east and sees the shape of a Messerschmitt falling out of the flapping rags of clouds. It begins firing.

"Kathy! Kathy! For God's sake, help me!" screams Freddie again and again as he runs headlong towards the ship's rail. He clambers up its slippery bars and looks down at the boiling, surging sea just a few feet below. Through the spray and the flying debris, he can see the lights of a town flickering fitfully a mile or so away. It must be better to take my chances in the water, for I can swim to shore, he thinks, than to stay here on a sinking ship where I'll either be drowned below decks or be shot to pieces by enemy fighters.

In any case, it would not be possible to hesitate for long on the top of the rail. The hurricane is tugging at him relentlessly and the bitter cold has frozen his fingers so that his hold on the top rail is failing fast. He loosens his grip, closes his eyes and, giving a push with his feet, drops into the foaming sea.

The furious tide spins him and turns him, bringing him to the surface and then sucking him down again amongst sand, cockle shells, broken boat spars, shards of crockery, rusting tins and the carcase of a drowned sheep carried from Foulness Island. He is swept this way for some distance. Eventually, after many minutes, his body, no more than a piece of flotsam to the angry sea, is propelled out of the main flow of the tide by an enormous soupy surge of mud, water and wreckage. He is cast carelessly ashore on the edge of Leigh Creek where his clothing snags on the snapped prow of a long-sunken dinghy.

He lies face down in the mud and sedge grass. As the tide begins to ebb some hours later, the wind abates and he is covered by a layer of snow, woolly pieces of a dirty blanket falling softly from a beaten-lead sky.

BOOK FIVE

THE WEAKENING EYE OF DAY

RAIN
Sunday 1st February 1953

I do, of course, remember that night, although it was the terror in my mother's eyes rather than the sound of the storm, or the rising waters, that gave Violet and I the feeling that the end of the world had come. To say that she was beside herself with fear and anxiety would be to put it mildly.

She had become used to my father disappearing for hours at a time, especially when he was feeling depressed or out of sorts. It wasn't unusual for him to walk from Southend, along the sea-front to Leigh and then across the fields of Belton Hills to Hadleigh Castle and back again, whatever the weather. Those were the times when he couldn't seem to bear human company. And then, at other times, he'd hole up in one of the pubs on the seafront or in the town and not return home until very late at night, usually long after we were in bed. So, when on the day of what came to be known as "The Floods of 1953" he was not at home, she was not unduly concerned; at least, not to start with.

She could have done with his help but it wasn't the first time she'd had to roll up her sleeves and deal with some emergency in his absence and she didn't expect it to be the last. Mr. Horsfall next door managed to get hold of some sand and we all spent several hours that morning filling sacks to make sandbags to put against the doors in case the waters should rise that far up the road. Then we set to and began to take what we could upstairs, out of harm's way.

By late afternoon, as the storm's fury increased and darkness began to fall, a conviction came upon my mother that all was not well with Dad. Despite her frequent tendency to ignore him or her bouts of contemptuous anger and resentment, there is no doubt she still loved him and that they shared a special affinity as they had always done. It was just that Mum had put her love in the back of a cupboard for a while and since he couldn't see it or find it, Dad's love wandered about the house, pining like a dog. Occasionally, the love would be brought out of hiding for a polish and all would be well for a while. Then something would go wrong and it was wrapped up and put away again.

In the terrible conditions prevailing on that Saturday, it was not easy to find Dad by popping round to The Minerva, for example, to see if he was there or if anyone knew of his whereabouts. At about seven in the evening, when Mum was arranging with Mrs Horsfall to mind us for a while so that she could go out and search, despite the awful storm, Grandad Soper turned up, cold, shivering and soaked to the skin. He'd tried to cycle but had been blown off his bike and then, since he felt he couldn't be sure whether public transport along the London Road was operating, he walked through Chalkwell and Clifftown all the way to Pleasant Road.

Mum was both horrified at the risks he had taken and at the same time overjoyed to see him and to know that some help was now at hand. Grandad wanted to turn round and go back out into the storm to search for Dad, but very sensibly, Mum would have none of it. She made him soup and sandwiches while he had a hot bath and changed into some of Dad's dry clothing.

Grandad soon discovered that all the seafront pubs were closed. Since he knew that the pier was also shut, it was difficult to know where to look next, but he decided on the pubs in Hamlet Court Road since that is on higher ground and Dad would sometimes go up there. He visited them all but nobody had any positive news. Apparently, he then tried to get back to the seafront down Shorefield Road but was horrified to discover that by this time there was no seafront along which he might search. The tumultuous sea had possession of the beach and the Esplanade in its entirety, not to mention the ground floors of many properties along that road. He was at a loss as to what to do next and returned to Hamlet Court Road for a shot of whisky in one of the pubs, thinking that this would warm him a little as well as giving him time to think.

He realised, as I suppose anyone would, that there was little more that he could do. He could hardly traipse the streets of the town all night and anyway, he reasoned, if Dad was still alive, he would surely have holed up somewhere, even if only under a bridge or some such and he would emerge when danger had passed. I say "if he was still alive" because Grandad told me, some years after, that he had come to the conclusion, having experienced the storm and fought with it for hours, that Dad might well have perished. This was no ordinary night of inclement weather and Dad was not exactly behaving and thinking rationally at that time: a possibly fatal combination.

So, he returned to Pleasant Road just after midnight, exhausted and depressed at his failure to find his son-in-law. Mum had tried to pack the two of us off to bed but apart from the obvious fact that the wind clawing at the house would preclude any sleep, we simply refused to co-operate until we knew what had happened to Dad.

"It's no good, Kathleen," said Grandad, standing on the doormat, dripping. "To be honest, I don't think I can take much more out there and in any case...well..." he looked at us anxiously, "...well, if he's anywhere, it won't be out in this lot. He'll have holed up somewhere so I wouldn't find him anyway. I've checked all the obvious places and some not so obvious."

"I think we should phone the police," Mum said. "We should report him missing."

Grandad agreed, although he said he thought the police would probably be inundated with such reports, but nevertheless, at least it would be logged. Not surprisingly, though, the telephone was not working because many lines and poles had been blown down. So, after yet more soup and another change of clothing, Grandad went out again to report Dad missing in person at the police station in the town, arriving back at Pleasant Road for the last time at two in the morning.

Grandad, Violet and I were all persuaded to go to bed, not that we got much sleep. Mum stayed up and sat in the back room by the fire, crying quietly to herself until a reluctant, grey dawn broke.

We finally received news just after midday on Sunday, by which time the extent of the damage caused by the storm was emerging through the news on the radio. We heard that Canvey Island had been inundated, that many hundreds of people had lost their lives, not just in England but also in Holland where the sea's invasion had been even worse than here. Houses had been swept away or made unsafe and uninhabitable and bodies were being washed ashore all along the coast. This last piece of information brought home to Mum just how serious the situation was and she sank into her chair, a terrible pallor having come over her face.

"Oh, God! Have I caused this to happen? Sent him out with my coldness into the storm? How can I live with this?" she wailed.

"Kathleen!" said Grandad sternly, "Now don't upset yourself. We don't know yet what's happened. We just have to wait...or I can go up to the police station again and ask. Don't jump to conclusions just because they're talking about people drowning." He leaned across her and turned off the radio.

In the event, there was no need for Grandad to go to the police station because the police came to us in the form of a harassed constable who'd obviously been up all night. He told us that Dad had been found lying in the marshes just by Leigh Station. It was not known how he'd got there or how long he'd been there and by rights, said the constable, he should be dead. But, by some miracle; the grace of God, I remember him saying, he wasn't dead. He was alive, but only just and he'd been taken to Rochford Hospital.

In later years I have often wondered, as Dad did himself when he was in a less troubled state, whether that kind of grace from God is a blessing or, rather, a curse.

MOONLIGHT

Dad was kept in Rochford Hospital for some weeks. He had a terrible gaping wound on his head where something had struck him while he was in the water. It refused to heal quickly. He had a badly fractured leg and many other cuts, severe bruises and abrasions. He developed pneumonia.

He lapsed in and out of consciousness for some days. Mum stayed with him when she was allowed to do so, holding his hand, or she sat patiently in the corridors or waiting rooms when she wasn't. She was determined that he was going to live and I think that determination communicated itself to Dad through their fingers. I know from my own work as a doctor that in these situations we often talk of the patient as a "fighter" who will not readily "let go of life" but in all honesty I don't think that was the case with my father. I believe that he probably was ready to let go, as much as he was able to think about the matter at all. But Mum was not going to let him do so and as so often in their lives together it was she, the apparently rather diffident character, who was actually the stronger of the two. Quite simply, she wouldn't let him go.

She talked to him constantly, mostly without any response at all, about all sorts of things from before the war and just after, when they'd been as one.

"It wasn't always like this, you know, Grace," she suddenly said to me one evening as we sat together at Dad's bedside. He was lying on his back, his head bandaged like an Egyptian mummy, tubes in his nose and his shattered leg in a hoist over the bed.

"How do you mean, Mum?" I asked.

"Well, arguments. Difficulties. Atmospheres. I think you know what I mean."

"Yes, I suppose so," I responded cautiously.

"I can barely remember a time when your Dad was not around. He's always been there. We were inseparable. Childhood sweethearts. Childhood lovers. Childhood parents, much to the disgust of all and sundry. But we came through it, because of each other. I never loved anyone else; couldn't have; out of the question," she said, dabbing her eyes.

"I don't think Dad ever did either, Mum," I said quietly. You usually don't know as a child what passes between your parents and I certainly knew almost nothing of the details of Dad's infidelity at that time, but nevertheless, I had some half-correct inkling of what had occurred. One could not but overhear their arguments and then piece things together.

"Something happened and then...well, I couldn't forget. I couldn't forgive either. My guilt, now. I don't know...maybe it sent him over the edge...and now this," she whispered, tears running down her cheeks.

I didn't really know what to say. I wasn't old enough to have the maturity to embark on such an exchange. Simple as that. I suppose I did my best as one does as a child in that situation. I then made an excuse that I needed to go to the lavatory and left them alone together in the ward. I sat in the corridor for a while.

It was dark outside by the time I decided I should go back. The nurses had closed the doors to the ward because visiting time was over. One of them said that they were sure Mum was just leaving, but she'd go and remind her for me. I stood looking through the door's porthole window. The lights had been turned right down in the ward but I could just make out Mum, still sitting where I'd left her by Dad's bed at the very far end of the ward. The nurse approached her and touched her on the shoulder.

There was a bright moon shining through the long window just beyond the bed. It cast an eerie, unreal glow across my parents and I wondered as I stood waiting, whether things would ever be alright again.

STARS
29th July 1976

As a child you do not properly have a sense of time. Adults talk of "tomorrow" or "next week" or tell you that it's your Grandfather's sixtieth birthday, but these numbers or periods of time have relatively little meaning for a small child. When my father fell or jumped from the pier I was eleven and to me all adults were "old", that is, clearly not children. There was, really, no more to it than that. My favourite teacher then, Miss Freeman, I now know was in her mid-twenties. (I recently saw her death notice in the "Southend Standard".) From my present perspective, almost fifty years later, that seems surprising but at the time she was just "old" or "a grown-up" rather than "only fifteen years older than me and still very much a young woman".

I think I was aware that my parents were considerably younger than other girls' parents when I went to Westcliff High School for Girls. I remember seeing a friend's father arrive to collect her one afternoon and being struck forcibly by the fact that his hair was grey and that he walked with a stick. I assumed it was her grandfather and was shocked and embarrassed to be informed curtly the next morning that it was her father. "He's only fifty five, you know," said Patricia with her usual acid tones. "He's not dead yet."

Indeed he wasn't, but he looked as though he might soon be. And I suppose that this is the point: as a child, you do not really have a concept of Man's threescore and ten and therefore you lack the ability to place yourself, or others, on such a continuum. In short, children do not generally have a full understanding of mortality. They know that things die (usually pets or other animals) or that Grandma has "gone to Heaven" and is therefore not around any more, but these things happen somehow at a distance. Of course, English society tends to tidy away or hide death (unlike some other cultures, for example) and so children are protected, if that's the right word, from its reality and inevitability.

My father's condition in early 1953 was therefore a very considerable shock above and beyond the simple fact that he had hurt himself and was in hospital. That he did not come home again after a day or two – indeed, initially, he seemed worse rather than better and he remained comatose – brought home to me the painful truth that he might die. But this was somehow not something I felt I could talk to Mum about, perched as she was on the edge of fear and eternal grief. I decided to ask Grandad.

"Is Dad going to die?" I blurted out one afternoon when he was looking after us while Mum was at the hospital. Violet had gone upstairs to play with her dolls, so I grabbed the opportunity.

He stopped what he was doing – washing the dishes, I think – and looked at me.

"Come and sit down," he said quietly. He took my hand and guided me into the back room.

"He's not getting better, Grandad, is he?" I quavered. "I can tell from what's happening when I go there."

"Grace, you are a bright little girl with a very bright future, so I'm not going to give you a lot of twaddle and wrap things in cotton wool. It's not my way, as I expect you know. I shall give you credit for your undoubted intelligence and perception." He paused. "Now, I don't think your Dad is going to die; well, not just yet, but we all must one day, mustn't we? But he's not recovering very quickly, it's true and so he is still in some danger, we're told."

"Why?" I asked.

"The storm knocked him about. He swallowed or breathed in a great deal of dirty water. He's had pneumonia and he's fighting other infections. He's been drinking heavily, so there maybe damage to his body associated with that. But he's young, so he still has reserves of strength which they hope will pull him through. And your mother is willing him to get better, with all her might," smiled Grandad. "Her love, actually."

At the time, I took greater note of Grandad's descriptions of Dad's medical problems than I did of his comment about Dad's youth. But in my own adulthood, I have frequently reflected upon the fact that my father was not even thirty when all these things happened.

"Things have not turned out for your Dad and therefore for your Mum, in quite the way that it was anticipated they would before the war, Grace. Just like you, he too was told he had a bright future. He was all set to try for university and to read law. But, well, you came along a little early, shall we say and the war itself got in the way, of course, so that seemed to knock it on the head. Watch out for events, Grace. Look before you leap."

"You mean Dad never did?" I asked.

"Well, he certainly didn't the other week when he slipped off the pier, did he?" responded Grandad, laughing sardonically. "But maybe neither your mother nor your father has managed to do so, I suppose we could say. Maybe your Dad can be impetuous and your Mum, well, maybe your Mum is usually happy with today, so she doesn't always see that there is something from which you could leap. If you see what I mean? But none of that's meant to be a dismissive criticism of them, Grace. They're human and all humans are weak and make mistakes."

I thought about this for a while and then asked Grandad about something which had been troubling me for some days.

"Grandad, people don't usually jump off the pier in a storm unless, well, unless they want to kill themselves, I reckon, or unless there is something else wrong? I mean, Dad behaves in a funny way, sometimes, doesn't he and it seems to make Mum mad but I don't really understand what's going on?" I said.

"Your father had been drinking, Grace. A good deal of beer and whisky and probably all day. So that in itself might have caused him to jump, or fall; we don't know for sure, do we – because alcohol can do strange things to your mind. But, as you imply, that's not the only problem, although the drink makes it much, much worse. Your Dad has a mental illness, I'm afraid, and at the present time it looks as though that condition is deteriorating. In simple terms, he is often confused about what he sees and hears; he imagines things that are not there; his behaviour is erratic; he's having trouble with...well...family relationships. They're all symptoms, apparently."

"You mean he's going mad?"

"Some people would describe it that way, I regret to say. There is no outright cure; there are treatments but how successful they might be is anyone's guess. And...well...I'm afraid to say that, depending on how things go, it may be necessary for your Dad to receive some of that care in...in a hospital. Now you probably know more than your Mum, because that last bit I haven't spoken to her about yet, even though the doctors have been making references to it for a few days because, of course, they have now married up the events on the night of the storm with his medical, psychiatric records. I don't think your Mum's taken it in. That's what I mean about her operating for today. So, Grace, whatever happens, it's not going to be easy for any of us, I'm afraid. But I've already promised your Mum that I'll do everything I can to help."

Grandad was, as usual, entirely correct and as good as his word.

Dad did manage brief periods living at home, sometimes spending all day writing one page in his journal, but these became fewer and further between as the years went by. It was not that Mum refused to try to cope with his deteriorating condition, it was simply that Dad was a danger to himself, let alone others, if he was at home where things could not be monitored all the time and where he might have an opportunity to slip out of the house. So, he spent long periods of time at Runwell Psychiatric Hospital and my belief is that the institutionalisation that inevitably accompanies such treatment hastened the progression of his illness.

Until Violet and I were in our late teens, Grandad effectively took over where Dad had been obliged to leave off. He was a remarkable man in many ways: selfless, astute, intelligent; affectionate and uncomplainingly dedicated to his family. Mum, to nobody's surprise, wanted to be where Dad was and although it was not easy, she managed to get up to Runwell several times a week. In those days public transport enabled one to move about to most places, albeit slowly, but in the end, she had driving lessons and bought herself a little car to make life easier for all of us.

Typical of Mum's determination, for she was not a natural motorist. We would go with her, perhaps once a week or a fortnight, but increasingly, I suppose, we didn't really recognise the man that we went to visit. He seemed to know us and then again he didn't. He would often spend the whole of our visit just staring vacantly into space, the one hand that Mum was not holding trembling or forever tugging and pulling at his sleeves or trousers which were frayed and ragged as a result.

He didn't speak much and when he did, what he said didn't seem to make too much sense to Violet and me, although Mum seemed to understand, replying softly and looking into his eyes.

"She's watching us again, Kathy," he suddenly said one afternoon, having not spoken or done anything for at least half an hour. Then he chuckled.

"Who is, Freddie?" said Mum.

"Next door; look: in the window! You'd better get dressed, girl," he gurgled.

At the time I thought this was just another example of his hallucinations but since having read his journals, I now believe that he was remembering an incident from their early married life at Paglesham. So he was not entirely disconnected from reality; and then again, he was.

Grandad suggested that we should all live at his place in Chalkwell Avenue because then he would be permanently on hand to assist. Mum resisted a little to begin with but in the end she could see the sense of it. Our little house in Pleasant Road was sold and we moved to Chalkwell in 1955. I'm still here, of course.

My gratitude to my grandfather for what he did in those years knows no bounds. Nothing was too much trouble; affection was never in short supply and he always told us the truth, including the truth about ourselves, no matter how painful. I determined to repay his kindness and his faith in me: I worked hard, passed the examinations, went to university and finally qualified as a GP in the sixties. Violet is not, by her own admission, an academic but she too blossomed under Grandad's encouraging hand. She is a very successful local businesswoman and member of the Town Council. More than once we have thought that perhaps Dad's ambitions have been realised in his daughters' lives.

My father died in December 1976, having spent more than twenty years of his life in and out of institutional care. I have already said that I have wondered many, many times whether surviving the Floods of 1953 was really the blessing that the young policeman on the doorstep had said it was. For those twenty years, my father suffered the unavoidable humiliations doled out by patronising or uncaring "professionals" and every day experienced the frustrations and anger that come from a mental condition that takes away your motivation, your personal esteem, your clarity of thought, your accurate memory and even your language, replacing them all with trembling confusion, dribbling incoherence and a head full of scurrying figures and whispering voices.

And yet...for those twenty years my mother was by his side whenever she could be, doing what she could to let him know that, despite everything, she loved him still, just as before and possibly more so now that she could finally understand that what had driven a wedge between them was not a cruel infidelity alone, but some sort of horror from his past, a horror that he could not help and which was not of his making. And I do believe that for much of the time, he knew that she was there and he tried to respond accordingly. It was those days that kept Mum going, that assured her that her love was not, and never had been, in vain.

One afternoon, a few weeks before he died and as if, perhaps, he knew that the end was coming, he suddenly drew himself up in his chair, clasping my mother's hand in a firm response to her own grip. His eyes lost their customary vacant, lifeless quality and seemed almost to sparkle.

"Kathy," he croaked, "Kathy...*let us be true to one another! For the world, which seems to lie before us like a land of dreams, so various, so beautiful, so new, hath really neither joy, nor love, nor light, nor certitude, nor peace, nor help for pain; and we are here as on a darkling plain...*"

And then he stopped, smiled at her and quickly reassumed his vacant stare. Mum and I looked at one another, open-mouthed in absolute astonishment and delight. Dad had spoken to us coherently for the first time in months. He had found something in his memory – a memory that by then we assumed to be an empty vessel – which said all that he wanted to say because, apart from my mother's devotion, he had precious little else to comfort him on his own darkling plain.

Interestingly, darkness and light were to be connected with the moment of his death. He had suffered a series of severe kidney infections and it was renal failure which brought his end. That is rarely swift but it is usually relatively quiet and painless. So, we knew he was going and were gathered around him at his bedside, Mum holding onto his hand and doing her best not to cry uncontrollably. He hadn't really moved much for a long time but, late that night, he opened his eyes and slowly seemed to focus on what was around him.

"Kathy?"

"I'm here, Freddie. And the girls."

"Good. It's very dark," he said. His voice was so dry and feeble, we had to bend towards him to make out what he was saying. "Kathy, I'm sure that...it's soon...I'm sorry, Kathy. Please forgive me."

I didn't think Mum was going to be able to respond to that without wailing, but she did. "It's alright, Freddie, it's alright. I understand. I forgave you years ago. I love you."

"I love you too," he whispered. "I think you'd better get into the shelter. Never mind the gas-mask. And I mean I'm sorry too that my life was such a mess..."

"Please don't, Freddie, it isn't a mess; don't upset yourself."

"Kathy! Kathy!" his voice seemed, quite extraordinarily, stronger. "Look! I can see the stars! Millions of them, just for us. We were lying in the grass! Remember?"

Mum smiled. "Of course."

"Let me go, Kathy. I can see the burning stars," he whispered and said no more.

Mum nodded, bent towards him and kissed his dry lips. He closed his eyes slowly, seeming to hold her in his gaze. He died a few moments later.

§

When we got home, we discovered that there had been a terrible fire at the pier head. It had destroyed practically everything there, including what we had known as Treasure Island although the premises had long since passed into other hands. My father did not, ultimately, regard his work on the pier as anything other than, "oiling the wheels of indulgence and frippery" as he once put it. It was a very far cry from the purposeful and productive professional career that he had promised himself and I believe that his self-esteem suffered as a result. Nevertheless, the pier was a significant part of all of our lives and Mum took the news badly since it seemed to her that on one day the two things that gave, or had given her life meaning were both wrenched away from her. I am glad that Dad did not live to hear of this fire or the other fires that have happened subsequently.

My mother survived him by more than twenty years. She enjoyed her children and her grandchildren, taking great pleasure in all the characteristics we had which she could ascribe to Dad. But it was an existence within which the real light had been extinguished. She was stoical and kept herself busy, but nevertheless, she never stopped grieving for him. She remained at Chalkwell Avenue with Grandad Soper long after Violet and I had left home, gone to university, come back, left home again and then got married.

Grandad died in 1980, leaving Mum all alone in that great big house. She couldn't quite decide what to do and then Mrs Horsfall happened to mention, in a telephone conversation, that the people who'd bought Pleasant Road all those years ago were selling up. Suddenly, Mum knew what she was going to do and within a month she'd bought it and moved back there. Jack and I moved into Chalkwell Avenue: it's ideal for a growing family. Circles within circles.

Mum said she felt closer to Dad at Pleasant Road and although for a while we were concerned that she was going to turn the place into a shrine and wear widow's weeds for the rest of her days, it did seem to help her to be there.

In keeping with the ironies that have accompanied my parents' deaths, Mum died in early 1997 as a result of severe burns. She had been beginning to shows signs of frailty and, perhaps, early dementia. Either Violet or I would "pop in" every day to make sure things were alright, as you do. But, also like many others, we put off doing what we should have done when we both could see the way that things were heading. Mum's small confusions became worse and she should really have gone into care of some kind.

I arrived there one evening to find the house full of smoke and Mum lying on the kitchen floor, much of her clothing badly singed. It appeared that she'd left something on the stove which ignited. She then flapped tea-towels about which made things worse as cornflakes packets and all sorts fell into the splattering, burning fat. No one noticed because she had all the windows shut and both sets of neighbours were out. She must have managed to extinguish the flames and then collapsed on the floor. She died in hospital a few days later. Whether my father's reference in one of his journals to a dream in which her clothes were burned is highly significant or just mere coincidence, one can only speculate.

We buried her with Dad, in the same corner of Sutton Cemetery that looks after Grandpa Soper and Great-Aunt Vi. It's one of the more restful parts of that place and is shaded by some beautiful yew trees. My mother once asked me, many years before she died, to ensure that when she did, we would keep her grave tidy and block any "little holes" around its edge. It's the least we can do.

BRIGHT SUN
August 1948

One wonderful day of cloudless blue sky, Archie announced that he was taking the girls off to Chalkwell Park for a run around, to be followed by ice cream and cakes somewhere as yet to be decided. We should push off for the afternoon, he said, and enjoy ourselves.

We didn't need to be told twice. Kathy packed a few sandwiches and we dashed off to get the bus out to Paglesham. It seemed like the right place to go; we hadn't been out that way for some time.

We saw Miss Harris in the Garden Field as we scrambled off the bus by the pub, glad to be out of its confining spaces and into the fresh air.

"Goodness me," she said, coming towards us, "hello, strangers!"

Naturally, she wanted to hear all our news and although we were itching to get down to the waterside, it would have been impolite to refuse her invitation to refreshments and so we spent an hour in the cool of her little cottage, sipping tea from delicate, china cups. When finally we did make our way down the lane towards Shuttlewood's Yard and the sea wall, it was high tide and an almost flat calm.

"Looks as though you could walk across there, doesn't it?" I said. "Looks solid, like a sheet of polished silver."

Kathy looked at me. "You'd drown," she said. "It's not solid, is it?"

"No, I know, it's just an illusion. I just meant...oh, well, never mind."

"Does it annoy you that I don't know what you're talking about sometimes? You know, that I'm stupid?"

"Look, Kathy, we can't all be the same. I don't think that you're stupid. Anyway, what matters is how we relate to other people, not how clever we are."

We carried on towards the spot where we'd had the picnic as children before the war. As we approached, we both saw the pill-box at the same time. Its solid, geometric concrete hulk was rooted deep in the soil, right where we'd sat in 1938, the spot from which I secretly watched Kathy's body under her wet clothing.

"Bloody hell," I said angrily, "just look at that damned thing!"

"Not very pretty. I don't like it, right here on our picnic place. Why did they put it here?"

"It's not our place, is it? I mean, not legally or anything. It has a terrific view right down the Pool, up the Roach and across to the Crouch. No bugger would have gone unnoticed past this, assuming the men on guard were not asleep, of course."

"Heaven forbid."

We took a step or two inside and wished we hadn't. Even if the structure had once served a noble cause, it evidently did no longer. It reeked sharply of urine and was full of rubbish. Bits of old shoes, torn clothing, tin cans, beer bottles and used contraceptives littered the mud under out feet. People had chalked or scratched crude, anatomical drawings on the walls. It was an ugly place.

We retreated quickly and sat down to one side of it, both feeling aggrieved that the beauty of our past had been despoiled by a relic from the war, itself fouled, one assumed, by modern youth. We began to eat our sandwiches, trying to ignore the monstrosity squatting by our shoulders.

We watched the play of the light on the Pool, listened to the curlews on Potton Island and remarked on the way that the tops of the sails of the yachts off Burnham-on-Crouch appeared to be slicing their way through the nearer fields of Wallasea.

"Another illusion," I mumbled through a mouthful of water-cress.

"Mmm," she said.

"Kathy, does it bother you that things haven't turned out the way we thought they would?" I asked.

"Oh, Freddie, you're not going to start on about moving to the Leasway or somewhere again, are you? I like it where we are. We should be satisfied."

"No, I didn't mean that," I replied, "although I think maybe my desire to move to Chalkwell may be a kind of reflection that I've somehow failed in life."

Kathy laughed. "You do talk rubbish sometimes, you know. Failed in life? You're only twenty two, Freddie. We both have a long time to go yet; lots of things we can do, unless you're proposing to jump off the end of the pier tomorrow?"

It was my turn to laugh. "No, of course not. Well, you know what I mean. I was supposed to go to university and become a solicitor or something. Make something of myself, I mean. Professional qualifications and so on. It was your Dad as much as anyone who encouraged me to think that way — right here, as it happens."

"I know. But you didn't. Something else happened, if you remember, which altered the plan! Don't tell me you've forgotten that?" she giggled.

"I'm not likely to forget that until my dying day," I replied.

"Anyway, you could have done with Aunty Vi's money, if you'd really wanted to. It doesn't matter, Freddie. We're doing what we're doing and that's all there is to it. If we're forever scrabbling to get back what we think we've lost, well, then we are lost."

A fitful breeze had appeared and a sailing dinghy made its way slowly towards the boatshed, its bow cutting a neat, triangular furrow in the glassy water.

"It's remarks like that which demonstrate that you're not stupid," I said, putting my arm around her.

"Just try to be content," she murmured into my ear. "I love you; there doesn't have to be anything else."

"I thought I was going to walk out over there," I said, pointing to the east as I had once done before. "That's what I told your Dad, anyway. And now it turns out that it's not solid enough to walk on. And then we find a beautiful little spot where we can delight in all that Nature has to offer and someone goes and builds a bloody great gun emplacement there. And then kids use it for...having it away."

"It's just a dirty pill-box, Freddie. A concrete shed in a way. And that's what kids do; it's what we...well, you know, don't get it out of...what is it? Perspective."

"I'll try."

"I love you. What else matters?" she whispered again, pulling me down onto the grass.

"I know and so do I. And, no, Kathy, we can't do it here. It's a public place! More or less."

"It never used to bother you," she laughed, thumping me on the chest. "I don't suppose you want to pop back in there?"

"You must be joking! And look what happened the last time we used a public space!"

The dinghy's owner was pulling his craft onto the slipway by the boatyard. As I looked in that direction, I saw a skylark darting and swooping over the fields behind us. Kathy saw it too, pointing up into the shimmering sky.

"Look, skylarks! Shall we see if we can find the nest? We didn't manage it last time. Maybe we'll have better luck today!"

"If you like," I said, rather ungraciously. "Come on then."

We levered ourselves into a standing position, brushing off dry grass, sandwich crumbs and pieces of water cress. Then, holding hands like a couple of young lovers, we set off into the field to search for eggs that the skylark had tricked us into thinking would be easy to find.

END

Paglesham Pool

The "pill–box" on the sea wall at Paglesham. It was half–buried
when the wall was raised following the 1953 floods.

The site of the picnic when Freddie and Kathy are children, July 1938 and where they return as young adults in August 1948. Shuttlewood's Boatyard is in the distance. The lane to the village and the field where Freddie toiled during the war are off to the right.

APPENDIX

FUTILITY

Move him into the sun -
Gently its touch awoke him once,
At home, whispering of fields unsown.
Always it woke him, even in France,
Until this morning and this snow.
If anything might rouse him now
The kind old sun will know.

Think how it wakes the seeds, -
Woke, once, the clays of a cold star.
Are limbs, so dear-achieved, are sides
Full nerved - still warm - too hard to stir?
Was it for this the clay grew tall?
O - what made fatuous sunbeams toil
To break Earth's sleep at all?

(Wilfred Owen, 1917)

DOVER BEACH

The sea is calm tonight.
The tide is full, the moon lies fair
Upon the straits; - on the French coast the light
Gleams and is gone; the cliffs of England stand,
Glimmering and vast, out in the tranquil bay.
Come to the window, sweet is the night air!
Only, from the long line of spray
Where the sea meets the moon-blanch'd land,
Listen! You hear the grating roar
Of pebbles which the waves draw back, and fling,

At their return, up the high strand,
Begin, and cease, and then again begin,
With tremulous cadence slow, and bring
The eternal note of sadness in.

Sophocles long ago
Heard it on the Aegean, and it brought
Into his mind the turbid ebb and flow
Of human misery; we
Find also in the sound a thought,
Hearing it by this distant northern sea.

The Sea of Faith
Was once, too, at the full, and round earth's shore
Lay like the folds of a bright girdle furl'd.
But now I only hear
Its melancholy, long, withdrawing roar,
Retreating, to the breath
Of the night-wind, down the vast edges drear
And naked shingles of the world.

Ah, love, let us be true
To one another! For the world, which seems
To lie before us like a land of dreams,
So various, so beautiful, so new,
Hath really neither joy, nor love, nor light,
Nor certitude, nor peace, nor help for pain;
And we are here as on a darkling plain
Swept with confused alarms of struggle and fight,
Where ignorant armies clash by night.

(Matthew Arnold, 1867)

'IN TIME OF THE BREAKING OF NATIONS'

I

Only a man harrowing clods
In a slow silent walk
With an old horse that stumbles and nods
Half asleep as they stalk.

II

Only thin smoke without flame
From the heaps of couch grass;
Yet this will go onward the same
Though Dynasties pass.

III

Yonder a maid and her wight
Come whispering by:
War's annals will cloud into night
Ere their story die.

(Thomas Hardy, 1915)

from Chapter 33 of 'TREASURE ISLAND'

And thereupon, we all entered the cave. It was a large airy place, with a little spring and a pool of clear water, overhung with ferns. The floor was sand. Before a big fire lay Captain Smollett; and in a far corner, only duskily flickered over by the blaze, I beheld great heaps of coin and quadrilaterals built of bars of gold. That was Flint's treasure that we had come so far to seek, and that had already cost the lives of seventeen men from the Hispaniola. How many it had cost in the amassing, what blood and sorrow, what good ships scuttled in the deep, what brave men walking the plank blindfold, what shot of cannon, what shame and lies and cruelty, perhaps no man alive could tell.

(Robert Louis Stevenson, 1883)

ANYONE LIVED IN A PRETTY HOW TOWN

anyone lived in a pretty how town
(with up so floating many bells down)
spring summer autumn winter
he sang his didn't he danced his did.

Women and men (both little and small)
cared for anyone not at all
they sowed their isn't they reaped their same
sun moon stars rain

children guessed (but only a few
and down they forgot as up they grew
autumn winter spring summer)
that noone loved him more by more

when by now and tree by leaf
she laughed his joy she cried his grief
bird by snow and stir by still
anyone's any was all to her

someones married their everyones
laughed their cryings and did their dance
(sleep wake hope and then) they
said their nevers they slept their dream

stars rain sun moon
(and only the snow can begin to explain

how children are apt to forget to remember
with up so floating many bells down)

one day anyone died I guess
(and noone stooped to kiss his face)
busy folk buried them side by side
little by little and was by was

all by all and deep by deep
and more by more they dream their sleep
noone and anyone earth by april
wish by spirit and if by yes.

Women and men (both dong and ding)
summer autumn winter spring
reaped their sowing and went their came
sun moon stars rain

(e e cummings, 1940)

Ellie is sixteen, beautiful, passionate and troubled. Mike is forty four and saddled (he'd say) with a dull marriage and a mortgage. They fall in hopeless, all-consuming love.

An age-inappropriate relationship? Infatuation or manipulation? Love or lust?

Ellie is still at school. She's clever and perceptive. Dr. Mike is her teacher, almost at the pinnacle of his career. An abuse of power? Technically, yes. But is it clear who is doing the grooming here, and why? Perhaps things are not always as they seem.

In any event, after a court trial in which Ellie's sexuality is put under a microscope, they elope and marry.

Time and place are suspended while they live in a little shack on a Devonian cliff – the magical but entirely unreal land where the bong tree grows. They watch the beach and the sea and dance in the moonlight. But things unravel as both of them confront their age-gap relationship and Ellie struggles with her past. Which factor is the most destructive?

In this forthright novel, the author challenges our assumptions and causes us to reflect on those stories we've read in the papers about students seduced by teachers.

It is a shocking, amusing, savagely humorous, often vulgar and yet thoughtful story concerned with, first and foremost, taboo love. But other things are interwoven too: time and landscape; religious hypocrisy; contradiction and paradox; disillusionment and reconciliation and the occasional absurdity and transience of human love played out against the enduring backdrop of the ancient Jurassic Coast.

Needless to say – F-word and naughty stuff warning!

(Originally published as "Please, Sir? I love you!")

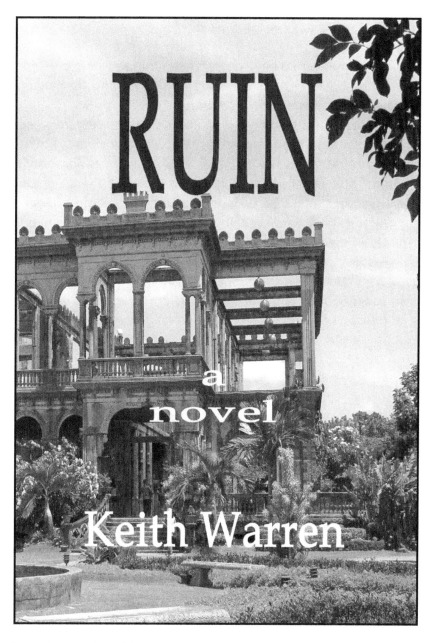

RUIN

a novel

Keith Warren

After the death of his controlling and violent father, Colin Fayn uncovers some items which his father has hidden in the cottage that was the family home. Some are simply mysterious; others are terrifying. They lead Colin on a voyage of discovery about his and his family's past.

His father would have no discussion of family history and his mother, incapacitated in the Blitz in 1940 and permanently frightened of her husband, will say very little.

Through his investigations and amateur detective work, Colin reveals a tangled family history which includes both his father's and his grand father's compulsive womanising and the deliberate torching of a beautiful mansion among the sugar canes on an island in the Far East. He is also forced to confront his own identity, for it is not what it seems. His world is increasingly peopled by spirits, visions and unpalatable truths.

With narrative skill and humour, the author weaves a mysterious tale in which human passion, brutality, deceit and evasion seem to be dominating forces, until we acknowledge too the influence of redemption, loyalty and enduring love.

§

PLEASE WRITE A REVIEW!

It is a great help if readers are able to write a review. This is not to make the author feel better, but to increase interest in his books! Many can be sold through websites that require a certain number of reviews before the title can be included. A "review" does not have to be long or scholarly. One word is OK and there is a star "approval rating".

To write a review or see other works by this author, please go to the location below and click on the title in question. Thank you!

https://www.amazon.com/author/keithwarren